RAVE REVIEWS FOR AWARD-WINNING AUTHOR CHRISTINE FEEHAN!

DARK FIRE

"Hot author Christine Feehan . . . is on a major roll!"

—*Romantic Times*

THE SCARLETTI CURSE

"The characters and twists in this book held me on the edge of my seat the whole time I read it. If you've enjoyed Ms. Feehan's previous novels, you will surely be captivated by this step into the world of Gothic romance. . . . Once again, Ms. Feehan does not disappoint!"

—*Under the Covers Book Reviews*

DARK CHALLENGE

"The exciting and multifaceted world that impressive author Christine Feehan has created continues to improve with age. By introducing this new band of Carpathians, she is setting the stage for more exhilarating adventures to come."

—*Romantic Times*

MORE PRAISE FOR BESTSELLING AUTHOR CHRISTINE FEEHAN!

DARK MAGIC

"With each book Ms. Feehan continues to build a complex society that makes for mesmerizing reading."

—*Romantic Times*

DARK GOLD

"The third in Christine Feehan's Carpathian series is her best to date. *Dark Gold* is imbued with passion, danger and supernatural thrills."

—*Romantic Times*

DARK DESIRE

"A very well-written, entertaining story that I highly recommend."

—*Under the Covers Book Reviews*

DARK PRINCE

"For lovers of vampire romances, this one is a keeper. . . . I had a hard time putting the book down. . . . Don't miss this book!"

—*New-Age Bookshelf*

"I WANT YOU."

She turned her head to study the glittering of his eyes. Dark. Dangerous. That was Gabriel, a legend come to life. He reached out, caught her wrist, and drew her to him. "I want you. All over again." He said it starkly, without embellishment. He brought her hand to his trousers, but the material was gone, sliding from his body in the way of their people so that her palm contracted the hard thick length of him.

"Undress for me, in the manner of humans," he said suddenly. His eyes had gone very black, burning with such intensity that she could feel tiny tongues of flame along her skin. "There is something very erotic in the way a woman removes her clothes."

Her eyebrows shot up. "I thought there was something erotic in the way your clothes melted away and left me to explore where I wanted." Her voice teased him, was sultry with invitation. She stepped away from him, her arm dropping slowly to her side, her fingers brushing the hard length of him as she did so. Francesca tilted her head so that her long hair slid in a silky black curtain over her shoulder. Her hands went to the small pearl buttons on her sweater. She eased each through its buttonhole so that the edges began to gape open to reveal the satin swell of her breasts.

Other *Leisure* and *Love Spell* books by Christine Feehan:

AFTER TWILIGHT
DARK FIRE
THE SCARLETTI CURSE
DARK CHALLENGE
DARK MAGIC
DARK GOLD
DARK DESIRE
DARK PRINCE

Christine Feehan

LEISURE BOOKS NEW YORK CITY

A LEISURE BOOK®

January 2002

Published by

Dorchester Publishing Co., Inc.
276 Fifth Avenue
New York, NY 10001

Cover art by John Ennis.
www.ennisart.com

ISBN 0-8439-4952-X

Printed in the United States of America.

Visit us on the web at www.dorchesterpub.com.

For my sister Ruth,
now and always the healer in our family.
You light up our lives.

DARK
LEGEND

Chapter One

Disoriented, he woke deep within the ground. The first sensation he felt was hunger. It was no ordinary hunger, but one of gut-wrenching, skin-crawling necessity. He was starving. Every cell in his body demanded nourishment. He lay there in silence while the hunger gnawed at him like a rat. It attacked not only his body, but also his mind so that he feared for all others, humans and Carpathians alike. Feared for himself. Feared for his soul. This time the darkness was spreading fast and his soul was in jeopardy.

What dared to disturb his sleep? More importantly, had it disturbed Lucian's sleep? Gabriel had locked Lucian into the earth, centuries ago, longer than he cared to think about. If Lucian had awakened when he had, if he had been disturbed by the same movements above ground, then there was every chance he would rise before Gabriel could find the strength to stop him.

It was intensely difficult to think with this terrible hunger gripping him. How long had he been in the earth? Above him, he sensed the sun setting. After all the long centuries, his internal clock could still feel the setting of the sun and the beginning of their time: *Creatures of the night*. The ground suddenly shifted. Gabriel felt his heart slam hard in his chest. He had waited too long, spent too much time trying to get his bearings, trying to clear his clouded mind. Lucian was rising. Lucian's need for prey would be as great as his own; his appetite would be voracious. There would be no way to stop him, not while Gabriel was so weak himself.

Because he had no choice, Gabriel burst through the layers of earth where he had lain buried for so long, where he had deliberately slumbered, choosing to bury himself in the ground as he locked Lucian to him. The fight in the Paris cemetery had been a long, horrendous battle. Both Lucian and Gabriel had sustained grave wounds, wounds that should have killed them. Lucian had gone to ground just outside the sanctified burial ground of the ancient cemetery while Gabriel had sought sanctuary within it. Gabriel had been tired of the long centuries of bleak darkness, the black empty void of his existence.

He did not have the luxury of choosing to walk into the dawn as most of his kind did. There was Lucian. His twin. Lucian was strong and brilliant, always the leader. There was no one else skilled enough, powerful enough to hunt and destroy Lucian. There was only Gabriel. He had spent several lifetimes following where Lucian led, hunting the vampire, the undead with him, relying on his battle sense. There had been no other like Lucian, none as brilliant at hunting the vampire, the scourge of their race. Lucian had a gift. Yet Lucian had finally succumbed to the dark whisper of power, the insidious call of blood lust. Lucian had given up his soul, choosing the way of the damned, turning into the very monster he had pursued for centuries. The vampire.

Gabriel had spent two centuries hunting his beloved brother, but he had never fully recovered from the shock of Lucian's turning. Finally after countless battles in which neither was victorious, he made the decision to lock his twin in the earth for all time. Gabriel had chased Lucian throughout Europe; their final confrontation took place in Paris, a city rampant with vampires and debauchery. After the terrible battle in the cemetery, where both of them suffered horrendous wounds and loss of blood, he waited until Lucian was lying unsuspectingly in the earth, and then he bound his twin to him, forcing him to remain there. The struggle was not over, yet it was the only solution Gabriel could devise. He was tired and alone and without comfort of any kind. He wanted rest, yet he could not seek the dawn until Lucian was fully destroyed. It was a terrible fate he had chosen, dead, yet not dead, buried for all eternity, but Gabriel could think of no other way. Nothing should have disturbed them, yet something had. Something had moved the earth above their heads.

Gabriel had no idea how much time had passed while he had rested in the earth, yet his body was starved for blood. He knew his skin was gray and drawn tight over his skeleton like that of an old man. At once, as he burst into the air, he clothed himself, adding a long, hooded cape to hide his appearance while he hunted through the city. Just that small action drained the energy from his wizened body. He needed blood desperately. He was so weak he nearly fell from the sky.

As he settled to the ground, he stared in astonishment at the huge contraptions that had disturbed the sleep of centuries. Those contraptions, so alien to him, had awakened a demon so deadly the world could never comprehend its power. Those contraptions had unleashed that demon upon the modern world. Gabriel took a deep breath, inhaled the night. At once he was assaulted by so many smells, his starving body could barely assimilate them all.

Hunger ate at him unmercifully, relentlessly, and he realized with a sinking heart that he was so close to turning, he had precious little control. When he was forced to feed, the demon in him would rise. Nevertheless he had no real choice in the matter. He had to have sustenance to hunt. If he did not hunt Lucian, protect humans and Carpathians alike, who would?

Gabriel drew the thick cloak closer around his body as he staggered through the graveyard. He could see where the machines had disturbed the earth. Apparently the grave sites were being dug up and removed. He found the spot, just outside the sanctified ground, where the soil had boiled up out of the earth as Lucian had risen. For a moment he sank down on his knees to bury both hands in the dirt. Lucian. His brother. His twin. He bowed his head in sorrow. How often had they shared knowledge? Shared battles? Blood? Nearly two thousand years they had been together, fought for their people, hunted the undead and destroyed them. Now he was alone. Lucian was the legendary warrior, the greatest of their people, yet he had fallen as so many had before him. Gabriel would have bet his life that his twin would never have succumbed to the dark whisper of power.

Gabriel stood up slowly and began to walk toward the street. The long years that had gone by had changed the world. Everything was different. He understood none of it. He was so disoriented, even his sight was hazy. He stumbled along, trying to stay away from the people crowding the streets. They were everywhere and they avoided touching him. He touched their minds briefly. They thought him an "old homeless man," perhaps a drunk or even insane. No one looked his way, no one wanted to see him. He was shriveled, his skin gray. He drew the long cloak even closer, hiding his withered body within its folds.

Hunger assailed his senses so that his fangs exploded in his mouth and dripped with anticipation of a feast. He needed nourishment desperately. Stumbling, almost blind, he continued along the street. The city was so different, no longer the Paris of old, but a huge sprawling complex of buildings and paved streets. Lights were blazing from the interior of the massive structures and from street lamps overhead. It was not the city he remembered or with which he was comfortable.

He should have caught the nearest prey and fed voraciously to bring him instant strength, but the dread of being unable to stop himself was uppermost in his mind. He must not allow the beast to control him. He had a sworn duty to his people, to the human race, but most importantly to his beloved brother. Lucian had been his hero, the one he placed above all others, and deservedly so. They had taken a vow together and he would honor it as Lucian would have done for him. No other hunter would be allowed to destroy his brother; it was his task alone.

The smell of blood was overpowering. It beat at him with the same intensity as his hunger. The sound of it rushing through veins, ebbing and flowing, burgeoning with life, taunted him. In his present state of weakness he would be unable to control his prey, to keep his victim calm. That would only add to the power of the demon rising.

"Sir, may I help you in some way? Are you ill?" It was the most beautiful voice he had ever heard. She spoke in flawless French, her accent perfect, but he was uncertain whether she was actually French. To his amazement, her words brought him comfort, as if her voice alone could soothe him.

Gabriel shuddered. The last thing he wanted was to feast on an innocent woman. Without looking at her, he shook his head and continued walking. He was so weak he stumbled against her. She was tall and slender and surprisingly strong. Immediately she wrapped her arm around him, ignoring his musty, dirty odor. The moment she touched him he felt a sense of peace seeping into his tortured soul. The unrelenting hunger lessened and as long as she was touching him, he felt a semblance of control.

Deliberately he kept his face averted from her, knowing his eyes would show the red haze of the demon rising in him. Her close proximity should have triggered his violent instincts instead she soothed him. She was definitely the last person he wanted to use as prey. He sensed her goodness, her resolve to help him, her complete selflessness. Her compassion and goodness were the only reasons he had not attacked and sunk his fangs deep within her veins when every shrunken cell and fiber of his being demanded he do so for his own self-preservation.

She was urging him toward a sleek contraption at the edge of the sidewalk. "Are you injured, or just hungry?" she asked. "There's a homeless shelter right up the street. They can give you a place to stay for the night and a hot meal. Let me take you there. This is my car. Please get in and let me help you."

Her voice seemed to whisper over him, a seduction of the senses. He truly feared for her life, for his own soul. But he was far too weak to resist. He allowed her to seat him in the car, but he huddled as far from her as he was able. Now that there was no longer any physical contact, he could hear the blood rushing in her veins, calling to him. Whispering like the most tempting seductress. Hunger roared through him so that he was shaking with the need to sink his teeth deep into her vulnerable neck. He could hear her heart, the steady beat that went on and on, threatening to drive him mad. He could almost taste the blood, knowing it would pour into his mouth, down his throat as he gorged himself.

"My name is Francesca Del Ponce," she told him gently. "Please tell me if you're hurt or in need of medical attention. Don't worry about the cost. I have friends at the hospital and they'll help you." She didn't add what he gleaned from her thoughts: she often brought in indigents and paid the bill herself.

Gabriel remained silent. It was all he could do to shield his own thoughts, an automatic protection Lucian had drilled into him from the time they were mere fledglings. The lure of blood was overpowering. It was only the goodness radiating from her that prevented him from leaping upon her and feasting as his shriveled cells cried out for him to do.

Francesca glanced at the old man worriedly. She hadn't seen his face clearly, but he was gray with hunger and shaking with fatigue. He looked starved. When she touched him she sensed a terrible conflict within him and his body raged with hunger. It took control not to race through the streets to the shelter. She wanted desperately to get him aid. Her small white teeth worried at her bottom lip. She felt anxiety, an emotion Francesca could not remember feeling in a long while. She *needed* to give this man aid and comfort. The urge was so strong, it was almost a compulsion.

"Don't worry, I can take care of things for you. Just sit back and relax." Francesca drove with her usual abandon through the streets. Most of the policemen knew her car and would do no more than grin at her when she broke all the laws. She was a healer. An exceptional healer. It was her gift to the world. It had made friends for her everywhere. Those that didn't care about favors or healing cared about the fact that she had a great deal of money and a great many political connections.

She pulled up to the shelter and stopped the car almost at the door. She didn't want the old man to have to walk too far. He seemed ready to topple over at any moment. The hood of his unusual cape concealed his hair from her, but she had the impression it was long and thick and old-fashioned. Rushing around the front of the car, she reached inside to help him out.

Gabriel didn't want her to touch him again, but he couldn't help himself. There was something very soothing in her touch, almost healing. It helped him to hold the terrible craving at bay for a little while longer. The contraption he was riding in, the speed at which it rushed through the streets, made him sick and dizzy. He needed to orient himself to the world he was in. Find out the year. Study the new technology. Most of all he needed to find the strength to feed without allowing the demon deep within him to reign supreme. He could feel it in him, the red haze, the animal instincts rising to overcome the thin veneer of civility.

"Francesca! Another one? We're so full this evening." Marvin Challot glanced uneasily at the elderly man she was helping toward the door. Something about the man raised the hair on the back of his neck. He looked old and gnarled, his fingernails too long and too sharp, but he was obviously so weak Marvin felt guilty that he didn't want anything to do with this stranger. He was ashamed of himself for the feeling of revulsion, but he was actually repulsed by the old man. He could hardly refuse Francesca. She contributed more money, more time and more effort than anyone else. If it weren't for her, there would be no shelter.

Reluctantly Marvin reached out to take the old man's arm. Gabriel inhaled sharply. The moment Francesca released his arm, he nearly lost all control. Fangs exploded in his mouth and the sound of rushing blood was so loud he could hear nothing else. Everything disappeared in a red haze. Hunger. Starvation. He had to feed. The demon within him lifted its head with a roar, wrestled him for total control.

Marvin sensed he was in mortal danger. The arm he had tried to seize seemed to contort, the bones popping and crackling, and fur rippled over the withered skin. Marvin smelled a wild, pungent odor like that of a wolf. He found himself dropping the elderly man's arm in terror. The head turned toward him slowly and he caught a glimpse of death. Where there should have been eyes, there were two empty, pitiless holes. Marvin blinked and the eyes were there again, red and flaming, like those of an animal stalking its prey. Marvin didn't know which impression was worse but he didn't want anything to do with the old man, whatever he was. The eyes bored into him like the slash of fangs.

Marvin cried out and jumped back. "No, Francesca, I can't allow it. There's no room here tonight. I don't want him here." His voice shook with terror.

Francesca almost protested, but something in Marvin's face stopped her. She nodded her acceptance of his decision. "It's okay, Marvin. I can take care of him." Very gently she slipped her arm around the old man's waist. "Come with me." Her voice was soft, soothing. She hid her irritation at Marvin's reaction well, but it was there.

Gabriel's first inclination was to put distance between them. He didn't want to kill her and he knew he was dangerously close to turning. Yet it seemed she anchored him. She soothed him so that he could leash the savage beast for the moment. Gabriel leaned heavily against her slender body. Her skin was warm, while his was ice-cold. He breathed in her scent deeply, careful to keep his head turned away from her. He did not want her to see him as he was, a demon, struggling with his own soul, struggling desperately for humanity.

"Francesca," Marvin protested. "I'll call someone to take him to the hospital. Perhaps a policeman. Don't be alone with him. I think maybe he's insane."

As Gabriel entered the car he turned his head to look back at the man standing on the sidewalk, watching them with fear in his eyes. He stared at the man's throat, his hand closing into a tight fist. For one terrible moment he almost crushed the man's windpipe just for warning her. With a soft ancient oath he curbed the impulse. Hunching one shoulder, he huddled deeper within the thick cloak. He wanted to stay close to this beautiful woman and let her light and compassion bathe his tortured soul. He also wanted to run as far from her as possible to keep her safe from the monster growing ever stronger within him.

Francesca didn't seem in the least bit nervous of him. If anything, she was trying to reassure him. Despite Marvin's warning, she smiled at Gabriel. "It wouldn't hurt to do a checkup at the hospital. Really, it would only take a minute."

Gabriel shook his head slowly in protest. She smelled good. Fresh. Clean. He was too weak even to clean himself up. It embarrassed him that she would see him in such a state. She was so beautiful, shining from the inside out.

She parked in an area where it appeared hundreds of contraptions like hers were sitting empty. "I'll be right back. Don't try to get out, it's a waste of your energy. This will just take a minute." She touched his shoulder, a small gesture meant to reassure. Immediately he felt the strange lightening of his heavy burden.

The moment she was gone he was assailed by hunger that clawed at his insides, demanding he feed. He could barely breathe. His heart was beating very slowly: one beat, a miss and another beat. His body cried out for blood. For nourishment. Screamed for it. He needed. That was all. So simple. He needed. Craved. Needed. It blended together into one desire.

He smelled it. Fresh. Heard it. Yet he smelled her, too, and her nearness helped to overcome the roaring in his head. His gut clenched, knotted. A male walked beside her. This one was different from the last. This man was young and he was looking at Francesca as if she were the sun, the moon and the stars. Every few steps the young man's body would brush Francesca's. Something wicked, something deep within him lifted its head and snarled with unexpected dislike. His prey. No one had the right to stand so close to her. She was his. He had marked her for himself. The thought came unbidden and at once he was ashamed. Still, he didn't like the male standing so close to her and it took every ounce of his discipline to keep from leaping on the man and devouring him there on the spot.

"Brice, I have to get home. This gentleman needs help. I don't have time to talk right now. I just stopped by for a few supplies."

Brice Renaldo put his hand on her arm to stop her. "I need you to look at a patient for me, Francesca. A little girl. It won't take that long."

"Not now, I'll come back later tonight." Francesca's voice was soft but very firm.

Brice tightened his grip, intending to pull her back, but as he did so, he felt something moving along his skin. Looking down he saw several small spiders with vicious-looking fangs crawling along his arm. With an oath he let go of Francesca and shook his arm hard. The spiders were gone as if they'd never been and Francesca was already walking quickly to her side of the car. She was looking at him as if he were a nut. He started to explain but when he couldn't see any evidence of spiders, he decided it wasn't worth the trouble.

Brice hurried to the car, deliberately taking her arm again, bending low to peer in the window at Gabriel. His mouth immediately twisted in a disgusted grimace. "My

God, Francesca, where do you find these bums?"

"Brice!" Francesca pulled her arm away from him with a small, very feminine gesture of annoyance. "You can be so callous sometimes." She lowered her voice, but Gabriel, with his superior hearing, heard the exchange quite clearly. "Just because someone is old or has no money does not make him useless or a murderer. That is the reason we never quite make it, Brice. You have no compassion for people."

"What do you mean, no compassion?" Brice protested. "There's a little girl who never did anyone any harm suffering and I'm doing everything I can to help her."

Francesca moved around him when he would have stopped her, and slid behind the wheel of her car. "Later this evening. I promise I'll look at the little girl tonight for you." She started the car.

"You're not taking that old man home, are you?" Brice demanded in spite of her admonishment. "You'd better be taking him to the shelter. He's dirty and probably covered with fleas. You don't know the first thing about him. I mean it, Francesca, don't you dare take him home with you."

Francesca gave him one haughty little frown before she drove away without a backward glance. "Pay no attention to Brice. He's a very good doctor, but he likes to think he can tell me what to do." She glanced at her silent companion. He was hunched very small on his side of the car. She still had not gotten a good look at him. Not even his face. He was hiding in the shadows, keeping his face averted from her. She wasn't even certain he understood that she was trying to help him. She had the impression of a great man, one used to wealth and authority, probably terribly humiliated by his present circumstances. It hadn't helped that Brice had been so rude. "It will be just a few minutes and I'll get you somewhere warm and safe. There will be plenty of food."

Her voice was so wonderful. It touched him somewhere deep inside, calming him, holding the beast leashed when he could never have done so alone. Perhaps if she was near him when he fed he would be able to control the demon when it rose. Gabriel buried his face in his hands. God help him, he didn't want to kill her. His body shook with the effort to control its need for hot blood pouring into shriveled, starving cells. This was so dangerous. So incredibly dangerous.

The car took him a short distance from the busy city streets along a narrow lane where trees and thick shrubbery grew. The house was large and rambled here and there with no particular style. It was old-fashioned with a wide verandah and long straight columns. Gabriel hesitated when he opened the door of the contraption. Should he go with her or should he stay? He was weak. He couldn't wait much longer. He had to feed. He had no choice.

Francesca took his arm and helped him as he staggered up the long stairway to the house. "I'm sorry, I know there are quite a few stairs. You can lean on me if you need to." She didn't know why it was so imperative she help this stranger, but everything in her demanded she do so.

With a sinking heart, Gabriel allowed the woman to help him up the numerous stairs to her dwelling. He feared it was inevitable that he would kill her. He would join the ranks of the undead and there would be no one to destroy Lucian. No one to destroy either of them. No one capable of destroying them. The world would have two monsters unequaled in evil. There were too many hours until dawn. The need for blood would overcome his good intentions. And this poor innocent woman with far too much compassion in her would be the one to pay the ultimate price for her kindness and mercy to one such as he.

"No!" The denial was a harsh growl. Gabriel tore his arm from her grasp and jerked away from the door. He staggered, lost his balance and fell.

At once Francesca was beside him. "What are you afraid of? I won't hurt you." He was trembling beneath her fingers, radiating stark fear. His head was averted, hidden deep within the folds of the hood, one shoulder hunched as if to block her out.

Gabriel got slowly to his feet. He didn't have the strength to get away from this young woman, from the warmth and compassion in her voice, from the life bursting in her veins. He bowed his head as he stepped through the doorway into her home. He prayed for strength. He prayed for forgiveness. He prayed for a miracle.

Francesca guided him through the large rooms to the kitchen, where she seated him at an intricately carved dining table. "There's a small bathroom off to your right. The towels are clean if you want to take a shower. You're welcome to use it while I'm heating food."

Gabriel sighed and shook his head. He rose slowly and moved across the floor to stand over her. Close. So close he smelled her faint enticing fragrance through the haze of his raw hunger. "I am sorry." He whispered the words softly, meaning them. "I must feed, but that is not what I need." Very gently he took the bowl from her hands and set it on the counter.

For the first time Francesca sensed she was in danger. She stood very still, her large black eyes studying his cloaked figure. Then she nodded. "I see." There was no fear in her voice, only a quiet acceptance. "Come with me. I have something to show you. You'll need it later." She took his hand, ignoring his long, sharp nails.

Gabriel was not using compulsion on her. He was not using any mind merge at all to calm her. She knew she was in deadly peril; he saw the knowledge reflected in her eyes. Her hand closed over his and she tugged. "Come with me. I can help you." She was almost tranquil, radiating a peace that enfolded him.

He followed her because every physical contact with her eased his suffering. He couldn't bear to think of what he was going to do to her. Inside he felt like weeping. A heavy stone seemed to be crushing his chest. Francesca opened a door on the left side of the kitchen to reveal a narrow stairway. At her urging he followed her down the stairs.

"This is the basement," she told him, "but over here, just above this little outcropping, is another door. You can't see it, but if you place your fingertips exactly here . . ." She demonstrated and the rock swung inward toward a dark cavern. She waved at the interior. "This leads beneath the earth. You'll find it to your liking."

Gabriel inhaled the sweet welcoming scent of the earth's richness beckoning to him. The coolness, the darkness reached out to him with the promise of peace.

Francesca swept her heavy hair from her neck and looked up at him with wide, gentle eyes. "I feel the fear in you. I know what you need. I am a healer and I can do no other than offer one such as you solace. I offer freely, without reservation, I offer my life for yours as is my right." The words were soft and gentle, so beautiful like the whisper of velvet over his skin.

The actual words barely registered. Only the sound. The

seduction. The enticement. Her neck was warm satin beneath his stroking fingers. Gabriel closed his eyes and savored the exquisite feel of her. Where he had feared he would rend and tear, he found the need to cradle her body close to his gently, almost tenderly. He bent his head to feel her skin beneath his lips. Heat and fire. His tongue stroked across her pulse and his body tightened in anticipation. His arms drew her into the shelter of his body, his heart. He murmured his apology and took her offering, his teeth sinking deep into the vein of her slender neck.

At once the rush hit him like a fireball, spreading through his starving shrunken cells. Power and strength blossomed within him. He felt it then. White heat. Blue lightning. His body tightened. She felt like hot silk in his arms, as if she fit perfectly into his body. He became aware of how soft her skin was. The taste of her was addictive. She had saved him with her generosity. She had successfully prevented the demon from rising. Her blood was freely given. *Freely given*. A new realization penetrated his feeding frenzy. He could *feel*. Guilt. He recalled the weight in his chest as he'd followed her down the basement stairs. He had been feeling since the moment he'd chanced upon her. His body was a hard, urgent ache as he fed. Sensual. Erotic. Feeding had never been in any way connected to sex. He should have been incapable of sexual feelings, yet now his body was one hard, unrelenting, urgent ache.

Beneath his hand her heart stuttered and Gabriel immediately swept his tongue across the pinpricks at her throat to close the wound with his healing saliva. He had drained most of the blood from her slender body. He had to act fast. He tore a wound in his wrist and pressed it over her mouth. He was strong enough to take control of her mind. She was fading away, her life force simply waning. Francesca was making no attempt to fight; rather she seemed to be quite calm and accepting, almost as if she embraced death. Gabriel forced the blood back into her. She had known the ritual words to keep the demon leashed. She had freely offered her life for his. What had she said? *As is my right.* How could it be?

Gabriel looked down at her face. She was very pale; her long lashes were thick and luxurious, a deep black to match the long silk of her hair. Her slender body was encased in men's pants, a light blue. Colors. He was seeing in color. He had not seen anything other than grays and blacks since he was a mere fledging over two thousand years before. Why hadn't he recognized her as his lifemate? Was he so far gone after all?

He stopped her from taking too much blood from him. He would need to hunt this night; he must be sure he took enough for both of them. He carried her into the cavern, and following her scent, he found the dark chamber that would be safe from humans and the undead alike. He laid her gently in the bed of soil and sent her to sleep, reinforcing the command with a hard "push" to ensure she would not awaken until he could give her more blood. Her heart and lungs were slow and steady, enabling her body to make do with the small amount of blood flowing through her veins and arteries, the chambers of her heart.

Gabriel glided through the house, expending as little energy as possible. He would have been more than happy to take Brice's blood. But Gabriel didn't have the time to indulge his whims; he had to find his prey quickly and get back to his savior. She had saved more than his life with her generosity. She had saved his soul.

Another moment and he was out of the house, into the darkness. His world. He had lived in it for centuries, yet it was all new. All different. Everything would be different now. He found prey immediately. The city was teaming with people. He picked three large men, making certain none of them were using alcohol or drugs and that the blood in their veins was not contaminated with any diseases. Gabriel easily led them into the shelter of a doorway and bent his head to drink his fill. He took enough to bring himself to full strength without endangering any one of them. When the first swayed with dizziness, Gabriel carefully closed the pinpricks and helped him to sit on the ground. He fed from the second and third almost greedily, his body craving the nourishment after so long without. He needed enough blood for Francesca to ensure her continued survival.

The moment he was finished he erased their memories and left the three of them sitting comfortably inside the overhang of the doorway. Gabriel took three running steps and sprang into the air, his body shifting shape so that wings spread wide and lifted him. He flew in a straight line back to her house. From the air he could see the estate for what it was. Obviously old, the house was in beautiful shape, the grounds meticulously cared for. Everywhere he looked were unfamiliar objects, things of which he had no knowledge. Life had continued while he lay sleeping under the earth.

He found Francesca as he had left her, her skin so white it was nearly translucent. She was tall and slender with a wealth of ebony hair that framed her face and tumbled around her body, emphasizing her lush curves. He picked her up with great gentleness, cradled her body close to his. How could it be that this woman was his true lifemate? After the wars, females had been scarce. A Carpathian male could search the world for century after century and never find his true lifemate, the other half of his soul, of his heart. Light to his darkness. Women of his species had become scarce by the twelfth and thirteenth centuries. What were the odds of finding her just walking down the street? Practically the first person he met after being locked in the soil for so long. It didn't make sense to him. Nothing that had happened made sense. But one fact was clear and simple. A Carpathian male could not see colors or feel emotions unless he was in close proximity to his true lifemate. Gabriel could see all kinds of color. Brilliant colors. Vivid colors. Colors he had long forgotten had ever existed. Feelings he had never experienced. He inhaled, dragging her scent deep into his lungs. He would be able to find her anywhere now. With his ancient blood running in her veins he could call her to him at will, talk to her, mind to mind, from any distance.

With his fingernail he opened his chest, holding her head in the palm of his hand so that he could press her mouth to his skin. He was powerful, in full strength once more, and in her weakened condition, Francesca was completely in his control. He took his time studying her. She puzzled and intrigued him. She looked like a Carpathian woman. Tall. Slender. Ebony hair. Beautiful eyes as black as night. She knew the ritual words. She had known he needed blood. She even had the chamber beneath the earth prepared for one of his kind. Who was she? What was she?

Gabriel searched her mind. She seemed human. Her memories were those of a human and contained many things he knew nothing about. The world had gained so much while he slept. She seemed wholly human and yet her blood was not exactly the same as humans. Her internal organs were not exactly the same. Still she had memories of walking under the noon sun, something his people could not do. Her existence was a mystery he intended to solve. This woman was far too important to him; he could take no chances.

Francesca's body once again had the correct volume of blood. Very gently Gabriel stopped her from feeding and placed her in the healing soil without closing it over her head. He wanted her to rest while he took the remainder of the night to study the new world he would be living in. He found a treasury of books in a library on the first floor. It was there that he learned of television and computers and the history of the contraptions—cars—they had been using to get around in. It was all amazing to him and he soaked up the technology like a sponge. Without thought he connected with Lucian. It just happened. For over two thousand years they had shared information. Gabriel was so excited he reached out to his twin and merged.

Lucian accepted the information and passed what he had been observing and studying just as if the last few centuries had never taken place. Lucian was at full strength and, as always, gaining knowledge at a rapid rate. His mind had always required new things to think about, to work on. The moment Gabriel realized what he was doing, he broke the connection, furious with himself. Lucian would be able to "see" where Gabriel was, just as Gabriel could easily find Lucian. Always Gabriel had been the one hunting his twin, tracking him to try to destroy him. He had never worried before when he had mistakenly merged with his vampire brother to share new information: If Lucian had chosen to use his knowledge to find Gabriel, it would only have made the job of destroying him easier. Now everything was different. Gabriel couldn't afford to allow Lucian to know where he was or whom he was with. Now he had to protect Francesca. Lucian could not find out about her. Vampires thrived on other people's pain. Francesca would be made to pay a terrible price for her interference.

Gabriel indulged himself with a human shower. He could simply be clean and fresh with a thought, yet now he could feel. He could savor cleanliness. It was an amazing feeling. Again he had to make a conscious effort to withhold the feeling from his twin. Even after all this time, he was used to slipping in and out of his brother's mind. Over the centuries he had used his ability to track his brother and even anticipate his kills in order to try to reach the victim before Lucian did. So far he had not been able to prevent any of Lucian's kills, but Gabriel continued to try.

After his shower, Gabriel went back to reading. He covered several encyclopedias and almanacs and every other book he could find. With his photographic memory this took very little time. He read at a rapid rate so he could get through the history and into the new technology. He wanted to read manuals and find out exactly how everything worked. And he wanted to learn everything the house could offer up about its owner.

He wandered around the vast rooms. She liked space. Open spaces. She appreciated great art and soft colors. She definitely loved the ocean and its inhabitants. There were books about underwater life and prints and watercolors of crashing waves. She was a meticulous housekeeper unless, of course, someone else came in to do the work. She lived like a human. The cupboards were full. She had beautiful china in the kitchen and rare antiques in the bedrooms. There was a room with a quilt in the making and he studied the work. The pattern was unusual.

Soothing. Beautiful. He was drawn to it, but he couldn't figure out why. In another room she had been working with stained glass. The designs were much like those on the quilt. Soothing and tranquil. Each one was intensely beautiful. He could stare at them for hours. She was a very talented woman.

The draperies throughout the house were unusually heavy, specifically made for the windows so that, if the occupant desired, not one bit of light could enter the room. That would make sense if she was a Carpathian integrating herself into mainstream life. Yet nothing in this house seemed to add up. It was a mixture of wealth and fancy, of Carpathian and human, almost as if two different people occupied the place. He looked for evidence of two residents.

In the study he found her personal papers, records of payments and private little notes she wrote to herself. There seemed to be quite a few notes, some of which were reminders to eat certain soups. A Carpathian would never eat human food unless it was imperative to do so to keep others from finding out the truth. Any Carpathian at full strength could eat and rid his stomach of the contents later, but it was uncomfortable to do so.

Who was Francesca? More important, what was she? Why wasn't her blood fully human? How had she known the ritual words to keep him from turning vampire in his weakest moment? Most important of all, why was he seeing in color? Why did he feel emotion? Why had she used the phrase "as is my right"?

Gabriel sighed and replaced her things, his fingers lingering for a moment to caress her small, neat handwriting. She would have answers for him. And if she didn't want to give them to him, he had ways of extracting information. He was of ancient blood, of a lineage of greatness and power. Few of his people had the knowledge and skills he had obtained in his centuries of existence. She would not be able to hide from him or his questions.

Chapter Two

Gabriel stared down at the woman lying so quietly in the dark rich soil. His body responded the moment he was in close proximity to her, something that had never happened to him before in all the long centuries of his existence. He felt tight and hot, his body making urgent demands just from observing her. His entire being, heart and soul reached out to her; his emotions were so powerful, he was shaking with the unexpected intensity of them. It was disconcerting to find that anyone would have such an effect on him. Feeling a little out of his depth, he woke her with a command.

Francesca stirred, a small frown slipping across her face. Her heavy eyelashes fluttered just before she lifted them. Her eyes were enormous and deep black. They went to him instantly, almost as if she had known he was there. Her small teeth tugged briefly at her full lower lip, a quick nervous gesture that she covered by sitting up. Dizziness swept through her and she swayed, a hand going to her head.

At once Gabriel's arm curved around her to steady her. Every protective instinct shrieked at him, demanded he take care of her.

Francesca pushed at him. "Get away from me. You've ruined everything. All those years, everything I worked for. Get away from me."

Gabriel moved back to give her room, surprised by the reproof in her voice. She was obviously upset with him. "What did I ruin?" he asked mildly. Her lack of fear shocked him. He hadn't shielded her from what he was. He had openly taken her blood. She knew it. There had been no compulsion to force her and he had not commanded her to forget what he had done.

Francesca studied his face. He certainly didn't look like the elderly man she had first thought him. His skin was healthy now and he looked young and strong. There was an air of power clinging to him. He stood straight and tall, looked exactly what he was, a warrior unsurpassed by any other. He had strong features and black gleaming eyes. His long black flowing hair was tied with a leather thong at the nape of his neck.

"I offered my life in exchange for yours. You had no right to give me your blood. That's what you did, isn't it? You had no right." Her enormous eyes flashed at him, smoldering with hidden fire. Her small fists clenched until her long nails dug into the palms of her hands. Her slender body was trembling with suppressed resentment. It was Gabriel. She should have known him anywhere, anytime, no matter his appearance, yet she hadn't recognized him until he had taken her into his arms. She had been so afraid he might see through her disguise, she hadn't allowed her senses to reveal the information she so desperately needed.

"You would have died." He said it starkly, without embellishment.

"I know that. I willingly offered my life so that you could continue your fight to save our people."

"You are Carpathian then." Very gently he reached out and took her hand, carefully prying open her fingers one by one and exposing the fingernail marks on her palm. Before she could guess his intention, he bent his dark head, his mouth brushing the marks with exquisite gentleness.

Her heart nearly stopped at the touch of his lips, the warmth of his breath. Snatching her hand back, she scowled at him. "Of course I'm Carpathian. Who else would recognize you? Gabriel. The defender of our people. You are the greatest vampire hunter our people have ever known. You're a legend come back to life. It took me some time to realize who you were, but you were in bad shape. You have been thought dead these last few centuries."

"Why did you not immediately identify yourself to me? I would never have allowed you to place your life in danger." His voice was very soft, a clear reprimand.

Color swept into Francesca's pale face. "Don't you presume to have rights over me, Gabriel. Your rights have been long since revoked."

He stirred, a slight ripple of muscle warning of his enormous strength. Francesca's black eyes flashed at him; she was not in the least intimidated. "I mean it. You had no right to do what you did."

"As a Carpathian male, I can do no other than protect

you. Why do you live here alone, unclaimed, unprotected? Has our world changed so much that our males no longer care for our women?" His tone was soft yet all the more menacing.

Her chin lifted. "Our males have no idea of my existence. And it isn't your business either, so don't think you're going to get involved."

Gabriel merely looked at her. He was over two thousand years old. It was ingrained in him to protect women above all else. It was part of who he was, of what he was. And if this woman was his lifemate, it was more than his duty, it was his right. "I am afraid, Francesca, that I can do no other than watch over you properly. I have never neglected my responsibilities."

She felt very much at a disadvantage sitting there with him towering over her. Francesca stood up and moved gracefully across the room to put distance between them. He was making her heart pound with nervousness. Francesca had forgotten what it was like to be nervous. She was no fledgling. She had done what no other Carpathian woman had ever done: managed to escape undetected from both Carpathian males and marauding vampires and live her own life by her own rules. She was not about to allow this male to walk into her life and just take it over. "I think we should get something straight, Gabriel. I am not your responsibility. I'm willing to allow you to use this chamber until you get your bearings and find your safe place, but after that, there will be no contact between us. I have my own life here. It doesn't include you at all."

His eyebrow rose, an elegant, polite way of calling her a liar. "You are my lifemate." He felt the certainty of those words. She was his other half, the light to his darkness, the one woman created just for him.

For the first time Francesca showed fear. She swung around, her eyes wide with fright. "You didn't say the ritual words to bind us, did you?" Her hands were trembling so, she put them behind her back. From the very moment she had recognized him, this was the moment she had feared most.

"Why would you fear so natural a thing? You know I am your lifemate." Gabriel watched her closely, noting every expression. She was definitely frightened. And she had known before he had that she belonged with him.

Her chin went up almost defiantly. "I *was* your lifemate, Gabriel, many centuries ago. But when you made the decision to hunt vampires with your brother, you sentenced me to a life alone. I accepted that sentence. That was a long time ago. You can't just come back into my life and decree something else."

Gabriel was silent, touching her mind easily with a light merging. He discovered a vivid memory of Gabriel striding through a human village with Lucian. The two legendary vampire hunters. The people were moving out of their way in awe. Gabriel saw himself moving quickly, his strides sure and long, his hair flowing in the night air. The movement of a young girl caught his attention and he turned his head without slowing his pace. His black eyes slid over a group of women, and then Lucian said something to distract him. Gabriel turned his head in the direction they were walking, not once looking back. The young girl remained staring after him for a long time in hurt silence.

"I did not know."

Her eyes flashed at him. "You didn't want to know. There's a difference, Gabriel. In any case, it doesn't matter. I survived the humiliation and the pain. It was all a long time ago. I've lived a good life for many centuries. I am tired now and wish to seek the dawn."

Gabriel regarded her steadily. "That is not acceptable, Francesca." He said it quietly, without inflection.

"You have no right to tell me what is and what isn't acceptable in my life. As far as I'm concerned, you gave up all rights to me when you walked away without looking back. You know nothing about me. You know nothing about the life I've lived or what I want or don't want. I made a life for myself. I've been relatively happy and more than a little useful. I've lived long enough, thank you. Just because you've suddenly decided to come back from the dead doesn't change anything at all. You didn't come for me. You came for him. Lucian. He has risen, hasn't he? You are hunting him."

Gabriel nodded his head slowly. "That is so, but you must realize, finding you has changed everything."

"No, it hasn't," Francesca denied. She wrenched open the door to the chamber and hurried away from him along the tunnel toward the basement. It didn't improve her temper when he kept pace with her easily, his muscles rippling powerfully, suggestively. How dare he be so casual about her life? "It hasn't changed a thing. You still have your job and I have my life. It belongs solely to me, Gabriel, and only I can make my decisions."

"The Prince of our people has much to answer to me for," Gabriel said in his soft, mild voice. "He has not watched over you as was his duty. Is Mikhail still in power?"

"Go to hell, Gabriel," Francesca bit out, anger erupting at his statement. She pushed her way into the kitchen and moved straight across the room to the hall mirror. Sweeping her hair aside, she examined her neck for any telltale marks.

"You are going out?"

His voice was so low and soft, her heart thudded hard in her chest. She kept her face turned away from him. "Yes, I told Brice I would look in on one of his patients. I can't have him worried and coming to look for me."

"Brice can wait," Gabriel said smoothly.

"There is no reason for Brice to wait," Francesca told him. "I expect you to be gone when I get back, Gabriel."

A small smile softened the hard edge of his mouth. "I do not think that will happen." He watched her go out the front door, amusement never once touching his smoldering black eyes. The moment the heavy door banged shut behind her, Gabriel flowed through the room to the window. Francesca was moving down the street quickly on foot. She hadn't used her car as a human would and she hadn't dissolved into mist and streamed through the air as a Carpathian might. As Gabriel watched, she began to run. Her body moved lightly and fluidly, poetic in its beauty.

He reached out with his mind and merged with hers so that he was a quiet shadow. Francesca was very afraid of him. She meant every word she had said. She had been conducting some kind of experiment, one that had allowed her to remain in the sun with the humans. She had spent a great deal of time and energy researching, looking for a way to make the change. It had taken several centuries to get her body to the point that she could do so. She had been so adept at appearing human in her thoughts and actions that she had fooled even such an ancient as he. Now he had ruined it for her by giving her his ancient blood. She was very upset over that. And she was determined that these were the last few years of her life. She had been considering spending her last years with Brice, growing old in the manner of humans. She intended to meet the dawn when those last few years were gone. She had been planning it for some time.

"I do not think so, Francesca," he whispered aloud. His body slowly wavered, shimmered into transparency. He dissolved into a fine mist and streamed from the house through the partially opened window. At once the mist took the form of a large white owl, his favorite method of traveling. Strong wings spread wide and took him high over the city.

Francesca ran as fast as she could along the sidewalk. She could hear her heart thudding wildly, heard the soles of her feet hitting the walkway, the air rushing in and out of her lungs. In her wildest dreams she had never once thought this could happen. *Gabriel*. Her people whispered of him. *Twins. Legends*. They were dead, not alive. How could this be? He had taken her life away from her, forced her to live an endless solitary existence. Now that she had finally found a way to live like a human, to perhaps have a human relationship, to live and die like the others she had watched come and go throughout the years, Gabriel had come back from the dead. What if he insisted on claiming her?

There was no way to run from one such as Gabriel. He was an elite hunter. Gabriel could track the ghost of a trail, let alone his own lifemate. Francesca slowed to a fast walk. Maybe he would just go away again. He had all but admitted Lucian had risen. He was still hunting. He would have no interest in her. She would never accept his claim on her. He had forced her to exile herself from her own people, her own homeland. She'd had no choice in the matter. A solitary female living among men so desperate for lifemates would have made their lives an endless misery. And she knew she could not tolerate the loss of freedom. The Prince of their people would have guarded her carefully in the constant hope one of the men would be her true lifemate. They needed children desperately. She knew she was compatible with only one Carpathian male and he had rejected her to devote himself to the protection of their people. She had lived as she wanted these centuries, secure in the knowledge that she was strong and powerful and no human could match her and no vampire could detect her. It was easy enough to hide from her people because such behavior was so unexpected.

They had lost so many of their woman and children over the centuries that every woman was guarded closely; the women were needed to bring children, especially female children, into the world. Most of the children born were males, and most did not survive beyond the first year of life. Their species bordered on extinction. Francesca had come to terms with her solitary existence. She wasn't about to change her entire life because Gabriel had suddenly decided to show up out of nowhere.

She felt moisture on her face and glanced up at the sky. It was perfectly clear above her head; the stars were out in full force. Surprised, she reached up and touched the tears on her face. That made her all the more determined that Gabriel would have no say in her life. Already he had made her cry. He had ruined everything. He had taken the sun from her recklessly, without thought. That was Gabriel. He made decisions and expected the rest of the world to fall in line with him. He was a law unto himself and he would expect Francesca to do whatever he dictated.

Francesca turned the corner, took a deep breath and walked into the hospital parking lot. She didn't want anything to appear to be abnormal. Brice met her soon after she entered the building, leading her to believe he had left strict orders that he be alerted immediately upon her arrival. He led her through the halls to a private room. There were teddy bears and balloons and flowers everywhere. The little girl in the bed was very pale with dark circles under her eyes. As always, Brice never told her exactly what was wrong with the patient; instead, he allowed her to perform her own "strange" examination.

"Do her parents know you asked me to look at her?" Francesca asked softly.

Though her voice had been low, the child stirred and opened her eyes. She smiled at her visitor. "You're the lady Dr. Brice says is such a help to people. My mom said you would come and see me."

Francesca glanced at Brice with a quick frown of impatience. She had told him a thousand times not to mention her to anyone. She could not afford publicity. They had argued more than once over the issue. She touched the child's thin little hand with a fingertip. "You're in pain, aren't you?"

The little girl shrugged. "It's all right. I'm used to it now."

Cold air stirred the curtains unexpectedly and Brice glanced at the window, checking to assure himself it was closed. The last thing they needed was a draft in the room. Francesca was concentrating wholly on the child. Nothing else touched her mind at these times. It was as if only the child and Francesca existed. "My name is Francesca. What is yours?"

"Chelsea."

"Well, Chelsea, would you mind if I held your hand for a few minutes? It would help me understand what's going on inside of you."

A slow smile lit up the little girl's face. "You aren't going to poke and prod and stick me with needles?"

Francesca returned the smile. "I think we can safely leave that job to Brice." She took the small hand in hers. The skin was very thin, almost translucent. This child was wasting away. "I'm just going to sit here with you and concentrate. You might feel warm in spots, but it won't hurt."

Chelsea's eyes rested on Francesca's face, studying her expression before she decided to trust her. She nodded solemnly. "Go ahead, I'm ready."

Francesca closed her eyes, focused on the child and only the child, driving every other thought from her head. She sent herself seeking outside her own body, becoming as insubstantial as energy, heat and light. Entering the child, she began a slow, careful examination. The child's blood was a mess. Massive attacks were being launched in the bloodstream and her pitiful antibodies could not possibly make inroads against the invading army. Francesca continued to look at each organ, the tissue and muscle, the brain itself. Sorrow swamped her for a moment, endangering her position within the child's body. She felt great empathy with this little girl who had suffered for so many years of her young life.

She swayed, blinking rapidly, bringing herself back into her own body. As always, she felt disoriented and weak after an out-of-body experience. She sat for a moment in silence before she looked up at Brice.

"Francesca." He said her name softly, in great hope. It wasn't a question. He was a doctor. He knew medically that Chelsea was dying, her body succumbing to the terrible army so ferociously attacking it. He looked exhausted, and sorrow etched his face. He had done everything within his power and it was nowhere near enough.

"Maybe." Francesca glanced at the clock on the wall. It was three-thirty in the morning. How much time would it take to heal this child, to rid this worn-out body of every scrap of cancer? Would she be able to finish and still make it home before the sun came up? Did it matter? The child's life was worth the risk. And she didn't mind walking into the sun.

"Leave me alone with her, Brice, and let me see what I can do." Francesca stroked back Chelsea's hair. "You go to sleep, honey, and we'll see if we can make you a little more comfortable." She waited until Brice had closed the door before she once more sent herself into the child's body.

Time meant nothing at all when she worked as a healer. She was in Chelsea's small human form, holding her safe and warm with her mind, even as her energy fought the terrible battle for Chelsea's life. She was meticulous in her work, tireless, careful to ensure that not one vestige of the vile disease remained in Chelsea's body. She had no idea of the hours that passed or of her own strength waning until she found herself faltering, her body wearing out before her spirit had time to finish the task. At once she was flooded with power, a strong surge of enormous energy coming from a source outside her. She accepted the energy without question, certain of the origin. Of course Gabriel would know when she was risking her health; he was tied to her through their blood bond. Naturally he would reach out to help her. He was, after all, a male

Carpathian. There was no deeper meaning to his aid. He certainly wasn't doing it because he cared for her.

Francesca utilized the energy immediately, grateful even though she wanted nothing to do with Gabriel. Only one thing mattered: healing Chelsea's worn-out body and restoring her to good health. When she was certain she had eradicated every last bit of disease, Francesca returned to her own body.

She was breathing heavily, trembling from head to toe. For a moment she remained slumped over the little girl, slowly recovering from the difficult task she had set herself. Added to the drain of healing was the effort necessary to shield her activity from all outsiders. Over the years she had learned to put up a barrier to hide the surge of power from Carpathians and vampires alike.

Glancing up at the clock, she realized it was nearly five in the morning. She had to get home. As tired as she was, it wouldn't do to be caught out when the sun came up. As often as she said it didn't matter, Francesca was still secretly afraid of dying in such a painful way. Gabriel had seen to it that the sun could harm her again.

"It was not intentional, sweetheart."

"But the result is the same."

Brice was waiting for her, leaning against the wall just outside the door. "So, could you help her?"

"I hope so." Francesca was noncommittal even though she knew very well the child would recover fully. "Please do me the courtesy of not mentioning me to anyone. Really, Brice, we had an agreement. I can't afford to have people knocking down my door expecting miracles. Give her a day or two before you perform any tests on her. You know I hate publicity. You take the credit if it works."

He fell into step beside her. "I'm off. Would you like to

have breakfast? A little thank you for staying up all night for one of my patients."

Francesca pushed back the heavy fall of her blue-black hair. "I'm tired, Brice. You know it always wears me out."

"If I knew what you did, maybe I could help and you wouldn't get so tired," he teased. "You walked here, didn't you? Come on, I'll give you a ride home." He took her arm and led her to his car.

Francesca went willingly. It would only take minutes to get home by car, and she was exhausted. Settling into the leather seat, she snapped her seat belt in place automatically and smiled up at him. "You do like your luxury, Brice."

"Nothing wrong with that. I know what I want and I go after it." His dark eyes moved over her suggestively.

"Don't start," she cautioned, a laugh in her voice. "What is it with you, Brice? I've told you over and over we can't see each other."

"We see each other every day, Francesca," he pointed out with a grin. "We do quite well seeing each other."

"I'm too tired to argue with you. Just take me home and be nice."

"What did you do with the old man? You've got to quit picking people up off the street, Francesca. That's why you need me. You're too nice for your own good. Sooner or later you're going to pick up an ax murderer."

"I don't think there's much danger of that." Francesca watched out the window as her house loomed large at the end of the driveway.

"He isn't in your house, is he?" Brice asked suspiciously as he parked the car and threw his seat belt off.

She flashed him a quick smile. "I take it you think I'm going to invite you in."

Brice rushed around the car to open her door. "I'm definitely going in. I don't want to find out you've got that flea-bitten old man in there. It would be so like you."

As if on cue, the front door suddenly opened and Gabriel's large frame filled the doorway. He certainly didn't look like a flea-bitten old man. Francesca felt the color drain from her face and her heart definitely somersaulted. She glanced uneasily at Brice. Gabriel looked invincible, a predator. He looked capable of eating Brice alive. He stood tall and elegant, his sensual features carefully expressionless. Gabriel looked like a dark prince of old; the power in him was so obvious it clung like a second skin. He was incredibly handsome and she couldn't help noticing despite her resolve not to do so.

Brice effectively stopped her by grabbing her arm and holding her still. "Who the hell is that?" He actually thrust Francesca behind him protectively.

The gesture was so sweet it brought a lump to her throat. No one had ever been so protective and attentive to her as Brice. No matter how often she rebuffed him, Brice was determined in his pursuit of her.

Gabriel came down the stairs. Glided. Flowed. He moved with the grace of a large jungle cat, powerful muscles rippling beneath the thin silk of his shirt. "Thank you so much for bringing her home. I was beginning to worry," Gabriel said smoothly. His voice was velvet soft, gentle, impossible to ignore. It paved the way for whatever compulsion he chose to implant in his listener's mind.

Gabriel moved right up to Francesca, ignoring her little feminine retreat. His hand closed over her wrist, drew her beneath his wide shoulder. "You stayed out all night, sweetheart, you must be exhausted. I hope she was able to help your patient." His arm slipped possessively around

Francesca's shoulders, firmly anchoring her to him.

If she struggled or protested, she would be placing Brice in an untenable position. He would feel he ought to come to her defense and there was no one on this earth, she believed, who could successfully defeat Gabriel, unless it was his fallen twin Lucian.

"What do you think you're doing?" she demanded, using their mind merge to chastise him. He was tall, his strength enormous. He made her feel small and delicate when she was not that at all. He made her feel vulnerable.

"Who are you?" Brice asked uneasily.

"He senses your fear, Francesca. Do not make me do something you will have a difficult time forgiving."

"Don't you dare hurt him."

"I am Gabriel." Gabriel thrust out his hand toward Brice, as friendly as a full-grown panther. He looked elegant. He looked dangerous. He looked untamed. He looked very courtly and old-fashioned with his thick flowing hair caught at the nape of his neck by a leather thong.

Brice shook the offered hand, uncertain how to handle the situation. Francesca wasn't giving him any cues. Her young face looked stiff and frightened, her eyes enormous, deliberately avoiding his questioning gaze. She remained nestled beneath Gabriel's shoulder and looked very much as if she belonged there. Certainly there was no mistaking the possessive way Gabriel touched her, the warning in his eyes when he looked at Brice. Gabriel was letting him know, man to man, that Gabriel considered Francesca his and wouldn't allow any other man in her life. It was in his very body posture as he sheltered Francesca's slender feminine frame against his own muscular one.

"I guess you know who I am," Brice said grimly. The stranger reeked of danger. It clung to him, emanated from him. And Francesca just stood there silently, helplessly, as if she had no idea what to do.

Fully aware of the imminent rising of the sun, Gabriel was moving her up the stairs, his larger, heavier frame urging her smaller one toward the door. Francesca went only because Gabriel gave her no real choice in the matter. If she protested in any way, she would be putting Brice in a terrible position. She forced a smile. "I'll talk to you this evening, Brice."

"Do not count too heavily on it."

Francesca continued the charade with a halfhearted wave before she ducked beneath Gabriel's arm into the safety of the house. "How *dare* you interfere in my life?" Adrenaline was surging through her veins. She paced across the floor, back and forth in quick, hurried steps, betraying her frame of mind. She couldn't have stayed still if she had wanted to.

Calling on the patience born of a thousand battles, Gabriel watched her through half-closed eyes, his body as still as the mountains. "You are extremely angry with me." He said it very softly without a hint of expression.

Her black eyes flashed fire at him, and she swung her head so that her hair flared out like a thick curtain of silk. At once his body reacted. She was intensely beautiful, every movement sensual. "Don't do that, Gabriel. Don't start patronizing me. You are nothing to me, nothing in my life. I helped out a fellow Carpathian, that's the extent of what is between us. It was my duty, no more, no less."

"You sound as though you are trying to convince yourself, Francesca." He tilted his head, regarding her steadily. "You were going to invite that man into your house."

"That man is my friend," she pointed out. He didn't blink. Not once. He just watched her. Francesca found it very disconcerting. He was as still as a statue, looking lazy yet dangerous, and the longer he stood there, the faster her heart beat. He had some kind of power over her. It was because he was her lifemate. She was still Carpathian enough to realize his soul cried out to hers. So did his body. She could feel it, the hunger, the desire washing through her with a slow molten burn. Carefully she averted her eyes, staring at the carpet beneath her feet instead of at his fascinating body.

"Francesca." He said her name softly. Gently. His accent was very Old World and produced an unfamiliar fluttering in her heart. His voice was so beautiful and pure, she felt a compulsion to look up at him but she kept her eyes cast resolutely downward.

Intellectually, Francesca knew Gabriel was an extremely powerful being. His voice was compelling, his eyes mesmerizing. Because he was her true lifemate, it would be even more difficult for her to resist him, but she had no choice. "I have lived my life, Gabriel. I no longer wish to continue my existence. I certainly do not want to start over with an entirely different lifestyle. I've been alone, made my own decisions all these long centuries. I could never be happy being dictated to by a male. You can't ask me to change what I've become by your own decree. Tell me, will you still devote yourself to destroying your twin?"

"That is my duty, my vow to fulfill."

Francesca sighed with relief. She was extremely tired, her body once again feeling the enervating effects of the sun as it began to climb. "We have nothing further to discuss."

"If I had not aided you while you healed that child, you would never have had the strength to make it out of the sun." He said the words as he said everything, with no inflection, yet she felt the weight of his censure.

Deliberately she shrugged, a careless movement of her shoulders. "It didn't matter in the least to me whether I did or didn't. I have said it more than once and I don't wish to repeat myself continually."

"You leave me no choice but to bind you to me." Actually, he had intended to do so from the moment he'd realized she belonged with him. For two thousand years he had not *lived,* he had merely *existed* in a dark, ugly world. It was completely different now. Everything. Emotions. Colors. Francesca. He had thought to court her first, she certainly deserved that much. But if her life was at risk, he would wait no longer.

She looked at him, her eyes like black opals, beautiful and glittering. "It won't matter, Gabriel. I won't hesitate to go to the dawn. I won't be responsible for your life. If you make the decision to bind us, it is your decision alone. I refuse to be a part of it. If you choose to follow me when I go, so be it. But my life will be *my* choice."

Gabriel touched her mind; her resolve was genuine. She meant every word she said. "Francesca, tell me about your relationship with this doctor. How far has it gone?"

She curled up in a deep cushioned chair. "I'm not sure what you want to know. I haven't slept with him if that's what you mean. He wants to. I think he'd like to marry me. I *know* he would like to marry me." She hesitated a moment before admitting the rest. "I've considered it."

His eyebrow shot up. "And you allowed a human to develop such a strong attachment to you?"

"Why not? My lifemate rejected me and later I believed him to be dead. I had every right to find affection if I desired it," she replied without remorse.

"What do you feel for this human male?"

There was a soft growl in his gentle voice, just enough to send a shiver along her spine. She would not be intimidated by him. She had done nothing wrong. She would not feel guilty because he had come back from the dead. She owed him absolutely nothing.

Gabriel, remaining a shadow in her mind, could read her thoughts easily. He accepted that he was to blame for her solitary existence. He believed she had every right to feel as she did. He also could see her point that she would not live comfortably with a dominating male. None of it mattered to him. He had spent a lifetime in service to his people. Battles. Wars. Destroying the undead. It had gone on endlessly. He had lived a gray and bleak existence, always the predator crouched in wait to hunt and kill. Darkness had spread within him, yet his iron will had held it off, century after century as it attempted to take over his soul.

There was a promise that had kept him going. A hope. He believed he would find his lifemate. At least he had believed it until a couple of centuries earlier. His faith had been shaken then. Perhaps she was correct. Perhaps some part of him *had* recognized her all those centuries ago and that was why he had been so certain she existed. And maybe it was her decision to change her Carpathian body and live like a human that had prompted the growing darkness in him to become so strong that he had locked himself and his twin in the soil for years.

He studied her mind carefully; he could allow no mistakes. He had fought his demons alone—that was the curse of the Carpathian male—but Francesca's life had been so much worse. He had not been able to feel the loneliness, the emptiness, that he'd experienced. She'd felt every moment of it. She had longed for a family, for children. For a man to love her and share her laughter and her heartaches. The young girl had felt his dismissal as rejection; the woman knew times were terrible for their people and was proud of his decision to give his life in service for their dying species. She had done her part by leaving the Carpathian Mountains, by making it easier on the remaining males.

Francesca had coped with her lonely existence by using music and art, science and study. She had learned how to mask her presence from other Carpathians in the area. From the vampires so that she would not draw the undead to her city. She had dedicated her life to healing others, serving others as he had done. She had made up her mind that these were her last few years on earth. She was tired and wanted eternal rest. His return had not changed her mind. She could not conceive of another lifestyle. She had no intention of trying to fit into the Carpathian world, where she believed she no longer had a place.

Gabriel couldn't help admiring her. She lived her life well. And she was every bit as strong-willed as he was. He would tolerate much from her. But another male was too much. "Francesca, are things so different from the time I remember? Do our people have all the women they need? Can we afford for one of our own to become involved with a human male? Has Mikhail solved the problem of female births, has he been able to cut down on the number of our males turning vampire?"

She lifted her chin, trying hard to ignore his voice. It had a way of seeping into her skin and flooding her with warmth, with unfamiliar longings. "I could not help one single Carpathian male with his anguish. Do not think to reprimand me with so foolish a statement. My presence would only serve to make their lives more difficult."

"What of my life? My struggle against the darkness?"

"You chose your life, Gabriel, and you are strong enough to decide when you wish to end it. There is little chance you will lose your soul as so many have before you. You have held out longer than any other of our kind. At this late date, the danger has long since passed."

He smiled then, a quick flash of his immaculate white teeth. The smile softened the hard lines in his face and brought unexpected warmth to his black eyes. "Perhaps you give me far too much credit."

For one moment Francesca smiled back at him as if he'd struck a chord in her. "More than likely."

In that small moment Gabriel felt how right it could be between them. The way it was supposed to be, the way it would be. They would move together, breathe together, laugh and love together. Maybe he owed her a final peace, but he acknowledged deep within his soul, he was too selfish to give up emotions and colors and the beckoning call of happiness. It was there before him, the endless dream, the promise given to the males of his kind, the reward for resisting the terrible call of power, of darkness. She was there and he would not give her up.

Gabriel held out his hand to her. "We can sort this out on the next rising. Come to ground with me."

Francesca stared at his hand for what seemed an eternity. For an instant he thought she might argue with him. Slowly she allowed his fingers to tangle with hers, to pull her to her feet. The moment he touched her, she felt the answering jolt in her body, the way her heart tuned itself to his, the way her breathing sought to match his. The way her body came to life, soft and sensuous and needing his. At once she tried to let go, jerking her hand as if he'd burned her, but Gabriel didn't allow her retreat and simply walked close beside her toward the kitchen.

"You did not answer me. I have a need to know what it is you feel for this human male. I have treated you with respect and not taken the answer from your mind. Perhaps you would do me the courtesy of answering." Gabriel's voice was mild, but the threat of his taking the information betrayed the smoldering possession of the Carpathian male.

Francesca glanced up at him as they walked side by side. He was studying their surroundings, taking in every aspect of her home. It amazed her that he could be so calm after waking up in a new century with technology so different, with the world so different. Gabriel seemed to take everything in stride. He had such complete confidence in himself, she found it a little disconcerting.

"I'm very fond of Brice. We spend a lot of time together. He likes operas and theater. He's quite intelligent," she answered honestly. "He makes me feel alive even though I know I'm already dead inside."

Gabriel looked down at the top of her bent head. He felt the pain of her words stab through him. Pain. Real, not remembered or imagined. Genuine pain at how she had suffered because he had not actively sought her. His fingers tightened around hers and he curled her hand against his chest, against his heart. "I am so sorry, Francesca. It was wrong of me not to think what might be happening to my lifemate when I did not find her. But you are wrong to say you're dead inside. You are the most alive person I know."

The flood of warmth she felt at his words alarmed her. She laughed to cover her confusion. "You don't know anyone else."

Gabriel smiled at her, savoring the feeling of happiness. He could look at her for all time. Listen to the sound of her voice. He would never tire of watching the expressions flit across her face or the sweep of her lashes against her cheekbones. Everything about her was a miracle to him and he was just beginning to realize she was real and not a fantasy. He could reach out and touch her skin, marvel at its softness. "That was not nice."

"I know." Francesca was very much aware of the power in his body as they descended together to the sleeping chamber. She had not used the underground hideaway for many years, but she knew it was necessary now. She could not sleep the sleep of the mortals or walk in the sun again. Gabriel's ancient blood had changed all that. She was exhausted and only the welcoming arms of the earth could rejuvenate her, restore her to full power once more.

Gabriel waved his hand to open the soil. Francesca stood there for a moment, hesitating to move forward. Gabriel simply caught her around her small waist and floated into the waiting earth with her. He locked the house in a strong safeguard few would be able to unravel. Lucian. Only Lucian. What Gabriel knew, so too did Lucian. It was only his twin he worried about. Only his beloved twin who could destroy them. For a moment his heart clenched with the torment of betrayal, a heavy burden he felt as an actual physical pain.

Francesca did her best to put space between them, but he felt her exhaustion and he simply drew her close, curling his body protectively around her while he swept into her mind and issued a command to sleep. He was incredibly strong and she succumbed without too much of a struggle. He would have to face her on the next rising, but for now he simply savored the opportunity to hold her body close to his, to rest his head on hers, feel the silk of her hair against his own skin.

"Gabriel? You are injured in some way. I feel your pain."

Lucian. Even now, locked within the earth during these vulnerable hours, his twin felt the wrenching pain in his heart. There was no gloating as one might expect from the undead, but in all the centuries of the chase, Lucian had never sounded anything but beautiful. Gabriel kept his mind blank, not wanting to take a chance that his brother might discover Francesca.

"Gabriel? This battle is between the two of us. No other can interfere. Should you have need of me, say so."

Gabriel's breath caught in his throat. There was compulsion in that voice, in that command, and it was so powerful he could feel the sweat on his forehead as he fought to break the contact. In the end it was easier just to answer. *"It is a minor injury due to carelessness on my part. The earth will heal me."*

There was a soft silence as if Lucian was deciding whether to believe him or not, then emptiness. Gabriel lay for some time thinking of his brother. How could this have happened to Lucian? Lucian had always been the strong one, the one Gabriel depended on, believed in. Lucian had always been the leader. Even now, as a vampire, wholly evil, wholly depraved, Lucian did the unexpected. He always studied, he was always unfailingly courteous, always sharing knowledge.

Gabriel had never considered the possibility of his twin turning vampire. He had known Lucian had lost his feelings and the ability to see colors at a much earlier age than most, many years before Gabriel; yet he was so strong, so self-reliant, so completely powerful. How had it happened? If only Gabriel had seen it coming, perhaps he could have aided his brother before it was too late. His terrible guilt was oppressive.

With a little sigh, Gabriel pulled Francesca closer to him and buried his face in her wealth of soft, fragrant hair. It gave him a sense of peace to hold her, to have his body wrapped so possessively around hers. He needed her so desperately, far more than she needed him. His last breath took the scent of her into his heart and lungs, carried it with him into the healing sleep of his people.

Chapter Three

Gabriel awoke to fire, hunger, need. Obsession. Every particle of his skin was alive with fiery tongues of heat. His body was hard and aching, urgently demanding he claim what was rightfully his. Beside him she lay pale and still, her skin cool against his. Ignoring the consequences, he disposed of the thin barrier of clothing between them with a single thought. She took his breath away. Her body was slender, perfectly molded for his.

He lay holding her, carefully calculating his options. He was not willing to allow her to choose death. He wanted a chance at life together. He could not exist without her. But even binding her to him with the ritual words would not be enough to keep her from facing the dawn. He had read her mind, her will. He could think of only one way to deter her. There was only one way to force her compliance. *Unforgivable.* He would have to accept that. She would not forgive him, but she would choose life for both of them. It would give him the time to tie her to him emotionally.

Gabriel thought about his lack of options for some time. While he lay holding her his determination only increased. He would have her. It was selfish and wrong and beneath him, but he would not allow her to choose death over life. He could pretend it was for the saving of their race, that both of them owed it to their species to do all they could to continue, but he knew there was nothing noble about his decision. He wanted her. She belonged with him and he was going to make sure not only that he possessed her, but that she no longer had a choice in the matter.

He closed his eyes and sent himself seeking outside his body and into hers. He moved slowly and surely, determined there would be no mistakes. He was an ancient with incredible power and knowledge. He made certain to arouse her body even as he found what he sought. There was only one thing left to do. As he emerged once more into his own body, he recognized that she was a healer, a woman long on the earth. He would have to be certain she had no time to think or feel anything but the hunger raging between them. He was completely confident he could manage that easily enough. Carpathian mating rituals could be fiery and intense.

Gabriel positioned his body over hers so that he could feel the cool satin of her skin against the unbearable heat of his. He bent his dark head and fastened his mouth to hers to take her first breath as he issued the command to wake, to come to him needing him. His mind fully merged with hers, he was unstoppable, a fully aroused male in the heat of the Carpathian mating ritual. His lifemate's heartbeat found the beat of his, her lungs followed the direction of his and her mind was instantly captured by the hunger radiating from Gabriel. He built the fire into a fierce conflagration. He needed her desperately just to survive. He had to have her. His body raged for her, demanded her. No one else could quench the flames threatening to devour him completely.

His hunger was her hunger, his need became hers. Her body burned and ached, her breasts swelling in invitation against his chest, her hips moving restlessly. Gabriel found some solace in the silken heat of her mouth. His hands explored every inch of her skin, every shadow and hollow. He wanted to take his time, savor each discovery, but he couldn't give her time to emerge from their mind merge. He stroked his tongue down the column of her throat, lingered over her rapid pulse. His hand moved to the junction of her legs, his knee pushing her legs open to give him better access.

Francesca could only feel fierce longing and terrible, empty hunger. There was a red haze of madness, a fire sweeping through her. Everywhere he touched her, flames danced. She heard a moan come from her throat as his fingers found her hot, moist center. It only made her longing more intense. His teeth scraped gently over her breast, teased her nipple into a hard peak, moved back to the satin-soft swell. She felt him, thick and hard, pressing into her. His mind was feeding her erotic images, projecting his fierce urgency to possess her. She couldn't think, she could only feel endlessly. Feel and hunger and burn.

Her hair was everywhere, brushing over both of them, the silken strands unbearably erotic on their sensitized skin. There was a strange roaring in her ears. She reached for him a little desperately, her arms circling his head, cradling him to her while his mouth drove every sane thought from her mind, until there was only him. There was no earth or sky, no time or place, only Gabriel with his wide shoulders and hot skin and demanding body needing her as no one ever had. Her body didn't feel as if it belonged to her; it was soft and pliant, aching every bit as much as Gabriel's.

He whispered something to her. She recognized the ancient language, but his words were muffled against her breast. He lifted her hips, and paused while one small heartbeat of time passed. She stared up at him, bemused by his sheer sensual beauty. His black gaze held hers. "I claim you as my lifemate." His body surged forward and took possession of hers.

Francesca cried out, her hands tangling in his dark flowing hair in protest of what he was doing. "Relax, Francesca." Gabriel breathed the words, his voice beautiful, mesmerizing, enthralling. His hips moved with a slow, sexy surge forward, giving her body time to adjust to the invasion of his. He bent his dark head to kiss her satin skin, his mouth moving over her pulse. He focused on breathing in and out to stop himself from plunging into her. She was tight and hot, surrounding him with velvet fire. She was so utterly perfect. He closed his eyes for a moment, savoring the feel of her all around him.

Francesca knew she should protest, but his mouth was making her crazy with need. Then white lightning flashed through her as he sank his teeth deep, joining them together in the most erotic way of all. Heart, mind, soul and body. Her life force flowed into him even as his body took hers, his hips moving in a deep, hard rhythm, taking them both toward a shattering release. Gabriel was shaking with the effort to hold on to his control. She tasted like nothing he had ever had. Heady, sexy, everything he could possibly want. Hot. Sweet. Addictive. His body was going up in flames, burying deeper and harder, making them one.

Gabriel swept his tongue over her breast. "Please, Francesca." The words were husky with need. At once she responded to the urgent plea. Her mouth moved over the heavy muscles of his chest. His body clenched as her teeth teased his pulse, scraped back and forth, nipped. "Francesca." He spoke her name with desperate urgency. Francesca found she had to comply. It was more than a black magic spell; the age-old lure was on her. His body was so strong, so hard, so perfect. She smelled his blood, his life force calling to her, beckoning. Her mouth moved sensuously over his muscled flesh, her teeth teasing him until he groaned with need. She sank her teeth deep. Lightning splintered through him and he buried himself in her hot, tight sheath, losing himself in the sheer ecstasy of her body. "I claim you as my lifemate. I belong to you. I offer my life for you. I give you my protection, my allegiance, my heart, my soul and my body. I take into my keeping the same that is yours." He could barely manage to get the ritual binding words out. Her body was rippling around his, shattering, fragmenting, milking his with hot fiery velvet so tight he thought he would go up in flames. "You are my lifemate, bound to me for all eternity and always in my care."

Francesca swept her tongue across the tiny pinpricks she had made in the heavy muscles of his chest and clung to him. He was the only safe anchor as her body was swept away on wave after wave of sheer molten pleasure. She was drowning in it; her body was not her own anymore. It never would be again. She lay beneath him, her heart hammering loudly in her ears, her blood racing, the taste of him in her mouth, his body buried deep inside of her, and for the first time in her endless existence she was truly content.

Gabriel lay over her, pinning her beneath him, and felt he never wanted to move away from the beauty of her body. He lifted his head to look down into her eyes, fully expecting censure. Francesca stroked back his damp hair. "So, that's what we've been missing all these years." She said it softly, in wonder.

He bent his head to place a kiss against the soft, vulnerable line of her throat. His hands bunched in her hair possessively. "You are so incredibly beautiful, Francesca." His voice whispered seductively over her skin.

She closed her eyes and allowed him to seep into her body and mind. He had bound them together. She had hoped he wouldn't, but it made no difference. None of this made a difference. Francesca was glad she had experienced what should have been hers, but it wasn't enough to hold her to earth. Hundreds of years had passed; her life had gone on endlessly. She could not start over as a Carpathian woman bound to a domineering male. She relaxed her body, soaking up the feel of his. He was so different from her, so much more muscle and sinew, all masculine and hard, angles and planes.

He was moving again, slow and gentle, building the heat between them once more. Francesca had studiously avoided all thoughts of sex and the sexual act once she realized it would never happen to her. Now she wished she had included it in her extensive education.

"I did," Gabriel assured her and once more took complete control of their bodies. He directed her with his mind; his hands, cupping her rounded bottom, moved her body to meet the rhythm of his.

There was no denying him; Francesca didn't even want to. In all the long centuries of her solitary existence, she had never betrayed her lifemate. As long as she knew he lived, she had waited, hoped in the way women often do. But as the empty years passed by, she'd realized he wouldn't come for her. Then she had turned her attentions to finding her way into the sun. Her life with Brice would have come next. But now it was so different. No other could ever make her feel as Gabriel did. He was flame and ecstasy, his hands moving over her as if committing every line and curve to memory. As if he were worshipping her. As if he *had* to have her.

He wanted her. He needed her. Only she could assuage the fiery burning in his body. And she knew absolutely that only Gabriel could make her come alive like this. Completely alive. Only Gabriel could make her body burn with such intensity that ripple after ripple of pure sensual pleasure shattered her into fragments and made her lose control. It was like nothing she had ever experienced or imagined, his body moving in hers with a commanding rhythm, leading hers ever closer to the edge of the highest cliffs.

Gabriel's mouth moved over her full breast, hot and hungry, so that her body did a meltdown, her insides turning to molten lava. She wanted him to touch her, to explore every inch of her skin with his mouth. His tongue was swirling around her hard nipples and her velvet sheath tightened and tightened so that she was drowning in pleasure. He moved with sure, hard strokes, their bodies coming together, his hands biting into her hips while he held her still for his invasion. She wanted him like this over and over. She could read the erotic pictures in his mind, the things he intended to do to her, the things he wanted her to do to him, and she wanted every one of them. Her body was spinning out of control and she clung to him, a soft sound of sheer pleasure escaping before she could stop it. She didn't want to stop it, she wanted this moment to last for all eternity. She wanted to take her time and explore every inch of his hard, perfect body. She wanted to drive him out of his mind with pleasure as she knew she could.

Her arms slipped around his neck and she held him close as he thrust into her, surging in and out, reaching ever higher while she careened over the cliffs into a free fall that went on and on until he exploded into her, falling with her, their bodies entangled so that neither could tell where one started and the other left off. Gabriel held her to him, slowing their heartbeats, more than satisfied with her reaction. Rather than being angry with him at his deliberate seduction, she was pressing her beautiful mouth into the hollow of his shoulder, her body soft and pliant. In her mind he read her satisfaction, her growing desire for more. She wanted this heat and fire. She wanted his hands on her. It was unlike anything either of them had ever experienced.

Suddenly she stiffened and pushed at the wall of his chest. Gabriel allowed her a few inches of freedom. A bead of sweat was trickling down the valley between her inviting breasts and lazily he leaned his head down, tracking the bead with his tongue. He felt her body shudder and tighten around his. She pushed at him again and at once he sought her mind. Guilt was invading her, guilt and confusion that she should feel such a strong sexual attraction when she had never before experienced such a thing.

"It is natural, Francesca," he whispered soothingly, his

teeth scraping back and forth over her sensitive breast, then moving to the corner of her mouth.

"Maybe for you it is, but not for me. I need time, Gabriel, to sort all of this out. I need to be alone. I need to think this through. Please let me up."

Were there tears in her voice? He studied her averted face for a long moment, willing her to meet his dark gaze, but she steadfastly refused. Reluctantly he eased his body from hers and at once felt bereft. She did too, but she was refusing to admit it to herself. She wanted to be alone. Gabriel moved his large frame off her body, his hand trailing over her soft skin once more because he couldn't help himself. He lay staring up at the ceiling of the chamber, a small smile of satisfaction curving his mouth.

She wanted him every bit as much as he wanted her. There was a sensual, very passionate woman hidden in Francesca. Gabriel closed his eyes and thought of what it would be like to hold her every dawn, to wake each night with her beside him, to bury his body deep into the welcoming heat of her at will. He had never imagined such a paradise in all his centuries of existence, and now more than ever he was determined he would not lose her.

Francesca had retreated to the bathroom. She stood in the shower with tears running down her face. How could this have happened now, so late in her existence? How could Gabriel still be alive when the entire Carpathian world believed him dead? He was a legend, a myth, not someone living and breathing and demanding his rights.

"It will not do you any good to hide in there." She sensed that Gabriel was close. Hastily she fought back the tears and turned off the water. Stepping from the shower stall, she wrapped her slender body in a large towel. Her skin was so sensitive she found herself blushing for no

reason at all. He had done this. Changed her for all time. He had given her blood and brought her back fully into the Carpathian world. He had bound her to him, completing the ritual so that the two halves of their soul were melded together, their heart was one. She would need him now, need to touch his mind and need the heat of his body for the remainder of her time on earth. Francesca, who had never needed anyone. Francesca, who never answered to anyone.

Gabriel was lounging lazily against the door frame, his black eyes watching her warily. She was so beautiful she took his breath away, but the tears clinging to her long lashes tore at his heart.

"I am not hiding," she replied as she stepped resolutely in front of the full-length mirror. Did she look any different? Did it show that she had been loved so thoroughly by a man? "I was merely collecting my thoughts."

"You believe nothing has changed." He made it a statement.

"I cannot give you what you want from me. Do not push the issue, Gabriel, or you will force me to bring this matter before our Prince."

Gabriel smiled, a predator's baring of teeth. There was no humor, only a wolfish menace. For the first time she was afraid. "No one will take you from me, Francesca, certainly not Mikhail. In any case, you would not bring another into our personal battle. This is between the two of us. You believe that as deeply as I do. Make no mistake, my first allegiance is to my lifemate, to safeguarding her health."

"What of her happiness?"

"Give me time and I will ensure that also. Do not think to cross swords with me. You will not win."

"I admire your arrogance," Francesca said smoothly and allowed the towel to drop to the floor, simultaneously clothing herself in the manner of her kind as she did so. "I have to go out this night." She was not going to be drawn into an argument with him.

"If you seek nourishment, I will provide for you," Gabriel said smoothly.

She fought to keep color from sweeping up her neck and into her face. She didn't want to think about the way he would provide for her. He turned the simple act of feeding into a sexual intimacy. "Thank you very much for the offer, but I am going to the hospital. There was a message from Brice about another patient."

Gabriel reached out and wrapped his fingers around her slender wrist, a shackle she couldn't possibly break. He wasn't hurting her; in fact his touch was gentle, but even if she had struggled desperately, she would never have broken his grip. "I will keep what is mine, Francesca. Do not put this doctor in the middle of our battle."

"There is no battle, Gabriel," she replied softly. "Brice is my friend. I go to the hospital often to give aid where it is needed. It is a large part of my life, of who I am. It has nothing to do with Brice, other than that he happens to be a doctor and we're friends."

"You are reaching for him in your mind because he is simple. He is someone you are familiar and comfortable with. I frighten you."

Her dark eyes rested on his face. "I don't know exactly what you're planning to do, Gabriel, but I can read your intent. You think to stop me from doing the things I have planned for so long."

Gabriel shrugged casually, not bothering to deny the

obvious. "Perhaps it would help if you considered other possibilities, another way of life."

"Because you think you've changed your lifestyle. You haven't, you know. In a day or two there will be a killing in this city and you will be on the hunt without a backward glance, without a single thought for me, just as you did before."

Gabriel smiled at her, his teeth very white. "I will have no choice but to hunt the vampire, but I will not only look back, I will come back."

Francesca twisted her wrist experimentally, reminding him to release her. "There's no real need to hurry," she said coolly. Even as she said it, even as she tried to dismiss him, she was reaching up to smooth his collar.

At once Gabriel felt the same soothing calm he had experienced from the moment she had first touched him. He had not realized just how tight he was inside. Francesca recognized it and knew what to do to relax him. "You are a great man, Gabriel, a legend among our people, and your reputation is well deserved. I wish that I could give you all that you should have." Francesca's long lashes swept down to conceal the deep sorrow and guilt in her eyes. "But I had a life before you came here. I don't know you. My body reacts as a Carpathian lifemate's should, but my heart is not yours."

Gabriel brought her hand up to her chest and held it over his heart. "You feel admiration for this human doctor, Francesca, I can read it easily in your mind, but do not mistake it for love."

"Why do you believe I could not love a human man?"

"Because you are my lifemate and there is only one man for you. I am here now, Francesca. I should have been here sooner, but I am here now. Do not allow fear to send you running to this man."

"I have felt affection for Brice for a long time, Gabriel. It is true I was entertaining the idea of sharing my last years with him. I deserve some semblance of happiness in so long a lifetime." Francesca could not understand why she was feeling guilty. She owed Gabriel nothing. She had asked him not to bind them together, yet he had done so. She felt cornered and confused.

"You enjoy this doctor's company because you share his interests. You are a born healer. He, too, heals people. But that commonality is not love, Francesca. Affection, admiration and friendship do not add up to love."

"If he had asked me to marry him, Gabriel, you would have found him living with me."

Gabriel's black eyes moved over her face. Very gently he reached out to tug her chin up. "I do not have to read your mind to know just how often he has asked this question of you. No man, human or otherwise, would take long to try to make you his. You do not love him, Francesca."

"I don't love you, Gabriel. And that matters to me. I have lived far too long to enter into a relationship at this late date because I wish to experience sex."

His eyes laughed at her. "Great sex," he corrected.

A small answering smile flirted with her mouth. "All right then, great sex," she conceded. "Don't get any ideas, I'm just giving the devil his due. All this time our people called you the angel of light and Lucian the dark angel. I think they might have it backward." She withdrew her hand and turned away from him. "I do not mind if you find another sleeping chamber, Gabriel. Do not count too heavily on winning this battle between us. Even after what has occurred between us, I am still determined to carry on with my plans to grow old. I have lived long and I tire of watching others die."

"There is no battle, honey," he murmured softly and watched her walk out into the dark night. She had no chance of escaping him. He had made sure of that. No one, human or otherwise, could take her from him now. And his insurance policy would prevent her from seeking the solace of the dawn as nothing else could. He glided through the room to the door and stood staring out at the lights of the city. So many. It was lit up as brightly as the heavens above.

Gabriel had been locked beneath the earth a long time; there was much to catch up on. He had to relearn the layout of Paris, find every alley and every bolt-hole in it. This was a perfect hunting ground for a demon such as Lucian had become. Soon it would start. The killings, the deaths, the endless hunt and the many battles. Somewhere out there in the slumbering city stalked a merciless, relentless killer. No one was safe, no one would be safe again until Gabriel destroyed him. Now with Francesca to protect, Gabriel knew it was imperative he win this time. He had to find a way to destroy his brother. If he had hesitated out of misguided loyalty in the past, he no longer had the luxury of being able to do so now. Francesca must be protected at all times. With a heavy heart, he took three running steps and launched himself into the air.

Francesca took her time walking to the hospital. She loved the night. As much as she had longed for the sun, had worked to be able to walk in it, she loved the night. There was peace and tranquillity after sunset, whereas chaos often reigned during the day. She loved the sounds of the night creatures, the rush of wings overhead that only a select few ever heard. There was a secret world she had always been part of, and now Gabriel was demanding she return to it.

How long had it been since she had seen her homeland, the Carpathian Mountains? What would it be like to walk among her own kind? To dig her fingers deep in the rich, healing soil? She had long ago given up that dream. Why had he come back after all this time? Why now? What was it she felt for Brice? Could she give her body so willingly, so completely to Gabriel and really have affection for Brice? Gabriel hadn't taken what she wasn't willing to give. He might have awakened her to his need, might even have planted the seeds of desire in her body before waking her, but she was no fledgling. She could not place the blame on Gabriel's shoulders. She could have stopped him, or at least made things extremely difficult. No, she couldn't place the blame on Gabriel. She had wanted him almost from the first moment she had awakened with his blood coursing through her veins.

What did that mean? Was she a woman who could be with more than one man at the same time? Could she love Brice? If she really loved him, why hadn't she said she would marry him long before now? Was Gabriel right? Was she rushing to Brice because he was safe and someone she knew? Someone who could never dominate her? Was she still harboring a young girl's hurt and humiliation? She had thought herself long over those silly feelings.

She was bound to Gabriel. Her mind tuned itself to his. Her body cried out for his. They were tied, yet her wayward heart seemed to have a mind of its own. How could that be? Had she made herself so human, she could no longer be tied by the ritual words? No, she had felt the burning need, the terrible hunger only Gabriel could assuage.

Sighing, Francesca rubbed her pounding temples. She had betrayed her own beliefs. She had never committed herself to Brice, but she had secretly entertained the idea that there was a chance for them. Brice cared a great deal for her; she felt his genuine affection every time they were together. It would be impossible for him to lie to her, she could read his mind so easily. He would be so upset if she suddenly withdrew from their relationship. She had allowed him to feel for her. Didn't that make her responsible? She felt confused and lonely. And she was so very tired of living so completely alone.

"Not alone, Francesca. I am here to talk with you. There is no need to feel betrayal. I came into your life unexpectedly. I cannot say I am happy you think constantly of another man and worry more about his happiness than mine, but I do understand. I complicated things for you."

Francesca blinked back tears. There was something comforting and very intimate about another speaking so softly in her head, whispering soothing words of understanding and camaraderie in the face of her personal crisis. It had been so long since she had used such a means of communication. Gabriel's voice was a powerful tool, stroking like a caress through her mind. For the first time in many centuries she felt she was not alone. The women of her species needed their other half. *Gabriel.* She closed her eyes briefly. Why had he come back now?

"Francesca! Thank God." Brice came hurrying out of an alcove just around the corner from the entrance to the emergency room. "I've lost half my life worrying about you. Who was that man?"

Brice's arm curved around her shoulders and at once she felt the heavy weight of Gabriel's disapproval. Carpathian males did not share their women well. Gabriel was Old World. He had spent centuries of his life chasing demons, protecting others. He had the instincts of a predator, yet he was also courageous, a courtly, elegant lord. She could feel his struggle to remain balanced and understanding when his very nature demanded he eliminate his competition efficiently and very swiftly. It had been a long time since Francesca had lived in his world. She had almost forgotten the way the men of her race were with their women. Protective. Possessive.

"His name is Gabriel, Brice. I'm sorry, I had no idea he was going to be there. If I'd known, I would have told you about him before you met him."

"He looks at you as if he owns you." Brice hugged her to him, suddenly feeling as if he had already lost her. There was a wariness in her eyes that had never been there before. Francesca was different, but he couldn't exactly say how. "He thinks he does, doesn't he? What is he to you?"

"He was my husband. I thought he was dead," Francesca said softly, truthfully. "I was more shocked to see him alive than you must be. I'm sorry, Brice, he's been gone forever. I had no idea he would come back. I truly thought him dead all these years."

"You never mentioned a husband." Brice was clearly in shock.

She nodded. "I know I didn't. It was a long time ago and I had accepted that he was gone. His return is a shock and I have to deal with it. All of us do."

Brice swallowed hard, visibly upset, so much so that she automatically soothed him with her touch. He immediately laced his fingers through hers. "What does it mean? He can't think after all this time he can just walk back into your life, can he? You know how I feel about you. Was he legally declared dead? What does this mean for us?"

"I don't honestly know what to think right now, Brice. I told you, I'm in a state of complete shock." Because Francesca could not bear to be dishonest with him, she forced herself to go further. "But it does change things. How could it not? Gabriel is a very overpowering man and he certainly was never declared dead."

Brice stepped away from her, his eyes moving over her face in censure. "You're still attracted to him, aren't you?" It was an accusation.

Francesca looked away from him, guilt washing over her in a rush. "He was my husband, Brice. What do you think?"

"Damn it, Francesca! You should have married me a long time ago. You certainly thought about it, you can't deny that you did. So what if he's come back? He doesn't belong in your life anymore." Suddenly he went very still. "He isn't staying at your house, is he?"

Francesca remained silent, her gaze studiously avoiding his.

Brice slapped his forehead. "Francesca! Are you out of your mind? You don't even know anything about this man anymore. Where has he been all this time? Do you even know what he's been doing lately? I'll bet you don't yet you just take him in as if no time has passed. For all you know, he could have been in jail. He probably was in jail." His hand on her arm detained her progress into the hospital. "Is that it, Francesca? Was he in jail somewhere and you just don't want to tell me? I think you owe it to me."

"If I wanted to tell you, I wouldn't be able to. You won't

let me get a word in edgewise," Francesca protested. "Where Gabriel was and what he was doing is his business, only his, and I don't owe you that information."

"You slept with him." Brice made it a statement.

"That isn't your business either." Her chin was up, her eyes flashing a warning signal. Francesca might feel guilty but she couldn't find it in her to allow Brice or any other man to chastise her. She had always been honest with him, always. More than once she had encouraged him to find another woman, one who would adore him as he deserved. Francesca was just not that kind. It made her feel sad that she wasn't. It made her feel inadequate that she couldn't give her heart completely and totally. There was something wrong with her, something missing. It was just as well Gabriel had chosen to follow another path; he would have found her less than perfect, his life with her less than satisfying.

"Has it occurred to you he may have been living with another woman all these years? He could have another wife and even children somewhere and you wouldn't know it." The words slipped out maliciously, before he could stop them.

Her large black eyes flashed with sudden anger at the suggestion. "That's beneath you, Brice," she pointed out softly.

"Francesca, please. Don't do this." Brice circled her waist with his arm, but as he drew her close to his body he was very much aware he had crossed some line.

At once she was uncomfortable, stiff. She could smell his cologne and though it was expensive, it made her feel slightly nauseated. It was strange, she had always rather liked his cologne, yet now she thought only of the way Gabriel smelled, his musky, male scent. Was that part of the ritual, the binding? Did it make it impossible for her to touch another man? Was that the secret the men of their race held over the women? She shoved an impatient hand through her hair, found her fingers were trembling. Maybe there was a way to undo what the ritual words had wrought. After all, she had done the impossible: she had found a way to walk among humans in the noonday sun. Gabriel might have reversed her accomplishment, but that didn't negate the fact that she had done what no other Carpathian ever had.

"I'm not doing anything, Brice. I don't know what to do, so I'm not doing a single thing. I'm not asking you to put your life on hold or asking you to wait. I've always told you to find a sweet girl and settle down." Francesca brushed her hair away, a nervous gesture she rarely made.

"I love you, Francesca," Brice said unhappily. "I'm not about to run out and find another woman. You're the one I want. I can't say I like the idea of a former husband staying at your house, but I don't want you shutting me out because you think I can't handle it."

Francesca shook her head. "I can't handle it, Brice. You have no idea how confused I feel. I'd rather not talk about it any more right now. What if I just look at this patient for you?"

Brice caught at her arm and slowed his pace to prevent her from entering the hospital. "Do you love him?"

Francesca let out her breath slowly, wanting to be entirely truthful. "How could I when I haven't seen him for so long? I don't know him. I haven't let myself know him; I don't want to know him right now. I can tell you I think he's courageous and I admire him as I've never admired anyone else in my life. And he deserves to have a good life. I just don't necessarily want to be part of it."

Brice swore silently to himself. "You don't owe him anything. I don't care if he was your husband. You sound as though you think you owe him, but you owe him absolutely nothing. I don't care if he was a secret agent and saved the world. He can't just come back here and decide he wants you again."

Gabriel *had* saved the world, probably more than once. And with a powerful vampire loose in the city, he would once again protect humans at great risk to his own life. He had given up his chance at happiness, had given up family, emotions and colors. He had done more than risk his life, he had risked his very soul to keep mortals and immortals alike safe. He had no real existence; even his own kind feared his power. He was completely alone. *Gabriel.* Her heart ached for him as much as her mind rebelled against his hold over her.

"Gabriel is different, Brice. I can't explain him to you. I've had a difficult evening and I'm asking you to drop the subject for a while. I can't give you the answer you want to hear and if you push me, I would have to say no, there's no hope for us and just forget it." She rubbed at her throbbing temples. "What about this patient of yours? Do you want help or not?"

Brice shook his head, trying to hide his frustration. "All right, Francesca, have it your way. We'll shelve it for now, but I wish you'd throw him out or take him to one of those shelters you're always funding. One of them ought to have a bed for him."

Francesca knew very well Gabriel was probably quite wealthy. No matter how long he had been sleeping beneath the earth, he would have a stash of gold or something of equal value to sustain him. Those in his line would keep his properties intact for him. If he had none, all Carpathians would contribute significant amounts to ease his way back into society. It was their way to aid one another at all times when there was need. In Carpathian society, wealth meant nothing. It was to be shared as a means of continuing their kind, of keeping them a secret. Gabriel had not yet had time to collect what was rightfully his, but he would. In any case, Francesca could do no other than live by the code of her people and share what was hers with him.

"I have asked him to find his own place as soon as he gets his bearings, but I will not force him to leave my home. Now tell me about your patient or I'm leaving." She meant it too. If Brice pushed her any harder she was just going to walk away and not come back for a very long time.

He recognized the finality in her voice. "She's fourteen years old, and looks as if she's been in a train wreck. X rays show a multitude of broken bones, some set by physicians and some knitted crookedly on their own. She's practically comatose. She looks at me, but won't say a word. I can't even tell whether she actually hears me. She's in bad shape. She has some wicked-looking scars on her back and some particularly bad ones on her hands and arms as if she fought back many times. She looks as if she's been battered repeatedly. Her father brought her in, a brute of a man, nasty, doesn't say much. No other relatives. Cops say he's a career criminal but no history of child abuse. We can't prove the father's a sadistic abuser without the child's account, and she can't talk to us. He wants to take her home, says she's retarded, but I don't think so."

Francesca felt her heart turn over. She hated this kind of thing, had fought for centuries to establish safe havens for women and children, yet there were never enough. Fourteen years old. Why would a father torture and abuse his own child while her species fought so hard to preserve their children? Carpathian males always protected women and children above their own lives. It just didn't make any sense and her heart bled for the poor teenager with no one to protect her from the very person who should have loved her the most. "Was there sexual abuse?"

Brice nodded. "Absolutely there was. This child has been so abused it's sickening."

"You have need of my aid, honey?" Gabriel's beautiful voice brushed gently at the walls of her mind.

"Show her to me, Brice," she instructed softly. *"A child has been abused. I am going to see her now. Brice said they suspect the father."* Without really thinking about it, she sent him all of the information Brice had given to her. *"I will be fine."*

"I expect you to call should there be need." Along with the soft command she was immediately flooded with warmth and comfort, strong arms to anchor her as she faced another emotional battering.

Chapter Four

Brice pushed open the door to the young woman's room and stepped back to allow Francesca entry. Fortunately the girl's father was not present. The man was a bully and Brice was afraid of him. He crossed the room, smiling gently at the young woman huddled on the bed. She hadn't looked up or indicated in any way that she noticed their entry.

"Skyler, I'd like you to meet a friend of mine. I know you can hear me, Skyler. This is Francesca. She's an extraordinary woman. You don't have to be afraid of her."

Francesca watched Brice, noticed how gentle his movements has become around the teenager. That was one of the things that drew her to Brice. The way he was with children, with those who were hurt and wounded. He cared. It couldn't have anything to do with money, she was certain of that. Brice really wanted to make things right, wanted to help these little lost souls. Her heart warmed and she smiled at him as she glided forward to seat herself in the chair Brice had placed right beside the bed.

"Hello, Skyler. Your doctor has asked me to come and visit you. I thought we'd ask him to leave so we can be alone together. Just the two of us." She nodded at Brice.

He bent close, his mouth so close to her ear she could feel the warmth of his breath. "I'm going to keep an eye out for her father. If he catches you in here, there's no telling what he might do."

"You think he'll become violent?" Francesca whispered the question, not wanting the child to hear her. The last thing the girl needed was an ugly scene involving her father. "Are you expecting him?"

"Not anytime soon. He usually spends this time of night drinking," Brice assured her. With a reassuring wink at the unresponsive teenager he left the room.

Francesca observed the child closely. The girl was lying in the fetal position, her hair hanging in ragged lengths as though someone had chopped it off indiscriminately. There was a crescent-shaped scar on her temple, white and thin. There were bruises all over her face. Her eyes were swollen and her jaw was several shades of green and blue. "So your name is Skyler." She lowered her voice so that it was soft and beautiful, hiding the underlying compulsion with a silvery sound.

Francesca took the girl's limp, scarred hand into hers, reaching at the same time for her mind. She wanted to examine the child's memories, to see what had happened to her to make her lie without moving, so lifeless and without hope. At once a flood of violence and depravity stormed into her. Tears burned, clung to Francesca's lashes. Such a terrible existence. She felt every blow the child had received, every burn, every rape, every act forced upon her, every single torture, mental and physical, as if it had been done to her. The scars were on the inside as well as the outside, scars that might fade with time but would never really go away. Her own father had sold her to other men, beaten her repeatedly if she fought them and punished her each time she had attempted to run away. He beat her if she cried, beat her when the men returned her, complaining that she was a wooden doll, uncooperative and frigid.

The images were terrible, of fingers forcing their way into the little body, hands squeezing and groping, men fumbling at her with alcohol on their breath. There was breathtaking pain as they rammed into a body far too small to accommodate them. Large, hamlike fists coming at the little face, her small body being flung against the wall. The nightmare went on and on, illustrating the hideous fate of a child impossibly young, without help, without hope. Locked in a stifling hot closet, locked in a freezing cold bathroom. Hungry, thirsty, knowing each time she heard footsteps it would start again.

Francesca pressed one hand to her stomach as it knotted and twisted in sympathy. For a moment, she was afraid she might actually be sick. This child had not only suffered physical hell, but had completely lost the will to fight. Francesca pushed past the total despair and reached for more. She wanted to find the real Skyler, the one that had existed before her spirit had been beaten out of her. Skyler had been a fighter once. A lover of life, of poetry, finding joy in the things around her, simple things, just as her mother had. Skyler Rose, her mother had named her. A beautiful rose without the thorns. She had a voice that could sing to the heavens, yet her brutal parent had managed to silence it. The man was every bit as evil as a vampire. Cunning and cruel and totally depraved. His very existence sickened Francesca. He lived for alcohol and crack. That was his life, his only life.

"Listen to the sound of my voice, Skyler, more than my words." Francesca projected her voice into the girl's mind, reached to touch the huddled, cringing spirit. "I cannot lie to you. I know you don't want to come back to this world and I don't blame you. You've gone far away from this body so you don't have to see or hear him. You don't have to feel what he does to you anymore. I can heal you. I can take away the things he has done to you, the scars on your body. I can lessen the impact of what has been done to you so you can live again whole. I can even make it possible for you to conceive a child later if that is your will. You can have a family of your own. You will believe me in this one thing, above all others: you are in no way responsible for the things that have happened to you. I know he made you believe you are worthless, but the truth is, Skyler, he couldn't stand your natural goodness, your very beauty shining at him, reminding him every day of his own sick depravity."

Stroking back strands of dull hair with gentle fingertips, Francesca leaned close to the girl's head. She wanted to hold her forever, keep her safe and love her as she should have been loved. Why hadn't she found this child earlier, before her cruel parent had done such extensive harm? She could feel the tears trickling down her face, the heavy sorrow pressing in on her chest. Ancients felt pain, emotions, much more intensely than fledglings. Francesca wanted to lie beside the girl and weep, but instead she forced herself to look beyond the pain both of them now shared.

She closed her eyes, focusing entirely on the young teenager, her own body dropping away from her until she became energy and light. At once she moved to merge with Skyler. Her young body was a mess of torn muscle, broken bones, bruised tissue. There were internal scars everywhere. Most of all the body felt dead, as if Skyler's spirit had long ago departed. Francesca knew it wasn't so; she had connected with the girl, knew the child was listening to her, somewhere deep inside her mind. A small huddled spirit drawn only by the compulsion in Francesca's voice. Francesca knew the girl was waiting very still in the shadows, just waiting to see whether Francesca was telling the truth. How could she believe? It was only the strangeness, the pure silvery sound of Francesca's voice and the fact that she was "different" that had captured her attention at all.

"Baby," Francesca whispered softly, her heart aching. "Baby, I'm so sorry I wasn't here for you before, but I won't abandon you. I will watch over you always, throughout your young life. I will make sure no one can ever hurt you again like this." She moved closer to the life force huddled so small. "Come back and live, Skyler. I can give you back your life. I'm not your mother, I know that, but I will never allow any harm to come to you again. I give you my word, and it is not given lightly or often." She moved closer, bathing the huddled, miserable child in her light, her compassion, the full force of her goodness. "Believe in me, trust in me. I know I can keep you safe as no one has ever done. Hear my voice, Skyler. I'm incapable of lying to one such as you. I know you feel my words are true."

Her voice was compelling, drawing the child's shattered spirit to her like a magnet. She swamped the teenager with warmth and reassurance, a promise that she would never again have to face the brute that was her father. She would be protected from him at all times. All she had to do was come back. Just allow herself to trust someone.

Softly, Francesca chanted a healing ritual in the ancient language, the words as old as time itself, as she began to work from the inside out to repair Skyler's damaged body. She worked swiftly and meticulously, paying close attention to details, not wanting any foul evidence of the beatings or rapes in her body. After a time she became aware of a discordant note. Merged as she was with the child, she became aware of the girl cringing, suddenly radiating fear. She was not frightened of Francesca, never of her. If anything, the huddled spirit was moving reluctantly toward her for protection. The child seemed to sense her father's presence. He was somewhere close inside the hospital, coming toward the room.

Francesca caught some of the young woman's fear. It would have been impossible not to feel it when the girl was so terrified and they were connected. Francesca had tremendous control, born of centuries of patience. She knew that she was powerful and could handle dangerous situations, yet at the same time she was also aware that she must appear to be human. She had trained herself to appear human, to make her responses totally normal. Even her thoughts had to appear human. Such precautions had protected her from the undead. They had also kept the Carpathian males from finding her. Even a mind scan would identify her as human, not Carpathian. She had never been able to risk a surge of power that might draw her own kind or the undead to her.

"It's all right, sweetheart. I won't let him touch you. I know everything, all of it, every terrible thing he's done to you. The police will take him away and lock him up so tight he'll never get out again." Once more she used her voice, the pure tones of truth and honesty, so that the girl would not retreat too far when her father entered the room.

Francesca slowly returned to her own body. As always when she healed out of her body, she was drained to the point of exhaustion. She rose with calm, unhurried movements, pushed open the door and beckoned Brice inside. "It's her father. He's committed terrible crimes against this child. Call the police and make certain they come down here at once to arrest him. Ask for Argassy, use my name. Tell him I said it was an emergency."

Brice glanced at Skyler, still in the fetal position, her eyes blank and dull. "If she can't tell them, Francesca . . ." He trailed off as Francesca's black gaze began to smolder. At times the compassionate healer could look quite intimidating.

"She will not have to testify." It was a decree. Francesca turned away from him.

Brice had one hand on the door when it suddenly crashed open, flinging him backward to fall against the bed. A huge burly bear of a man staggered in, blinking at them with hate-filled eyes. His hands were huge, opening and closing into fists. He barely looked at Brice, clearly dismissing him as an obstacle. His gaze settled on Francesca, whose hand was linked to Skyler's.

"What is this?" he bellowed. "How dare you come into my daughter's room when I said no one was allowed in here. Who are you?"

Francesca lowered her voice until it was as soft and

clean as a gentle breeze. "I am this child's advocate. She is very ill, Mr. Thompson, and I want you to leave this room before you distress her further."

Her voice was so compelling, the man actually turned to leave, one hand up to push at the door. Then he spun around shaking his head, a cunning feral hatred gathering in his eyes. "You little bitch, you can't tell me what to do with my own daughter." Deliberately he stalked across the room toward her. Skyler was essential to him, his only way to get his drugs now.

He was good at intimidating others, Francesca admitted. He had perfected his technique with years of practicing on Skyler and her mother. He was an ugly brute of a man with a special need to inflict pain and fear on others. She read him easily, recognized his enjoyment of hurting others—men, children, women, it didn't matter. He needed to do so. Francesca could see Brice making himself very small, cowering in the corner, trying to edge toward the door. If he made it, he could call security and bring help immediately.

Francesca controlled the beating of her heart, knowing Skyler was still clinging to her, still waiting to see if she was true to her word. Francesca sent waves of reassurance, a calm tranquillity she didn't actually feel. This man should have walked out the door at her command. He was human and the hidden compulsion in her voice should have been enough to control him, but it hadn't worked. She could handle the situation using other powers and skills, but it was a chancy thing to do with Brice in the room and a legendary vampire somewhere in the city. Lucian would feel the surge of power, know the touch was feminine. It could very well bring instant trouble to the hospital, to her friends as well as to her.

The man stood so close she could see the hair on his chest through his dirty shirt. He smelled of cheap whiskey and rye. The taint of drugs seeped from his pores. She met his gaze with a calm acceptance of his rage. If he struck her, her friends would see to it that he would be locked up for a very long time. And he was going to strike her. The air was thick with tension.

"You bitch. You need a real man to show you how to behave. Your simpering little doctor probably runs to you every time you crook your little finger." Deliberately he cupped his crotch lewdly. "You smell good, lady, and I'll bet your skin is as soft as it looks." He was breathing too fast, already stiff and licking his lips with anticipation. His hand moved to touch her face, to feel if her skin could possibly be as soft as it looked. "Don't!" It was a sharp command. Francesca didn't move. Her eyes blazed at him, glaring with contempt. He was incapable of performing sexually. She knew that much about him.

Vulgarly he spat out a string of swear words even as he swung his fist at her. Francesca stood very still waiting calmly for the blow. Brice yelled at the top of his lungs for security. Only a heartbeat went by, a tiny space of time, but in that space the air in the room thickened to a black malevolence. The door burst inward at the same moment that Thompson's fist connected with flesh.

Gabriel was smiling even as he crushed Thompson's fist in his hand. He had caught it before the brute could strike Francesca. Moving with preternatural speed, he had inserted his body between Francesca's and Thompson's, catching the punch before it could connect with his lifemate's face. Only Gabriel's black eyes seemed alive in his still face. Deep within their depths burned the bright red flame of the demon. It revealed his true nature, that of a predator.

To Brice's astonishment Skyler's father seemed to crumple before Gabriel. Brice read the terror in the man's face and forgot to continue calling for security. He felt fear himself, a mounting surge of adrenaline that refused to abate. Gabriel looked like an avenging angel, a warrior of old, invincible, merciless. He was staring directly into Thompson's eyes. "You do not want to strike Francesca, do you?" The voice was very soft, almost gentle. Although pleasing to the ear, it was all the more frightening because there was no emotion.

Thompson was shaking his head like a child. There was pain etched on his face and Brice could see that Gabriel retained possession of his fist. Gabriel's knuckles weren't white, he didn't look as if he was exerting any pressure at all, yet Thompson's face grew gray and he began a low-pitched moaning that fast rose to a cry. Gabriel bent his dark head to the man and whispered something Brice couldn't hear, but Thompson ceased to weep, managing only a moaning whimper. His eyes remained fixed on Gabriel's face, eyes filled with horror, with sheer terror.

Security burst into the room and immediately Gabriel stepped away from the man, his larger body protectively shielding Francesca's. They took Thompson out into the hall, astonished that he went with them so docilely. There was the sound of something heavy hitting the floor and a terrible coughing, then a rattling. Almost at once, a nurse called for Brice, her voice tense. He hurried out to find Thompson lying on the floor, both hands clutching his throat, his face gray as he fought desperately for air, his eyes rolling back in his head.

"What's going on? What happened?" Brice was on his knees beside the man.

"He just started gasping and grabbed his throat. He went a little crazy, acting as if he were wrestling with someone for a minute, almost as if he were being strangled, and then he fell," the security guard blurted out.

Francesca heard the explanation and sat down once again in the chair beside Skyler's bed. "Thank you, Gabriel," she said sincerely. He had no idea how relieved and happy she was at his unexpected arrival.

His hand moved over her silken hair in a slow caress. "You should have known I would never allow anyone to lay a hand on you." His voice was very gentle, almost tender. It gave her an unfamiliar feeling. This was what it felt like to be protected by a male Carpathian. Cherished. She knew Thompson was dead. Gabriel knew everything, all of it, every terrible thing that the beast had done to his daughter. Gabriel had been there, a shadow in her mind all along, monitoring her surroundings as the male of their species often did to insure his lifemate's safety.

He had felt the child's terror, had suffered right along with Francesca every single torment the teen had experienced. He had shared every tear Francesca had shed and the fear she'd felt when Thompson burst into the room. She was oddly grateful not to be alone. At the same time she resented the idea that she liked being protected.

Francesca watched the way Gabriel touched Skyler, his hand so gentle, his voice like a musical instrument. The tenderness of this enormously powerful man put a lump in her throat. "He cannot harm you, little one. Francesca will watch over you and so will I. You are under our joint protection and I give you my word of honor it is for all time. Come back to us, join us."

There was no way to ignore the compulsion in Gabriel's voice. The child stirred, blinked rapidly, made a soft sound of distress. At once Gabriel moved back so that the child would focus on Francesca. Skyler needed a woman. Francesca was all compassion and honesty, goodness and purity. Skyler would see it. Francesca's soul was so beautiful that anyone meeting her could see it shining in her eyes.

Skyler looked up at the ceiling first, shocked that her body didn't feel pain. She remembered the voice of an angel reassuring her, making her promises. A voice she had to listen to, but she was very afraid she had made it up. She turned her head and found her angel. She was beautiful. Every bit as beautiful as any angel Skyler had ever imagined. Her hair was long and flowing, as black as a raven's wing. Her face was that of a Madonna. She had classical bone structure, delicate, almost fragile, so beautiful she took Skyler's breath away. Skyler had not spoken a word in months. It was difficult to find her voice. "Are you real?" Her voice trembled, wobbled, a mere thread of sound.

Francesca felt Gabriel's surge of pride in her and it humbled her that she could receive such high praise from him. *Gabriel. The hunter.* No one had accomplished the things he had in the centuries of his existence. She didn't want to feel warmth at the knowledge that he was so proud of her, but he made her feel as if no one else had her talents, her capabilities. No other woman had survived as she had on her own for so many centuries. And no other woman was so beautiful or so courageous. He made her feel like that in spite of her determination not to let him get to her. He didn't say it, he just resided in her, a merging of minds and souls. She felt it. *We belong together.* Unsaid, but there all the same.

Francesca ignored him, a small smile curving her mouth. "I am very real, sweetheart. I meant every word I said. You have nothing to fear anymore."

Skyler shook her head, her eyes suddenly wild with terror. "They'll give me back to him, they always do, or he just takes me back. I can never get away from him. He finds me. He always finds me."

Gabriel's voice came from behind Francesca. It was tranquil, calm, soothing. "He is gone from this world, little one. Gone for all time. He can never find you or come near you again. He went into cardiac arrest when he was confronted with his sins."

The girl gripped Francesca's hand in hers. "He's really gone? Is this man telling the truth? Where will I go? How will I live?" She was panic-stricken. She knew how to retreat from life and pain and a brutal tyrant. She had no idea how to live in the world. She didn't even know if it was possible.

Francesca stroked back Skyler's hair gently. "There's no need to worry about anything. I have friends who will help us. You will be well taken care of, I promise you. For now, all you have to do is lie here in this room and get well. I'll bring you some clothes and books, maybe a stuffed animal or two. We'll get you some things to make your stay a little less boring. I will come back tomorrow evening and visit with you. We can talk more about what you would like to do with your life and where we'll go from here."

Skyler tightened her grip on Francesca. "Is he really dead?"

"Gabriel would not tell an untruth." Francesca said it very softly but with great conviction. "You need sleep now, child. I will be here tomorrow as promised."

Skyler couldn't quite make herself let go of Francesca's hand. As long as they were physically connected, she believed she was safe. She believed she had a chance at living a normal life. It terrified her to let go of that lifeline. Something about Francesca soothed her, made her believe she actually had a chance. "Don't leave me alone," she whispered, her eyes frankly begging. "I won't be able to make it without you."

Francesca was sagging with weariness. Gabriel circled her shoulders with a strong arm, pulled her beneath his broad shoulder so that she could lean on him. He bent close to Skyler, capturing her gaze with the black intensity of his eyes. "You will sleep, little one, a long, peaceful, healing sleep. When they bring you food, you will be hungry. You will eat what they bring. We will return tomorrow evening and you will have no worries until we are here to help you sort out your life. Go to sleep, Skyler, beautiful, peaceful dreams without fear."

At once the girl's lashes fell and she retreated from the world, this time into a healing sleep, where she'd been sent by the magic in Gabriel's voice. She would dream of angels and beautiful things and a world completely new and exciting to her.

The moment the child was asleep, Gabriel turned his full attention to Francesca. "You must feed, sweetheart." His voice was mesmerizing, filled with concern, infinitely tender. His hands moved up her arms to frame her face. "What you have wrought here is nothing short of a miracle. You know that. A miracle." As he spoke, he was drawing her into the circle of his arms, pressing her face into the warmth of his neck where his pulse beat so strongly.

The lure of it was sharp and tempting. She was exhausted from her energy-draining work. More than that, more than the call of her depleted cells crying out for nourishment, was a new addiction to his taste. He held her so gently, so possessively, so protectively. He was heat and light, safety and companionship. He made her feel complete. She closed her eyes and inhaled his scent, taking just a moment to rest her head against his shoulder. Her mouth was against his bare skin, the material of his shirt brushing against her cheek. He was so close. His skin. Her skin. His blood surged and flowed, beckoned to her.

"You are so tired, Francesca. Please give me the honor of doing this small thing for you. I will not take it as a surrender. I know your mind. You have not attempted to deceive me in any way. I fed well this night." His whispered words were a seduction, a temptation; he was a dark sorcerer brushing at her mind like the touch of butterfly wings.

Francesca merged with his warmth, both physically and mentally. The feel of his body so close, so protective, next to hers was a gift. When had a man held her in arms of steel? When had a body, so hard, so defined with masculine muscle and sinew, sheltered her close?

"Why didn't he respond when I commanded him to leave?" That had surprised her, even alarmed her. She had promised the child. It had never happened before. Humans had always listened and obeyed the "push" in her voice.

Gabriel recognized her distress, understood that she judged herself less than him, a failure. *"You are of the light, my love. I am the darkness itself. Thompson was wholly evil. You can restrain and delay evil, but you cannot completely touch its core because you cannot connect with it. Most humans are both good and evil. Not pure evil. You can connect with them because you can touch that which is good. I have the demon in me; it is my nature. He resides there, crouched low, waiting to leap out when I forget to leash him. I know evil every day of my existence. When you control it every day, it is not such a great feat to destroy it."* Gabriel dismissed his actions easily. "You are not less than I, Francesca. You have never been less. You saved lives and I took them. Who is the greater?"

Her slender arms crept up around his neck seemingly of their own accord. "You saved our people. You saved the human race. Not once, but decade after decade. It was your nature that allowed you to do so." Her voice whispered over him, a soft sound of admiration, a seduction in itself.

The faint stubble on his jaw caught the silken strands of her hair as he rubbed his chin on the top of her head in a little caress. "You must feed, honey. You are drooping with weariness." His coaxed her gently.

"Brice is right outside the door. They've given up on saving Thompson. He'll be in any moment." Her soft voice brushed his body like her fingers, producing a savage, unrelenting ache, but Gabriel kept himself strictly under control. She needed to be held, to be comforted, to be taken care of, not assaulted.

"Take what you need, I am quite capable of sustaining an illusion for humans." There was a faint husky note in his voice, one that was aching and lonely, turning her heart over. He needed the intimacy of providing for her as much as she needed the nourishment.

Almost blindly Francesca turned her face into his throat, inhaled the spicy masculine scent of him. His heart beat strongly, in rhythm with hers. The blood ebbed and flowed in his veins calling to her, an enticement. The warmth of her breath against his skin heightened his pulse, tightened his body to such a painful ache, he clenched his teeth in response, his hand bunching in the thickness of her hair.

Her mouth moved over his skin, soft, sensuous, seductive. At once need slammed into Gabriel so hard it shook his entire frame so that he trembled with urgent desire. Her teeth scraped once over his pulse, her tongue swirled in a velvet soft caress. Gabriel's fist tensed in her hair, pressing her closer to his suddenly heated skin. In response to his urging, her teeth sank deep, lancing him with white-hot lightning and a blue flaming fire that would never be quenched again. It was in his body for all time, in his mind, in the taste of his mouth, a fiery ache in his heart that danced in his very blood.

Warmth spread like thick molten lava. His heart was aching for her. It was not simply the physical demands of his body beating at him like a jackhammer, but something that went far deeper. The closeness of her mind, the rightness of the way she fit against him, crawled inside his skin. He recalled the tears she had wept for a stranger, her courage in facing the monster that posed as a man, and realized she was far more than a body to sate his wild appetites and an anchor to keep him safe from the growing darkness.

He was aware of Brice in the hallway turning slowly to stare at the door with a frown on his face and suspicion in his mind. Brice would have to be handled carefully. But not too carefully. A slow smile curved Gabriel's mouth, and there was little humor in it. He waved his hand and cloaked his body and Francesca's so that they were invisible to the human eye. He built the illusion of Francesca leaning close to Skyler, whispering softly to her with encouragement. His clone was in the corner, giving the two women a semblance of privacy.

Brice pushed into the room, revealing something very close to fear in his eyes when he looked over at Gabriel's clone. He glanced at Francesca talking so intimately with the teenager, and stopped himself from speaking. He glared at Gabriel, who smiled rather sardonically at him, arrogance etched into his classical Greek features. It annoyed Brice that the man was so good-looking, so tough. Gabriel's rescue of Francesca made him look bad. He couldn't afford to take a chance on breaking his hands. He was a doctor, for heaven's sake.

Gabriel half closed his eyes as Francesca swirled her tongue over the tiny pinpricks in his neck to close them, savoring the moment, the feeling. She lifted her head, her gaze drowsy, sexy, satiated, almost as if they had made love. He bent his head and kissed her forehead gently, holding her close for one more heartbeat before reluctantly allowing her to slip away, to take the place of the clone in the chair by the bed. *"Thank you, Gabriel, I feel much better."*

From the corner he bowed, an elegant, courtly gesture as Francesca turned with a small, secret smile. Brice's hands clenched into two tight fists. There was something different about Francesca, something he couldn't quite put his finger on. She was more beautiful than ever, but it was something elusive. Something she shared with Gabriel.

"I must speak with Francesca about my patient," Brice announced and then was annoyed with himself for sounding like a loud, defiant child. Abrasive. Harsh even. He made an effort to lower his voice. "Privately if you don't mind, Gabriel."

"Of course not."

Brice winced at the purity and goodness in that voice, at such odds with his own. It was as gentle as a summer's breeze, as soft as velvet.

Brice took possession of Francesca's elbow and all but pulled her out of the room. Francesca tried not to notice the difference in the way the two men touched her, but it was impossible. "What is it, Brice? You're upset." She spoke calmly even as she removed herself from his grip.

"Of course I'm upset. I just lost a man who had absolutely nothing wrong with him. Except a crushed hand. It was pulverized. The bones were crushed like matchsticks." It was an accusation and once more Brice realized he had raised his voice.

She lifted one perfect eyebrow. "I don't understand what you're saying. Skyler's father died of a crushed hand? How strange. I didn't know that was possible."

"You know damned well it's not," he snapped. "He strangled. His throat swelled, was completely closed, just like that, for no apparent reason."

"Are they going to do an autopsy?"

He raked a hand through his hair. She drove him crazy. She just didn't get it. "Of course they're going to do an autopsy. That isn't the point." He clenched his jaw. In his head he swore he heard Gabriel's taunting laughter, low and amused. "It's that man."

"What man?" Francesca's black eyes were wide and beautiful, entirely too innocent. Of course she wouldn't know, she would never suspect anyone of wrongdoing.

Exasperated, Brice took a step toward her, wanting very much to shake her. At once he felt an oppressive malevolence gathering in the hall, thickening the air, the exact same feeling that had been in the room before Gabriel entered. Nervously Brice glanced at the door. He cleared his throat, jerked his head toward Skyler's room. "Him."

"Gabriel? Are you implying Gabriel had something to do with Thompson's death?" Francesca sounded somewhere between outraged and amused. "You can't be serious, Brice."

"He crushed his hand, Francesca. Your Gabriel did that. Crushed his fist with one hand. I watched him do it and he wasn't even straining. I never even saw him come into the room. He was just there. There's something not quite right about him. His eyes. They aren't human. He's not human."

Francesca stared at him wide-eyed. "Not human? As in what? A phantom? A ghost that flies through the air? A gorilla? What? Maybe he lifts weights. Maybe he's strong because he lifts weights and his adrenaline was pumping. What are you saying?"

"I don't know, Francesca." Brice raked a hand through his hair again. "I don't know what I'm thinking, but his eyes were not human. Not when he was confronting Thompson. He's different."

"I know Gabriel. I do. He's perfectly normal," Francesca insisted softly.

"Maybe you *knew* him. People change, Francesca. Something happened to him. Of course he's no phantom, and he can't fly, but he's dangerous."

"Gabriel is one of the most gentle men I know." She started past him back to the room.

Brice caught her arm in a bruising grip, a surge of anger making his grip much harder than necessary. Instantly something pinched a nerve in his own arm, causing it to go completely numb. He cried out, was given no choice but to release her as his arm dropped uselessly to his side. "What the hell? Francesca, my arm! Where are you going?"

"I'm too tired to deal with this right now. You're jealous, Brice. I don't blame you for what you're feeling, but I'm exhausted and I don't want to discuss Gabriel any more, especially if you're going to say such awful things about him. You don't know the first thing about him." She jerked open the door and nearly ran into Gabriel's arms.

He bent over her, his body posture protective. "What is it, sweetheart, what has upset you?" His arms circled her slender body and pulled her into the shelter of his large frame. He had heard every word Brice had said to her, every accusation and each innuendo that remained unsaid. Over her head his eyes met the doctor's. In the depths burned a fiery flame of sheer menace.

Brice stopped dead, terror seizing him. More than ever he was convinced Gabriel was a dangerous man. His arm had suddenly returned to normal and he made a mental note to have it checked out. He held on to the door for support, determined to see this through. "Francesca, we have to decide what we're going to do about Skyler. I doubt very much if her father left her a thing, and from what he said he's her only relative."

Francesca turned immediately to face him. "She'll be well taken care of. I intend to become her legal guardian. I've promised her I'd be there for her."

Brice threw his hands up in the air in total exasperation. "You can't do that, Francesca. There you go again, trying to save every wounded soul in the world. You aren't responsible for this girl. You don't even know her. She could turn out just like her father. She'll need therapy for the next twenty years."

"Brice—" Francesca sounded as if she was on the verge of tears. Taking a deep breath, she calmly tried to reason with him. "What's the matter with you?"

He made an attempt to get himself back together. "I know you want to help this girl; God knows I want to help her too, but we can only go so far. She needs professional help, not the two of us."

"So what do you suggest, Dr. Renaldo?" Gabriel asked softly, his voice gentle.

There was nothing gentle in his still, watchful eyes. They reminded Brice of a predator's. A wolf with deadly intent. The look gave Brice an eerie feeling. He struggled to maintain his composure. "I suggest she be left to the professionals. There are people who deal with this sort of thing. If Francesca wants, she can donate money."

Francesca looked at Brice. "I gave her my word, Brice. She came back because she believed in me."

"Then visit her every now and then. You don't owe her your life. We have plans together, Francesca. You can't make these kinds of decisions without me."

Gabriel stirred, a ripple of muscle, no more, but it was intimidating. *"I can see to the child, Francesca. I will remove the memory of your promise and replace it with my own. I will see to her care and happiness while you take your time deciding what you are going to do about this human. I do not wish to complicate your life any further than I have already, but like you, I cannot abandon the child."*

"I keep my promises, Gabriel." Francesca shook her head. "I'm not going to argue, Brice. I'm too tired. I'm going to go out into the night and stare at the stars or

something. I need fresh air. I gave Skyler my word. There is nothing else to say."

"I think there is," Brice snapped, angry that Gabriel was witnessing this argument between them. They rarely argued, but he couldn't keep quiet now. This teenager would affect their lives together. He was not taking a chance that a nutcase would be living in their home with them. No way. And Gabriel had to go.

Gabriel simply took the matter out of Francesca's hands. He could feel her exhaustion beating at him, the sadness in her, the overwhelming need to leave this confined space and be out in the open. Brice couldn't comprehend what she went through to heal his patients, what it took for Francesca to merge with them and know every detail of their lives, every moment of their suffering. It was beyond Brice's comprehension, but not Gabriel's.

With his arm around her shoulder he walked quietly out of the room, taking her with him, his hold gentle but implacable. Francesca hardly seemed to notice. She went with him willingly. Gabriel turned his head slowly, looking back over his shoulder as he glided silently from the room, his black eyes moving over Brice's face. His stare was merciless, relentless. For one moment his white teeth flashed in a humorless smile, exposing a glimpse of razor-sharp fangs.

Chapter Five

The breeze washed over Francesca's face as she looked up at the night sky. A thousand stars twinkled and glittered overhead. She inhaled to take in the crisp clean air, washing the hospital smell from her lungs. Gabriel walked unhurriedly through the streets, his stride slowing to match hers perfectly. He didn't talk, didn't demand answers, didn't dictate to her. He simply walked beside her, asking nothing of her.

She unerringly found the path to her favorite place, turning down narrow twisting lanes until the paved streets gave way to old-fashioned cobblestone. She followed the pattern up a small hill to a bridge spanning a small lake. It was only a walking bridge and at this late hour, no one was on it. They had the large park and the lake to themselves. Francesca walked out to the center of the bridge and stopped to lean against the railing. "It seems as if I always have to thank you for something." She said it quietly, without looking at him. Instead, she stared out over the lake.

The water was shimmering almost black in the moonlight. She could hear the fish jumping every now and then. The sounds of the water lapping at the banks and the fish leaping were somehow reassuring and soothing. Francesca smiled over her shoulder at Gabriel. "I come here quite often."

"When you feel alone." He said it softly.

She turned back to the water, her smile fading. "I guess you read that in my memories."

He leaned down to find a round, flat rock and skipped it expertly across the surface of the water. "No, I have not had a great deal of time to read your memories; I am still attempting to get to know the woman you are now. As I am still a stranger to you and you have commitments in your heart elsewhere, I felt it would be wrong to invade your privacy more than absolutely necessary."

Francesca found laughter inexplicably spilling out her lips. "Invading my privacy is sometimes a necessity?"

"I am, after all, a Carpathian male and your lifemate. I cannot change what I am; certain things are necessary for my peace of mind. But I am trying not to intrude where I am not wanted." He stood tall and lonely with the wind blowing his long black hair around his broad shoulders. He was not asking for approval, only stating a fact.

Francesca studied his face, the way the moon bathed it in silvery light. He was very handsome, his angular face that of a man, not a boy—his mouth was sensual, his eyes by turns smoldering with passion or as cold as ice. His eyelashes made her smile. They were long and black and heavy. Any woman would envy him those incredible lashes. He held himself aloof, careful not to pressure her. She liked him for that. She felt pressure everywhere, from all directions, and she was glad that Gabriel simply wanted to keep her company.

"I needed a place that wasn't exactly part of the city. I pretend I'm in the mountains. Sometimes I can hear the wolves calling to one another." She brushed back her cascading hair but the wind tugged at it playfully. "I really miss home. Just once I would like to go back there, although I've lived in Paris for so long now, I'm not certain I would enjoy it as much as I remember it."

He nodded. "I know what you mean. It has been centuries since I was there. The people were uneasy with my presence and once Lucian turned, I could do no other than follow where he led."

"As you have done all your life," Francesca pointed out without rancor. "I am proud of you, Gabriel. I know I have not behaved as well as I should have, but in my defense, your sudden appearance was quite a surprise and fit in with none of my plans. In my way I have always supported your fight for our people. I accepted your commitment and knew you incapable of shirking your responsibility. I tried to do something with my life that counted also. I never wanted you to think I had wasted my life." She looked down at her hands. "There was so much time for me to be alone."

"Were you afraid?" He asked it gently.

The tone of his voice turned her heart over. "Often, especially at first. I knew I had to disappear for the sake of the other males of our race. I did so during the terrible wars when so many of our people were lost to us. It took great planning. I was still quite young then, a mere fledgling. I was afraid Gregori would discover me and bring me to Mikhail. It was my greatest fear, yet sometimes I was so alone I prayed they would find me and then I was ashamed of my selfishness."

"I am sorry I put you in such a terrible position." His voice was sincere, contrite. He looked sad, his mesmerizing eyes revealing his inner turmoil.

Francesca touched his mind; she couldn't stop herself from doing so even though she was secretly ashamed of herself for doubting him. She needed to know whether he was speaking the truth or saying what he thought she wanted to hear. She examined his mind carefully. She was nowhere near his age, nor did she have his skills and power, but she was no fledgling to be tricked. Gabriel felt genuine sorrow for his part in causing her loneliness. He knew he could not change what he had done—too many would have suffered—but he wished it could have been different. He had been alone in a stark black void. With each kill the darkness had spread over his soul, forever seeking to claim him. It had been an endless battle.

Francesca gasped when she realized he had almost lost the war with the beast. It had occurred around the same time she had made her decision to attempt to become human. Had her decision influenced the outcome of his fight? Had there been a connection and she had inadvertently made his life more difficult?

"Francesca," he said softly, gently, "has it occurred to you that my near disaster with the beast may have influenced *your* decision? Why do you insist on blaming yourself? I was the one who sentenced you to a solitary existence. I would not want you to feel one bit of blame. It is not yours. Even if such a connection existed—"

"And it probably did," she interjected.

Gabriel nodded his concession. "It could be so. But

there can be no blame attached to you. Not ever. I am a Carpathian male. I lasted much longer than the majority of our males and that was probably due mostly to you, and the fact that you were somewhere in the world. My soul knew it. So all that time you gave me solace and kept me strong."

"I'm a thousand years younger than you," she said and then burst out laughing. "Living so long in the human world, thinking in human terms, do you know how silly that sounds? We cannot possibly be compatible. You're way too old for me."

Gabriel found himself laughing, too. There was warmth in his heart, a genuine joy in her company. He found comfort, a soothing tranquillity he had never experienced before. For so long he had felt nothing at all. Now there was light and laughter and vivid colors and textures and life itself to be lived. *Francesca.* She had given that to him. "I think that remark borders on the insubordinate. Youth can be so impetuous."

"Do you think?" Francesca bent down and found a flat round rock, her fingers closing around it, the pad of her thumb rubbing back and forth over it. "I'm pretty good at this. You're not the only one that can skip rocks. I'll bet I can put one of these across the lake with ten skips."

Gabriel's eyebrow shot up. "I cannot believe my ears. The arrogance of youth."

Francesca shook her head. "Not youth, woman power."

He made a sound somewhere between laughter and a growl of derision. "Woman power? I have never heard of such a thing. Woman magic maybe, but never woman power. What exactly is it?" he teased.

"You're asking for a sound thrashing, Gabriel," she cautioned. "I'm a champion."

He nodded toward the lake. "Let me see what I am getting myself into."

"You want a preview? I don't think so. Let's make a wager. If I win, I get the sleeping chamber. If you win, you get it."

He rubbed the bridge of his nose thoughtfully, his black eyes laughing. "You are attempting to trick me into something I will regret for the rest of my days. If we must wager, the prize will have to be something other than the sleeping chamber. If I lose I will brush your hair at every rising for a month. If you lose, you will brush mine for the same length of time."

"What kind of dumb bet is that?" Francesca demanded, laughing. She couldn't help herself. He was far too good-looking for his own good. His black eyes were dancing and in spite of her determination not to be drawn in by him, she thought him terribly sexy. The moment the adjective entered her head, she pushed it out, but betraying color flushed her skin.

She was not going to share her body with him again. It had nothing to do with love and everything to do with chemistry and Carpathian heat. She wanted someone who wanted her for herself, not because he *had* to take her. Not because he had no choice in the matter. Just one time, before she left the world, she would like to be loved. Really loved. For herself.

"Francesca." That was all he said. Her name. There was an ache in his voice. Velvet seduction. Black magic.

She closed her eyes against unexpected tears. "Don't, Gabriel. Don't pretend with me. I am no longer human. I know your thoughts."

"You were never human, honey. Perhaps on the verge, but not wholly human. You belong in my world. You have done things no other has done and I salute you, but you were made to be the other half of my soul. Do you really think I do not love and honor you for yourself? That I would not know you better than the good doctor or any other human or Carpathian for that matter? I see into your heart and mind. I should have been there all those years, protecting you, caring for you, building a family with you. Punish me, blame me, I deserve it, but do not think you cannot be or will not be loved for yourself."

He was breaking her heart with the sincerity of his words. She couldn't touch his mind; if she did, her composure would shatter. She had been through so much—discovering he was alive, their blood exchange, which had taken the sun from her for all time, the earth-shattering experience of making love with him, the terrible ordeal of the two patients in the hospital. Brice. Thompson. All of it.

He moved then. Glided. He was power and coordination combined, so fluid he took her breath away. He moved like an animal, a great wolf stalking silently toward its prey. She closed her eyes as his hand wrapped around the nape of her neck. Exquisitely gentle. Possessive. "I am not trying to take over your life, I only want to share it. I ask for a chance. Only that. A chance. You had not planned to end your life for several years. Share those years with me. Let me try to make up for the wrong I did you."

"Don't pity me, Gabriel. I couldn't stand it if you pitied me. I've had a good life, remarkable really, for a woman of our species." She made a small movement of retreat.

His hand tightened around the nape of her neck. "You are a beautiful woman, Francesca, with many talents. There is nothing to pity. In any case, we need not discuss this matter just now. You have had to face far too many difficult situations lately. The last thing you need is to worry about how a stranger feels about you and what you do or do not owe him." His hand moved gently over the silken strands of her hair in a small caress. "I know that is what I am to you right now: a stranger. Give me the chance to become your friend."

The touch of his hand sent a swirling heat spiraling through her. Maybe it was the fact that he realized she needed space and cared enough to give it to her. "I think that might be a good idea," she replied. Warning bells were shrieking at her. He was entirely too handsome, too courtly. Too everything. What if he managed to steal her heart, after all? She was tired and wanted to go home.

Gabriel suppressed a sudden surge of triumph he was ashamed of feeling. He smiled at her, a flash of white teeth that softened the hard edge of his mouth. "You did not answer me. Are you willing to wager?"

She nodded, desperate to change the subject. "Fine, I'll make the wager with you, but only because you have never learned about real woman power." This time when she moved away from him, he allowed her to retreat. Francesca studiously avoided looking at him, concentrating instead on the surface of the lake and her rock. With a quick flick of her wrist she sent the rock skipping across the lake. Ten skips exactly.

She couldn't help grinning up at Gabriel triumphantly. He took his time finding the perfect stone. His large hand shielded its exact shape from her. "I have to skip it eleven times to win?"

She nodded solemnly. "Absolutely."

He smiled again. This time it was definitely the predator's smile. Wicked. Sexy. Altogether too tempting. Francesca tilted her chin and forced her fascinated gaze away from his perfect body to the shining surface of the lake. Why did he have to look so utterly masculine? His body was well muscled, hard, and looked way too good. "I'm waiting," she said, all too aware of how close he was standing to her. How he smelled. The taste of him. She wanted to groan but instead, she looked steadfastly out over the water, pretending she wasn't in the least affected by his close proximity.

The rock spun out of his hand so fast, she heard it buzz through the air. It skimmed across the water, hop after hop like a leapfrog racing across the water. It went on and on until it had crossed the lake and had hopped onto the opposite shore. "Well," he mused softly, a masculine taunt in his voice, "I would say that about wraps things up. Twenty-two skips all the way to the other side." He sounded very complacent. "I believe you get to be my slave and brush my hair for me at each rising."

Francesca shook her head. "What I believe is, you rigged this wager. You did something to win."

"It is called practice. I have spent much time skipping rocks across the lake."

Francesca laughed softly. "You are not telling the truth, Gabriel. I don't believe you ever skipped a rock in your life until now. You tricked me."

"You think?" He asked it innocently. Too innocently.

"You know you did. Just to win a silly bet. I can't believe you."

He reached out to tuck a wayward strand of hair behind her ear, making her heart leap wildly. "It was not just a silly bet, honey, it was a way to get you to brush my hair. No one has ever done such a thing for me and I think I crave attention." He rubbed the bridge of his nose again and grinned at her almost boyishly. "I asked Lucian to do so once and he threatened to beat me to a bloody pulp." He shrugged his broad shoulders. "Some things are just not worth it, you know."

"You're nuts," Francesca decided, but she was laughing, unable to help herself. "Fine, I'll brush your hair," she conceded, her fingers itching to bury themselves in the silken strands. She was unaware that she was agreeing to far more than brushing his hair. He would be spending the days with her in the sleeping chamber. They would retire together.

Gabriel was very much aware of that fact. He was making progress. "What are we going to do with this young lady of ours, Francesca? Little Miss Skyler. We can insure that her mind heals, but we cannot remove all scars unless we empty her memories. It might be that lessening the impact of them is best. We can provide her with schooling, clothes, everything she needs, emotional support, but we cannot be there for her during certain hours of the day. Have you considered what we will need to do to cover those times?"

Francesca reached behind her for the railing, intending to pull herself up on it. Gabriel's large hands spanned her waist and lifted her effortlessly, seating her on the structure. It was amazing to her that he knew what she wanted almost before she did. The idea was both exhilarating and terrifying. She had not shared her thoughts, her mind, herself in so long, she had forgotten what it was like. *Temptation*. It whispered over her, tugged at her heartstrings.

"I know, I know, it was rash of me to promise I would be there for her, but to be honest, I had been able to walk in the sun for some years and I didn't remember that I could no longer do so. I can't bear the idea of Skyler going to some place where they won't give her love and affection. She needs that, the support she should have had. I shared her life." She looked up at him in sudden wonder, in comprehension. "Both of us did. I know I can feel the love she needs. Can you?"

Gabriel nodded slowly. "She is a child, Francesca. We can do no other than offer her our love and protection. No one else will ever understand her or understand the enormity of what she has suffered. I do not think we can turn her over to others."

Francesca let out her breath in a rush of relief. She hadn't realized she had been holding it, waiting for his answer. "We both agree. Now we just have to figure out what to do with her."

He shrugged powerful shoulders. "In your mind is the idea that your lawyer will handle the necessary legal actions to gain custody of her. We will take her home with us. It will be necessary to find someone to aid us in her care. I seem to recall there was one family in our homeland that had humans caring for the household. The humans were exceptionally loyal to them. It was several centuries ago. Perhaps it would be worthwhile to find out about them. I was going through various things you had on the computer and this seems like a possible use for such a machine."

Francesca heard her own laughter. Carefree. Happy. It startled her. "You just want an excuse to use the computer. A techno junkie, that's what you are."

He grinned at her. "You have to admit, it is a good idea. There must be some of our people who remember this family and can tell us what they did. If not, we can always take blood from human servants and command them to do our bidding. It is not the way I would prefer to proceed, but it is a viable possibility. We can offer protection in return."

Gabriel had been leaning against the rail beside her. Now he straightened slowly, stretching like a lazy cat. There was no real change in his expression, yet all at once Francesca found she was shivering with fear. Something about him had changed completely. His hands settled around her waist and he lifted her to the bridge. *"We are being watched, honey. It is not Lucian, and for that I am most grateful."*

"The undead is here." She made it a statement. She felt it now, the creeping evil spreading like a hideous stain across the air. *"What can we do?"* She had always managed to hide her presence from the vicious killers. Now she was out in the open and it frightened her. She had seen the evidence of their depravity and it sickened her.

"The first thing is to get you to safety. You are a Carpathian woman. You will be his target." His hand was at the nape of her neck, soothing the tension out of her. He was bending over her protectively, like a lover, his mouth very close to hers.

Francesca knew it was all show, but it still made her feel cherished. She had a sudden wild urge to cling to him, to his strength and tranquility. The vampire in no way disturbed him. Gabriel exuded complete confidence in his ability to destroy the creature. *"I will draw him out to open ground. When I do, wait until I am certain there is only the one. When I know, I will alert you. You will dissolve into molecules, very tiny, untraceable by any but the best of our hunters. Go to the house and set safeguards. I will stay with you in a mind merge unless I must break away for the kill. Do not try to touch my mind unless you are in danger. There is no need for you to expe-*

rience such violence." His mouth brushed hers. Velvet soft. He found the corner of her mouth and lingered for just a moment as if he was savoring the feel and taste of her.

Francesca reminded herself it was all for show. Her body didn't need to burst into flame and her heart didn't need to somersault so treacherously. *"Tell me what to do to help you. I don't want to leave you alone to fight this thing."*

He laughed softly, his warm breath stirring the tendrils of hair at the vulnerable line of her neck. It warmed him that she offered when he could feel her fear beating inside him. He couldn't help himself, he knew he was taking unfair advantage of the situation, using it as an excuse to touch her, to kiss her, to inch forward his claim on her. He told himself to take it slow, not to push her too hard. If only she hadn't been so kissable, it would make his plan much easier. A sneak attack. Surround her and move in and take over before she realized what was happening.

"I am an ancient hunter, sweetheart. I will have no problem dispatching this unclean one." He kissed her forehead, infinitely gentle, reluctantly releasing her.

Gabriel turned and walked away from her to the end of the bridge. He glanced up at the sky. "Come out, small one. Come out and face the one you have challenged so openly." His voice was so soft and gentle and compelling, it crawled inside one's head and pushed and pushed until there was only one recourse. Obedience. Gabriel moved farther away from Francesca, toward the open grassy area. "You have asked for the justice of our people, unclean one, and I can do no other than oblige you. Come to me."

Francesca could not take her eyes from the ancient warrior. He stood tall and broad-shouldered, his hair flowing in the slight breeze. His face was stern yet gentle. He seemed relaxed, yet gave the impression of immense power. His voice was mesmerizing, his manner confident. He looked invincible. She gasped as she saw the vampire emerge from the thick bushes to Gabriel's left. The creature inched forward, fighting every step of the way, growling and spitting, hissing with hatred. She had never seen a vampire so close and he was hideous. The eyes were sunken and red-rimmed. The teeth were rotted, jagged, and stained a dark color. The flesh on him seemed to sag as if it didn't quite fit.

More than the looks of the man, it was the cunning, crafty hatred in the repulsive creature that frightened her. Francesca, as far away from him as she was, could still sense the stench of depravity that surrounded him. She made herself look at the creature, made herself feel its evil. It was important to realize just what Gabriel had faced his entire life. This monster. How many of them? How often? How many had he known personally, grown up with before they had turned? She had thought her life difficult and solitary, yet staring at the undead, she began to understand just what his life must have been like.

All those centuries she had viewed him as a hero, a revered legendary protector of immortals and mortals alike. Now she recognized just what being a hunter entailed. His own people had feared his power and skills. Males would have kept away from him, fearing he might later have to hunt and destroy them. He could never afford to have friends. Worse, his beloved brother had become a vampire and Gabriel had been forced to track him, battling him again and again over the centuries.

"I can help."

"You can do as I instructed. I am in more danger having

to worry about protecting you. He will seek to use you. When he realizes he cannot defeat me, he will try to destroy you in retaliation." He sent her a wave of warmth. *"Thank you, Francesca. I will join you soon at home."*

Gabriel turned his attention to the vampire, who, free from the enthrallment of his voice, was beginning to stalk him. Gabriel smiled, his teeth immaculately white. "I see that you are in a hurry to have your sentence carried out. I am of ancient blood, a true defender of our people. I am Gabriel. You know of me, you have grown up on the tales of my exploits. There is no way to defeat one such as I. Come, accept your sentence quietly, with dignity, remembering the great Carpathian you once were."

The vampire hissed again, flames leaping in his red eyes, his feet dragging him ever closer despite his resolve to attack on his own terms. The sound of Gabriel's voice was so pure and true it grated on him, actually caused him pain. He could not face that voice any more than he could have looked at a reflection of himself in the mirror. He could not ignore the compulsion woven in the notes of the voice; he had no choice but to move ever closer to the hunter. The words undermined his confidence in his own ability to battle and destroy. Who could defeat such a hunter? How many others had fallen before him to this centuries-old warrior?

The vampire shook his head hard, chanting in his mind in an attempt to counteract the spell the hunter had ensnared him in. No matter how hard he tried to break away, his feet continued to walk forward. The terrible voice continued, low and pure and very gentle. "You are not capable of denying me. I forbid you to shift your shape. You will come to me and receive the justice of our true Prince."

Gabriel didn't move, not one step. He stood quietly,

hands at his sides, his face portraying no emotion. No rage. No remorse. Only his eyes were alive, smoldering with intensity. Relentless. Merciless. The watchful eyes of a predator. They gleamed with menace, with ferocity. Still, the vampire could not stop his approach. He was snarling now, his legs dragging as he thrashed and fought to keep from moving forward, to keep from obeying that soft, gentle voice. The voice of death. It went on and on. Soft and persuasive, persistent, compelling.

Francesca knew she should obey Gabriel. She dissolved into a fine mist, and moved farther away from the combatants. She had never seen anything as terrifying as the vampire. He exuded evil, yet Gabriel stood calmly, tall and straight, unbelievably beautiful in his light and truth. She saw him as an angel with a sword, a dark guardian of the gate, defender of those less powerful. He took her breath away. And she was truly proud of him. Proud of his decision to make the sacrifices that he had.

The vampire did his best to evaporate, found he could not do so. It was as if his cells and tissue would no longer respond to his commands. The hunter had somehow managed to ensnare him, to trap him with his voice so that his flesh-and-blood body would only respond to the purity of those notes, to that perfect tone.

Furious, the creature turned its hideous face back toward Gabriel, its head swaying back and forth like a reptile's, his eyes glowing with fury. A long slow hiss escaped between his jagged, broken teeth. Over Gabriel's head a large tree branch cracked ominously and plummeted to earth.

Francesca felt her heart slam painfully, the air catch in her lungs, but Gabriel merely lifted his hand so the branch was deflected away from him, flung off to the side a good distance from where he remained so calmly. "You are young to have chosen such a path. Losing one's soul is for the aged and weak, yet you made your choice so soon. Why is that?"

"The only chance of salvation any of us have is to acquire a woman. The Prince has chosen his favorites to give the women to. There is no hope for the rest of us unless we take one for ourselves." The undead surreptitiously dropped his hand to his side to see whether he could shape-shift if he concentrated on one area of his body. His arm rippled with fur, his nails lengthening.

There was a rush of wind, unexpected, off the surface of the lake. The wind hit the creature full in the chest, driving deep, a heavy blow more heard than felt. The vampire blinked and stared at Gabriel, who was standing directly in front of him, his arm extended at full length. Shock spread across the undead's face. He looked down, wondering why he couldn't see the hand on the end of Gabriel's arm. It was buried deep in the wall of his chest.

There was a loud sucking sound as Gabriel extracted the vampire's heart, stepping away at the same time. The vampire screamed and screamed, the sound hideous. Tainted blood spewed into the air like a geyser. The creature reached for the hunter as he fell, his body flopping helplessly. Above their heads lightning arced from cloud to cloud, slammed to earth in a bluish white streak of pure energy. It incinerated the heart even as it bathed the hunter's hands clean of the poisonous blood.

Gabriel's movements were graceful and flowing, revealing power and coordination like those of a dancer, a warrior. He lifted his hand once more and directed the bolt to the body of the hapless creature. It turned to ash at once, disintegrating before his eyes.

He turned then slowly, a lonely figure against the night sky, his face in the shadows as he looked at the spot where Francesca remained. She shimmered into solid form, her large eyes locked on his. "Are you all right?" She moved fast, a mere blur as she came close to him. Her hand found his, her fingers lacing through his.

At once he felt peace stealing into him, deep within his tortured soul. She had a healing power unlike any other he had ever experienced. He had taken a life, one of so many. Gabriel had dedicated the remainder of his life to hunting his twin. Over the years he had chased Lucian almost exclusively, only rarely stopping to destroy the undead he came across. It had been years and it was the first kill he had made since finding his lifemate. He felt emotion. Not guilt exactly. He accepted his duty as a sacred responsibility. But the taking of a life in front of someone like Francesca bothered him. She was so pure, so compassionate, so good. She had been healing for all the centuries that he had been destroying.

Gabriel avoided her enormous black eyes, the innocence there. Without emotion, it was far easier to face those around him, those who feared him. He was used to the whispers, to the way people moved out of his way. He was used to the fear in their minds and hearts. He was needed, yet never accepted.

Her small hand moved up his arm, a curiously intimate gesture that left him weak and warm inside. She was crawling inside him. Winding her way deep into his very soul. He was unprepared for that. He knew now just what a lifemate was. How important she was. Intellectually he had known Carpathian women were the light to their men's darkness. He had accepted Francesca and what must be between them. Their union meant not only his continued survival, but also guaranteed he would not join Lucian in the ranks of the undead.

For that alone he had respected Francesca. Wanted Francesca. He was totally unprepared for the jealous streak that made it difficult not to dispose of Brice. He was totally unprepared for the savage demands his body made when he was near her. More than anything, he was unprepared for his heart melting when she was sad or hurt or felt tired. He had not counted on his reaction to her at all. He wanted to hear her voice all the time, watch her smile, see the way her face lit up, her eyes so soft and melting, so beautiful. He thought about her far too much.

"Gabriel." Francesca's voice whispered over him like a soft summer breeze. At once he felt sweat beading on his body in reaction. "You asked me to leave this place and I should have, but please don't feel ashamed or embarrassed that you had to do such an important job in front of me. You think your talent less than mine."

"You save lives, I destroy them." Just the touch of her fingers was a miracle to him. The scent of her, clean and fresh and feminine. He had never noticed that about women before. The way they smelled; yet now she filled his lungs and he wanted to always have her there. "I am not certain killing is considered a talent."

"The undead are no longer alive. You know that. They have chosen to lose that which makes them live. Vampires are monsters without equal, merciless, living only for depravity and the rush of the kill. Without you to stand guard, Gabriel, there would be no way to hide the existence of our people. Even now, a small minority of humans hates the very idea of us. They have a society of people, professionals and others, who hunt us down to kill us. It seems to me that without you, our people would long ago have been hunted to extinction."

A small, pleased smile escaped before he could stop it. She had a way about her. There was no doubt in his mind why Brice wanted her. It wasn't because she was a healer, as Brice was. It wasn't because her Carpathian beauty drew males to her. It was the entire package. Francesca. *His* Francesca. "You give me far too much credit," he answered her softly. "Thank you for that. Thank you for making a difficult situation easy. I did not expect to feel this way." He flashed her another smile. "These emotions are difficult to control."

She tilted her head to look up at him. It should have been declared a sin to look as good as he did. He made butterfly wings brush at her stomach, made her heart somersault at the most unexpected times. His eyes could create a firestorm in her with just one smoldering, brooding look. He could melt a woman, any woman, at twenty paces. Francesca cleared her throat, trying hard not to blush, suddenly remembering he was more than likely a shadow in her mind, reading her all too intimate thoughts. "We should start for home."

"You want to walk or do you feel like flying?" He asked it gently, unwilling to influence her decision one way or another. She always chose the human way. She would have allowed herself to be struck by Skyler's monster of a father in order to preserve her way of life. Her image. He wanted her to accept that she was Carpathian. Wholly Carpathian. It was too soon for that, he knew, but a sign that she was weakening just a little would give him hope.

Francesca linked their fingers once more. "We have plenty of time before the sun rises. Perhaps we should walk and discuss further how to manage Skyler."

Chapter Six

Francesca averted her eyes as they walked along the empty streets hand in hand. He was so intensely male, moved so fluidly. She found herself wanting to brush the waves of his hair, smooth the lines from his face. His mouth was so perfect. She glanced at him from beneath her lashes. Her lips tingled, softened, aching to feel his. There was the sound of his voice when he talked to her, soft, sexy, intimate as sin. Gabriel flashed a smile at her and Francesca felt her instant response. He brushed against her while they walked, the slightest of movements, yet it set her heart pounding and sent tiny tongues of fire flicking over her skin. Her palms itched to feel the hard muscles of his body, to run her hands over his chest, his belly. She glanced lower at the material stretched so tight. She ached to stroke and caress, to slide her mouth over him just to see his reaction. To hear his groan.

She could think of nothing else. Her breasts ached and between her legs liquid heat gathered in invitation. Her clothes felt cumbersome, far too tight. She wondered what he would do if she suddenly yanked her blouse off and offered him her breasts right there on the street. All she could think about was Gabriel. His hard body, his hands as they moved over her skin. The way he said the most beautiful things to her. The way he wanted to help a young stranger who didn't know what love was supposed to be. The way he had stepped in front of her body, shielding her before a brute of a man could strike her. Everything about him was extraordinary and she was consumed by a sudden need to hold him, touch him, kiss every inch of him.

A store appeared in front of them, deserted now, long after business hours. "My friend owns this store. She's given me a key and the code for the alarm. I just leave the inventory slip for her and she charges it to my account." Her voice was husky, sexy, a blatant invitation. "We can go in and find a few necessary things for Skyler." Her hand was shaking as she turned the key in the lock.

Gabriel watched her intently with his black velvet eyes as she punched in the code for the alarm system. The store was dark, deserted. The silence was broken only by their ragged breathing. She turned to him, her hand brushing his face. Her hand found his hair unerringly, fingers tunneling in the thick strands.

A soft sound escaped his throat. "Francesca, you have to stop before there is no going back for us. I am no angel as you often persist in thinking me. I can read every thought in your mind and what you are doing to my body is nothing less than a sin." His thumbs stroked caresses over her jaw, traced the outline of her lips.

"Really?" Her hands tugged at his shirt until it was free from his trousers. Immediately her palms slid over his bare chest, her fingers splayed wide to take in as much of his skin as she could. She traced every defined muscle, aching for him. "I've always thought sinning might be an interesting experience." There was invitation in her voice. Blatant seduction.

His hands bunched in her hair, drew her head back so that his glittering eyes raked her face. "I *hunger* for you, Francesca, *hunger*. You cannot touch me with your mind and your body and not expect me to react. It is like a raw craving in my bloodstream and I know it is there for all time. Do you know how many times I dreamed of you? How many times I woke in the night alone without you?"

"I did the same," she said softly, her eyes meeting his steadily. She did not flinch away from the concentration of sheer passion gathered in his gaze. "Gabriel—" She whispered his name, leaning forward to press her lips against his chest. Her mouth swirled heat over his pulse. "You talk too much when I need action." She lifted her head so that her dark eyes laughed at him. "You do action, don't you? My clothes are heavy and troublesome," she added as she leaned forward to flick his flat nipple with her tongue. She stood on her toes to press her swelling breasts tightly against his chest.

Gabriel couldn't bear even the thinnest of materials separating their bodies. He pushed her blouse from her shoulders, tossing it aside in the heat of the moment. His palms slid gently over her bare flesh, tracing the delicate line of her bones, the curve of her breasts. His breath escaped his lungs in a long rush as he cupped the soft weight in his hands, his thumbs stroking her nipples.

The store was silent, mannequins staring blankly

through the racks of clothes. Gabriel drew her deeper into the interior of the room, away from the windows, into the shadows where they would have privacy from anyone walking along the street. The heat and hunger of the Carpathian mating ritual was upon him, brought on by his lifemate's erotic thoughts. She was beautiful, inside and out. It was exciting and arousing to know that she wanted him so badly, that she knew exactly what she wanted and would demand it of him.

Her lifemate. Francesca reveled in her right to touch his body, to be able to bring him to a firestorm of need so that he burned for her in the same way she burned for him. His touch on her bare skin was torment and pleasure. When he slowly bent his dark head to find her breast with the heat of his moist mouth, she trembled with an urgency she had never known before. Her fingers crushed his hair, holding him to her. "It's almost too much feeling, Gabriel. I don't know if I can take it."

His hands were shaping her body, pushing aside her clothes while his palms and fingers lingered and savored, stroked and caressed. "Yes you can, you were made for this," he whispered softly. He bent his head lower to lick her flat stomach. "You were made for me." Easily he lifted her to the top of the counter, seating her on the edge. "You were made for long nights, Francesca, long lazy nights of making love." His hands caressed her thighs, and he pressed his palm to her hot wet core, smiled when her body clenched and she shuddered with pleasure. His head dipped lower so that his silken hair brushed her sensitive thighs and a soft moan escaped her throat.

Francesca cried out at the first touch of his warm breath, the first lap of his tongue. *"Do you know what you taste like?"* He asked the question softly, intimately, in her mind. His voice scorched the inside of her mind as his tongue was scorching the core of her body. She could feel her body winding tighter and tighter, pleasure building in force and intensity so that the release rushed over her with such power she could only clutch his hair as wave after wave swamped her.

"Gabriel." She said his name, breathed his name, drew the masculine scent of him into her lungs. *"Gabriel."*

"We are just getting started, beautiful one," he answered softly, raising his head to smile at her.

He was so handsome, so perfect for her, Francesca could feel tears burning in her throat. There in the night, the night that called to something wild in them, he looked at her with eyes burning with desire. Hot. Urgent. Demanding. She had waited so long for his eyes to look at her like that.

And then he was driving sanity from her mind, replacing it with frenzied passion. Francesca could think of nothing but having his body buried deep within hers. Once more his palm pushed against her sensitive core, and then he slowly inserted his finger, all the time watching her face, watching the pleasure wash over her as her tight sheath clenched around him.

"It is not enough." There was a smile in his voice; he bent his head to taste her again even as his finger slowly eased out of her. Two fingers stretched her, pushed deep so that she gasped with pleasure. "And that is not enough." There was pure masculine satisfaction in his voice, on his face.

She could feel it again, the hot pressure, molten lava building and building until her entire body was in danger of imploding. He pushed into her, caressed, stroked, his tongue teased and danced. "This is what I want, honey, more, come for me. I want to see it on your face, I want to know you feel it, too." His voice softened, went husky. "Come for me, my love, just let go."

With a choking cry she let herself be taken over the edge, her body clenching and spiraling out of her control. His mouth heightened the effect, bringing her an endless orgasm that seemed to go on forever and yet was not enough. She closed her eyes and just gave herself up to pure feeling, to the beauty of his hands and tongue in her body doing slow, merciless things that only made the fire hotter. She was writhing now, her hips unable to stay still beneath the assault on her senses. Then he added his mind, thrusting deeply into hers, picturing things he wanted to do before he did them, so that she could feel her body through his mind, the silken heat, the clenching, tight muscles.

Francesca could feel Gabriel's mounting desire, the way his body burned and ached, hardening to the point of pain. His hands were becoming rougher, more demanding, and she reveled in the thought of his own loss of control. "I want you inside me, Gabriel," she murmured softly, a demand. "I want your body in mine. I don't want you to treat me as if I might break either." She said it deliberately, knowing what it would do to his body, knowing he was caught up in the same storm of fire as she was.

She looked beyond him to the bank of mirrors, saw his perfectly formed masculine body, the defined muscles, the long shiny hair, and her body fragmented again, an explosion of such force it rocked her, shook her, so that she cried out with the fury of it. "Gabriel, now, right now."

"On the floor, where I can go deep, I want to be so deep inside you, you will never get me out." The admission was torn from him as he dragged her from the counter and laid her on the thick carpet. He followed her down, needing her so much he was thick and hard and aching with urgency.

Francesca lifted her hips to meet him as he surged forward, penetrating her, filling her, her body slick and wet and hot, coiling around his tightly. Her breath escaped; his left his body. The rush was addicting and complete. Gabriel caught her hips in his hands, and set a rhythm, using hard, sure strokes that drove deeper and deeper to find her soul.

She turned her head to look at them in the mirror, to see the beauty of their bodies coming together in perfect accord. His face was etched with concentration, with ecstasy, with total focus. She knew what he wanted before he did, every small adjustment of her body so he could penetrate even deeper, fill her until they were both gasping with the pleasure of it. She lifted her head, watching him intently as she flicked his chest with her tongue, lapped at a bead of moisture. His hands tightened, his body clenched. Her teeth nipped him gently, scraped in a caress over his skin.

Gabriel threw back his head, his long hair flying out in a silken halo for one moment. His body took hers, harder and faster, on and on, winding her body tighter until she thought they would both spin out of control. She swirled her tongue lazily.

"I will burn up!"

His voice was nearly pleading, a command, a plea, a husky, sensual caress. Francesca rewarded him, sinking her teeth deep to join them together body and soul and mind. White lightning arced between them and set them on fire. Her body was no longer her own, but his to do with whatever he needed, whatever he wanted. His body belonged to her. A fair exchange when she was crying out with her release, soaring into space, riding the waves of the sea.

Gabriel went with her, shouting her name to the heavens, to the silent watching mannequins, into an unnamed place of sheer feeling. Francesca swept her tongue across the two tiny pinpricks, gasping for breath, her heart pounding out the same rhythm as his, shocked at the intensity of their wild lovemaking.

Gabriel held her close to him, bracing himself with one hand to keep his weight from crushing her. "Are you all right?" he asked gently. He brushed her hair with his free hand, his dark gaze searching hers soberly.

"Of course I'm fine. It was beautiful, beyond words. I *wanted* you, Gabriel. You are so careful of me." She traced his mouth with a fingertip. "I appreciate your consideration, I really do, but I am a strong woman and I make my own decisions. I would not be lying beneath you, your body in mine, unless it was exactly what I desired."

She was in his mind, she could feel his guilt, yet he was a very adept ancient. There was something else there, something she couldn't figure out.

He bent his head and kissed her. Thoroughly. Completely. A kiss that melted her insides and brought unexpected tears to her eyes. "I am amazed at you, Francesca. I thought I would never be surprised in this world again, by anything or anyone, but you are beyond anything I have ever known." He kissed her again, gently this time, leisurely. Reluctantly he withdrew from her, moving away from her to climb easily to his feet. He reached down and drew her up. "The floor must be hard. I think we will need a bed next time." He said the words carefully, as if afraid she would think he was pressuring her.

Francesca couldn't help herself; it was rather exhilarating to have so much power over an ancient Carpathian. She leaned forward and gave him a kiss of her own. Slow and hot and blatantly wanting more. "I will never be able to come to this store again without thinking of this night." She moved away from him, cleaning and clothing herself in the easy manner of her people. There were tremendous advantages to being Carpathian, things she had been unable to do while keeping up the illusion of being human. It was fun, enjoyable, those little details she had tried to keep out of her mind.

"I'll find a few things for Skyler while you try to catch your breath," she teased, flashing him a saucy grin.

He followed her around the store, watching her carefully choose clothing she thought the young teen would be comfortable with. He knew she intended to buy her all the latest fashions, but this first shopping trip was simply to provide comfort. He found a stuffed animal, a fluffy wolf with bright blue eyes, and was immediately drawn to it. "I want to get this for her. It is telling me it needs to go home with us."

Francesca laughed at him. "That is from Dimitri's foundation. He guards the wolves in the wilds of Russia now and writes books with beautiful photographs. He was a child when you knew him, do you remember? A portion of the sales goes to his wolf foundation. He has saved many of our wolf brethren from an early demise or capture."

"It is good to know Dimitri is still with us. He was different as a child. A loner already, long before his fledging days were past, and there was a dark core of violence in him, the mark of a good hunter, yet often a sign of an early turning to the darkness."

"Well, he turned his life in this last century to preserving the wolves in the wild. He is a renowned scientist and his foundation is flourishing. I'm not surprised that you would be drawn to his lifelike stuffed animals. Each one is a work of art."

Gabriel bared his white teeth at her. "I have good instincts." There was a wealth of innuendo in his voice.

Francesca laughed softly and wrote out a quick inventory of their purchases and a note asking her friend to send the items to her address the following evening. She did a quick automatic check of the store before setting the alarm. "I like being with you, Gabriel. Come on."

Gabriel tightened his fingers around Francesca's, making certain there was only acceptance of what had transpired between them in her mind. She had wanted time to adjust to the idea of a lifemate but the chemistry between them seemed to sizzle with the slightest contact. He had intended a slow courtship, to win her gently, not leap on her body every time he looked at her. Her strides were not nearly as long as his, so he consciously shortened the length of each step. It amazed him how right it felt just to walk through the night with her. "If I never have another chance to do this with you again, Francesca, thank you for this walk." It came out before he could censor the words. He glanced down at her bent head. "I do not mean to make you uncomfortable. But I have never done this. Just walking in the night, no hurry, no plan, just drifting along. And I certainly never had the opportunity to have a beautiful woman at my side. It may seem a simple pleasure to you, but it is unique for me."

She glanced up at him, so that he had a quick glimpse of the sweep of her long lashes and then the perfection of her profile. "I'm certain you had plenty of opportunities,

Gabriel." He was extraordinarily good-looking in his dark, masculine way, and she knew he would attract women easily. "You can't make me believe you went centuries without . . ." She trailed off when he stopped abruptly. He was so good at pleasing her, so good at knowing exactly what she needed.

Gabriel caught her chin in his hand, forcing her head up to look at him. "I am a hunter, Francesca, a Carpathian hunter. I did not feel passion as you think I did. There was no desire for a woman. I wanted there to be desire and I merged at times to see what the feeling was like for those humans I occasionally met. But I never wanted anyone until I awoke from the dead and heard your voice." A faint smile touched his mouth briefly, then was gone. "The feelings you produce in me are far different from the ones created by humans. Much more intense and urgent." He dropped his hand away from her. "My words put pressure on you that you do not need at this time and I do not want it to be so. I really wanted to respect the distance you wish to put between us. I had every intention of waiting until you were more at ease with our relationship."

She laughed softly. "You can hardly take the blame for our lovemaking, Gabriel. That was entirely my doing."

A small smile flitted across his face. "I do not know if I can honestly say that is so, but I think you have had enough adventure for several risings."

"You must learn to say days or nights," she corrected gently. "This is the age of computers. It is dangerous how quickly information can be exchanged. You have been away a long time. I know you assimilate information at a rapid rate but technology is making things much more difficult to hide our presence from the world. You are used to a world where the human threat is nearly nonexistent, but that has changed with the age of computers." His hand brushed hers and without thinking she entwined her fingers with his as they began to stroll along the sidewalk.

"I must admit I have never considered humans a threat; they are easily managed."

"You sound very arrogant, Gabriel, although I sense you don't mean to be. Our people are in dire straits, our race all but doomed. I keep up on the news in a roundabout way, so I know what is going on. There are some human women with extraordinary psychic talent who are compatible with our race. The Prince of our people has a lifemate who once was human."

There were several moments of silence. Once again, without conscious thought, Gabriel had reached out to share this new knowledge with Lucian. He touched his twin easily, lightly, as he had done for nearly two thousand years. Lucian was immersed in a complicated text he was finding highly interesting. That always astonished Gabriel. That Lucian had retained his need for knowledge. He had always been a sponge soaking up information. Now he reciprocated, sharing all that he had learned of the modern world, flooding Gabriel with so many facts, he began to laugh.

"What is it?" Francesca asked softly, seeing genuine affection for just a moment in the depths of his eyes.

Gabriel broke the contact instantly, swearing softly in the ancient language. Why didn't he think? It had never mattered before, his ingrained habit of reaching out to his brother. Even after Lucian had turned, he hadn't fought the habit. Why should he bother? The more knowledge they each had, the better the battle. It was very different now. This time it could cost Francesca her life. Gabriel had battled Lucian many times over the last few centuries.

He had inflicted mortal wounds on more than one occasion, yet he had never bested Lucian, never managed to destroy him. He had no reason to think the outcome of their battle would be any different now. He could not afford the luxury of a mistake. Lucian must not know of Francesca's existence.

"What is it?" Francesca repeated, this time shaking his arm. "You went from smiling happily to looking like a wolf, your eyes still and watchful. What happened in so short a time?" Her voice was soft and compelling, a mixture of concern and compassion.

Gabriel shook his head. "I have made mistake after mistake. Resting these centuries has done me little good. It is confusing to wake and feel emotions, to see colors. Everything is vivid and bright. Emotions are violent and raw, hard to keep under control. There is an ever-present craving in my body for yours."

Gabriel was speaking so thoughtfully, so matter-of-factly, Francesca felt he was musing aloud.

"I led that vampire straight to you, you know that." Gabriel raked a hand through the shiny mass of his blue-black hair. "All this time, you successfully managed to hide. Now I have called attention to your presence, and he will not be the only one to seek you out."

He stopped and faced her, his hand curling around the nape of her neck. "I should never have made my claim without your consent. I should have sought your safety above my own needs and desires. I have wronged you in an unforgivable way."

Francesca touched his mouth. His words and the sincerity in his voice were turning her world upside down. She didn't know what she wanted anymore. Away from him it was all so clear, but when he was close and he allowed her to see into his tortured soul, she felt altogether different. "You could not have taken my body so easily, Gabriel, had I not wished it to be so. I was not under compulsion."

His fingers were massaging the back of her neck, his thumbs brushing intimately along the delicate line of her jaw. Each caress sent heat spiraling through her body and little flames dancing over her skin. Lost in his regret, Gabriel didn't seem to notice the way her body responded to his touch. "I woke you with the command to come to me in need. Your body responded to that command and to my deliberate arousal of you. I should have waited until you had time to know me. You should have been courted the way you deserved."

"It wasn't just you, Gabriel. I am no fledging. I recognized the 'push' as I awakened. I am not without power of my own. You couldn't have taken me so easily without my consent. I wanted you. I wanted to feel you, to feel what it was like." She confessed it bravely, taking her share of the blame without hesitation. "You were not forcing my compliance. In any case, sooner or later the Carpathian cycle would have begun and we would have had little choice in the matter."

"I said the ritual words to bind us without your consent."

"Males do so all the time, Gabriel. It is the way of our people and has been so for thousands of years. You have not done anything so unforgivable. This situation is difficult for both of us."

He dropped his arms and swung away from her. "Why do you accept these things so easily, Francesca? Why do you not condemn me as you should? Your anger would go a long way toward . . ." He shoved his hand through his hair again. "There I go again, wanting it to be easy. I am selfish, sweetheart, very selfish, and I have tied you to me."

"Gabriel? You are distraught. You have need of me?" The voice came unexpectedly, easily in his head. He fought with himself to keep his mind blank, to ensure that no information went toward that perfect voice. Lucian had always been able to command with his voice. He could make anyone believe anything with that voice. That weapon. Gabriel had never heard anything quite so beautiful. Lucian had retained that gift even when he had lost his soul for all eternity.

When Gabriel refused to respond, the laughter came, a taunt, almost lazy. It chilled Gabriel to the bone. He had to protect Francesca from Lucian's wiles. His twin was cunning and smart. Ruthless. Merciless. Gabriel knew better than any other. He had seen him in action for two thousand years.

Francesca laid her hand on Gabriel's arm. "You are trying to tell me something but you haven't gotten there yet."

"You are with child." He stated the four words clearly, starkly.

Francesca's enormous black eyes went wide with shock. "That cannot be. It is not so easy. Why do you think our race has bordered on the brink of extinction? Our women are able to bear children only every few hundred years. I am a healer. I studied this for many decades, determined to unlock the key to our bodies so that we could conceive more often and be more successful in the carrying. I had wished to be able to understand why we conceive males instead of females but I could not find the answers." She shook her head. "No, this cannot be."

"You know I speak the truth. I knew our women can

only conceive every so many years, and that they manipulate that time, but I also knew the chances were very good that, as you had never conceived, you would be ripe to do so and I took full advantage of that."

She stared up at him a moment in silence, in shock. "But I am a woman, a healer. You could never have done such a thing without my knowledge. . . ." She trailed off as she pressed her hands to her flat stomach in a kind of wonder. "It cannot be so." Even as she denied it, she closed her eyes and sought inside herself. There it was. The miracle of life. The thing she had longed for. Cried for. Wanted more than anything. The very thing she had given up ever having. Growing. Changing. Cells dividing. A child. She wanted to be upset. She had given up the idea several hundred years earlier. She was prepared to go to the next world. She was not prepared for such an event.

Francesca raised her head so that her eyes met his. "You really did this?"

"I would like to say I knew you wanted a child above all else. I had read that in your memories. I had also read your resignation and acceptance that you would not. I would like to tell you I did such a thing for you, or even more nobly, for a cause, for the continuation of our race, but the plain truth is much uglier than that. I did it so that I would not lose you. So that you would be tied to this world and not escape me into the next. Until Lucian is dead, I could not follow you. I did not want to be alone anymore. I acted out of selfishness. I changed the direction of your life inadvertently so many centuries ago and now I have deliberately changed it again."

Francesca just stood there, shock registering on her face. "A baby. I had all but forgotten the possibility of a baby." There was no condemnation in her voice, only a soft musing as if she couldn't comprehend such a thing.

"I am sorry, Francesca. There is no real way to make amends." Gabriel rubbed his forehead with the palm of his hand. "There is no excuse and there can be no forgiveness."

She wasn't listening to him; her mind was turned inward. She had longed for a baby, a family. More than anything she had wanted a child. Even if she had chosen to spend the last years of her life with Brice, she would never have brought a child to their union. Her pregnancy was a miracle, and she couldn't quite come to grips with the idea. "A baby. I do not remember what it is like to dream of such a thing. It cannot be, Gabriel. How is this? How did I not know?"

"You are not listening to me, Francesca," he said, his black eyes searching the sky overhead as if it might offer answers. He rubbed his temple. He needed a way out of the mess he had created with his arrogant decision, yet there was none. He had to be honest with her. He respected Francesca too much to give her anything less than the truth. In any case, she was his lifemate and eventually she would read his memories.

He should have waited, taken his time. He could have stopped her from choosing the dawn if there was such a need. But he had taken the attitude that she belonged to him and owed him complete surrender.

Francesca took a deep breath and laid her hand on his arm. She could easily read his inner turmoil, his anger at himself. In truth, she didn't know how she felt, but she didn't like the way his mind was so consumed with guilt. *Gabriel, her legendary hunter*. He had given so much to his people, had always done the right thing. Francesca didn't have it in her to condemn him. "In your defense,

Gabriel, it was not a conscious decision on your part."

"Francesca!" Gabriel stepped away from her, unable to bear her touch when he had so wronged her. "You are touching me, yet you do not hear me. You are not seeing what is before your eyes. I do not want to start a relationship with dishonesty between us. Of course it was a conscious decision. I manipulated the outcome of our joining just as I aroused you with more than my body." He shook his head in wonder. "You really are the opposite of me. You cannot conceive of such deception and I cannot conceive of such goodness. See me, Francesca, see me with all my faults. I do not want you to accept me even in friendship merely because I am Carpathian and you are lonely for your homeland. I thought that it would be enough for me just to have you, but I find it is not. You do not know just how wronged you really are. Lucian himself will be hunting you and I am not certain I can protect you from him."

Her eyes moved over his brooding good looks. "Of course you can, Gabriel. He has no power over you, not unless you allow such a thing." She tilted her head, her long flowing hair cascading down in a shiny raven's wing. "And you are far too hard on yourself. It is true I do not merge willingly or fully with you, but when I touch you I can read you. You wanted me to stay with you but you did not really act out of selfishness. You simply could not allow a Carpathian woman, *any* Carpathian woman, to destroy herself. That precept was imprinted on you before you were born. Had I been another woman choosing to meet the dawn, you still would have found a way to stop me."

He looked down at the hand curled over his forearm. Very gently he captured it, brought it to the warmth of his mouth, an intimate, tender gesture that made her heart contract. "You take my breath away, Francesca. If I live another thousand years, I could never find anyone with your natural compassion. I do not deserve you."

A small smile curved her soft mouth. "Of course, you don't. I've known that from the first," she teased, wanting to ease the tension in him. "Come on, let's keep walking. I want to show you some of the sights."

Obediently Gabriel fell into step beside her, retaining possession of her hand. "You have not chastised me, not one word."

"What would be the point? Can I change what is? I cannot change the past. Why would I want to make you feel worse than you already do? Your remorse and regret are genuine. Chastisement will help neither of us. I don't really know what I'm feeling right now. I'll look at it later when I'm alone. All I know is I am very tired and at this moment strangely happy. It is a beautiful night and this city is truly a beautiful one. And there is no other I would rather share it with than you."

He had to look away from her, from the inner beauty shining out of her. Tears were burning in his eyes and he was ashamed. He didn't deserve her, he could never make up the terrible wrongs he had done to her, no matter how hard he tried. He shifted his body more protectively toward her as they walked along the nearly deserted streets swinging their hands together.

Chapter Seven

"Tell me of your stained glass. It is very beautiful and peaceful. When I was examining the pieces in your studio I could feel the presence of power woven into the patterns. Safeguards of a kind." Gabriel was slightly in awe of her healing talent. Few had it so strongly. Her touch alone could impart a soothing peace and he detected that same sense of peace in her work.

She smiled, a quick flash of happiness that he would be interested in the things she enjoyed. She was glad finally to have someone she could talk to about her discoveries. "I started long ago working with small pieces. The idea was to use quilts and coverings of that nature to aid the sick. I often found when I examined a patient that there were other things involved than simply physical illness. Grief for the loss of a loved one, marital troubles, things like that. I began to experiment making specific items for individuals I had touched. I wove patterns that would aid my patients while they slept. Eventually my work became quite popular. People found they were drawn to the articles because they were so soothing." She glanced up at him. "I'm not explaining this very well. I just read people and know what they need and try to provide it. That's how it all started."

"You are truly an amazing woman," he said softly. She astounded him with her accomplishments. "And now?"

"I created a company. My identity is buried deep so if someone comes looking it will be difficult to find out who I really am." She grinned at him, her pride in fooling the ancient Carpathian males showing through. "I even added a safeguard to discourage human sleuths."

"A Carpathian would feel the dusting of power and certainly recognize the ancient symbols in your work," he pointed out.

"Naturally," she said complacently. "That is why I went to the trouble of creating a fictitious male Carpathian, an artist, who is a hermit. My work is often sought by Carpathians to safeguard their homes and bring peace to their environment. They send their orders through my company and I do the work. A few have asked to see the artist, but I always decline."

"Any Carpathian worth his salt can distinguish the difference between the touch of a female or male."

She raised her elegant eyebrow. "Really? Perhaps you underestimate me, Gabriel. I have lived for centuries in secret, undiscovered by the undead, by Carpathian males traveling through this city, and even by you and your brother. Although at times I suspected Lucian might have been aware of my existence. He returned often to this city and scanned more times than I care to count or remember."

"He did?" That made Gabriel nervous. If Lucian suspected such a thing as a female Carpathian in this city, he would dig and dig until he found her. Nothing escaped Lucian's attention. Gabriel recalled how Lucian had led him back to Paris time and again. Even their last terrible battle had been here. Had Lucian somehow been aware of a female's presence? They had shared information all the time. What one knew, the other did, too. Would Lucian hide such knowledge from him?

Francesca nodded solemnly. "Yes. I felt his presence often over the centuries, and I must confess I buried myself deep within the earth to hide from him. I was afraid of you finding me. I had lived alone so long doing whatever pleased me, and I no longer wanted a male in my life." She did not tell him that she had been afraid he might reject her again and she couldn't have borne it a second time.

"Francesca, Francesca," Gabriel murmured softly, "what a little liar you have become. What is the good doctor if not a man? Why would you want the taste of love from one such as he?"

She pulled her hand away from him, cutting him off from her soothing touch. Her face was averted, the curtain of hair concealing her expression from him. "That just happened unexpectedly."

"You have lived with humans so long, sweetheart," he said softly, gently, "you have forgotten what it is like among our people, among lifemates, males and females. I am a shadow in your mind, in your thoughts. You can tell an untruth to Brice, but never to me. You have lived as a human and do not want to extend your own feelings beyond their capabilities. You are afraid of the intensity of Carpathian emotions. I hurt you, Francesca, and you do not ever want to experience such pain again."

She pushed at her long, wild hair and her hand was trembling, betraying her, even as she shrugged her shoulders with studied casualness. "I don't know if you're right. I certainly never blamed you. I was hurt at first, I was only a child, but I *always* understood the well-being of our race was far more important than the happiness of one person."

He caught her shoulders, bringing her to an abrupt halt, the controlled violence in his grip setting her heart pounding. He had enormous strength. "Never think that I had a noble purpose in leaving you behind, Francesca. If I had known of your existence, I would never have left. I am far more selfish than you can imagine, because you are not. I would never have given you up then, any more than I intend to now. You are the only person who is important to me. I saw the memory of that day so long ago in your mind. I was striding through a village, as I had gone through so many other villages. I felt something unusual, but my mind was preoccupied with thoughts of war. I glanced back, I saw women, but did not really see them. The faces of women and children haunted me, I could never look directly at them. I turned away as my brother spoke. Had I seen you, our lives would have been very different. I have a duty to perform, but I would have forsaken it back then. I would have allowed Lucian to hunt alone."

She studied his face for a long moment; then a slow smile curved her soft mouth and she shook her head. "No, you would have willingly sacrificed your happiness for the good of our people."

"But not yours. You still do not understand. I would not have sacrificed yours. I would never have allowed you to be so unhappy. I hate myself for what you have gone through to survive alone, feeling so rejected and unwanted."

"That was the child, Gabriel, not the woman. My life has had purpose and meaning. Because I am tired does not mean I did not enjoy the years I had. I lived well and made my life count as best I could. I had experiences other women of our race could never have. I have been independent and loved it. Yes, I missed having a family, but I had other things to occupy me. It was not a terrible life. And I always had a choice. I could have revealed myself to you again. I could have sought the dawn. I could even have chosen to go back to my homeland where at least the soil and the company of our people would have given me solace. I did not choose to do so. And it was strictly my choice, not yours. I am a woman of power, not a child creeping and hiding in the shadows. All I did, I did of my own will. I'm not a victim, Gabriel. Please do not attempt to make me out to be one."

"You do not love Brice, you only admire him. You have something in common. You respect the way he is with children, his ability to heal, and his focus on his medicine. But you also have your reservations about him."

"I do not," she denied adamantly. "Why would you think that?"

"If you did not, Francesca, you would have committed your life to him. I have been in your mind—"

"Well, stay out of it."

"It is not such an easy thing to do, sweetheart. In fact, you are asking the impossible of me. You do not like the way Brice treats the patients who are less fortunate, those without homes. You do not like the way he is able to completely forget his patients once he has treated them. There are many things you have serious reservations about. You share so much with him, so many children who are ill, but part of you knows that he needs to cure them for his own ego."

Her dark eyes flashed at him. "Maybe that's why I do it, too." There was far too much truth in his words for comfort, and she was annoyed at herself even more than at him. She wanted to cling to Brice because he could never hurt her the way Gabriel had. Her lifemate *had torn out her heart*. His voice, so calm, so truthful, was enough to make her writhe with mortification. She was a woman of power, not a child to be hiding behind a mortal; yet, in the end, that was what she was doing rather than face her lifemate.

"You do it because you are a natural born healer with a gift beyond comparison. You would never leave Skyler in a home with strangers after what she has been through. It would never occur to you. If you could not care for her yourself, you would always watch over her. That is who you are. The doctor would simply forget her."

"You aren't being entirely fair to him, Gabriel. After all, he didn't share her memories. He doesn't know what she's been through." Francesca found herself defending Brice almost automatically.

"He examined her extensively," Gabriel said. "He saw how withdrawn she was. That comes from trauma. He knew. He probably knows all of it, the physical part anyway, and he can guess at the mental and emotional trauma. It does not touch him once she is no longer his patient. That bothers you."

Francesca turned away from him and began to walk

along the sidewalk. "Maybe you're right, Gabriel. I don't know. I'm very confused." *He had torn out her heart.* He would again when he left her to follow his twin, as he must. She could feel the touch of his mind gently reaching for hers. She hastily forced herself to think of Skyler, to focus on the teenager.

"I know you're confused, love, and it is no wonder that you are," Gabriel said softly, but he was watching her with his intent black gaze. "For now we should concentrate on how to bring Skyler home and provide a decent home for her. We will need to decide which memories to erase completely and which to minimize."

"I don't think we have the right to erase the things she's been through, but it wouldn't hurt to dull the memories so that she can deal with them. The most important thing is to help her feel safe, to trust us. I think she needs that more than anything else," Francesca said softly, worried. "Of course, she's missed most of her schooling, too."

Gabriel shrugged indifferently. "That is the least of our worries. We can impart knowledge should there be a need. At this point she needs stability and a decent home life. Once she has the things necessary to build her confidence back, school will come."

"Helping her will be a huge commitment, Gabriel. I do not ask that you share it with me."

"I felt her pain. She is a mere child. But she will soon be a woman. A woman who has psychic ability."

Francesca swung around to face him once again. "Are you certain? I thought she might, because the connection between us was so strong."

"I could not mistake such a gift. I am thinking she could not be in better hands than ours. We can see to her happiness, protect her, and safeguard her should the undead detect her presence. She is so young and has suffered so much already, we cannot allow her in harm's way. And when she is grown, she may be a lifemate for one of our people."

Francesca stiffened. "She will be free, Gabriel, to choose her own destiny. You will not call in the males of our race and hand her over. I mean it. She has suffered much at the hands of males, and our race is domineering and at times brutal. She has it in her mind to avoid all relationships of such a nature and we must respect her wishes. She may never fully recover from the damage done to her."

He laughed softly and curved his arm around her slender shoulders. "We males are never brutal to a lifemate. I believe we have a mama tiger on our hands. You are a very formidable lady. The kind I would choose to be the mother of my child."

She made a face at him. "I don't think you should bring that up just now. It could get you in trouble." She didn't sound as if it would. Her tone was mild, teasing even. Her dark eyes were smoldering but there was a softness about her mouth that belied her flare of temper.

"Skyler will be a well-loved young lady in our household. I will cherish her and offer her the protection I would give my own daughter. She will be happy, sweetheart, very happy. I would never allow someone to claim her ruthlessly without her consent as I have done to you. You forget she may not be compatible with any of our men. I believe in destiny. If she is to be claimed by one of our males, let him find and court her as he should. He will treasure her all the more. *As I do you.*" He thought it and the words shimmered in the air between them.

Francesca blushed a vivid scarlet, her long lashes

sweeping down to hide her pleased expression. There was such a sincerity about Gabriel. She loved his Old World accent and his intense smoldering passion barely hidden beneath the thin veneer of civility. His emotions were stark and devastating, raw and real. He looked at her with such need, such hunger, he took her breath away.

Francesca kept her eyes focused straight ahead. Gabriel could so easily overwhelm her, swamp her with his hungry passion. No one had ever needed her before, the way he seemed to do. She had always thought of him as being entirely self-sufficient, yet now she saw he was utterly alone. A warrior endlessly walking the earth in search of the enemy. She didn't want to sympathize with his loneliness, to admire his honor.

"You are smiling again. That faint mysterious smile that makes me want to pull you into my arms and kiss you. I promised myself I would behave in your presence, Francesca, but you are making it extremely difficult." He said the words softly, his voice a smooth black velvet whisper of seduction.

She was suddenly terrified of reaching her home, yet at the same time, she wished desperately that they were already there. "You can't kiss me Gabriel. You're already driving me crazy. I don't know what to do with you. I had a nice comfortable life with a nice comfortable future all planned out and now you've come and turned my world upside down."

He grinned at her, a quick, almost boyish, mischievous flash of immaculate white teeth. "I cannot help myself, sweetheart. You are so beautiful, you take my breath away. What man would not have such thoughts walking in the night beside you, with the stars overhead and the breeze teasing him with your scent?"

"Do be quiet, Gabriel." Francesca tried not to let any pleasure sound in her voice. He certainly didn't need any encouragement. "For a man who claims little knowledge of women, you certainly know all the right things to say."

"It must be inspiration," he replied.

Francesca burst out laughing; she couldn't help herself. He was becoming more outrageous by the minute. "The dawn is creeping up on us and I'm tired. Let's go home."

He liked the sound of that. Home. He had never had one. Gabriel could acknowledge to himself that he had been lucky in the unique relationship he shared with Lucian. He had been lonely, but never truly alone like the other males of his species. Even after Lucian had turned, they merged often. A two-thousand-year habit could not be broken so easily. It was automatic.

It bothered Gabriel that he had not found Lucian's first kill in the city. Any kill. Lucian had risen starving from their long imprisonment beneath the earth. He would have gorged himself on the first human he had come across, yet Gabriel had scoured the city for evidence and had found nothing. He knew there was more than one vampire in the area. He read the papers for news of strange murders, but none of those murdered had been killed by Lucian. Lucian was an artist with a very distinctive style. There was nothing sloppy about Lucian. Each kill held his personal signature, as though he were taunting his brother to come after him. Sometimes Gabriel thought it was all a game to Lucian.

"You've gone away from me again," Francesca said softly. "Where do you go, Gabriel? Is he talking to you?"

Gabriel didn't pretend not to know whom she was talking about. "Sometimes we merge inadvertently. At those times you are in great danger."

"You love him very much, don't you?" Francesca curled her fingers around his wrist, brushed her body close to his to offer comfort.

At once he felt her soothing presence, and peace stole into him as it always did when she was touching him. He wondered, just for one moment, if she could have healed Lucian before he turned. Could she have imparted the same peace to his soul as she did to his twin?

They turned up the road leading to her house. He liked the look of it, the way it seemed to reach out and beckon to them. Home. This was home. Was there any possibility of a family for him? Could they actually live here together? Raise their baby? Care for Skyler? Would Francesca ever be able to love him? She wanted him, her body craved his, but would she love him? Forgive him?

"You go very quiet when you think about him," Francesca murmured softly. "I can feel the pain it causes you. Yet if I touch your mind, you have only good thoughts of him. He must have been quite a man."

"There has never been another like him. He was a master at battle. At anything. I never had to look to see if he was there, I always just *knew* it. Lucian was a legend. He saved so many lives down through the ages, human as well as Carpathian, it would be impossible to count them. He never faltered in his duty. Not at all. We were close, Francesca," he admitted softly. "Very close."

They were walking along the property toward the front entrance. "Tell me about him. It might help to share your memories. I feel your reluctance to speak of him; you think it is disloyal to him. But I would never presume to judge him. You loved him and admired him and I can only do the same."

Gabriel pushed open the front door, stepped back to

allow her to precede him. He was continually scanning the area around them, a habit long since drilled into him by his lost brother. Sorrow welled up out of nowhere. "I sometimes think I could have destroyed him by now if it weren't for the fact that I can't bear to be in the world without him. I gave my word of honor to him long ago that I would be the one to destroy him should he lose his soul. We both did. If one turned, the other would hunt and destroy, yet I have been unable to fulfill my promise to him. Is it deliberate, Francesca? Is it?" He sounded lost and very alone.

She closed the door firmly against the light beginning to streak through the early morning sky. "No, Gabriel, you would have honored your promise if you were able to do so. And I believe that you will. You honor him."

"Lucian lost feeling while he was a mere fledgling, long before our males normally do, yet he endured for two thousand years. I had emotion far longer than he did, so I shared what I felt with him. I still cannot believe he turned. I have seen the evidence of his kills. I have even come on him when he was making a kill. But something in me will not believe it. I cannot comprehend that so strong a man, such a leader, a defender of our people, would have chosen to give up his soul to the darkness for all eternity."

"You love him, Gabriel. It is only natural that you would want him to remain in your heart the way you have always known him," Francesca said softly. She tugged at his hand and moved through the house, taking him with her. "I need to call my attorney and ask him to draw up the appropriate papers making me Skyler's guardian. Before we retire to our chamber, we must send inquiries to ask if any of our people have human families they would trust to aid us in caring for Skyler during the day while we sleep."

He followed her to the study, watched as she spoke quickly and firmly to the lawyer. She gave him no real chance to argue with her; there was compulsion in her voice, and Gabriel automatically aided her, adding the weight of his power to hers. Her attorney would have everything in order for them by evening. No one would protest. Who would want Skyler Rose Thompson? She was an orphan with no relatives. Francesca had money and influence. Any judge would gladly grant her wishes.

Gabriel watched carefully as she turned on her computer and began typing at a rapid rate. It amazed him, the capabilities of the new technology. Her fingers flew on the keyboard with total confidence. She had watched this technology as it had grown. She had experienced the things he could only read about. He could read about them, but he could not go back and watch them as time unfolded. Francesca was comfortable with speeding cars and airplanes that blasted across the sky. With spaceships and satellites. With the Internet and computers.

"I've got a hit, Gabriel," Francesca said. "Savage, Aidan Savage in the States. I've made several lovely pieces for his house. I am certain I heard his lifemate was once a human psychic. Aidan has a twin brother, Julian."

A slow smile spread across Gabriel's face. "Julian, I remember him. He was just a boy with wild blond hair, very unusual for our species. He was eavesdropping on a conversation Lucian and I were having with Mikhail and Gregori. He was quite a handful even as a boy. I sensed a darkness in him, but there was no time to examine him closely." His white teeth flashed. "Gregori was very protective of him, and I did not wish to challenge my own kin. We were hundreds of years apart, but our blood is the same. I would like to know what happened to both of them."

"Well, I do not know much of Julian's fate—I am careful not to rouse curiosity with my inquiries—but I have done business with Aidan on more than one occasion. He does not know me, only my fictional Carpathian male, the artist who owns my company. I'll e-mail Aidan and see what he can tell us of his human family and how it works. I can include a question about Julian. As far as Gregori, it is well known his lifemate is the daughter of our Prince."

"Please do ask about Julian. It is interesting that you can talk so quickly to someone halfway around the world. One of our own people. You must be very careful about the way you talk to our people. Anyone might be able to intercept your mail," he cautioned.

"Trust me, Gabriel, I am very careful. I've always had to be careful." She turned off the computer and took his hand once more to lead him to the chamber beneath the earth. Her heart was beating so loudly she knew he could hear it. They walked through the halls at a leisurely pace, through the large kitchen passageway leading to the sleeping chamber.

Gabriel brushed her temple with his mouth, lingering for a moment against her pulse. "I want you, Francesca, I will not pretend that I do not, but I have told you I want us to be friends. I will be satisfied with holding you." He wanted the comfort of her arms, her closeness.

Francesca tightened her fingers in his. She was just as capable of reading his mind as he was at reading hers. He was determined to put aside his own needs and see to hers first. He wanted to give her as much time as she needed to accept his claim on her. Her heart gave a curious lurch at his consideration.

"How did you manage to walk in the sun at midday? Our ancients are unable to do such things, yet you managed to find the secret."

There was so much admiration in his voice, Francesca felt color steal into her face. "I knew the only way to avoid recognition by my own kind was to train myself to think like a human and walk and talk like a human at all times. When I reached the point where I wanted to be able to go out into the sun, I had already given up so many of our gifts, it seemed like a kind of return, a treasure. I had been researching why our women cannot usually conceive more than one child successfully. I came to the conclusion it was nature's way of balancing our population. Then I turned my attention to why we lose so many children during the first year of life. Our children are much like human children—they do not drink blood, their teeth are not developed, and they cannot go to ground, shape-shift, or do anything we can do as adults. Their parents, however, must rest during the daylight hours, and the children are certainly at risk without supervision because they must be above ground when their parents put them to sleep."

"That is very interesting, but it does not explain how you managed to go out in the sun." His chin rubbed the top of her hair in a little caress. Tendrils of her hair caught in the stubble on his jaw, tangling the two of them together with the silken strands.

She smiled up at him. "I theorized that if we could do so as children, then we could do it again. What changed us? Our body chemistry altered, and we required blood to sustain our lives and our gifts. Yet we could survive for long periods of time with transfusions and with animal blood. I experimented and eventually changed my actual body chemistry. I was weak and unable to shape-shift or do most of the things that are necessary to our species."

Beside her he stirred. She felt the sudden pounding of his heart. His lifemate had been alone, unprotected, performing dangerous experiments to enable her to walk in the sun. He was proud of her, but the thought frightened him. Francesca found herself a bit pleased at that reaction. She hid her smile as she moved the large bed with a command so that they could open the chamber below the ground.

The chamber was cool and welcoming, the darkened interior inviting. Francesca waved her hand and the earth opened to reveal the dark, rich soil. Gabriel glanced at the bed. The quilt was thick and soft with intricate swirls and ancient symbols. He slipped free of Francesca's fingers and went to examine the fine craftsmanship. Francesca had accomplished so much in her time on earth. "How did you change your body chemistry?" he asked. "It is a tremendous feat and one that might be very useful to our people."

Francesca shook her head regretfully. "I experimented over many years, Gabriel, but it was a trade, my gifts, for the sun. And I was very vulnerable. I found herbs and made them into soups and used different compounds in an effort to duplicate the metabolism our children have, not human yet not Carpathian. Just as they could spend time in the sun but could not go to ground, so it was with me. For Carpathians at the end of their days and wishing to try new things, it might be good, although the process is painful and very long. It requires nearly a hundred years. And my eyes really never got used to the sun. There was still some weakness. I recorded it carefully in our ancient tongue and would have sent the information to Gregori before I died."

She turned her head to study the glittering of his eyes. Dark. Dangerous. That was Gabriel, a legend come to life. He reached out, caught her wrist, and drew her to him. "I want you. All over again." He said it starkly, without embellishment. He brought her hand to his trousers, but the material was gone, sliding from his body in the way of their people so that her palm contacted the hard thick length of him. He was hot, throbbing with need.

She wrapped her fingers around him, simply holding him for a moment, and then her fingers began to move of their own accord, a small experiment as she watched his face intently, as her mind merged deeply with his to share what he felt. At once she was rewarded with the sheer pleasure etched into the lines of his face, in his mind. "The bed does have possibilities," she murmured softly.

"Undress for me, in the manner or humans," he said suddenly. His eyes had gone very black, burning with such intensity that she could feel tiny tongues of flame along her skin. "There is something very erotic in the way a woman removes her clothes."

Her eyebrow shot up. "I thought there was something erotic in the way your clothes melted away and left me to explore where I wanted." Her voice teased him, was sultry with invitation. She stepped away from him, her arm dropping slowly to her side, her fingers brushing the hard length of him as she did so. Francesca tilted her head so that her long hair slid in a silky black curtain over her shoulder. Her hands went to the small pearl buttons on her sweater. She eased each through its button hole so that the edges began to gape open to reveal the satin swell of her breasts. Deliberately her hands traced the path of the opening, pushing the sweater slowly from her shoulders and allowing it to fall on the floor unheeded. She was rewarded with the darkening of his eyes, the swelling of his body to alarming proportions.

She eased her slacks from her hips to reveal her silken panties, a scrap of fabric that barely covered her tight black curls. She kicked off her sandals as she stepped out of the slacks and stood for a moment in her underwear. Her nipples were already hard in anticipation, pushing at the lace of her bra, adding friction to sensitize her further. With a slow, unhurried movement she released the catch and dropped it aside. "I ache for you," she said softly, cupping her breasts as an offering. "I want you suckling me. Your mouth is always so hot, Gabriel." Her hands traced a path down her flat stomach to strip the panties away.

His eyes blazed with desire. "Are you wet and slick with wanting me, Francesca?" His voice was husky, his eyes raking her body possessively.

Her hand slipped between her legs, sampled the moisture there, and held it out to him. His eyes on her face, he stepped forward and deliberately sucked her fingers. At once Francesca's legs went weak. He melted her. Anything and everything was beautiful with Gabriel. She loved how he wanted her.

His arm circled her waist, dragged her close to kiss her, devouring her mouth. "You taste so sexy, Francesca, I want to feed on you for eternity," he whispered into her open mouth. "Taste yourself, sweetheart, feel what it is like for me when I have you. When you take me in your mouth and suck on me, hot and tight, when I am deep inside your body. Whatever we choose to express how we feel, it is so beautiful." His mouth wandered to her breast, his hand kneading her buttocks, pushing her deliberately against his arousal.

Francesca cradled his head to her, giving herself up to the shared ecstasy. Gabriel pushed her down on the bed, dragged her to the edge. "What do you want, my love?"

She didn't hesitate. Why should she? She was his lifemate and there should only be pleasure between them. She had every right to total fulfillment and she wanted it. She opened her legs wide, her hand going to the hot wet core of her. Once more she brought her fingers to his mouth. "I want to feed you for eternity. Make me come, Gabriel, long and forever. I want you buried deep inside me and I want to wake the same way."

He lifted her legs to his shoulders and bent his dark head, his tongue stroking, caressing, and probing until she was writhing on the bed, unable to hold still. His fingers inspected, explored, probed deep, only to be replaced by his tongue. She cried out then, shuddering with pleasure, closing her eyes as he lowered her body to his hips and surged forward, taking her, filling her as she fragmented, catching her at her most sensitive.

He plunged into her hard and fast, as hungry and ferocious as she was for their joining. He wanted her like this, craving him, needing him, her body glowing with pleasure, her sheath a tight hot home for his own engorged body, relieving the ever-present raging need in him. He wanted it to last forever, riding her hard, her hips rising to meet his, his body and hers coming together in perfect union, her breasts full and firm and quivering with each hard thrust, her hair spread out around her, and her eyes fixed on them. Together. As they should be.

When the release came it swept both of them up into the flames, hard and long, an endless spiral, an earthquake with strong aftershocks. They lay in each other's arms, kissing, their mouths melding together, expressing a fierce need and hunger they couldn't seem to assuage. It was Gabriel who floated them to earth, still entangled together, his mouth dominating hers, his hands holding her close.

They settled to earth and still couldn't stop. He took her a second time, harder and faster than the first, and even then he couldn't quite let go. He lay beside her for a long time, his hands in her hair, his mouth at her breast. They lay together until the light in the sky made it impossible to stay awake. Reluctantly, Gabriel set the safeguards on their chamber and covered their resting place. Their bodies needed the rejuvenating sleep of the earth during daylight hours. Sometimes they slept in chambers above ground, but they needed the benefits of the healing soil for rejuvenation.

She curled up in his arms, feeling secure and protected. Feeling as if she was not alone anymore. Francesca snuggled closer, breathing in his masculine scent. His body was made for hers. Perfect. The way she fit against him, the way he seemed to shelter her, making her feel so much a part of him. Inside her was their child, living, growing, developing, warm and safe, a gift from her lifemate so precious, no treasure could ever surpass it.

"Sleep, my beautiful lifemate, rest while you can," Gabriel said softly. She felt his mouth brush a kiss in her hair. His arms tightened around her and they both allowed the breath to leave their bodies and their hearts to cease beating.

Chapter Eight

When Francesca pushed open the door to Skyler's room, she was carrying the package of clothes and the stuffed animal, the blue-eyed wolf she'd bought the night before. The teenager was lying on her back staring up at the ceiling. Her long lashes fluttered once in acknowledgment that she was no longer alone, but she didn't turn her head. Francesca could see that her small, battered body had tensed. The child's fear permeated the room.

"Skyler." Purposely Francesca used her softest, gentlest voice. "Do you remember me?"

The girl's head turned slowly, and her large soft gray eyes fixed on Francesca's face as if she were clutching at a lifeline. "I could never forget you." Like Francesca, Skyler spoke in French, yet Francesca had the feeling it wasn't her first language. There were several heartbeats of silence before the girl forced herself to continue. "Is it true? Is he really dead?"

Francesca glided across the room, her movements as fluid and graceful as those of a ballet dancer. There were no sharp edges to Francesca, only a whisper of sound as she moved. She dropped the package of clothes on the end of the bed. More carefully, she tucked the stuffed animal close beside the girl and took Skyler's hand in her own. Gently. Lovingly. "Yes, my dear, he has passed from this life and can no longer touch you. I am hoping you will want to come and live with me." With her free hand she stroked back Skyler's wild hair. "I very much want you to live with me." There was a trace of compulsion in the silvery purity of her voice.

To her astonishment, Skyler's steady gaze wavered. She closed her eyes, the long lashes sweeping down so they lay like two thick black crescents against her pale skin. "I felt you inside me, reaching out to me. I know you aren't like most people." Her voice was so soft it was a mere thread of sound. "I know things I'm not supposed to know about people. When I touch them, I know things. You do, too. You know what he did to me, the things he let his friends do to me. You want to make it all better, but even if you could take away the memories, you can never make me innocent and good again."

"You don't believe that, Skyler. You're smarter than that. They may have touched your body, but not your soul. They could have destroyed your body, but never your soul. You are already good and innocent. You have always been that. The things done to you cannot change your basic nature. They can shape you, make you stronger. You know that you're strong, don't you? You found a way to survive what would have destroyed others."

Skyler's small teeth touched her lower lip in agitation but she didn't answer.

Francesca smiled at her, a gentle smile of commitment to Skyler's healing. "You're right about me. I am different, just as you are different. Perhaps the world around us can shape us, but we are strong inside. You are whole. There is no stain on your soul to cause you to be afraid to be with me. I shared everything with you, your pain, the degradation, the beatings, the fear, all of it. I want you with me where I can shelter you, offer you the things you should have had, things you truly deserve. You're holding my hand, you know the things I am saying are true."

"There were others with you when you were sharing my memories. I felt them, two men with us."

"There was only one man," Francesca corrected gently. "Gabriel. He is a very powerful man. Under his protection there is no one who can harm you."

Skyler looked puzzled. "There was another. I am sure of it. There was one staying very quiet, lending his strength to you and to me. But the other remained passive while you were here with me. After you left, I remember him holding me, yet he wasn't touching me at all. His arms were strong and felt very different than any other's. He wanted nothing from me, only to comfort and help. Who is he?"

"Only Gabriel was with us, sweetheart. Maybe you were dreaming."

"I felt all three of you distinctly. He was very strong. There was no anger or rage, only a quiet acceptance. He examined my memories. I know he was learning about you through me, I felt it." Skyler sighed in resignation. "You don't believe me. You think I'm making it up."

"No, I don't think that at all, Skyler," Francesca said. *He was learning about you through me.* "I simply do not know who it was. I only felt you. Later I realized Gabriel had shared your ordeal with me, but I was so caught up in it at the time I was focused solely on you. I believe you have this gift. How could I do otherwise? You cannot lie to me. Even though I cannot 'see' this man in your mind, that does not mean he was not with you. You knew I shared your memories when few others would have known. You are aware I am different from others. Stay with us, Skyler, with Gabriel and me. We are different. I'm not going to pretend otherwise, but our feelings for you are genuine." She sent a quick mental report of the conversation to Gabriel. It alarmed her that Skyler remembered so vividly the feeling of another sharing their mind merge.

"How can I ever face myself, look in the mirror again?" For the first time the thin, small voice held emotion, a sob of burning pain, quickly beaten back. Skyler's torment immediately claimed Francesca's full attention.

She tightened her hold on Skyler. "Look at me, sweetheart. Look at me." It was a soft command.

Skyler turned her head once more and lifted her impossibly long lashes. She could see her face reflected in Francesca's black eyes. Like a mirror. Skyler looked beautiful. "That's not me."

"Yes, it is. That's how I see you. That's how your mother saw you. That's how Gabriel sees you. Who else matters? That man who claimed he was your father? A drunken shell of a human being who wanted only to use drugs to escape what he had become? His opinion cannot possibly matter to you, Skyler."

"I didn't want to come back. I was safe where I was." There was a plea in the young voice, a heartbreaking plea. "I can't face it all over again."

Francesca stroked back the fringe of hair tumbling over the girl's forehead, her touch soothing and healing at the same time. "Yes, you can. You're strong, Skyler, and you're no longer alone. You know I am different, I have certain abilities. I can dull your memories, give you time to heal properly. You will still feel the pain, but it will be bearable. You are surrounded by those who love you and you see yourself the way you really are inside, not the way that man tried to teach you. He was dead inside, a monster made of drugs and alcohol."

"He is not the only monster in the world."

"No, sweetheart, he is not. The world is filled with such creatures and they come in all forms and sizes. We can only do what we can to stop them and rescue the innocents from their hands. Gabriel has dedicated his life to doing so and so have I in my own way. Give us the chance to love and care for you as you should have been."

"I'm afraid," Skyler said. "I don't know if I can ever be whole again. I can't bear the sight of men. Everything frightens me."

"Deep within your heart and soul, Skyler, you know all men cannot be condemned for the despicable things your father did. All men are not alike. Most are fair and loving."

"I'm still afraid, Francesca. It doesn't matter that I know what you're saying might be the truth. I can't take the chance, I don't want to take a chance."

Francesca shook her head gently. "You retreated so that you would not become like them. You wanted to be like your mother, seeing the good in people and having compassion. I read that in you easily."

Her eyelids fluttered, then bravely remained open. "I wanted him dead."

"Of course you did. I wanted him dead, too. That does not mean we are monsters, sweetheart, only that we are not angels. Join with us. I want you with me, I have been inside your head and know you as your own mother did. Better perhaps. I would count myself blessed to share my life with yours. If that is not what you wish, I will provide the money for your education and upbringing. Either way, it is your choice. I will not abandon you."

Skyler twisted her fingers tightly around Francesca's. "You know what you're asking of me. I know you do. I'll have to go out into the world, be with others. I'll never be the same as they are. I'll never fit in."

"You'll fit in with me," Francesca insisted. "With Gabriel and me. We appreciate talent such as you have, we really do. We can help you develop it. There are ways to tone it down or expand it if it is necessary to do so. And you will have plenty of time to heal before you need to face the world. Try to sit up, Skyler. You're strong enough."

"I don't think I want my ability developed any more than it already is. When I touch people, I know things about them I shouldn't. Sometimes I see terrible things. No one believes me when I tell them." There was no trace of self-pity in Skyler's voice or in her mind. The teenager was simply stating facts as she saw them. Skyler reluctantly withdrew her hand and with Francesca's aid managed to sit up.

"I brought you a few things, some underwear and T-shirts and a robe." She held up the stuffed wolf. "And this. Gabriel thought you might like a friend."

The girl stared at the stuffed animal for a moment, her

eyes widening. "For me? Really?" She reached for it, pulled the animal into her arms. At once peace seemed to steal into her heart, a little at a time. "No one but my mother ever gave me anything before. Thank you, and please thank Gabriel," she said in a tearful voice. She pressed her face against the wolf's face and stared for a moment, entranced by the blue eyes. She had awakened from a long nightmare and the world seemed more fantasy than real. She struggled to stay in it, not to slip back inside her own head.

Francesca studied the teenager. Skyler was so thin, Francesca could see every bone in her body. She seemed so fragile, Francesca was afraid she might break. Francesca placed pillows all around Skyler, tucked the blankets up high. Skyler's face still held traces of bruising, but she was remarkably healed from her single session with Francesca. She was all eyes, and she had beautiful eyes of soft dove gray. They were haunting eyes, eyes that had seen far too much for such a young girl.

"Well, how bad do I look?" Skyler asked it indifferently, her voice more tired than interested. She didn't let go of the stuffed animal.

"I think Gabriel is right, we will have to invest a great deal in food for you. Were you starving yourself?"

"I considered it. I thought even if I didn't actually die, his friends wouldn't want me if I was really skinny." The comforter bunched in Skyler's fist as she curled her fingers tightly around it. "There was one who didn't care. He called me ugly all the time, but he came around just the same. I think he was worse than my father."

Francesca sent her waves of reassurance but remained silent, wanting Skyler to continue talking, wanting her to get it all out. She knew the man, the one the girl was referring to. She had shared memories of him, of his brutality to a small innocent child he held completely in his power. Paul Lafitte. Skyler would never forget him, never forget the three others who had used and battered her. Their faces were burned into her mind, the sound of their voices recorded forever in her memory. They would be etched into Francesca's memory for all time also.

"He was here again," Skyler said suddenly. "He was just here with me."

Francesca's head went up. She scanned the area quickly but found no one who could be considered an enemy. There was no taint of power, no voids to indicate an evil one was near. Whoever or whatever was reaching out to Skyler was powerful enough to elude Francesca's search. "What do you mean he was here? Lafitte? One of the others? Tell me, Skyler."

Skyler shook her head. "The one like you. The one that was here before and stayed quiet while you healed me. He touches my mind when my memories are overwhelming. He makes me feel safe."

"Gabriel?" Francesca had thought he'd gone into the city looking for evidence of Lucian. He had read the newspaper, given a quick exclamation, and was gone before she could ask. When she picked up the paper there was an article about an unidentified man found in an alley with his throat slashed. He had been found in a part of town where few decent people ever went. Francesca was certain she would have recognized Gabriel's touch in Skyler's mind. She reached for Gabriel and found him at once.

"You are safe?" She asked it softly, a little hesitantly, knowing from his deep concentration he was in the middle of something important.

"He was here. Lucian. This was his kill. He is still in

the city. I do not know why he was not waiting for me as he should have been."

"Were you here with us just a moment ago? Skyler says she felt the presence of another while we were talking."

There was a moment of silence. Gabriel examined Francesca's memories of the conversation she had had with the teenager. *"It was not me, sweetheart. This worries me. Lucian is extremely cunning and he likes games. If he is aware of Skyler, he would be aware of you. He would not pass up the opportunity to use either of you to get to me. You must be very careful. He is killing now, leaving his prey for me to find."*

"Why would he comfort Skyler?"

"I cannot say. Perhaps to use her against you. I do not know, Francesca, but we cannot underestimate Lucian. We must assume he has found Skyler and is aware she is linked to me through you. He is extremely powerful and sensitive to the smallest hint of power. We both were vulnerable to his detection last rising. I should have been more careful."

"Would you feel him if he had linked with us while we were with Skyler? She says she felt a third presence. She definitely felt another male, not you, and he held her, yet was not present physically."

Again there was a long silence. *"I do not like this, Francesca. It had to be Lucian. Only he is capable of slipping in and out of my mind without my knowledge. You are in great danger, you and Skyler. He is up to something. This kill was deliberate. A message to me that he has opened the game and it is my move."*

"How do you know?"

"His victim is one of the men from Skyler's memory."

Francesca bit her lower lip hard enough to bring a dot

of ruby-red blood welling up. She let her breath out slowly. Now it was Skyler who reached out to comfort her. "What is it? Why are you upset?"

"I don't know who this man is, the one who came to you this morning. It was not Gabriel as I had hoped. There is one in this city like us, with the ability to connect without his physical presence, yet he is not like us. He is dangerous." Francesca tried to keep the fear out of her voice. She knew what the vampire was capable of. He was a ruthless, merciless killer who played with people and their emotions for his own amusement. The undead could appear to be handsome and courteous, friendly and gentle, when in fact they had only dark, demonic thoughts. Lucian was the most powerful Carpathian alive other than his twin. Now that he had chosen to lose his soul he was doubly dangerous. He had been feared before; now he was considered the most menacing enemy of all time. It was a frightening thought that Lucian might be stalking them for his own deadly purpose.

"He didn't *feel* evil," Skyler said softly. "I'm always afraid of men. Even the doctor makes me nervous, but for some reason this man's different. He almost feels like Gabriel, sort of safe. I've never had a safe feeling before so I'm not certain."

Francesca nodded. "I hope you're right, sweetheart, but I want you to be cautious with this man. Very cautious. Now tell me about your talent."

Skyler's eyelids were drooping. "I'm already tired, Francesca. It isn't exactly a talent, it's just knowing things. And I can sometimes read people's thoughts, just like you can. Like Gabriel and the other. I prefer animals to people. I couldn't keep any pets, but I knew all the neighborhood animals and they were my friends, even the dogs that were supposed to be mean. I connected with them, you know."

"How do you see Gabriel and me? What can you tell about us?" Francesca asked curiously. How much could Skyler actually see?

Skyler slid once more down between the sheets. Trying to be civil after living in silence so long was a difficult task and very exhausting. "Do you really want me to answer that question, Francesca? I see far more than you think."

"I believe if we are to live together and become a family, there should be truth between us, don't you?" Francesca asked gently.

"You are not like me and not like the others. I don't know what you are, Francesca, but you can heal the sick and comfort those in need. There is only good in you. Only that. I wish I was like you. I wish I really was your family." Skyler added the last sadly, her lashes fanning her cheek as sleep overcame her.

Francesca brought the limp little scarred hand to her mouth. She kissed the scars on the back of Skyler's hand and turned her arm over to inspect the palm. The child had fought off someone who'd slashed at her with a sharp piece of glass. Had it been her father? Gabriel had dealt him swift, merciful justice. Francesca examined the teen's memories once more. Not her father that time. It had been a tall, thin man with coarse, dark hair and large hands. He was furious because Skyler refused to voluntarily kiss or fondle him. She couldn't have been more than eight or nine at the time.

Sickened, Francesca dropped the girl's hand, afraid she would awaken her with her violent reaction to the child's ordeal. She pushed her hand against her throbbing temples and her palm came away smeared with blood.

"Breathe, Francesca, you can do her no good reliving

these memories. Lucian may have sought to throw down the gauntlet but he is inadvertently aiding me in bringing about justice for this child. Our child. We will love her." Gabriel flooded her with warmth and solace. She could feel the sensation of his arms around her, the strength of his body as if he were holding her close even though they were miles apart.

"Where are you?" She caught a glimpse of a busy room filled with desks and people, mostly men.

"At the police station. I am unseen at the moment. I need to know everything about this kill. I want to hear the personal comments and read the reports. I have already visited the site. I do not know what Lucian is up to, but I want you to be very careful. Scan Skyler's memories each time you visit her."

"She is asleep and becoming restless."

"I want you safe, my love. Perhaps you should go back to the house and set safeguards. But do not think it will do more than slow him down if he attempts to come after you. Should you be in danger, you must call to me. Do not wait."

"I have to see my lawyer. He has drawn up the papers and the judge will see me this night. It is a special favor he is doing me and I must attend. The judge will ask Skyler if she agrees and as soon as Brice okays it, we will be able to take her home with us. There has been a reply from Aidan Savage via e-mail. A few members of his household are in London at the moment. He will contact them and see if they would be willing to aid us, housekeeping for Skyler during the daylight hours."

"Please be careful, Francesca," Gabriel cautioned as he slowly allowed the connection between them to fade. He liked none of it. It could only be Lucian merging with

Skyler. Gabriel knew he would easily detect any other of their kind or the undead. Everything pointed to the handiwork of his twin. This kill. It was classic Lucian. Neat. Tidy. Unidentifiable to anyone except Gabriel. The opening gambit in their game.

He considered an attempt to lead Lucian away from the city and the two women. Both of them were at risk.

Gabriel examined the pictures of the body from all angles. In a few minutes he would go to the morgue and make sure that there were no telltale signs of vampirism. Most vampires were messy with their kills and the remains usually had to be incinerated to a fine ash, leaving little for the human police to trace. Lucian had always been different. It was as if he deliberately kept the game between Gabriel and himself.

This body was Lucian's kill. He was like a surgeon, never leaving so much as a pinprick behind. The blood was drained from the body, not a single drop spilled on the ground. Around the neck was a clean slice like a giant smile. The medical examiner could never quite figure out exactly what was used. The evidence pointed to a single razor-sharp claw like that of a long-extinct raptor. The only blood remaining in or on the victim was the thin line like a necklace around the throat. That macabre mystery was Lucian's calling card, his idea of a joke. In the past no one had ever determined what had caused the injury or how the blood loss had occurred. When Gabriel was a step and a half behind Lucian, as he was now, and the police found the bodies, these kills always created a major sensation. Everyone liked a good mystery.

Right now they were all speculating about the injury. It was so precise they were betting it was done with a surgical instrument by a surgeon. Gabriel walked among them unseen to the human eye. As he moved through their midst, he noticed that some of the detectives were more sensitive than others. One or two of them shivered unexpectedly, looking around to see where the cold draft came from.

Computers could make things much more dangerous now. With their ability to trace everything from DNA to voice to fingerprints, they could make the job of concealing evidence of Carpathians extremely difficult. Gabriel realized he needed to learn every aspect of the latest scientific discoveries. A great number of the topics being discussed were things he had no real knowledge of. He automatically shared the information with Lucian, and much to his shock found that Lucian already had studied the latest in medical research. The flow of data returning to him was astonishing, although he shouldn't have been surprised. Among their kind Lucian had been shockingly intelligent, assimilating information at a much more rapid rate than others. It was as if his brain constantly craved more data. Naturally Lucian had already discovered the scientific advances, the extraordinary technology that could make things so difficult for their people. Carpathians and vampires alike would undoubtedly have a much more difficult time hiding their existence.

"Do not worry so much, Gabriel, I am more than careful. They will not find what I do not wish to leave behind."

Gabriel took the opportunity to "see" through his twin's eyes. If he could lock in on his brother's position, he might have the opportunity to fulfill his vow. At once Lucian's soft, taunting laughter echoed in his mind and the view was distorted so that Gabriel had no chance to see anything that would help him. *"You do not think I would make our game so easy for you, do you? You must follow the clues I leave. That is the way it is done. You cannot cheat, Gabriel."*

"This is between the two of us, Lucian. There may be other hunters in the city. I would keep this between us, as it should be."

"Do not worry so much for the safety of your brother. I am certain I will defeat all who come to threaten me. I am learning about this world fast and the knowledge is rather exhilarating. There is much to play with here. I like this place and do not want to hurry our battle."

Lucian was gone just like that. Gabriel felt a peculiar wrenching pain in the region of his heart. His brother. He missed their closeness. Missed the man he had followed for so many centuries. A great mind. A warrior unsurpassed. No one could orchestrate a battle as Lucian could. Sorrow engulfed Gabriel, nearly drove him to his knees. To destroy such a great man. To destroy the one who had always been there with him, for him, the one who had saved his life so many times. It was more than should be asked of anyone.

"Gabriel, you are not alone." Francesca's voice was gentle and soothing. *"You know that is no longer truly Lucian. You are honoring him by fulfilling your commitment to him, by destroying the very thing he fought against for so many centuries."*

"I remind myself of that fact often. Intellectually I know it is true, yet my heart is heavy with the burden."

"Fortunately, you have only to reach out to find me here. I am, after all, a healer." There was the merest hint of teasing in her voice.

Gabriel instantly felt warmth surround his heart. It was supposed to be this way. Never alone, the two of them walking through life together, helping each other with the emotional entanglements, with each crisis that came their way. That note in her voice gave him a measure of comfort, gave him hope. He touched her mind to see if she had talked with Brice. He didn't want to ask and he was ashamed that he was jealous enough to invade her privacy to find out if she was sharing her time with the doctor. *"Perhaps you should leave Skyler to her rest and attend to the business of gaining custody of her so you may return to the safety of the house."* He made the suggestion carefully, choosing his words so they would not sound like an order.

Francesca's laughter was very soft. *"I am touching your mind as you are touching mine. You are not nearly as subtle as you think you are. I will leave the hospital, Gabriel, because I have much business to attend to."*

She was not about to give him the satisfaction of knowing she was avoiding Brice on purpose. She no longer viewed Brice in the way she had before Gabriel had entered her life. It made her feel guilty. Francesca had no idea what to say to Brice. She knew Skyler was destined to live with her, yet Brice didn't want anything more to do with the teenager. He didn't know what Francesca was, what she needed to do to survive. Everything was different now that Gabriel had returned. She was very confused and needed time to sort everything out properly.

Francesca touched her stomach with the palm of her hand, a light caress. A child. Gabriel had given her a child when she had gone so many centuries certain she would never have such a gift. And now Skyler. Able to touch minds as she could, Francesca knew everything about the young girl. Everything. She already loved the girl as a daughter.

There was soft male laughter brushing her mind. *"You*

do not look old enough to have a daughter Skyler's age."

"I am old enough to be her ancestor. She knows we are not human."

"Not really. She knows we are different. She thinks we are psychic as she is. Eventually we will explain the full truth. In the meantime, we must treat her the way humans with money treat their children. She will need a bodyguard during the daylight hours when we cannot be with her, along with a housekeeper to see to her needs."

"I have to do this, Gabriel. I cannot leave her alone to face the world. She needs me." Francesca was unsure whether she was apologizing or not.

"She needs the two of us," Gabriel corrected her gently. *"She must learn from someone that all men are not the monsters she has encountered. She is still of two minds. She wishes to retreat back into that place where nothing can touch her, yet the hand you are holding out to her is very tempting. She has felt you, the love you have for others, the compassion in your heart, and it calls loudly to her."*

"She will choose to come with us, Gabriel. She is tremendously courageous."

Francesca flagged a cab to take her to the judge's office. Her lawyer would meet her there. *"We will meet back at the hospital as soon as the paperwork is finished so that the judge can ask Skyler if she is agreeable to my guardianship. I am concerned that Brice may make a scene over you. Are you prepared for such a thing?"*

Gabriel censored his thoughts immediately. It was ingrained in him not to call unwarranted attention to himself. This was a situation he was unfamiliar with. His instinct was to remove the threat to himself and Francesca and even Skyler. Brice would not interfere with their plans. He would not allow such a thing.

"Gabriel?" Francesca's voice was soft with worry. *"Why have you closed your mind to me? You will not harm Brice, will you? He has been a good friend to me when I needed one."*

Gabriel swore to himself in several languages, mixing them up as he did so. Francesca had a way of forcing compliance on his part. It felt rather like being hobbled. What was he to do when she was always placing restrictions on his actions? *"Attend your meeting, woman, and leave me in peace. I will be there should you need me later. For now, I am hunting and cannot take the time to give you reassurance."*

"Don't growl at me, you fraud. I was not the one monitoring your thoughts. You opened this conversation, not me."

She was laughing at him. Gabriel. The hunter of vampires. A warrior two thousand years old. Men feared him but Francesca was laughing at him. It was a new experience but one he could definitely get used to. She had a way of turning his heart over and melting his insides until he barely knew himself.

Gabriel streamed through the city, checking every haunt remembered from centuries earlier. He knew the layout of the huge sprawling city now. Every rat trap, every narrow alley and bolt-hole. He knew the cemeteries, the cathedrals, the hospitals and blood banks. He looked in every place he could think of for signs of Lucian. He knew his twin was in the city yet it was as if he were searching for the wind itself; there was no trace of Lucian's existence other than that body left for the police.

Gabriel touched Francesca's mind, knew she had returned to the hospital and was entering Skyler's room. He decided to meet her there. Francesca needed to lean on someone, whether she wanted to admit it or not. He fully intended to be that someone. He moved through the night air, a stream of mist blending with the bands of fog rising from the ground. He was not about to allow the doctor to be there alone with Francesca if anything should go wrong. He did not want to take a chance that Brice might attempt to influence the judge against allowing Skyler to live with Francesca. A small smile curved his mouth, but did not touch his coal-black eyes. Gabriel had a way of making sure the judge would give Francesca anything she wanted. He entered the room as fine molecules so he could easily slide under the door. As he moved inside, his powerful frame once again came together, still unseen by those in the room.

She was sitting on the edge of Skyler's bed holding the young girl's hand. Just the sight of Francesca took his breath away. He knew it always would. The judge was a tall, thin man with graying hair and kind eyes. The lawyer was altogether much too young and good-looking for Gabriel's peace of mind. He, also, was staring at Francesca with a kind of rapture on his face. Another fan. She seemed to have them everywhere.

"So you see, Skyler, if you want to live with me, the judge is willing to agree, but you'll have to talk to him," Francesca coaxed gently. She was not using her voice to sway the teenager in any way.

The judge moved to within a few feet of the bed. Skyler was visibly trembling. Gabriel reached automatically for her mind. She was under his protection, a female child with psychic ability, a precious treasure to be guarded at all times. He did not like her agitation, the terrible distress on her face. Francesca was also in her mind, bolstering her courage, soothing her, aiding her to face the male strangers invading her room. The terror of her childhood was far too fresh in her mind to be able to handle such an event alone.

At once he gathered Skyler into his mental arms, pouring his strength and power into her so that she blinked in amazement. He was surrounding her mind, repeating a healing chant in the ancient language of their people, whispering teasing nonsense so that Skyler could hardly keep a straight face. Her large soft eyes darted around the room searching for him, but Gabriel was nowhere to be found. She glanced at Francesca questioningly but Francesca could only smile and shrug her shoulders. She didn't know his exact location either, only that Gabriel's presence was strong enough to indicate he was very close to them.

"Well, Skyler," the judge prompted gently. "Don't be afraid. We want to do what's best for you, whatever will make you happy. Francesca has indicated quite strongly that she would like to be responsible for you, to be your guardian. She has room in her home and can easily give you every advantage, but you are old enough to choose for yourself. I would like to hear what you have to say."

The door to the bedroom swung inward and Brice walked in. "May I inquire what is going on in here? This girl is my patient."

The judge turned slowly, one eyebrow shooting up. "I thought you had agreed that we could question her today." He glared at Francesca's lawyer.

Gabriel reached for Brice's mind. The man was a whirling chaotic mass of contradiction. He was angry with Francesca, certain she had already chosen to be with Gabriel. It was in his mind to sabotage her efforts to gain custody of Skyler. Gabriel forced down his own desire to allow the man to completely ruin his chances with Francesca. At once he made the decision to interfere. He solidified outside the door to Skyler's room, shoved it open, and strode in.

Brice swore aloud, stepping back hastily to allow Gabriel entrance. Gabriel's tall, powerful frame dwarfed the doctor's. As he brushed by, he leaned close so that his words were heard by Brice alone. "You will tell the truth in this matter." He gave the command softly, his voice compelling the other man to do his bidding.

Brice found himself responding with words he'd had no intention of saying. "I did say Skyler could answer your questions," he admitted reluctantly. He glared at Gabriel. "She is high strung. All these visitors could very well upset her and send her into a regression." He avoided Francesca's dark eyes and the censure he knew he would see there. "I have serious reservations about Francesca providing a home for Skyler. I happen to know her home situation has changed and she no longer lives alone." He said it in a belligerent tone, his jealousy making him reckless.

The judge glanced at Gabriel. "You must be Francesca's husband." He reached out, offering his hand. "She has been saying some wonderful things about you. It is quite a privilege to meet you."

"What did you tell him?" Gabriel took the offered hand with a firm, courteous shake. His black gaze caught and held that of the judge. The man stood mesmerized, felt as if he were falling forward straight into that gaze.

"The only record they will find of you has a top-security clearance. I created a file on you explaining your absence.

You were heroically serving your country. It is not too difficult to do such things when you know your way around the computer. It also helps to have people in high places owe you favors. You look like a hero to anyone who might inquire." Francesca's soft voice brushed rather smugly in his mind.

"I hope my living at Francesca's house will not be a problem." Gabriel said, staring directly into the judge's eyes. "After all, we are still married. She was kind enough to give me a place to stay. Francesca is obviously the best person in the world for Skyler. I would not want to do anything to jeopardize such an arrangement."

The judge had never heard a voice so pure and beautiful as Gabriel's. His entire being reached out toward that voice, wanted to please the speaker.

"Francesca, there is no need to stay married to him. You're not obligated just because he came back from the dead," Brice put in, furious. "Has he done something to make you lose your mind? You don't know this man anymore. You haven't seen him for years. You don't know anything about him. He should have stayed dead!" Suddenly aware of the things he was shouting, of the difference between his voice and Gabriel's, Brice made an effort to calm down.

Skyler was gripping Francesca's hand hard, her incredibly long lashes shading her large gray eyes, hiding her mounting terror. At once Francesca touched her mind to reassure her, recognized Gabriel's comforting encouragement.

"We are with you, Skyler, right here."

To the shock of both Gabriel and Francesca, the young girl was able to reply on a mental path neither had ever used before. *"What if the doctor won't let them give me to you? I can't live without your help. I know I can't. It would be better to just let go."* There was a desperate fear in her. Someone had touched her life with gentle understanding, someone she recognized as good. Someone who understood how different she was. Someone who valued her despite the terrible things that had happened to her. Now she might lose her rescuers.

Gabriel's dark eyes swept the child huddling close to Francesca for protection. *"Look at me."* It was a soft command, but impossible to disobey. Skyler's large eyes met his instantly. *"You will trust in me, in Francesca, and believe that we can sort this out. There is no need for fear. Those under my protection cannot be abused in any way. Francesca will continue to heal you and you will cease to worry over trivial matters such as this ugly argument. They cannot touch your life, little one. They will never be allowed to do so. They only believe they have such power."*

Skyler visibly relaxed, allowing her breath to escape in one long sigh of relief. Francesca found herself beaming at Gabriel, her heart in her eyes.

Chapter Nine

Brice was watching Francesca's face. He found himself cursing silently at her expression as she gazed at Gabriel with pride. He knew he had to back off or lose her. He had never experienced jealousy and found it to be an extremely ugly emotion. What had gotten into him? Was this his true character? Of course it would be best for Skyler to live with Francesca, how could it not be? But Brice didn't want to share Francesca with anyone, it was that simple. Francesca had many acquaintances who called themselves her friends, but he was the only one she had allowed close to her. He was used to having a special place in her life. A teenager didn't figure into his plans for the future. Francesca knew many people; she had money and moved easily in the inner circles. She was beautiful and well liked by both men and women. By escorting her to charity balls and parties, he had become accepted also.

Gabriel moved. It was a mere shifting of his muscles, subtle but frightening all the same. There was something very dangerous about Gabriel, though Brice couldn't quite put his finger on what it was. Something about his eyes that wasn't entirely human. He tried to look away from those black, empty eyes, but instead he was falling forward, straight into their centers. At once he felt ashamed of himself. Brice had a very strong urge to retract his words. He cleared his throat and spoke almost without his own volition. "Francesca is the perfect guardian. Of course there's no question about that."

Brice managed to tear his gaze away from those cold black eyes. He had the feeling Gabriel was secretly laughing at him. To his amazement, Brice found himself clenching his fists. He was not a violent man, but he desperately wanted to hit someone. He also had the strangest feeling Gabriel knew exactly what he was thinking, knew it and was deliberately antagonizing him. It was in his every look, his smile, his pitiless eyes. Why couldn't Francesca see that those eyes were as cold as death itself?

Gabriel smiled, a flash of perfect white teeth. "Of course Francesca is the perfect guardian. You think so, too, is that not correct, Skyler?" His voice was soft and gentle, so beautiful it made Brice sound harsh in comparison. But it was more than that, it was the way he said Francesca's name that made Brice want to throw things. There was something very intimate, very possessive in his tone.

The judge turned to look at the young girl. "Is that so, Skyler, would you like to live with Francesca? It's up to you. If you prefer to answer in private, we can clear the room and just the two of us will hear what you have to say."

Skyler shook her head, hugging her stuffed wolf close to her. "I know what I want," she answered softly, but very clearly. "I want to live with Francesca."

The judge beamed at her as if she were a brilliant child. "Naturally. I can see you and Francesca have already established a close bond. I trust we can see to the proceedings as quickly as possible?" He fixed a stern eye on first the attorney, then Brice.

While Francesca's attorney nodded solemnly, Brice squirmed. "We haven't settled the matter of Francesca's living circumstances to my satisfaction. After all, *I* am ultimately the one who must decide if Skyler's environment is safe or not before I release her. She has suffered a tremendous trauma. I don't know if living with a male, a stranger, is conducive to her recovery."

"Brice—" Francesca put a wealth of feeling into his name. "Please don't force me to go to court over this. Skyler and I need to be together as a family."

Brice raked a hand through his hair. "I'm not arguing that point, Francesca. I just think we shouldn't move too soon. A background check is usually done on anyone seeking custody of a child and I don't think dispensing with it is proper since we know nothing about your friend here."

"But Francesca is the one seeking custody," the judge said, "not Gabriel. I have had ample time to read the files prepared by Mr. Ferrier on Gabriel, and I believe he is a good and decent man, well suited to caring for a child."

"What file? I didn't see a file," Brice protested.

Once again the judge was caught and held in Gabriel's slashing black gaze for a long minute. He smiled warmly. "I assure you, I read the file thoroughly and know everything necessary about Gabriel. It is a confidential document, not open to the public." He leveled his gaze at Brice.

"I am certain you will take my word for it."

Brice was more than certain Gabriel was manipulating the judge. Blackmail? Money? Was the man wealthy? Was that it? Each time Brice thought he had come up with a compelling argument, Gabriel would somehow catch the judge's attention and turn everything back against Brice. He glared at his rival. When Gabriel returned his stare, those damnable black eyes slid over him with malice, sending a shiver of fear down his spine. *Who is he? Where has he been the last few years?* Was he a killer for the government? Did they really have killers that walked around freely? Was he a criminal and the judge knew him from a past experience? Brice felt sure Gabriel was holding something over Francesca's head. That had to be it. He was forcing her compliance. Maybe it was a good thing Skyler was going into that home. She could see what was going on and report back to him. It would be necessary to get into the girl's good graces and persuade her to watch over Francesca. He would have to make her his ally.

Brice nodded slowly. "I will give my consent then, Judge, as long as you have knowledge of his background."

Gabriel smiled pleasantly. "Thank you, Doctor, although I was unaware your approval was needed in this case. Skyler is technically a ward of the court." He sounded mildly amused at the presumption that Brice was needed at all.

Brice turned a dull red. Damn the man and his manner. His voice was so beautiful and compelling, so perfectly amiable no one could fault him, yet he was deliberately insulting. "Skyler is my patient. She needs my clearance to leave the hospital. I take my job very seriously." He moved at once to establish his authority.

Gabriel bowed with an Old World courtesy, a courtly

gesture, as though he were a prince dealing with a peasant. Brice gritted his teeth to keep from swearing. He hated everything about Gabriel. His tall, well-muscled frame, his broad shoulders, the long shiny hair tied with a leather thong at the nape of his neck. How could a grown man look so well dressed with his hair like that? Brice hated the elegance of his clothes, the sensuality of his mouth, the inhuman look of his eyes. Most of all he hated the power that clung to Gabriel, the complete self-confidence. He carried himself like a man used to commanding others. It was easy to imagine him as a feudal lord in another lifetime. Brice felt as if Gabriel was secretly laughing at him, as if he was a source of amusement and no more.

Gabriel smiled at him easily, a show of those immaculate white teeth. How did he get them that white? Brice wanted to smash those glistening white teeth right down Gabriel's throat. "Skyler is well on the road to recovery. Francesca tells me she is stronger every day. I am certain it will not be much longer before she is able to be home with us."

To everyone's surprise it was Skyler who replied. "I am feeling much stronger." She said it defiantly, her voice soft and trembling but quite clear. "And if anyone cares about my opinion, I want to live with Francesca *and* Gabriel." She had no idea why she felt a sudden compulsion to add Gabriel's name when she really meant Francesca. Men frightened her. Even Gabriel, although she sensed only compassion and caring in his feelings for her. She was more astonished by her outburst than anyone. She hadn't spoken to anyone in months, yet now she was in a room filled with adults, strangers really, and they were deciding her life. It was terrifying and she was grateful for the stuffed animal and the strange soothing comfort it offered her.

"I'm glad to hear that," Brice said immediately, recognizing he needed to back down. "The stronger you are, the happier we are, Skyler." He turned his back on Gabriel as he spoke. He knew Gabriel would read the lie in his eyes otherwise. Skyler should have been grateful to him: he was her doctor; he had been the one who had risked his license by bringing Francesca in to see his patient without parental consent.

Brice made himself smile down at the child. After all, he could charm women. It was his best asset. "I'll have you out of here in no time, young lady, and that should please you immensely." His gaze swung around to encompass the officials. "If you're finished here, I suggest you leave and allow my patient to rest. She is quite pale."

Francesca leaned down to hug Skyler. "I'm going to have such fun preparing a room for you. I know the things you like."

Skyler caught her arm, lowered her voice to a soft whisper. "I hid my mother's locket in my old bedroom. It's behind the paneling next to my bed. I don't want anything but that. I don't want anything of *his*."

Francesca nodded solemnly. "Don't worry, honey, the locket will be waiting for you at home. I'll see to it personally." She murmured the promise softly as she brushed her mouth against Skyler's forehead.

Gabriel reached right passed Brice as if he weren't there and captured Francesca's hand, twining his fingers through hers as if they belonged together. "You need to sign the papers, sweetheart, and then, I think we will visit several shops for our young lady." He flashed his smile at Skyler, the one that could light up the sky and take Francesca's breath away. She loved him in that one single moment. She loved the way he reassured Skyler with genuine caring. She felt it in him. He was her lifemate and could not lie to her or mislead her in any way about his true feelings. He wanted Skyler to share their life and their protection. He wanted her safe from all harm. There was true goodness in Gabriel.

Francesca allowed him to pull her from the room, down the hall into the waiting room where she could finish her business with the judge and her lawyer. Gabriel remained at her side, silent but supportive. He didn't try to catch her eye or hold her attention in any way, yet she could think of little else. He was there, larger than life. He was life. And laughter. She wanted to smile just thinking of him. How had he managed to create such a shifting of her loyalty in such a short period of time?

As a young girl so many centuries ago, she had been certain of what she was, proud of who she was. She knew she was created to be the lifemate of someone extraordinary. She had always known it. She had been proud of Gabriel, always proud of him, even when she thought him lost to her. He was a legend, a great vampire fighter, a hunter unsurpassed by any other. Francesca had known the call of the lifemate was powerful, yet she had been certain the passing of centuries would diminish that strong pull. She had counted on it. She bit her lip, attempting to concentrate on what her lawyer was saying; yet all the time, *he* was in her mind, filling her senses and confusing her completely.

She wanted peace. Rest. After all the emptiness, all the long years of being alone, she deserved rest. She had been useful, she hadn't wasted her life or her gifts.

"No, my love, you did not. I could not be more proud

of anyone. You accomplished a great deal, all for good. While I was taking lives, you were saving them." The voice was soft in her head, filled with respect, tinged with regret. As if he considered himself unworthy of her.

At once her large dark eyes turned to capture his. *"You were saving lives, too. Gabriel, you are the guardian of our people. You must know you stood between mankind and the undead. You gave up your happiness to do so."*

Watching them from the doorway, Brice saw the raw emotion in Francesca's beautiful eyes as she gazed so lovingly at Gabriel. She had no idea of her own feelings, how deep, how intense they ran within her, but he could see the truth in her eyes. It looked as if they lived in their own secret world. They seemed to communicate without words. His fingers bunched tightly at his sides, curling until his knuckles were white and his body shook with anger and disappointment. He had courted Francesca for so long, devoted himself to her, yet never once had she looked at him in such a manner. And she was more beautiful than ever, more alluring. Watching her, he realized she was sexy beyond anyone he had ever encountered. He had always thought her beautiful, a perfect ornament to display in the social circles he intended traveling in. Brice had never thought of her in terms of hot steamy nights and sex, yet now, looking at her, he could hardly restrain himself.

Just then Gabriel lifted his head and looked at him, a long cold look that sent a shiver racing down Brice's spine. Brice turned on his heel and walked away. There was no way Gabriel could actually read minds, no way he could judge the extent of Brice's hatred of him. No way he could have seen the erotic pictures in his head. Brice needed Francesca in every way and he deserved her. He was not going to allow Gabriel to waltz in and take over. Maybe no one else could see it, but he knew there was something wrong with Gabriel, something dark and dangerous. A monster lurked inside him and every now and then, Brice caught a glimpse of it in his eyes. Brice intended to protect Francesca from her own compassionate nature.

Gabriel shook hands automatically with the judge and with Francesca's lawyer. He was used to thinking and even speaking on two different levels. He made small talk easily, all the while turning the problem of Brice over and over in his mind. The doctor was jealous and obsessed with Francesca. He was becoming a threat to their well-being. Brice's hatred seemed out of sync with his bland personality. Was there a subtle taint of power that Gabriel had not caught? Few of the undead could hide such a thing from him. *Lucian.* Was it his twin playing games again, using his human enemy against him? He examined Brice's mind. If it was tainted with the power of the undead, the user was extremely skilled. He should recognize traces of his brother, yet he did not. Yet Brice seemed twisted with hatred. It was centered on Francesca, as Gabriel knew it would be. Brice was determined to get her back, to turn her against Gabriel. If the undead was using the human, Gabriel could not detect the subtle power.

"What is it?" Francesca asked softly, placing her hand in his.

He smiled at her. She was his world. The only one in it. Very slowly he brought her palm to the warmth of his mouth, lingering for a moment to inhale her scent. "You are an extraordinary woman, Francesca."

She was glad the others were already out of the room. She could hear them as they walked down the hall together, pleased with the outcome of the meeting. Color was moving up her face like a schoolgirl's; she was blushing simply because he had kissed her palm. Francesca tried to tug her hand back.

Gabriel retained possession, his white teeth very much in evidence. "You are shy with me even after all we have shared?" Deliberately his voice held a husky seduction, a teasing temptation.

"I am not," she lied, embarrassed by her reaction. She had once thought his eyes so empty of emotion, yet when they rested on her they were filled with such hunger, such intensity, she could barely think straight.

His white teeth flashed at her. "I think we need to find a store and furnish a room for our teenager. I never thought I would have to 'father' a girl of her age, and a human at that. I pity any young man who thinks he might like to take her out on a date. Reading minds is very helpful in certain situations."

Francesca reached up to rub his chin. "Thank you for wanting to do this with me. I'm really excited about bringing Skyler home with us and it's nice you share that with me. She's such a beautiful girl."

"Yes, she is. She should have clothes that make her feel good about herself." He suddenly grinned. "I know quite a bit about the world, almost any subject, but I have no idea what a teenage girl would want in her room. I must rely heavily on you in that department. There were no images in Skyler's head of what she would like."

"I don't think she's ever thought about such things. Her life has been one of survival. I have been thinking we could give her the upstairs room with the balcony, the one with the small turret attached to it."

He nodded solemnly. "I believe she would like that very much, Francesca." He took her hand. "Fly with me this night. We can go to the shops and walk unseen until we decide what we would like to purchase. Allow yourself to feel the freedom of our race once more. You have not done such a thing in a very long time."

Francesca found a small smile forming at the idea. It was true. She had given up many of the gifts unique to their people in order to think and feel and act human. It had been very necessary in order to hide herself. But now the temptation was too strong to resist. Allowing her senses to flare out into the night, scanning the entire area, she waited until she knew there was no one in the vicinity, then took a running leap skyward. As she launched herself into the air, feathers shimmered, iridescent and beautiful, so that she flew silently across the starlit sky.

The feeling of soaring through the night was so incredible, she could hardly take it in. It had been so long since she had allowed herself the luxury of thinking like a Carpathian. She had wanted her thought patterns to be wholly human at all times. Now it seemed she could enjoy the special privileges of her race once again. She laughed with joy as she moved through the sky.

Gabriel joined her, a large raptor, silent and swift and deadly, winging through the sky toward the heart of the city. He knew her mind, knew she would go first to the home of Skyler's father to retrieve the precious locket. He flew close to Francesca, determined to protect her even from her own exuberance if necessary. He was in her mind, ensuring that she held the image of the bird in flight so she could make no mistakes. He shared her joy and reveled in her freedom, but he remained a shadow, determined to protect her.

Francesca settled on the rooftop of the old building where Skyler's father had lived. It was severely run down.

There were bars on the windows and the door, something that was no barrier for the two powerful Carpathians. The little apartment was was a wreck of smashed liquor bottles and filthy dishes. There was no food in the refrigerator, only beer. The cupboards held a box of crackers and two cans of soup. Francesca touched one of the cracked mugs sitting in the sink.

She turned to look at Gabriel with tears in her eyes. She could feel the violence locked in the tiny apartment. A child's terror. The brutality a man could impose. She saw flashes of Skyler's life, the father, a huge man, swinging a belt at her in the bathroom. Skyler huddled in a corner while a man approached her with an evil smile.

Gabriel grasped Francesca and shook her gently. "Leave this evil place. You are too sensitive for such as this."

"Skyler was, too. That beautiful child was subjected to this depravity. They drove her to the edge of madness, Gabriel."

The tears in her voice were almost more than he could bear. "She is safe with us, Francesca. We will not allow harm to come her way again."

"She is a human psychic, a rare treasure to our males. She would have been invaluable to our race, but after such atrocities, I cannot imagine her being able to love one so dominant and wild as any of our males. What are we to do?" There was despair in her voice.

"That dilemma is a long way off, honey, not something we have to solve at this moment. In any case, we do not know if she is the lifemate to one of our species. Our first duty is to her now. She is our daughter and deserves our protection. Go, I will find her mother's locket," Gabriel assured her.

She linked her fingers with his, needing the comfort of his closeness. She didn't question why his touch felt so right to her. She only knew she wanted to be held in his arms and feel his enormous strength when all around them was the evil of mankind. Gabriel fitted her beneath his shoulder, instinctively knowing she would rather be with him in this wicked place than outside alone in the clean air. The realization made him humble. He brought her hand to the warmth of his mouth, breathed a kiss onto her skin, his mouth telling her without words that she was the magic in his life.

They found Skyler's locket and he secured it around his neck as they made their way to the shops. Francesca was in her element there. She knew the city, knew the vendors. She often bought thousands of dollars' worth of clothes to donate to the poor. Gabriel twined his fingers with hers as they entered one of the stores. This was not Gabriel's forte, but he was more than willing to share the excitement with her. He watched Francesca blossom, her beauty almost ethereal. She lit up the shop and he couldn't help thinking of their night alone in her friend's boutique. When he flashed her a grin, she blushed and quickly looked away from him, sharing his thoughts of their wild encounter together.

Closing hour came and went, but all of the merchants Francesca called cheerfully opened their shops for her. Gabriel found he enjoyed watching her move through the stores, examining clothes and furniture, selecting youthful styles appropriate for the newest member of their family.

"Are you planning on getting her an entire wardrobe?" he teased when she showed him pair of faded blue denim pants. "What is this fascination modern women have with these men's pants?" He rubbed the bridge of his nose thoughtfully. "Must our daughter wear such things? Dresses and skirts would be much more appropriate."

Francesca's eyebrow shot up, and her mouth curled in a small smile. "Perhaps you're right; perhaps we need to look at more feminine clothes for her."

It was her voice that warned him all might not be as he would like. He followed her with some apprehension into a different area of the store. Francesca took a navy blue sheath from a hanger and held it up. "This is darling, Gabriel. Don't you love it? You're right, I think we need to concentrate on much more feminine articles of clothing."

He reached around her and fingered the soft material. "Where is the rest of it?" He was very serious, his dark eyes searching her face for signs she was teasing.

"This is the entire dress. Girls wear them quite short these days. Haven't you noticed?" Francesca couldn't believe he had never noticed the women in the city and the clothes that often revealed a generous portion of leg.

"You do not wear such clothes." He made it a statement.

"Of course I do. Short and long dresses. Anything goes in this age."

"You wear things like that dress in front of men?" There was a curious churning in the pit of his stomach. He didn't quite understand why he suddenly wanted to rip the doctor's head off. Had the man seen her in such garments? The thought of it brought an unfamiliar volcanic feeling to his gut.

Francesca laughed at him. Straight out laughed at him. Her dark eyes were shining with merriment. "You sound just a tiny bit on the jealous side."

His hand reached out, almost of its own accord, his

fingers circling her throat. "I know you are not making fun of me, are you, Francesca?"

Francesca tried to keep a straight face. "I'm sure I wouldn't do that," she said sweetly. "But I do look like dynamite when I dress up."

"My heart cannot bear the image," he said, "at least not if you are dressing up for another male. Do not tell me anything more."

"Your age is showing." She laughed, the sound carefree, piercing his heart like an arrow. "Get over it and help me find her some dresses she'll love."

"I will find her dresses she will be allowed to wear in public," he countered gruffly, looking for the first time at the little frocks on the mannequins. "Where are the ankle-length garments?"

"Are you going to be one of those guardians who insists on bodyguards and strict curfews?" she asked with one eyebrow raised.

"Absolutely. You can count on it." He made no attempt to pretend otherwise.

Francesca's smile washed over him, making it clear she was not in the least impressed by his stony features and grim mouth. She found the underwear section and spent time choosing lace and satin while he simply shook his head in wonder. She arranged for her purchases to be delivered the next evening and followed him out into the night.

Skyler would have a room designed especially for her, the items chosen as much as possible from her memories of things she had seen and liked. The rest they chose for her, wanting her happiness and comfort. The pattern for her quilt and sheets was a design fashioned by Francesca to aid healing and promote soothing comfort and a feeling of well-being. The room they had decided to give her was a round turret where the intricate stained glass contained a powerful spell to protect the occupant from outside harm and nightmares.

Francesca smiled up at Gabriel as they settled onto the balcony of her home, once more taking their own shapes. "I had a wonderful night, Gabriel. Thank you so much for sharing this with me. It is much more fun experiencing life with another."

"You are growing used to me, despite your intentions not to," he ventured as he led her down the stairs to the kitchen.

"We have to remember to stock the house with food that will appeal to a teenager," Francesca said, determined not to be drawn into a conversation about their relationship. She wasn't ready to think too much on the subject.

"Skyler should eat what is the most nutritious for her. She is skin and bones. And you must do something with her hair. She wears it in her face because she thinks the scars make her ugly."

Francesca followed him to the chamber beneath the earth. "I know she does, although I think it is more what they represent, the memories that are so ugly. I can't wait to bring her home. This house will be so different. Music, noise, a housekeeper, probably guards—our lives will be very different, Gabriel."

He circled her shoulders with his arm, grateful she didn't pull away from him. He was making progress without her being aware of it. "Change is good, Francesca. My existence was bleak and barren for two thousand years. I welcome change." His hand slipped down her arm, crept around her stomach so that his palm lay over their growing child. He closed his eyes for a moment, savoring the feel of her, of their unborn child.

She smiled up at him. "The dawn is approaching, Gabriel, you must rest."

"You are the one with child." He opened the earth and floated with her into the welcoming soil, his arms pulling her into the protection of his body. "Sleep, honey, tomorrow we will fix her room for her." His body and soul, heart and mind, were content. She was with him, his arms around her, her scent filling his lungs, and it was enough.

You are the one with child. She repeated those words in her mind, hugged them to her, wondering at such a miracle. Francesca felt his mouth against her forehead, his hand over their child, and she closed her eyes, content to rest.

When she woke, Gabriel was already out, searching for evidence of Lucian's whereabouts. Their world was fragile and filled with danger as long as his brother hunted in their city. Francesca felt Gabriel stirring in her mind, felt his warmth, yet she shivered as she moved through the familiar rooms of her house. During the day the deliverymen had arrived, leaving boxes of every size and shape. She had forgotten just how many things they had purchased for Skyler the night before. Francesca enjoyed every moment of arranging the room and placing Skyler's clothes neatly in the dresser and closet. She took great care working on the heavy quilt, putting love into each stitch as she fashioned it especially for Skyler.

She was beginning to worry about Gabriel now. From Gabriel's thoughts she learned that already Lucian had struck again; there would be another unsolved murder for the police. She sensed Lucian was deliberately baiting Gabriel, leading him toward a trap of some kind. She moved about the house, taking care of business before her trip to see Skyler. She made calls to various organizations, to members of society, to old acquaintances. It was always necessary to keep up appearances, now more than ever with Skyler as her ward.

The first order of business was to secure a housekeeper they could trust. Aidan Savage in the United States had recommended a trustworthy couple, his own housekeeper's son, Santino, and the man's wife, Drusilla. They would move in and protect Skyler during the day. Santino knew Aidan was Carpathian, and Aidan assured Francesca it would be safe to confide in him.

Satisfied, she made her way to the hospital. Skyler smiled tentatively as she entered the room. "I thought maybe you changed your mind," the girl said. The stuffed animal was in its usual place in her arms.

"No, you didn't," Francesca corrected with a smile. "You had a panic attack. Things are falling in place, honey. Gabriel and I found your locket for you. It's in a jewelry box in your room. You have everything you need waiting for you to come home. All you have to do is get better. Are you eating?"

"I'm trying to eat," Skyler answered honestly. "It isn't easy. I didn't for so long, I'm never hungry now. Where's Gabriel?"

Francesca thought it a good sign Skyler had inquired after him. "Out hunting."

Skyler was silent a moment. "Hunting?" she echoed. "I didn't think he was the kind who would want to kill a living creature." She seemed disappointed.

Skyler obviously had an affinity for animals. Francesca smiled gently. "Not animals, silly. Things." She brushed the hair out of the girl's eyes, her touch tender and soothing. The contact gave her access to Skyler's emotions.

The child was frightened but was making every attempt to be brave. The future terrified her, life terrified her, but not Francesca and not Gabriel. She had made up her mind to try to give life another chance. "I can't go to school," she blurted out suddenly. "I can't be around anyone. I don't want anyone to see me."

Francesca nodded soberly. "I understand, honey. I think it best we stick together for a while, the three of us and our housekeeper. I'm going to hire a couple who will work for us, keep an eye on you."

Francesca took her hand and simply held it, allowing her special gift to flow out of her and into the girl.

"Now I want you to rest, young lady. I'm going to ask Brice to release you as soon as possible, but you have to do your part. If you have trouble eating, or you're afraid, reach for Gabriel or for me in your mind. Like you, we are telepathic and we will hear you and come to your aid. Call if you are in need. I expect it, is that understood?"

The girl nodded solemnly. "I'm tired all the time."

"That's to be expected. You suffered a trauma, Skyler, and you were beaten very badly. Your body and mind need time to heal as well as your spirit. I'll be back later. For now, rest." With a wave of her hand she pushed open the door and glided out.

"Are you Francesca Del Ponce?" There was a stranger standing outside Skyler's room. She sensed he had been lurking there for some time. Francesca had scanned him, of course, that was as natural to her as breathing, and she had known he was waiting to talk with her.

She smiled pleasantly, her long lashes veiling the expression of annoyance in her eyes. For a brief moment she considered using a mental "push" on him, but there was something about him that wasn't quite right. She couldn't quite put her finger on what it was so she stopped to face him. "Yes, that's right. I'm Francesca." She flashed a smile at him, one that caught his attention immediately.

"Barry Woods, Miss Del Ponce. I'm a reporter looking for a good story. I understand you heal people."

Her eyebrows shot up and a small smile curved her soft mouth. "I'm sorry, I must have heard you wrong. What do I do?"

"Heal people. I was told you healed a little girl who had cancer."

Francesca hesitated for a moment before answering him. There was something about the man that bothered her, that wasn't quite right. A craftiness. Something subtly evil. Perhaps she was mistaken, but he sent a shiver along her spine. She touched his mind very delicately.

At once her breath caught in her throat. She forced a smile to her lips, her large dark eyes widening so that they were as black as night. "I wish I had such a wonderful ability. The truth is, I have no such talent." With her stomach lurching, Francesca made herself touch his mind. Gabriel would need information. This man was not what he seemed on the surface. He was a fanatic, his mind filled with images of vampires and stakes and garlic.

The reporter continually clutched at the golden chain circling his throat. She knew in his hand he held a cross. "My source is very reliable, Miss Del Ponce."

"The doctors here are quite remarkable," she said softly. "Don't you think it is much more likely they healed the child if her cancer is in remission? I go and read to the children often, but I cannot heal them, much as I would like to. Have you seen them on the cancer ward? They are so beautiful and brave. It's rather heartbreaking. Perhaps you should visit them. The story would have tremendous human interest, don't you think?" She buried the subtle compulsion in her suggestion carefully.

The reporter shook his head as if to clear it. "I have to get the story."

She nodded gently, her long hair moving like a silken curtain around her shoulders. "Yes, the story about the doctors here in the hospital and how remarkable they really are." Her dark eyes stared directly into his. "You really must write about their work."

Woods caught himself as he was turning toward the cancer ward. He shook his head hard to clear out the cobwebs. For a moment he was disoriented, unable to remember exactly what he had been doing. Uppermost in his mind was the overwhelming urge to write a story about children with cancer. He shook his head again, certain he had not come here for that reason. A woman was walking away from him, her hips swaying gently. Her hair hung below her waist, thick and rich and shining with high lights. She was so beautiful she took his breath away and he hadn't even seen her face.

He stood a moment, reluctant to move. He couldn't think what he was doing. He wanted her to turn so he could see her. He wanted to follow her, but his feet felt like lead. He had come here for a reason, an important reason, but he could only remember that he wanted to write a story on children with cancer. There was a doctor he needed to talk with. Not French, but English. Strange name. Brice something. Woods scratched his head and turned resolutely away from the cancer ward. He felt very lost, very confused. He had no real idea what he was doing.

Chapter Ten

"How long do you think you can keep avoiding me?" Brice demanded as he came up behind Francesca.

"Don't flatter yourself, Brice," Francesca said exasperated. "This isn't the best time to confront me. I just had a little visit from a very unsavory reporter. He was making me out to be some kind of nutcase. I suspect I have you to thank for that."

Brice had the grace to look ashamed even as he tried to shrug her accusation off casually. "I only told the truth. You examined my patient. At the time she was terminally ill. There is no question that was so. It was fully documented and I have all the records to prove it. Afterward every blood test came out clean, Francesca. She's completely cured. I didn't do it and I have no idea how it was done."

"So you just gave me up to reporters, the freak miracle

worker. You made sure my privacy was completely destroyed. Is that supposed to make me look upon you with favor?" Francesca tossed her head, her thick curtain of blue-black hair flying. "I'm busy avoiding your reporters, Brice. I don't have time for a little chat."

"Francesca, it didn't happen like that. Come on, you know me better than that. I admit I like to grab the headlines, but it wasn't me who talked to the reporters." He caught her arm, bringing her to a halt. "Stop running, Francesca, you're wearing me out. It wasn't me. It was the girl's parents. Her name is Chelsea Grant. Her father is a United States senator. I mentioned you to her mother without thinking. There was no hope for Chelsea. None. Her parents knew that. I wasn't the only doctor who had examined her. I was only one in a long line of opinions. Mrs. Grant had you investigated. Several former patients were only too happy to be able to talk about you and the miracle you worked for them."

Francesca glanced down at the fingers trapping her arm. There had been a time the brush of his fingers had warmed her heart; now he irritated her. Was she so shallow that her feelings could change so easily, so quickly? Or had she somehow deceived herself about his true character because she had been so lonely? She had wanted to share her life with someone once before she allowed herself to die. Now Francesca could clearly see how important headlines were to Brice, how important pleasing a senator's wife really was to him. "Important enough to sell me out," she mused aloud. "You wanted her to owe you a favor."

"I'm sorry, Francesca, I wanted the best for my patient. And yes, she happens to have parents who could smooth my way to the hospital I want. A place where my skills can really make a difference."

"I thought you cared about these kids."

"Of course I care about them, I've dedicated my life to them. You haven't learned that it's okay to want to make a decent living. You have money, Francesca. You have more than enough, although you're giving it away at an alarming rate. I need to make a living. It's as easy and as heroic to help a rich sick child as it is to help one that's homeless."

"Like Skyler," Francesca said softly. "She can't do a thing for your career. You didn't want her in your life so you tried to make certain she wasn't in mine. That is beneath contempt, Brice. That child needs a home and I can provide her with a good one. For you to try to keep me from taking her home was absolutely unforgivable. How could you do such a thing?"

"Damn it, Francesca. You're the one who's changed, not me. You knew I wanted certain things. This isn't about me, it's about him. Gabriel. What is he, exactly? A government spy? A mob boss of some kind? Is he holding something over your head? Over the judge's? Are you all afraid of him? Don't think I haven't noticed something's not quite right about him. Was he in prison for a crime? Where has he been all the years he was gone?"

"You heard what the judge said. He has all he needs to know about Gabriel. His life is a matter of security. It's classified."

Brice bit back an explosion of swear words. "Is that what he told you? And you just believe him? Don't you see, Francesca? He could be a criminal of the worst sort. You're too trusting. He just waltzes back into your life after dropping off the face of the earth and you accept him. The judge accepts him. Your attorney accepts him. My God, don't you see? He's not like us."

"No, he's not. He's good and kind and has no ulterior motive when it comes to Skyler." Francesca's dark eyes were flashing fire at him. She was so beautiful Brice found himself reaching for her, wanting to take her into his arms. He must have blinked because she moved so fast he didn't actually see her move, but his arms dropped empty to his sides.

"That's a hell of a thing to say to me. I wanted Skyler to get better. I was the one who asked you to look at her in the first place. Her father had no money. Don't forget that, Francesca, while you're so busy condemning me. And don't think for one minute your precious Gabriel has no ulterior motive when it comes to Skyler. His motive is you. He wants you and he'll use anyone to get you. Is Gabriel holding something over your head? Are you afraid of him? Is that what it is? You can tell me. I can help you. He can't be so powerful we couldn't fight him together."

Francesca almost burst out laughing. Brice had no concept of what power really was. The two of them and an army could not defeat Gabriel. "No, Brice. I'm not afraid of Gabriel, but thank you for asking. I'm grateful you would want to help me."

"Why have you taken him back into your life without so much as a fight?" Brice demanded. "He just showed up on your doorstep and you let him in. Why? Why didn't you take some time to get to know him again? Don't you see what a mistake this is? I'm your friend and I can see him more clearly than you. He's dangerous, Francesca. I mean really dangerous. He's a criminal of some sort. He reeks of it."

Francesca shook her head wearily. "I don't want to fight with you any more, Brice. I can assure you Gabriel is no criminal. If the judge has information on him and is willing to allow Skyler to stay with him, you must accept that he is a good man. You know he's no criminal. You're just angry because I've allowed him back into my life. I don't know what I'm going to do about Gabriel, but it's for me to decide. I've never deceived you, not once in our relationship. I never told you I loved you, I never committed to a relationship with you."

"You've always known how I felt. I haven't changed. I'm sorry I'm jealous. Just spend some time with me." His voice suddenly turned cajoling, appeasing. "Come home with me. Spend the night." Brice bent over her, his mouth hovering close. His face was suddenly filled with a kind of crafty, greedy lust, his eyes flat and unfamiliar.

Francesca's heart slammed in alarm. It was all she could do not to jerk away from him. She was very aware of his suddenly strong grip on her upper arms as he drew her body into his. He seemed different somehow, a stranger, not at all like the Brice she thought she knew. Could she have been so wrong? Had she been so desperate for companionship that she had overlooked his true character? It didn't make sense. It wasn't in Francesca to make a scene and it was ingrained in her to act human at all times. She stood very still, like a deer caught in the headlights of a speeding car. Just as his lips were about to touch hers, he coughed, both hands going to his throat as he began to choke. His eyes glazed with instant alarm.

"What's wrong?" Francesca deliberately touched his arm to read what was happening in his body. Was it Gabriel? She didn't feel the surge of power his presence should cause, but he was an ancient. She had no real idea of his true power. All she could tell was that Brice's airway was blocked. She couldn't tell what was wrong. His throat seemed swollen, almost as if he was having an allergic reaction to something.

Brice went limp, his eyes rolled back in his head, and his knees buckled so that he began to topple to the floor. Francesca easily caught him with preternatural strength, easing him to the floor, reaching to open his shirt, frantically seeking to find if his airway was open. *"Gabriel!"* She reached for him almost automatically. *"Help me."*

He was there instantly in her mind, a soothing calm in the eye of the storm, assessing the situation. Francesca was attempting to breathe for Brice, but no air could make it through his passageway. When she tried to enter his body using pure energy and light, there was some obstruction she could not pass. Gabriel was grateful that she had suspected him only fleetingly, had turned instantly to him for aid. She was beginning to trust him far more than she realized.

"Lucian, I know you are there." Gabriel was very calm. *"You are killing this man. Let him be."*

"You do not fight your own battles." It was a taunt, a reprimand. Francesca renewed her efforts to enter Brice's body to heal him, but the obstruction was like a brick wall. Sharing Gabriel's mind enabled her to "hear" the exchange between the twin brothers.

"Who is this man that you do not remove him when he causes you such annoyance? You have grown soft, Gabriel. You expect to hoard these two women when you cannot even destroy your enemies?"

The voice was beautiful. So beautiful that Francesca had to try to block it out. It was compelling without the vampire even trying to make it so. She was frightened to think what power he wielded so easily. *"Hurry, Gabriel."*

She whispered it on their own private mental path. Brice had been without air for far too long.

At once she heard the soft, beautiful laughter echoing in her mind. *"She is begging for the life of this worthless human. Your woman, begging for the life of another male. What does that mean, brother? You cannot even keep your woman."*

It was shocking to discover that the private path used between lifemates had been so easily invaded by the vampire. It was unheard of. Her heart began to beat loudly. She felt very vulnerable and she was desperate now to save Brice. Gabriel, however, remained as calm as ever, completely unruffled. *"Keep this between the two of us, Lucian. You are becoming rather tedious with these displays. Showing off for women is beneath you. Are you so afraid, then, that I am not paying enough attention to you? I will come to you at once if that is your desire."* He was searching for a path to locate the vampire.

All at once, Brice coughed and choked, gasping for breath. Francesca felt the unmistakable ripple of power. It filled the spaces around her, vibrated in the air, and then it was gone. She shuddered, sitting back on her heels beside Brice, her hand on his shoulder, her large dark eyes anxious. "Should I call someone?"

"Water," he croaked, his voice strangled and hoarse. His hands groped their way to his neck rather weakly.

Francesca could feel Gabriel's frustration as he realized that once again the vampire had slipped away before he could pinpoint his exact location. Since there was nothing she could do to help Gabriel, she hurried to find a cup of water for Brice, nearly spilling it as she helped him into a semisitting position.

"It was Gabriel," he accused, his voice rasping. "I felt his hands on my throat strangling me."

"Brice, it was not Gabriel. He is nowhere near this hospital. You were choking. I cleared your airway so you could breathe." She made the suggestion calmly and clearly.

Brice's eyes flashed at her. "It was Gabriel. I even smelled him. It was his hands around my throat and he tried to murder me. I saw him. I know I did and you're trying to cover up for him."

"There is no use trying to persuade him otherwise, Francesca." Gabriel said it softly, matter-of-factly, not bothered by Brice's opinion of him. *"Lucian is far too powerful for you to overcome the compulsion he has buried in this man. I have seen him destroy an entire army. When we hunted together he often ordered a vampire to rid the world of its existence using only his voice and it was done without a fight. The vampire ended his existence without so much as a struggle. You know vampires will do anything to continue their life, yet Lucian is able to control them with only his voice. You have no idea of his power. Allow Brice to think what he wishes. I will have established a perfect alibi with the judge. It will not be hard to do so."*

Francesca climbed slowly to her feet, turning her full attention to the problem at hand. "You may think anything you wish, Brice, but remember when you accuse Gabriel of this terrible crime, you are also accusing me of aiding him by my denial. I was here with you, I helped you. What motive would I have for lying to you?"

Brice shook his head, rubbing his sore throat and neck. "I know he's evil, Francesca, and I know you have to do as he tells you. I know you wouldn't want me hurt. He's making you say and do the things you're doing. You're afraid of him, aren't you? You probably did save my life, but you're covering up for him because you're afraid. If you'd just tell me what he's holding over your head, I could help you."

Francesca sighed, swept a hand through her long silken hair impatiently. "I thought you knew me, Brice. Really knew me. If I was afraid of Gabriel and thought him capable of outright murder, if he was threatening me in some way, even with so trivial a thing as blackmail, do you think for one moment I would expose Skyler to such a person? Never. I could never, under any circumstances, be persuaded or induced to place her in jeopardy. If you know nothing else about me, you should know that. And if Gabriel had tried to strangle you, you would be dead. I would not be able to fight him off, nor would anything induce me to protect him if he had attempted to murder you."

"I don't know what he's done to you, but you can expect a visit from the authorities, because I intend to press charges against him." Brice massaged his neck and throat, coughing several times.

"Do whatever you think you have to do, Brice," she said softly. "Obviously you think me capable of being an accomplice to murder." Regally, she turned and swept down the hall toward the double doors, leaving Brice to stumble unsteadily to his feet by himself.

"I do not know where Lucian is, Francesca." Gabriel's voice was as calm as ever but she was beginning to know him well enough to hear he was worried. *"Do not leave the hospital until I am once again with you. I am on my way."*

"What if that's just what he wants? What if he is using

me to lure you out where he can harm you?" There was real fear in her voice.

"He has never defeated me in battle, sweetheart. You should have more faith in your lifemate. Lucian is a very unusual vampire, just as he was an unusual Carpathian. There is no other like him. It does no good to try to second-guess him. He always does the unexpected. He could just as easily have attacked you or Skyler. He is intelligent far beyond your imagining, just as he is more powerful than the legends have told. To guess what he is up to is impossible, but he has found you and he has found Skyler. I do not want you to set one foot into the night without me by your side."

For some reason, Francesca was annoyed. *"I am not about to allow this vampire to change my life, Gabriel. This is my city. There is much I do here, much I love. Over the centuries there have been many vampires who have come and gone. For that matter, there have been many Carpathian males, yet I live on and do as I please."*

"Lucian likes games, Francesca. His mind craves action at all times. He is not one you can 'play' with and expect to win."

"I will not live my life in fear of him."

She said it defiantly, both to him and to the vampire if he was monitoring their conversation. She didn't think it was possible, but then she had not thought it possible that anyone but Gabriel could "hear" their private path. All Carpathians communicated on a common mental path, but this was different. Gabriel was her lifemate. Their path was an individual, very intimate, personal one. No other should have been able to penetrate their private communication. Lucian was indeed powerful and unique. As she emerged into the darkness of night that was her world, into the fresh air where she could breathe without the stench of human suffering, Gabriel materialized beside her, his strong arm encircling her slender waist.

Francesca's heart nearly stopped, his presence was so unexpected. "I thought you were establishing an alibi somewhere."

"It is not so hard, honey, to send vivid images to those humans I have touched already. The judge and I have spent a pleasant evening together in his home. He plays chess, did you know that? Naturally I was the victor, but it was a close game. He believes I drank his favorite brandy with him and conversed on all sorts of subjects. As he resides alone, it was not at all complicated to plant the memories in his mind."

"There was another murder?" Francesca asked unnecessarily. "It was Lucian, wasn't it? What is he doing? What does he hope to gain?"

Gabriel shrugged easily, the movement a subtle ripple of power. "He seeks to draw me into his web. Do not worry, honey, he will not defeat me at the scene of one of his kills. He may be high and powerful from one of his kills, but I know his ways. I know the way he does battle, how he thinks and moves and plans. He will be far more clever than an ordinary vampire. He has a master plan. This is just beginning, rather like the opening moves in a chess game." He bent his head to inhale her fragrance, needing in that moment to bury his face in the warmth of her neck. He could feel the age-old call of her pulse, her blood, the essence of life calling to him. His body was hard and aching and his hunger intensified.

Francesca was shocked at how her body was responding to his. Every cell was alive. Inside, heat was spreading at the mere sight of him. Even with the vampire stalking them and Brice out to blacken Gabriel's name, all she could think about was Gabriel's hard body, the heat of his skin, the softness of his long hair, the perfection of his mouth.

"Stop it." There was a husky sensuality to Gabriel's voice. The words were low and his hand bit into her ribs just beneath her breast so that every step they took she could feel the brush of his thumb against the underside of her swelling flesh. "I am trying to be the hunter, the legend you have named me. Do not tempt me. I am not nearly as strong as I would like to think."

She smiled up at him, her long lashes concealing the sudden hunger in her eyes. She liked the way she felt beside him, safe and protected. Cared for. She had been so alone for so long. Let him hunt another time.

Gabriel stopped abruptly and caught her chin in his hand. "I was alone, too, Francesca. All those empty years. Totally alone. You are cared for now. And safe. And protected. You are my reason for existing, the air I breathe." His thumb feathered along the side of her face. His black gaze burned over her, needing. Needing. He took her breath away whenever his eyes moved over her so possessively.

"I want you." She said the words in the same low tone he had used. She wanted him on fire, unable to resist temptation. She no longer wanted him in control. It was contrary of her and she knew it was wrong of her. He had a job to do, she shouldn't distract him, she shouldn't seem to know that he needed to be with her in the same way she needed to be with him. She knew she was playing with explosives, but it didn't matter to her. The world was caving in around her and she wanted his arms and his body and the hot flames only he could ignite. She wanted him no longer thinking and in control; she wanted him needing her beyond anything else. Beyond hunting Lucian.

He made a sound low in his throat, easily reading her every thought. "You are not making this easy, Francesca. We are in an open place and it is becoming difficult to take a step without pain."

A slow smile tugged at her mouth. Her hand brushed his chest, dropped lower to caress the inviting bulge that was already hard and thick. Her long fingernails raked the fabric, teasing him, deliberately arousing him further. She took the lead toward the river, her body enticing him with every step. Her breasts were aching and swollen with need and her hunger was rising sharply. Inside her mind were hot, erotic pictures. "It isn't as if we will not know if someone comes along," she whispered softly. Francesca reached up and began to slowly unfasten the buttons of her blouse as they approached the shelter of some trees.

Gabriel watched in complete fascination as the edges of her blouse slowly parted to reveal her creamy breasts thrusting so invitingly toward him. Her smile was pure seduction. "You think to resist me, lifemate?"

"We are not in a safe place," he replied, but his black gaze was burning over her naked skin so intensely, her nipples hardened in response. He had scanned the area just as she had. He knew they were alone, and the knowledge didn't help his discipline at all. He knew that if someone came along the river, he was perfectly capable of shielding their presence.

She dragged the shirt from his shoulders, wanting to see the ripple of power in his hard muscles. Her hand moved over his skin, her fingers imprinting the memory of him on her brain for all time. "I want to feel what you're feeling," she said softly. "I want to know what I can do to your body, to your mind." Her hands went to his waistband and with deliberate slowness she opened the material so that he spilled out thick and hard and throbbing with fullness and need. At once the warmth of her hands cupped him, her fingers committing him to memory.

Gabriel groaned with pleasure, allowed her mind to fully merge with his so that she could feel the intensity of his enjoyment, the lust rising sharply in him, the hunger threatening to consume him. Her long silken hair brushed his sensitive tip as she found his chest with the warmth of her mouth, her soft lips following the path her fingers had taken. Another groan escaped as she moved ever lower, so slowly he thought he might die before she touched him.

Her lips moved over the hard length of him, her tongue tasting him, gently at first. Then her mouth, hot and tight, took him to a place he had never imagined, took her there with him. Francesca could feel every pleasure she gave him, knew exactly what he wanted, what he needed. Her hand found the tight muscle of his buttocks through the material of his trousers and urged him deeper into her, reveling in the power she wielded in that moment. She reveled in the fact that he could do nothing but thrust his hips helplessly, his fists clenched in her silken hair. It felt like nothing she had ever experienced, hot and sexy and so erotic. It seemed incredible to have such power over a legendary being.

He muttered her name, his head thrown back, his voice husky with need. He dragged her up to him, fastening his mouth to hers, hard and relentless, dominating, hungry, intensely masculine.

He kissed her until he was drowning in her, merged so deeply he didn't know where she started and he left off.

Francesca. His life. The air he breathed. His arms tightened possessively. His lips drifted from the heat of her silken mouth to her throat, down lower to find her creamy breast, soft and full and inviting. His lips closed over the hard peak, pulled strongly, a torment for both of them.

She circled his head with her arms, cradled him to her. "Tell me this is real, Gabriel, this is us, you and me, not the Carpathian heat rising between us." There was a plea in her voice, an aching need for it to be real.

"Only you, Francesca," he whispered fiercely. "Look into my mind and see the truth; it is there for the taking. I want you and only you. For yourself, not just your beautiful body. For me there will never be another. No other could satisfy this desperate craving. A craving as old as time itself. Beautiful and magical." His hand wandered over her skin, pushed low into the waistband of her jeans. "I look at you and remember the endless centuries, all those wars and battles, my people turning undead and the countless times I was forced to destroy them. You are the reason I did it, the reason I endured it. Just you. Not some noble purpose, but somewhere on this planet I knew you might be, a child just beginning and it was necessary to keep you safe."

His palm moved along the curve of her hip as he pushed her jeans aside, traveled down her soft skin following the slender line of her legs. "I thought of you every time I made a kill, when my life was dark and bleak, without hope. I thought of you in a village or town somewhere, high in the mountains or down in a valley. I whispered to you that I was coming, that no harm would find you as long as I existed. And I continued to exist, century after century." Gabriel closed his eyes as his hands moved over her body, savoring the feel of her, the perfection of her,

committing every curve to memory. To carry with him always. For all time. For all eternity. "For you, Francesca, I continued to exist for you." To carry with him wherever he went after his death.

Francesca felt tears burning behind her eyes, shocked that his words could move her so deeply. The feel of his mouth drifting over her breast, the heat of his breath as he whispered beautiful things against her skin were as compelling as any black-magic spell he could have used. "You make me ashamed that I gave up all hope," she whispered, tears in her throat, as she cradled his head to her.

He lifted her easily with his enormous strength. "I do not want you ever to feel such a thing," he chastised softly. "You are the strength in my mind, the iron in my will, you are so brave and beautiful, inside and out, and I do not deserve one such as you. So many centuries of living alone, cut off from your people—for someone else it would have been a living hell, yet you managed to do good with your life."

Francesca clasped her hands around his neck, threw back her head as she wrapped her legs around his waist, and settled over the hard length of him. Her hair fell in a dark curtain of silk, enveloping them in a private world. She wanted this, the union of their bodies, so perfect in the night air. The night where they belonged, where their people lived and thrived. She held him to her, rode him, at first slowly, savoring the hot slick feel of him filling her with his strength, sending pleasure coursing through her slender body. She clutched him, trembling with ecstasy.

She bent her head slowly, seductively toward his throat. He had fed well this night, and she was shaking with her longing to have every part of him, to consume him in her own fiery need, in the fires of her dark desire. He whispered her name, his arms like iron bands, holding her close. He closed his eyes as her breasts moved over his chest, as her tight sheath enveloped him, clutching with a hot velvet friction. Unbelievable pleasure. Her teeth sank deep into the side of his neck and white-hot lightning lanced through him, through both of them, welding them together.

He began to move then, taking the lead, picking up the pace, surging deeper and deeper, striving to find the very core of her. Her hair was sliding over his skin, sensitizing him even more. She seemed to be his world, his breath, his blood, his body, his every pleasure. The rush built like a fireball, a firestorm out of control. He felt her gasp, close the pinpricks with her tongue, a sensuous caress, her body clutching at his, milking him until he wanted to shout his joy to the heavens. To feel this. To experience this. The love that welled up in him overflowed. His body was exploding into the universe, following hers, stars shooting in all directions and colors whirling like a kaleidoscope.

He held her to him, their hearts beating as one, their bodies united. They belonged together. He stood there in the darkness holding her close. "I love you, Francesca. I really do."

She went very still, her head buried against the warmth of his neck. "Gabriel."

"I do, Francesca, very much, more than I ever thought it possible to love anyone. I did not know how strong such an emotion could be. I am not asking anything of you, sweetheart, do not think that. I only want you to know what I feel. I want to say the words to you aloud. And just so you know, I love your body, too."

She laughed softly. "I was the one who seduced you." She wanted to make that very clear. "Time and again."

"It was not for lack of wanting, lady, and you well know that. I was being a gentleman." Very gently he allowed her feet to touch the ground. "And I told you first that I loved you. Just remember that when you are being smug."

Francesca stretched sensuously, turning her face up to the stars. "Take me home, Gabriel. Set safeguards for Skyler and take me home. I want to spend the rest of this rising making love to you." She grinned at him mischievously. "And you remember when you're being smug, I was the one to make the suggestion first."

"It is only fair that you spend time with your lifemate. Soon our home will be filled with others. I think it is time you stayed with me and admitted you made a terrible mistake looking at that poor excuse for a human man."

"He is not as bad as he is looking at the moment." There was genuine puzzlement in Francesca's voice. Without giving any more thought to Brice, Francesca straightened her clothes, her body very close to Gabriel's.

"It is all right with me that you showed poor judgment in this one small area before my arrival," he said with a straight face. "After all, you showed your common sense in all other things."

Francesca began laughing so hard she had to fling her arms around Gabriel's neck to keep on her feet. "I can't believe you're such a schmuck after two thousand years. I would think you'd have a clue how to talk to a woman."

He bent his dark head to hers. "Sweetheart, do you want to hear me talk to you?" His voice was softer than the night sky. At once her dark eyes found his. He was looking at her with hunger. Nothing else described it. *Hunger*. "Because I very much want to talk to you." His hand cupped her breast, his thumb moving gently, insistently over the hard peak of her nipple. "Can you hear what it is I am saying to you?"

Francesca shivered and wrapped her arms around him. "Let's go home, Gabriel. Skyler needs a few more days in the hospital and I want every minute we have alone with you. Every minute." Her mouth found his, every bit as hungry as his eyes.

Chapter Eleven

Something terrible was going on in the city. Francesca could hardly bear to look at the news. There were strings of murders, mutilations, terrible things that seemed to be breaking out all over the city. Was it Lucian? Was he responsible for the crimes sweeping her beloved Paris? If she and Gabriel left, would he follow them? It was more than the brutal murders, it was the *feel* of the city, as if something evil resided there. Something dark and malevolent, crouching, awaiting its moment to rise. Somehow it seemed to permeate the city until the residents were affected. Fights broke out, wrecks occurred on the streets, and conflict erupted everywhere.

It was important to her to spend as much time as possible with Gabriel. She wanted to be with him each rising, when the night was so beautiful it took her breath away. She wanted the early morning hours. She wanted to make love to him, watch his gaze become so intent that she felt a rush of heat through her body. They had spent every moment they could together, their only responsibility checking on Skyler. Francesca wasn't yet ready to relinquish her time with Gabriel, but he was a hunter and the newspaper reported that evil had found its way into her city. He could do no other than destroy what threatened his family.

Gabriel moved up behind her, silent as was his way, his palm shaping the nape of her neck, his touch warm. "It is not only Lucian, my love. I believe Skyler and you are targets of the undead. You are now out in the open. I have exposed you to a danger you managed to elude for long centuries. Skyler is not of age, but her ability is strong and she has come out of her own mind where she had so successfully remained in hiding. The undead seek ones such as Skyler. We need to move her to this house immediately and set up strong safeguards for her."

"Brice said one more day," Francesca murmured, all too aware of his hands on her. She was always so aware of Gabriel. His rich scent, the power in his body when he moved. Most of all, the way he *needed* her. The way it was so necessary for him to touch her, to allow his fingers to drift through her hair, to touch her skin. The connection between them. She loved the way he glided up behind her and circled his arms around her, his hands locked protectively over their child.

Their child. It was growing inside her, a part of her, a part of him. A miracle she had never expected. He thought he had committed an unforgivable crime, yet she wanted to weep with the joy of it. He had given her a gift beyond measure, beyond her dreams. Francesca wanted to laugh aloud at herself. How silly and childish she had been to think she would walk into the dawn.

She was a healer, a woman of power, one who knew her body intimately. Gabriel could not have deceived her unless she had wanted to be deceived. She had taken his dark desire willingly, returned it tenfold. He thought he wielded so much power over her, yet on some level she had known all along what was happening. She had known. She was no fledging; she was an ancient. He could not have seduced her without her consent.

Was the call of a lifemate so strong? Or was it the lure of Gabriel himself? The legend. The myth. The Carpathian wanting to share her life, no, needing to share her life. She leaned into him, her body finding the exact niche it sought as if they had been made for each other.

Gabriel, a shadow in her mind, refrained from reminding her they had been made for each other. Exclusively. Francesca was the other half of his soul, his heart. She was his world, the reason he had spent two thousand years in darkness. She was the reason he fought so hard to rid the world of the undead. She needed to know he was the reason she had held on to life for as long as she had. They *belonged* to each other.

Francesca glanced over her shoulder at him, her large dark eyes very expressive. "I am reading your mind, Gabriel," she said softly, a small smile tugging intriguingly at the corners of her mouth.

"If you were reading my mind," he responded wickedly, "you would be blushing right now."

She found herself blushing just at the sound of his voice, the brush of velvet, the whisper of his breath. She didn't need to see the images in his mind, so vivid in detail, so completely erotic. "Stop it, we have work to do this rising." She took a deep breath. "Especially you." She could feel her heart skip a beat at her words. She was sending him out into the city to hunt the vampire, to try to find out what was happening to her beloved home. Evil was stalking Paris. *Lucian.* Dark angel, the fallen angel. At once she felt incredibly sad and knew she was catching Gabriel's sorrow, so intense it washed through him like a turbulent storm.

Gabriel turned away from her, removing his touch as well as his mind to spare her the intensity of his grief, but Francesca immediately swung around and captured him within the circle of her arms. Soothing, tranquil, his healer as well as his lifemate. Her mind found his unerringly, sending him waves of peace and comfort. "I am with you, Gabriel, always with you. Do not feel as if you are alone in your task."

"If you are sharing my mind, Francesca, then you will see him as he was, a warrior unsurpassed by any other. He gave his life for our people, for mankind. I believed in him always and he never once let me down. After all the battles, all the times I witnessed his kills, it is still impossible for my heart to accept what I know to be true." Gabriel raked a hand through his long black hair, his dark eyes stricken. "He fought the vampire night after night. He suffered many wounds, terrible wounds, and often he took my place when I would have been injured. He moved that swiftly, inserting his body between mine and the undead when we battled. I never heard him complain, not once in all those endless centuries. He always did the right thing, no matter the cost to himself, yet now I am sworn to destroy him."

Francesca chose her words very carefully. "It is no longer the man you are hunting, Gabriel, but a shell left behind. What once was great, the soul and mind and heart of your twin, is long gone from this earth. You cannot think of him as being the one you loved so much, the one you held in such high esteem. This is a vampire, the undead, and is not your twin."

Gabriel caught her hand, held it to his chest over his heart. "I know what you say is true, yet he is not like the undead I have hunted and destroyed for my entire life. He retains certain qualities I would never have expected."

She moved closer to him, a small protective gesture he treasured. "Perhaps those small things have been your downfall with him, Gabriel. Perhaps he was cunning enough to know the memories would defeat you where he could not."

He brought her hand to the warmth of his mouth. "I know only that he was a great man and I loved him much. We were together two thousand years, Francesca, even during the last few centuries when we battled long. He was always there, touching my mind, sharing information, a challenge in a world of emptiness. It was Lucian who allowed me to continue when the darkness threatened and the whisper of power called to me. He was always there, my mission on this earth. To allow another to destroy him would be a sacrilege and I have given my word of honor to him." He shook his head, his sorrow so great it weighed both of them down, a stone on their hearts.

"Gabriel?"

The voice shimmered in his mind and Francesca heard it as clearly as Gabriel did. It was soft and beautiful. Lonely. Concerned. It sent a shiver deep inside her very soul. How could one so evil possess such a gift, such a weapon? If he commanded her obedience, would she be strong enough to resist the lure of that voice?

"If you seek me, Lucian, simply reveal where you are and I will come to you in all haste." Gabriel sounded weary, and his tone alarmed Francesca. She took a firmer grip on his arm, terrified that that beguiling voice was somehow wearing Gabriel down so that he no longer believed in his abilities.

"You are tired, brother. I would not want to take unfair advantage when there is much more entertaining prey. I will leave you to your rest."

The contact was broken as easily and as swiftly as it had been made. Gabriel buried his face in the warmth of her neck. "Do you see what I am saying? It was my sorrow that brought his mind to mine. He retains a strong connection with me that I cannot sever." He lifted his head, his black eyes searching her face with such intensity she could hardly bear his scrutiny.

"I want you to know something, Francesca. You have given me more happiness in the short time we have been together than I have ever known in all the centuries of my existence. I am honored that I was given such a wonderful lifemate, a woman of courage and beauty when I have only known evil. I have never had a home before. I look around this dwelling of yours and I see you everywhere. I went into the room you put together for Skyler and it was so beautiful it brought tears to my eyes. I touched the quilt you had wrought for her. It was you. Soothing. Compassionate. Courageous. It was filled with life and love and laughter. I felt the safeguard to keep her nightmares at bay. It was strong, as you are strong."

Embarrassed by his words, Francesca looked away from the black depths of his eyes. In a way, his words were frightening, almost as if he were saying good-bye. He caught her chin in his fingers, stilling her so that his gaze could capture hers. "Do not look away from me. You deserve to look into my heart and mind and know the truth of my words. There is no other woman in the world like you. I would want no other. If something happens to me, I know you will choose to stay in this world, you will be strong enough to raise our child with enough love for both of us. You will see to it that our child knows who I was and what I stood for."

"Gabriel, don't!" Francesca jerked away from him. "You are talking about yourself in the past tense. You will destroy Lucian, I know that you will."

He nodded slowly. "Yes. I have no choice."

Francesca found herself clutching his arm, giving him a little shake. "You don't believe you will return to me."

"No, Lucian will take me with him." His hands framed her face. "You are in my heart, and wherever I go, I will take memories of you with me until such time as you are able to join me. It is enough that you and Skyler and our child will remain safe."

"I am your lifemate, Gabriel. You insisted on the ritual, you bound us together, you gave me a child. You cannot go into battle with the idea that you will not return. Lifemates remain together," she protested. He believed what he was saying, and all at once she realized he was everything she had ever wanted in her life. Gabriel. Her lifemate. Her legend come to life.

A small smile tugged at his sculpted mouth. "You are so brave, my love, you will remain even when others would not. You have known a life on this earth few others could have managed. You would never abandon Skyler when she is in such need. She must be guarded at all times and brought up to know her own power and strength. Without you, Skyler would retreat back into her mind and be lost to our people. You know that. In your heart you know it is only the link you forged with her that keeps her with us. You cannot leave her. And there is our child, growing inside you, part of me, part of you. You must be the one to raise and guide him so that he has the strength so many others do not. I would want no other to perform this task. He must know you, and through you, me." Gabriel kissed her forehead gently, his hands tunneling in her hair.

"And you must be here to help me with these tasks, Gabriel," Francesca replied, striving to remain calm. He was calm. Tranquil even. She felt his deep sorrow, but there was acceptance in him, complete acceptance of the future. "I mean it, Gabriel. Call the others. Call Gregori. He is a great hunter of the undead. You do not know his reputation, but vampires walk in fear of him. There are several others who could help. Aidan would come from the United States. He is feared by those he hunts. His brother is powerful and the Prince would come to aid you. All would do so. Lucian could not defeat all of them."

Gabriel brought her hand to his mouth, lingered over the pulse beating so frantically in her wrist. "This is all a game to Lucian, Francesca. Right now he is soaking up what this century has to offer, feeding his intellect, but he will soon grow bored and the game will begin in earnest. If I broke my vow to him, my word of honor, I could not live with myself, and worse, he would use his power in such a way as to destroy all those who sought him. The Prince has a lifemate; I believe the others do also. Their loved ones might be his targets. We cannot take such a chance. You would not want me to do such a thing."

She rested her forehead on his chest, struggling not to cry. "I am very afraid, Gabriel. You attribute all kinds of wonderful traits to me, but I am a woman who had chosen to end her lonely existence before you came. Now you think I will not only choose to stay without you, but I will do so for at least two more centuries. Alone."

"Or longer if you must. The child is most likely a male. He will need you to give him memories that will last until his lifemate is found."

"You can defeat Lucian. I know you can do it. There must be a way, Gabriel. We have to find a way." She raised her head to look directly into his eyes. "I have examined your memories of him. I know that you bested him once. You caught him by surprise and locked him into the ground with you. He did not expect such an attack by you and it worked. We have only to think of something similar, something he would never expect. I will work with you. He will not think a woman would do such a thing. Do not smile, Gabriel, I am serious."

He bent his dark head to kiss her. She was so beautiful to him in every way. When he looked at her, she warmed him. When she talked this way, she melted his heart. "You are incapable of harming a fly, Francesca. You would want to aid me; indeed you would try, but the healer in you would prevent you from destroying another. Even the undead. And Lucian is not like the vampires you have seen or heard of. He appears beautiful and is more deadly than all others. You would hesitate, and he would kill you. I would never allow such an event to take place."

"Then do not confront him until we come up with a plan that will work," Francesca said decisively. "I will not give you to him so easily. I will not, Gabriel. You must defeat him and live."

"We have been tied together two thousand years," he replied sadly.

"*We* are tied together now. What happens to you happens to me. I will not allow him to take you with him," she said furiously. Her silken hair went flying in all directions. "He cannot have you, Gabriel. He is using his voice to defeat you, using your own emotions. You are an ancient and the strength of your love is vast. He knows you feel for him while he cannot. It is his advantage. You must separate what remains on this earth from what was lost to you. He is no longer Lucian, your twin, your hero; he is foul and unclean and it was his choice."

Gabriel shook his head. "I wish that were true, my love. It would make my task so much easier, but Lucian did not have a choice. He waited long with me, far past the time he would have met the dawn. He waited to protect me even though he lost his emotions centuries before I did. He waited too long for my sake. In the end he was unable to make a rational choice. He was too close. He rose without me and it was done." He bowed his head in shame. "I was struggling with the demon. It was with me endlessly, calling, whispering that all was lost to me. I thought I would rise undead if I did not choose the dawn. There was so much death around us, so much violence. I often wonder if my struggle pushed him over the edge."

Francesca flung her arms around his neck. "Do not do that to yourself, Gabriel. We have enough burdens to bear in our lives without taking on those that belong to others. You must honor Lucian's last request and defeat him. Remember your true brother, the one who shared your life for those two thousand years. He fought to protect you that you might find me, and you have. Your real brother would want your life, not your death."

He brushed at the silken ebony strands tumbling around her face. "You have given me food for thought,

Franesca. In the meantime, I must hunt this night for the lesser vampires that have invaded the city. They are a foul stench in the air, impossible to ignore."

"I will send out the quilts and stained-glass pieces I have been working on. I do have a business to run," Francesca said, trying to think of mundane things so that she wouldn't live in terror of what Lucian might do to Gabriel.

"There is no need for worry," he said softly, his voice magic and so pure Francesca felt instantly better. He was like a clear breeze blowing through her body, removing the terrible fear.

Francesca knew he was using his voice, his magical voice to aid her, but she didn't mind. She pressed her hands to her stomach and thought of their baby for further comfort. Gabriel, like all of their race, would believe she carried a male child. Yet she knew she carried one of the precious females. She had a daughter. Fragile. So very vulnerable. Francesca took a deep breath and let it out slowly. Was their baby one of the rare females because she had succeeded for a short while in changing her body chemistry enough to walk in the sun? As a healer it was all important to find that answer. Female children were so unusual within their race, and very few managed to survive the nine months' gestation. The one in a century that did, still had to face that difficult first year of life. Francesca did not want to have to face that fight without Gabriel. She did not want to lose her child and not have him beside her, rock steady, to lean on.

Gabriel's eyes met hers with sudden understanding. He caught her to him, nearly crushing her slender body in his arms. Yet at the same time, he held her so tenderly he made her want to cry. "It is impossible. Our family produced only one daughter in eight hundred years. Before that, it was nearly a thousand years and she did not survive. We cannot be so blessed as to have a girl."

Francesca leaned into him, savoring the heat of his skin, his masculine frame, so different from her own. "I examined her earlier while you went out to feed. The child is female and she clings to life stubbornly. I do not want to face this test alone, Gabriel. Find a way to live for us. You are right about Skyler. Without my aid, without her belief in me, she would slip back into her mind. We would surely lose another of our males to the undead. More than that, we would be without a brilliant, rare treasure. I cannot do it without you, Gabriel. Live for us."

He buried his face in the silken curtain of her hair. "I can do no other than as you command, my love. It is my duty to see to your happiness. I will find a way."

He meant it. She could hear the resolve in his voice. The weariness was gone, as was the acceptance of his own destruction. Lucian had held him for two thousand years. Francesca would not give him up so easily to his dark twin. She would fight with every cell in her body, every weapon she possessed to keep him with her. Lucian would not win. It didn't matter that he was Gabriel's twin and had been a great man once; he was now the biggest threat to her family. She would find a way to combat him. There was a way. Somehow. There was a way.

They clung to each other for a few minutes longer, each aware of the other's thoughts, each determined to find a way to defeat the ultimate vampire. "You must go," Francesca finally whispered reluctantly. "I have so much to do this rising, and I must attend to Skyler. I have neglected so many of my responsibilities."

Gabriel's smile was slow and sexy, heart-stopping. "I

am very pleased that I was able to provide such a distraction for you."

For no reason at all, Francesca found herself blushing. At once she ducked her head so her hair fell around her face, protecting her. He laughed softly. "My beautiful woman, I cannot believe you are blushing after all that we have done together."

"At least you didn't mention my age," she said.

"I am not that unbalanced, although I will admit I do not have much practice with women." He bowed, that curiously courtly bow that always made her breath stop.

Francesca glared at him. "Go away, Gabriel, you have that look in your eyes and I have much to do."

His hand moved possessively over the long curtain of her black hair. "Nothing is more important than satisfying the needs of your lifemate." His face was innocent and very serious.

Francesca blinked once, then gave him a good hard shove. "Go tell it to the last century, ancient one. I am a modern woman with many commitments."

"You are a woman much sought after by these human males and I am beginning to find it tedious."

Her eyebrow shot up. "Tedious?" she echoed. "Do I hear a veiled threat in there somewhere?"

He bent his head to kiss her. "It was not all that veiled." His grin was boyish and seductive at the same time. "I cannot very well admit I am bothered by those who seek your attention when I am your lifemate. As an ancient I am above such trivial things."

Francesca found herself laughing. "You're above something all right, but I'm not entirely certain what it is."

"Watch yourself tonight, Francesca," Gabriel cautioned as he glided through the room toward the door. "You must always remember you are a target now, and so is Skyler."

"I'll send word to Aidan's family, asking them not to delay. That way if Skyler is home, she can be protected while we sleep." Her dark gaze was suddenly anxious. "Gabriel, don't let Lucian undermine your confidence in yourself. I really need you and so does our child. Our children."

He paused at the door, looking back at her, his world, the only real joy he had known. "I love this home of yours," he answered softly.

She watched him leave. "Ours," she corrected, knowing he could still hear her even though the door was closed. Gabriel's hearing was phenomenal and he often shared her mind.

It was their house, their life. Gabriel had to separate himself from his twin if he were to survive the battle that was to come. Francesca was carefully folding quilts into large boxes when it suddenly occurred to her that Lucian might lead him out of the city and far away from her. Her hand went protectively to her throat.

"Stop worrying over what has not happened." There was a wealth of love in Gabriel's voice. It felt like a caress.

She glanced at herself in the mirror. "Quit mooning about and get to work. You have much to do and little time to do it in." She was very stern with herself but a curling heat stole through her body as Gabriel's warm laughter echoed softly in her mind.

Francesca completed as many tasks as she could. She took orders for her stained-glass pieces and her quilts. She sent out the ones she had completed and paid her bills meticulously. There were the shelters to call and the hospitals. There were charities she had neglected and friends she wanted to keep in touch with. Because they had risen late and spent a great deal of time talking together it was already well into the evening and past time to call too many. She kept each conversation brief, but very upbeat. It was necessary to maintain the appearance of being human at all times. She was firmly entrenched in society and it wouldn't do to simply disappear. Her contacts would be helpful to Skyler.

Once her phone conversations were concluded, Francesca drove to the hospital, scanning the surrounding area along the way. She was worried about Skyler, worried that something was going to upset their careful plans for her. She had been vaguely uneasy ever since her encounter with the reporter. Something about him bothered her immensely. He was the type of man who could cause her tremendous trouble.

She walked into the hospital, greeting the nurses with a little wave of her hand as she made her way down the hall toward Skyler's room. Her heart dropped when she caught a glimpse of the reporter lurking just a few feet from the room. Francesca paused for a moment, waved her hand to create a clonelike image as she blurred her own. She sent her soft musical voice out ahead, so that her body seemed to be moving quickly along the hall as she called to an unseen nurse around the corner.

At once the reporter turned his head, catching a glimpse of her slender shape and long hair. He hurried down the hall in an attempt to catch up to her. Francesca laughed softly, waiting until he disappeared before entering Skyler's room.

The girl turned her head, her soft dove-gray eyes wide and beautiful. There was a welcoming look in her gaze that hadn't been there before. "I was waiting for you." Her voice was stronger and Francesca noticed for the first time how melodious it was. "I thought you'd never get here."

"I had quite a bit of work to do," Francesca said, seating herself and reaching for Skyler's hand. "I make stained-glass windows and also quilts for people in need."

A slow smile curved the young girl's mouth. "I had my friend here to keep me company." She hugged the stuffed wolf to her. "I like the way you say that. 'People in need.' People like me. I've noticed you have a way of making me feel like everything is going to be all right. Sometimes, when my mind is very chaotic, I think of you and feel you in my mind." Her long lashes swept down, concealing her expression, but Francesca was holding her hand and could read her mixed feelings. The girl was struggling to come to terms with the idea of entering life again.

"I'll be with you every step of the way, Skyler," she softly reassured her. "You won't be alone, and you won't be expected to take on more than you can cope with. I see you are worried about school. It isn't necessary to think about it at this time."

Skyler turned her face to wall. "Dr. Brice said I would have to go to school immediately so I wouldn't fall behind. I didn't want to tell him, but I hardly ever went to school. I'm different. I could never fit in."

"You are different," Francesca affirmed, "but that is not a bad thing. It doesn't matter about school. You are gifted, quite brilliant actually. We can provide tutors for you and I can help when there is need. It is certainly nothing to worry about. Dr. Brice is a good man and he wants what is best for you, but he doesn't have a clue about your special talents and gifts. He does not understand what it is like to be a woman and be abused as you were. He does not understand what it is like to be a child and have no guidance, no one to love you unconditionally. He has no say in your future, Skyler."

Skyler's fingers twisted together, a small betrayal of her nervousness. "I don't like it here. I never feel safe unless you're here, or . . ." She trailed off as if she had done something wrong. "Sometimes the other one touches my mind and I feel reassured."

Francesca's heart skipped a beat. "Not Gabriel?"

"He is there sometimes, but it is different. The other one never really says anything, he's just there, touching me, but I can feel I'm not alone and he only comes when I'm very frightened. Like when I have a nightmare and I wake up. In the middle of the afternoon there was a stranger in here. I didn't like him and I was so scared. That's when the other one touched my mind. It was soothing and comforting."

Francesca bit her lip. The other had to be Lucian. Was he so strong, then, that he could defeat the daylight and reach out to touch Skyler when she was frightened? Was he already so connected with her that he could read her fear even when his strength was at its lowest ebb? She forced air through her lungs, remaining calm. "What stranger entered your room, Skyler?"

"A man. He asked me lots of questions about you, but I didn't answer or look at him. I retreated like I do. Into my own mind." Skyler continued to look at the wall as if she were slightly ashamed of herself. Her hands were clutching the little stuffed animal until her knuckles turned white. "I don't know if I can keep from doing it when I'm really afraid."

Francesca gently pushed her hair from her forehead. She couldn't wait to get the child home, where she would be surrounded by love, by feminine things. She couldn't wait to do something with the wealth of hair that had been neglected for so long. "He's a reporter, honey, nothing more. Someone told him a story about me and he wants to write about it. It has nothing to do with you, but I'll make certain there's a guard posted outside your door at all times. No one else will get in." She should have posted a guard long before this.

A small sound escaped Skyler's throat, something between a laugh and a cry. "A guard? I don't think you have to go that far. I think it's a little late for guards."

Francesca leaned over the teenager and brushed her forehead with her lips in a small caress. "You are so silly, young lady, to think it is too late for a guard. You are beautiful and unique, a rare treasure. I intend to guard you and keep you safe for all time. There is no need to have idiot reporters breaking into your hospital room and questioning you."

"He asked strange things. He wanted to know if I had ever seen you during daylight hours. Isn't that a strange thing to ask?"

Francesca went very still inside. There were many people throughout Paris who would testify they had seen her during daylight hours; and there were photographs to prove it. Her picture had appeared more than once in the newspapers at various charity functions around the city. The reporter would soon lose interest in her if he was no more than a simple reporter; she wouldn't fit the profile of what he was looking for. But if he was more than a reporter, if he was a member of the society hunting the Carpathian people, seeking proof of their existence, she needed to know.

"Francesca?" Skyler sounded tired and forlorn. "I want

to go home with you. When can I get out of here? Everything scares me, even Dr. Brice, and I know he means well. I just can't stand to be around him anymore. He doesn't feel the same."

Skyler was very sensitive to the emotions of others. All around her, the plots were thickening. Francesca had to get Brice to agree to allow the child to go home with her. She would have to face him and use the power of her voice if necessary. They could better protect her if she was in their home.

"I think you're right, honey. I'll track down the good doctor and get his permission to allow you to leave. You'll like the house. It's big and roomy and filled with all kinds of books and treasures."

"I've seen stained glass in churches before. Is that what you do?"

"Most of the time I create pieces for private homes. Sometimes I'm asked to do windows for a church or cathedral. I mostly like to do residences. I want to know all about the people and get a feel for who they are and what they need. I try to incorporate feelings of safety and comfort into the patterns." Francesca shrugged casually. "Sometimes I'm successful."

"Can you teach me how to do it?" There was interest in her voice. Real interest. "I drew pictures of wolves one time. They're so beautiful. I used to read everything I could find on them. That's why I love my blue-eyed wolf. I always wanted to study them, but I know it won't ever happen. Not here anyway. But maybe I could do a picture in stained glass."

"You can do anything you want, Skyler, anything at all. If you wish to study animal behavior, I am behind you one hundred percent. And I know you can make stained glass. I would love to work with you. Rest now while I go to find Brice." She patted the wolf gently and bent to kiss the girl's head before leaving.

Chapter Twelve

Francesca bit her lip as she quietly closed the door to Skyler's room. The reporter was waiting as she had known he would be. She had heard his footfalls, the sound of his pacing. She read his determination to confront her even as she was speaking to Skyler. It was okay, it was what she wanted, too. She needed information and he was conveniently outside the door. She wouldn't have to go looking for him.

The man spun around with a determined look on his face. "I need to talk to you."

Francesca's smile was mysterious and inviting. "What can I do for you?"

His eyes were devouring her, roaming freely over her body. There was something about her that made him a little crazy. The way she looked, the sway of her hips, the sultry smile. He had never seen a woman who moved him in quite the way she did. He liked women, in their place, but he had always bought the right to their bodies and kept it strictly business. No fuss, no emotional entanglement. This woman was very different from the average woman. There was something mysterious and sexy about her. He could stare into her eyes forever, listen to the sound of her voice for eternity. All at once his suspicions seemed totally ridiculous. This was no vampire preying on the human race. She was a woman of extraordinary talents and he wanted to protect her from those who sought her for study.

Francesca could feel Gabriel's power flowing through her when she looked into the reporter's eyes. It was not the same as hers, but far more aggressive. Gabriel would make sure this man would never harm her, would in fact die to save her. He did it easily as he did all things, the commands flowing through her mind into the reporter's. She had no idea how Gabriel could do the things he did. He was helping her at the same time as he hunted the undead and watched for traps along the way. He seemed capable of operating on more than one level at a time. Even when the stakes were as high as his own life.

"Nothing is more important to me than your life." His voice was fading away as if he was in motion somewhere.

Francesca did not seek to sustain the connection between them. She wanted to concentrate entirely on the reporter. She needed to know everything he knew about the society he was a part of, a society that had hunted and murdered humans and Carpathians alike, naming them vampires. She smiled at him. "It's Woods, isn't it? Barry Woods? You said you were a reporter. I'm so sorry about the other evening. I was in such a hurry, late for so many appointments, I can't recall exactly what we talked about.

I promise to give you my full attention now. Would you care to go somewhere and have a cup of tea or something?"

"Tone it down, Francesca. He is very susceptible to you and that in itself can be dangerous." This time there was a distinct growl in Gabriel's voice.

She tilted her chin, although she knew he couldn't see her. *"Go away, I can handle this problem all by myself. You have bigger fish to fry."* She sounded faintly haughty, snippy, warning him to back off.

Barry Woods was gaping at her, astounded that she was actively seeking him out. She leaned close, enveloping him in her mysterious scent. *"You will never attempt to see Skyler Rose again."* The command was one of the strongest she had ever issued.

She could read his acceptance of her authority, but all the same, Francesca guided the reporter to the seclusion of one of the empty rooms with every intention of ensuring obedience by taking his blood.

"You will not!" The command was sharp and authoritative. Gabriel was not playing now. The threat was very real. *"I will see to it this buffoon does no harm to our girl, but you will not do this thing."*

Exasperated, Francesca decided against arguing with Gabriel's tyrannical ways. At once she felt Gabriel relax, felt his amusement, and she shook her head over the silly idiosyncrasies of men. "Did you have some questions you wanted to ask me?" she queried softly, looking directly into Barry Woods's eyes. "Or did you have information that you thought was very important to tell me?"

He could feel himself falling forward, deeper, deeper still until he was so mesmerized he wanted to stay there for eternity. He cleared his throat, unable, unwilling to break away from the beauty of her eyes. "I have friends who heard things about you. They're dangerous men. We hunt vampires. Real vampires, not the make-believe things in the movies. No one believes the creatures exist but us. We've been collecting proof over the years. We just need to get one, a body, something tangible to make the world take us seriously. Right now they think we're fanatics, nuts to be laughed at, but we're scientists and we're trying to save the world."

Francesca wrapped him in waves of warmth, swamping him with approval, with the idea that she believed in him and what he was doing. He broke out in a sweat, but his gaze remained captured by hers. He wanted to do whatever she wanted of him, whatever it took to make her happy. He wanted her to believe in him. She tipped her head to one side so that her hair fell in a seductive sheet of silk across her shoulder and tumbled past her waist. "Why would anyone think such a thing of me? I have lived in this community for some time and have been involved in many things. I think my life is rather an open book. It is not so difficult to find those who know me."

Woods leaned forward, needing to hear the purity of her voice, or maybe he wanted to touch her hair. He really wasn't certain which was more important at that moment. "I think I can dig up indisputable proof that you're no vampire." There was a trace of humor in his voice. The idea of her being in the ranks of the undead was totally ludicrous. He could convince his fellows they were wrong about her and she would be crossed off their list.

"Are there many of you?" Francesca requested the information softly. "Are there any others named on this list of potential threats? Perhaps I can aid you in some way."

"We have to protect ourselves now. We've lost many of

our best people. It's a war, a real war, between them and us. We only know a few of each other's names; our meetings are small. We use phone numbers and a place on the Internet to leave messages back and forth. That way if our society is penetrated, we will only lose a few."

Francesca could see that something was making him very resistant to giving out the names of those on the vampire list, although he was deeply ensnared by her compulsion. She pushed further into his mind and found a strange phenomenon. Immediately she reached for Gabriel and shared the information, puzzled by what she found in Barry Woods's mind.

"He has undergone some kind of strong hypnosis." Gabriel relied. *"You can get around it, but he might have flashbacks. I can remove all traces of you from his memory. It is not so difficult to extract the information from his mind. He will never know."*

"Go ahead then, Gabriel. I don't want him to take up any more of my time." Francesca wanted to get her business out of the way and return to Gabriel. She didn't like him being out in the city hunting the undead. She wanted him back in the safety of their home. She wanted Skyler safe within the walls of their home. She wanted the reporter long gone.

"Are you attempting to distract me from my task with your wanton thoughts?" There was a curling caress in Gabriel's voice, brushing at the walls of her mind, flooding her body with heat and excitement.

"Wanton thoughts? You need a checkup, my boy. Your fantasy world seems to be growing larger with each passing day. I wanted you home to take out the trash." She was staring directly at Barry Woods, so that Gabriel could use her as his instrument, could "see" the reporter and

extract the information they needed from his mind. Gabriel's teasing had lifted her spirits, given her the impression of a cool cleansing breeze moving through her mind, erasing her worries.

Francesca smiled at the reporter. Gabriel had what they needed and it was time for her to reinforce her most important command. She leaned closer to him so that her eyes held his. "You will never, under any circumstances, go near Skyler again." At once she felt Gabriel's power moving through her mind, swift and deadly, unbreakable, relentless. He issued his own command, stronger than any she could have made. The reporter would protect her, ensure that others left her strictly alone.

Francesca shook her head over the vehemence of that command, but she felt very precious to him. *Cherished.*

"You are cherished. Now do something women are supposed to do, something I will not worry about."

"Look who's talking!" She tried to sound indignant, but he was making her laugh with his nonsense.

"It is not nonsense. These are commands from your lifemate, and you should listen and obey." He sounded very arrogant as only Gabriel could.

"You're showing your age again. You awoke in the twenty-first century. Women no longer listen and obey, worse luck for you. I have work to do, and you are in some place very musty and smelling of wet dirt. What are you doing?"

"Performing secret masculine rituals."

Francesca found herself laughing out loud. Woods startled her by smiling and reaching out to shake her hand. She had almost forgotten his existence. "Thank you so much for your time, and I enjoyed the tea." He sounded very brisk and businesslike. Gabriel had ensured his obedience and the reporter was doing exactly as he had been instructed. He was leaving Francesca and going to report his findings to his friends. They would believe him: Francesca was a human woman with extraordinary talents but she walked in the sunlight and drank tea. Woods was certain he had shared such a thing with her.

Francesca smiled gently. "I am pleased to have met you, Mr. Woods. Good luck with your work."

She turned and made her way through the corridors, moving silently. She was scanning for Brice. He often slept in one of the empty rooms if he had been working all day and late into the night. When he was not attending social events, Brice spent the majority of his time at the hospital. She caught his scent and turned unerringly toward the small room at the end of the hall. It was one of his favorite places to escape.

Gabriel moved silently through the cemetery, the very place where he had spent so many years locked in the ground. The earth was torn up where graves were being opened and the caskets removed to make way for progress. He shook his head at the way of life. A hundred years ago no one would consider disturbing a grave site in such a manner. It would be sacrilegious. Evil stalked Paris, and it slept within this ancient cemetery that held the bodies of so many of the dead.

As he moved through the graveyard like a silent wraith, he thought of that long-ago battle, nearly two centuries ago. He had found Lucian crouched over his latest victim, a man in his early thirties. The victim had been drained of blood, a lifeless rag doll that Lucian had tossed carelessly down on the ground when he turned to confront Gabriel. As always, Gabriel was struck by his twin's elegance, the way he moved so silently. There was never a stain of blood on his clothing or his teeth or nails. He was always immaculate. Nothing about him seemed different, yet he was a terrible monster, not the legendary hunter their people whispered about.

Just the memory of his brother, tall and elegant and so courtly, sent a wave of love through Gabriel. He had not felt it for so long, only remembered the emotion, but now it was stronger and more intense than ever. Gabriel bowed his head. *Lucian. His brother.* The grief was overwhelming him and he shook his head decisively to clear it. That way lay his own destruction. His mind had to be clear and fixed on the hunt. He needed every advantage ferreting out the evil undead. They were here in force.

A grave caught his eye. He turned back to examine it. Freshly dug, it was one of the newest in the cemetery. The heavy equipment had not reached this corner so near the rock wall. He touched the soil and at once felt the vibrations of destructive forces. So tuned, he snatched his hand away. The earth itself was groaning from the touch of the vile abomination. He remained hunkered down, his eyes casting along the floor of the cemetery even as his senses flared out to scan the region around him.

Gabriel sighed. He heard the soft shuffle of boots in the dirt, the heavy breathing of the ghoul a vampire had created. Dangerous creatures, ghouls lived to serve their masters, feasting on tainted blood and the flesh of humans. They were vicious and without mercy. He waited, his power building and building, gathering until it flowed through him and poured out into the air around him.

The ghoul approached from behind, shuffling closer, an evil being, clumsy but very cunning and impossibly strong. A human being would be in grave danger should he meet with a minion of the vampire. Gabriel was one of the ancients, powerful and far too experienced to give the ghoul much thought. As the grotesque creature closed the distance between them, Gabriel whirled around, caught the misshapen head between his hands and jerked hard enough to break the neck. The crack was loud in the silence of the night. The monster wailed loudly, flailing its arms, but Gabriel had melted away, his speed far too great for the macabre puppet.

The ghoul was shrieking in a brutal animal rage of pain and anger. It moved with jerky steps, swinging its body this way and that, searching for Gabriel, searching as it had been programmed. Its head flopped at a sickly angle, and the creature drooled continuously. Gabriel materialized in front of it, plunged his hand deep within the chest cavity, and removed the already dead heart. At once lightning slammed to the ground, incinerating the body to a fine ash. Gabriel flung the putrefied organ into the blue-white streak and turned away, shaking his head at the horror of the long-dead creature.

He felt their presence long before he saw them. Three vampires were moving silently toward him, gliding through the air so that their feet didn't touch the surface of the earth. He inhaled the stench of their foul, poisonous bodies. He turned slowly to face them. They were older than he would have liked and powerful.

"Come to me, then," he said softly. "I will give you the dark death that will free you from your chosen path."

Brice sat up when Francesca called his name softly. Raking a hand through his hair, he regarded her with speculative eyes. "Francesca. I didn't expect to see you tonight." He got to his feet and smoothed his rumpled clothes.

Francesca noticed his clothes were stained. Always before, he was immaculate and meticulous in his appearance. This shocked her. There was even a faint shadow of a beard, something Brice had abhorred in the past. He was almost compulsive about his appearance. He often said it was because he attended so many meetings and press conferences. He needed to know he looked good at all times.

Guilt swept through her. Had she caused this? Was she going to be the instrument of his destruction? "I wanted to see you, Brice. We've been friends a long time." Francesca sighed softly. Out of respect for their friendship, she had never "read" his mind unless it involved a patient or a crisis he needed help with. It had been important to her to be as human with Brice as possible. Now it was a temptation to look into his mind. Was he going to be all right? Had she really broken his heart? Maybe she should plant a subtle compulsion in his mind to get over her.

"I wasn't sure we were friends anymore," he responded. "Come on, let's get out of here and go somewhere quiet where we can talk this out."

Francesca glanced around the room. "It's pretty quiet right here, Brice." For some strange reason, Francesca was reluctant to leave the hospital with him. Gabriel was out in the city hunting the undead. She needed to arrange a guard for Skyler's room, and until she was certain the child would be safe, she wanted to stay close.

"You know if we stay in the hospital we'll be interrupted. I really want us to remain friends. Come on, Francesca. It's not like I'm asking all that much."

She nodded reluctantly. Brice immediately opened the door and waved her down the hall. He followed close behind her, occasionally resting his hand on the small of her back. His palm felt hot and sweaty right through her clothes. Francesca found herself squirming to get away from him, walking faster through the corridor and out into the night. Clouds were swirling ominously overhead.

"The weather is looking a bit grim, Brice. Where should we go?"

"You never were afraid of a little rain in the old days, Francesca, before you had to look perfect for your hero."

Francesca stopped right there at the edge of the parking lot. "If you're going to be snide, Brice, there's no point in this. I don't want to fight with you any more. I really don't. I've always valued your friendship and I prefer not to lose it, but if you can't be civil about Gabriel, or at least avoid the subject, then our conversing is a complete waste of time." Suddenly, she didn't want to go with him. A dark feeling of dread was stealing over her and she wanted to be back with Skyler, or better yet, wrapped safely in Gabriel's arms in the sanctuary of their home.

Brice deliberately took her arm. "I'm sorry. Jealousy is an ugly thing, Francesca. I'll behave. Just come with me. Please."

She owed him that much and she knew it. Brice had always been her friend. It wasn't his fault that she wasn't human. He had no idea of her true nature. He couldn't possibly fathom the relationship between true lifemates. Francesca glanced up at his face as she went with him. She thought she saw something flickering in the depths of his eyes, just for a moment, something sly and cunning, but he blinked and it was gone before she was certain. All the same, Francesca was uneasy.

Brice cleared his throat as they walked along the bank of the river toward the seclusion of the park. "I haven't liked myself very much lately," he admitted. "I didn't much like learning certain things about myself."

"Brice"—her voice was soft and sad—"I didn't want you hurt, not for the world. I'm the one who's sorry. I didn't tell you about my past with Gabriel because I truly thought him lost to me. Otherwise, I would never have allowed you to think there was a chance for us. You knew I didn't love you. I told you I didn't."

"I loved you enough for both of us."

His words stabbed at her heart. "Brice, no one person can make a relationship work. It takes two people together. I wish I was the right woman for you, but I know I'm not. There's someone out there, someone very special who will love you as you deserve to be loved." She used her voice, giving a little push even though she didn't like to do such things do with friends. She hated his pain, hated knowing she was the cause of it.

Brice was silent for a moment; then he let go of her arm and clutched his head. Francesca touched him. At once she could feel his pain, a sharp splintering headache growing and building at an alarming rate. She settled her fingers around his arm. "Let me help you, Brice. You know I can."

He broke away from her, breathing heavily. "No, Francesca, just let me be for a moment. I've been getting these headaches the last few days and they're killers. I even had a CAT scan done to see if I had a tumor." He pulled a tube from his pocket, took off the lid, and shook several small pills into his mouth.

Francesca could see his hand was trembling. "You don't need medication. I can take the pain away," she said softly, feeling hurt by his rejection.

He shook his head again, this time decisively. "Don't

waste your time and talent on me. The pills work just fine. Give me a few minutes and I'll be okay."

A small frown touched her soft mouth. "Brice, I know you're angry with me, but these headaches sound serious. You know I can help. How often are you taking these pills? What are they?"

He shrugged and cut through the park along a dark pathway, holding aside the low-lying branches to prevent them from hitting Francesca. "It doesn't matter. Why were you looking for me?"

"Where in the world are we going, Brice? This path leads out of the park toward the cemetery. Let's go back."

He swung around to face her and once again she thought there was something crafty in his eyes. Then he blinked and it was Brice looking down at her with sad eyes. But Francesca was very uneasy now. Nothing felt right to her, not Brice, not the path they were taking, not even the night itself. She bit down on her lower lip while she tried to think what he could be planning. Brice was not a violent man, she knew that much about him. He was gentle and caring, even if he was ambitious.

"We aren't going back, Francesca, not until we talk this out. If nothing else, I want to stay friends. I'm hurt, I won't deny that, and I've acted like a spoiled child, but I always thought you would come around and marry me. I really did. In my mind we were already engaged." He shook his head as he picked his way along the uneven surface of the road. "You never looked at other men, never. I thought that meant you truly felt something for me, but you had been hurt and were afraid to love again."

Francesca could see the first of the many headstones standing like silent sentinels of the dead in the graveyard. It was a beautiful place really, ancient, a place where it was believed the sacred and the damned had to be kept apart. One side of the burial grounds was sanctified, blessed with holy water, while the other was for those who had lived lives of sin and debauchery, criminals and murderers. It was now being torn up, the dead removed to the new cemetery away from the middle of the city. The machines hadn't yet reached the area where they walked. The imminet destruction made her sad; she had many human friends buried there.

"I never was interested in anyone else, Brice. I preferred your company, but it was friendship I felt, the love of a sister. I often wanted to feel more, and when I thought about the future, I wished I could love you as you wanted me to, but I never loved any man other than Gabriel. I thought him dead to me, all these years, but I was not over him."

"Why didn't you ever mention him?" Brice demanded, sounding petulant again. "Not once did you even say his name. If we were such good friends, why didn't you share with me such a terrible tragedy as losing your husband?" He spat the last word out distastefully. "I didn't know you'd ever been married to anyone." He was moving faster, now, taking the lead, pushing his way over the small rock wall to hurry along a little-used path leading to the mausoleum.

"I never spoke of him to anyone, Brice. It was too difficult." That was the truth. Even her mother had never known about that small incident in the village so many centuries earlier. When her family had been wiped out in the wars, she had fled the Carpathian Mountains, making her way to Paris, where she learned to hide herself from her people. Tears shimmered unexpectedly in her dark eyes, the memory of that time still raw. She blinked them away and followed Brice along the winding trail.

"I wasn't just anyone, Francesca. I was your best friend. But you always held a part of yourself away from me. No matter how hard I tried, I never could get close to you."

She hated that whiney note in his voice and that made her feel guiltier than ever. He had every reason to feel bad about what had happened between them. She *had* thought about spending her remaining years with him. She ducked her head, her long hair falling in a cascade around her face. "I didn't mean to lead you on, Brice. I hope you believe that. I tried to be honest with you, but there were times when I seriously thought about becoming involved with you. Because I was considering a relationship with you, I must have been inadvertently sending you messages that we might eventually be together. That was very wrong of me, but I didn't do it on purpose."

He turned his head for a moment, fury in his eyes. "That doesn't take away what I feel, Francesca, or absolve you of guilt."

She sighed. He seemed to be going back and forth between recrimination and genuinely wanting to retain their friendship. "Perhaps it is too soon for a conversation like this one. Maybe we should wait a few weeks until you can see I never would have been right for you, I never would have felt the way you wanted me to feel."

"We'll never know that for sure, will we?" he said. He was moving rapidly through the graveyard, moving away from the newer headstones into an older part of the cemetery where the stones were so ancient, they were crumbling and gray from the effects of weather.

Francesca slowed her pace. "Brice, do you have any idea where you're going or are you just walking as fast as you can because you're so angry with me?" She could hear the blood pumping furiously through his heart, the rush of adrenaline coursing through him as he moved.

He caught her wrist and yanked, a snarl twisting his handsome features. "Come on, Francesca, hurry up."

She moved with him a few steps, deliberately touching his mind as she did so. At once she was afraid. There was nothing in his mind except the overwhelming desire to get her to a certain place at the far side of the cemetery. He was willing to use any method, from cajoling her or humoring her, to brute strength. His need to get to this place was so strong, it blocked out everything else.

"Brice," she said very softly, "you're hurting me. Please let go of me. I can walk all by myself." He needed help desperately. Whatever was wrong with him, whether he had been shadowed by a vampire, or was using drugs, or was on the verge of a mental breakdown, Francesca wanted to help him. She feared for him now, more than for herself. There was something terribly wrong with him and she was determined to heal him.

"Well, hurry up then," he growled, still retaining possession of her arm. He loosened his hold because she had picked up her pace and was walking willingly with him. "Honestly, Francesca, you want everything your own way. You didn't want to talk to me about our friendship. You probably wanted to discuss your little patient."

"I do want to find out when I can bring Skyler home. She's anxious and bored in the hospital. And a reporter got into her room. She was very frightened." She kept her voice reasonable as she walked beside him, studying him intently. If she used her power, the vibrations of it would scatter into the night and draw unwanted attention. She would have to be persuasive to get him to her home, where she could control him and help him without the threat of interference.

"If she was so darn frightened, why didn't she tell me about it?" he demanded, angry all over again. "I'm her doctor, not you, not Gabriel. If she has a complaint, she can voice it to me. We know she can talk. Not that she talks to anyone but you."

"Brice," Francesca protested, slowing her pace again. He seemed to be pulling her at breakneck speed, almost as if he was so enraged he didn't know what he was doing. "Slow down, I'm going to fall. Do you have a pressing appointment somewhere? Let's go back to my house. I'll make us some tea, your favorite kind, and we can talk."

He instantly slowed his pace, shaking his head. "I'm sorry, I'm sorry," he repeated. "I don't know what got into me. It isn't good for that girl to depend so heavily on you. She won't talk to the counselors we send in, she won't speak to the nurses, or to me, just you."

"She has been severely traumatized, Brice. You know that. There's no quick fix for her pain. I'm taking it one step at a time with her. Once I have her settled at home, I will get her a counselor. I will follow your advice. You know I respect you as a doctor. I'm sorry we've gotten so off track together, but our feelings for each other are genuine. I still want us to remain friends. You might not be able to accept my friendship now, but perhaps you will in time. Meanwhile, we can still keep a professional relationship going, maintain that connection." Francesca tried to be hopeful. She put a gentle hand on his wrist to restrain him, to get him to come with her. She was really afraid for him now, certain he was losing control of himself.

Brice shook his head, turned onto a faint trail through thick shrubbery. Francesca felt as if she was in a maze.

Now the feeling of impending doom was growing. Overhead the storm clouds were dark and heavy. The wind was picking up so that it blew her hair into a wild mess. She caught at it, twisted and clipped it at the nape of her neck. With the wind came the scent of danger, and Francesca stopped dead in her tracks. Why hadn't she scanned the area as she should have been doing? She knew the undead were in the city somewhere.

"Gabriel!" She sent the call instantly. She had walked straight into a trap and poor Brice was with her. She had already ruined his life and now, because of her failure to be alert, he would most likely lose his life.

The stench of the undead permeated the air around her. Brice yanked on her arm once more, dragging her out of the shrubbery and into the open. At once, in the distance, she saw Gabriel. He was standing with his arms at his sides. Tall. Strong. Powerful. His long black hair was flowing to his shoulders. He looked relaxed.

On three sides of him were the enemy, circling, moving their feet rhythmically in an attempt to weave a holding spell. At first the three appeared to be tall, rather gaunt, handsome men, but at once Francesca saw through the illusion. Brice stopped abruptly when he saw Gabriel, suddenly confused. What was he doing in this dark, dreary place? Gabriel looked so powerful standing in the midst of the three other men.

Before Brice could make a sound, Francesca drew him back into the maze of shrubbery. Without conscious thought she took command of him, pushing his body along the path, turning onto another one so she could get above the combatants. There were three vampires, all flushed from fresh kills, high on the adrenaline rush. Gabriel might need her strength, or, if he was wounded, her blood in the aftermath of the battle.

She touched his mind, unable to stop herself from doing so. He was Gabriel, always the same. Tranquil. Calm. Without fear. His strength enabled her to breathe easier. Francesca pushed Brice along until they were well above the lower part of the cemetery. She moved out where she could better see what was happening. The scene below was frightening. From her vantage point she could see a dark shape on the ground near one of the graves. A young woman by the look of her, her throat torn. She lay like a broken doll, one hand stretched out toward the cross marking the grave. Gabriel would have sensed death and violence in the cemetery but he would not have been able to see the body with the machinery blocking his line of vision. She sent him a vision immediately, warning him of what had been done.

Francesca closed her eyes for a moment, sent up a quick fervent prayer for the victim and her family. How could she ask Gabriel to be anything but what he was, a hunter for their people, exterminating the vicious creatures who committed such senseless, cruel acts? Beside her Brice stirred, coming out of the semistupor he had fallen into.

"What the hell's going on?" he snapped, glaring down at the scene below. He could clearly see the body of the young woman and off to the right, far away from them, where the heavy equipment was parked, he could make out what looked like another body slumped near the bulldozer. A man, by his size. "I told you Gabriel was a criminal. He's involved with murder."

Francesca waved her hand to silence him, her entire focus centered below. The vampire to the left of Gabriel suddenly launched himself, wings bursting through his back as he leaped into the air, talons twisting his hands, his face contorting until he wore a razor-sharp beak. Even as he attacked, the second vampire's body rippled with fur and his face lengthened into a long muzzle to accommodate the teeth filling his mouth. While the bird went high, the wolf attacked low. The third vampire wavered until he was transparent, dissolving into droplets of mist streaking toward Gabriel.

To Francesca's horror, she could see a vine creeping along the ground, a long deadly tendril reaching out toward Gabriel's ankle. She pressed a hand to her mouth to keep from screaming. It wouldn't do to distract him. She had to trust in the fact that Gabriel was very experienced and would see each and every threat directed at him even though the attacks had been launched simultaneously.

"Get home now!" Gabriel's voice issued the command in her mind. It was sent sharply and with a strong underlying compulsion to obey. She knew he had no energy to spare to force his will on her.

Francesca felt the seriousness of his command deep within her body. His first concern would be her protection, not that of his own life, and with her out in the open, vulnerable, she would be a weapon to be used against him. The information flooded her mind out of nowhere; she wasn't even certain it came from Gabriel, but she turned at once to obey him.

Her hand caught Brice's. "Come on, we've got to get out of here now."

They began running down the embankment toward the river, away from the cemetery and the terrible battle taking place. As Francesca turned toward the lights of the city, a single figure moved out of the night and blocked the way between the two of them and freedom.

The beast was tall and gaunt with gray skin stretched tightly over his skull. His teeth were blackened and jagged, stained with the blood of so many innocents. He smiled at her, a terrible parody of a smile.

Chapter Thirteen

Francesca was screaming, although no sound emerged from her throat. Gabriel was engaged in a terrible battle with three ferocious enemies, his very life at stake. She closed herself off from him immediately, not willing to take the chance of distracting him from his duty. He could not help her.

"What the hell is going on?" Brice muttered, his voice strangled in his throat. He was terrified, certain someone had slipped him a hallucinogenic. This could not be reality, not with monsters fighting, demons turning into wolves, and winged gargoyles coming to life.

Automatically Francesca reached out to soothe him, her fingers settling lightly around his wrist so she could manipulate his mind. Her voice was low and compelling, the compulsion embedding itself deep within his brain. She might not be able to save Brice's life, but she could make the dying easier. He would never feel the teeth in his throat, ripping and tearing while the monster gulped fresh blood.

With her head held high, she faced the creature, her eyes blazing defiance, her soft mouth set with distaste. "How dare you come to me in such a way?" she said softly. "You are well aware such things are against the laws of our people."

The vampire's smile was a macabre parody. "Stand aside, healer, allow me to dine this night."

Francesca retained her light hold on Brice, kept her body positioned slightly in front of his. The enemy was calling to him, the command floating in the air, but she had successfully cut Brice off from the rest of the world. His head was down like a small child's, innocent of the things happening around him. "I will not. Go away from this place. You do not belong here."

The vampire hissed horribly, spittle spraying into the air between them. "Take care, woman, the hunter is otherwise occupied. He will not rescue you this night. I would not want to see harm come to you, but if you do not place yourself in my care, it will be necessary to force your compliance."

"*You* take care, evil one. I am no rank fledging to be forced into anything. I have no intention of going anywhere with you," Francesca said quietly. She pressed a hand to her stomach protectively. He would force her to accept his tainted blood. It would run in her veins, it would contaminate her child. She screamed again silently, using every ounce of self-control she possessed not to call out to Gabriel. Her only chance was for Gabriel to defeat his enemies and rescue her. But her baby, it would be far too late for her child. Vampires deceived themselves into believing that if they found a woman of the light, their souls might be restored. They sought Carpathian women and human women with psychic abilities in the hope of regaining what they had chosen to lose.

She would have to make the decision to sacrifice Brice to this thing; eventually she would have no other choice. It would be Brice or her daughter. Inadvertently her hand tightened around Brice's wrist as if she could anchor him to her. She kept her mind firmly away from thoughts of Skyler and disciplined herself to keep from calling out frantically to Gabriel. He would come to her as soon as he was able. It was up to her to stall the vampire.

"Do not anger me, woman. I am far more powerful than that one who claims you. An unknown upstart who believes he is a hunter. I know every hunter and this one has no reputation. I am an ancient. Do not think he can save you."

He didn't know who Gabriel was. She held that realization to her. It was ammunition, might have shock value when she needed it most. His head was beginning to move from side to side, a slow reptilian motion that was curiously hypnotic. Francesca knew better than to focus her attention too closely on the movement. Something about it fascinated her, yet at the same time repelled her. That was warning enough. He blinked his hooded, bloodred eyes just once.

She blurred her image and that of Brice, jerking the human with her as she sped with preternatural speed just as the vampire struck, grabbing for her with his clawed hands. She felt the wind of his strike as he missed her by scant centimeters. The creature shrieked his anger, whirling in a cloud of dirt and twigs, a powerful dust devil towering high, blackening the air around them.

Francesca's heart was pounding in alarm. She had succeeded in angering him. There was no telling what he might do to her now. Overhead the storm clouds were gathering, a dark ominous portent of things to come. Lightning arced from cloud to cloud while all around her the skies darkened until every star was blotted out, until the moon was nothing but a memory.

The vampire hissed again, a deadly sound while the wind whipped at his tattered clothing and raked the lank hair hanging around his skull-like face. "You will be punished for that. I will have this human, and his dying will be long and painful. I will destroy everyone who has ever meant anything to you."

Francesca's heart was pounding frantically and she took a deep breath to calm herself. Inside she felt her daughter leap in fear. Immediately she covered her womb with her two hands as she faced the beast. He was undulating his head again, a rhythmic motion designed to be hypnotic. He attacked again in a blur of motion and Francesca waited until the last possible second to escape, towing Brice with her. Before the vampire could reach her, something inserted itself between them so that the undead was forced to halt his attack. With a howl of rage, he jumped backward.

Between her and the vampire a form shimmered, solidified. For one heart-stopping moment she thought it was Gabriel. The figure was tall, broad-shouldered, with the same long black hair and hauntingly perfect features as her lifemate. His eyes were black and empty, although Francesca could occasionally see the beginnings of small red flames smoldering deep within the empty depths. Power clung to him as if he were power come to life, power personified. He moved with a flowing grace, yet when he stopped, he was as still as the very mountains, a part of the earth itself. He was like Gabriel, yet unlike him. He bowed to her, a courtly, princelike gesture, before turning his attention to the vampire.

Francesca's breath stilled in her body. This was Lucian. It could be no other. Gabriel's twin and a vampire without equal. Her heart began to thud painfully in despair. Where she had feared the other vampire, she was now terrified. It was something about Lucian, something she couldn't name, but he seemed invincible, seemed so powerful that a force of hunters could not defeat him. This was Gabriel's mortal enemy and the one he loved above all others. She bit her lip hard to keep from crying out to her lifemate.

And then Lucian spoke. It was as if music were playing, music not of this world, but so pure and beautiful it was impossible to forget. His voice was the most beautiful thing she had ever heard in her life. "You have come here to this place and you have annoyed me, undead. I have chosen this city as my own personal playground and yet you think you can simply ignore my claim. You sent your minions to challenge my brother while you attack this one that he has laid claim to. She is under his protection and I can allow no other to interfere in our game. You understand that." The voice was so perfect, so reasonable, *anyone* could understand him. "You lost your soul many centuries ago, dead one, and you yearn for the freedom of the final death. Go now. Your breath is no longer able to sustain you; your heart shall cease beating." He raised his hand into the air and slowly began to close his fingers into a fist.

Francesca watched in horrified fascination as the undead obeyed the compulsion in that sweetly lethal voice. The vampire gasped for air, and as the fist closed tighter, his face began to turn color as he choked and strangled before her eyes. The vampire clutched at his chest as his heart stuttered, but he made no attempt to fight the order, so powerful was that voice. Francesca could scarcely take her eyes from her lifemate's twin; she, too, was caught in the spell of his power, mesmerized by the true beauty of his voice. It was only when he plunged his fist deep within the cavity of the vampire's chest and extracted the heart, when lightning slammed to earth in a jagged bolt of blue white and incinerated the already dead organ and its host, that she managed to jerk herself awake, once again aware of her own very precarious situation.

Francesca waited in silence, one hand over her stomach to protect her unborn daughter, the other holding on to Brice, who was still under her mind control, unable to comprehend anything going on around him.

Lucian was a thousand times more powerful, more deadly, than the vampire she had just faced. She stood watching him with her dark eyes, her small teeth biting down on her lower lip, betraying her nervousness. He moved then, a flowing of grace and timeless beauty, a two-edged sword more destructive than anything she had ever known. Gabriel was right to hunt this monster. Nothing could stop him, nothing the humans had would slow him down if he should decide to give up the murderous game he played with his brother and turn to something even more vicious.

Francesca swallowed the tight knot of fear blocking her throat and lifted her chin defiantly. "I must thank you for coming to my aid, dark one."

"To my brother's aid," he corrected softly, moving around her with a flowing grace. He seemed not to touch the ground, but to glide through the air itself. He moved so softly there was no sound, no disturbance in the air. Lucian's black eyes moved over her face, and he seemed to see right into her soul. "My brother is the only one able to provide me with diversion. Life is tedious when one is so much more intelligent than all others."

"Why have you come to his aid?" Francesca asked softly, puzzled that he did not appear as foul to her as the other vampires she had encountered over the centuries. Was he so good at illusion that even an ancient such as she could not recognize what was foul and wholly evil? His power was very disturbing to her.

The broad shoulders shrugged in a lazy ripple. "I do not allow others to interfere in our game. You are an anchor he weighs himself down with. A pawn I can use against him when I so desire. What is between my brother and me shall remain so always. Any who dares to interfere, hunter or vampire or woman, will die at my choosing."

She tilted her chin. "What are you going to do with me?"

The perfect mouth slanted into a brief, humorless smile. "Call him to your aid. You would not want me to make you my slave. Call him." His voice was pleasing and subtle, an insidious whisper of purity. He seemed not to move, yet he was so close she could smell his scent, clean, not foul. She could feel his power.

Francesca swallowed hard and took a step backward, shaking her head to be sure she wasn't under compulsion. "Never. There is nothing you can do to make me betray him, not of my own free will. Gabriel is a great man and my lifemate. I willingly exchange my life for his." She waited to be struck down. There was a silence, long and empty. She couldn't hear him breathing, couldn't hear his heart beating, if he had a heart.

Her long lashes fluttered as she regarded the master vampire standing so motionless, looking like the statue of an ancient god. It took a moment to realize there was no entrapment in his voice, just plain black magic. His voice simply made one want to comply with his every wish. "Why aren't you forcing me to do your bidding?" she asked curiously, sweeping one hand nervously through her long blue-black hair.

"I do not need the aid of women in my battle." She felt a whip of contempt in his words. "I find it rather astonishing that my brother has grown so weak he has allowed this mortal you guard to remain alive. What do you see in this mortal that you would prefer his company to that of one of your own people? He is self-seeking; his mind is filled with plans of revenge. His main purpose in life seems to be to get at my brother." His black eyes were steady on her face. "But you know that, Francesca."

She shivered, running her hands up and down her arms. She was suddenly cold. It was his voice again. The tone was exactly the same. Soft. Pure. Beautiful. Yet somehow she felt threatened now. And worse than being threatened, she felt the heavy weight of his rebuke. It shouldn't have meant anything to her. He was the undead. Yet she felt as if she were a young girl censured by the Prince of their people. It hurt and it was humiliating. Francesca could not meet those empty black eyes. Instead she found herself looking down at the toes of her shoes. She wanted to make him understand, yet she didn't understand her own feelings. How could she possibly explain them to someone who had no emotions at all?

"I would stay and play longer, but the foolish one is forgetting all that was taught him." Lucian said the words softly as he shimmered for a moment, his once-solid form transparent so that she could see the trees right through him. There was a peculiar prism effect she had never seen before right before he dissolved into droplets of mist and streamed through the fog-filled terrain away from her.

Francesca let out her breath slowly and relaxed muscles she hadn't realized were cramped and taut. At once she reached for Gabriel to warn him. He was in a desperate battle, whirling among the three lesser vampires, all minions of the one Lucian had destroyed. They were darting in, seeking to wear him down with long, razor-sharp talons, attempting to slice small, deep cuts in his flesh to weaken him.

"Lucian is here."

Soft laughter echoed through her mind. At first she thought Lucian had somehow managed to get into her head, but then she realized he was in Gabriel's mind. Because she shared Gabriel's thoughts and memories, she could "hear" their strange conversation.

"You have forgotten all that I taught you, brother. Why would you allow these lesser vampires to surround you this way?" Lucian shimmered into solid form between Gabriel and the largest and most aggressive of the three undead.

Gabriel launched himself at the smallest vampire, the one directly behind him, moving so quickly he had plunged his fist into the chest and extracted the pulsing heart while the vampire was still staring in shock at Lucian. Gabriel was on the second vampire before he had dropped the heart of the first one. The creature screamed his defiance, lashing out, but was far too late. Gabriel had taken his heart and whirled away, even as bolt after bolt of jagged lightning beat at the earth, incinerating the two bodies and their tainted hearts.

It happened so quickly, Francesca was unable to comprehend how Gabriel had done it. There was no thought, no plan in his mind that she could read, not even a communication between the twin brothers, yet even as Gabriel had used Lucian as a distraction, so had Lucian used Gabriel. He had attacked the largest of the undead while it was gaping in horror at Gabriel. The third body was lying shriveled and lifeless on the ground while Lucian tossed the tainted heart into the fiery ball of energy Gabriel was using to destroy the other two.

It was then Gabriel suddenly comprehended that his brother, the mortal enemy of their people, had once again aided him in his battle. Francesca read his guilt, his annoyance with himself that he had not taken the opportunity to destroy Lucian. He was so accustomed to working with his twin, he had simply acted on instinct. Before he could launch himself in his brother's direction, Lucian had disappeared, leaving no trace behind. There was no trail of droplets, no minute particles, no suggestion of power or empty spaces that Gabriel might use as a path to follow the undead to his lair.

As he finished incinerating the three vampires and all evidence of their battle, he went over every detail of Lucian's appearance, the tone of his voice, the things he had said. Lucian had flooded him with more information about the city, hideaways commonly used by the underground people, those who were often used as minions by the undead.

Gabriel swore softly, eloquently in the ancient language. *"I am useless."*

"Do not say that, Gabriel."

"You see why I have not destroyed him. I have always followed where he has led. He knows it and taunts me

with my failure. If I had not done so tonight, I could have had a great advantage against him."

"You would have been fighting four vampires, Gabriel. He would have defeated you. You would be dead and I would be forced to flee to the Carpathian Mountains to have this child. You cannot take such risks." The very idea of his death frightened her. He was already a part of her, buried deep within her soul. She would live a half life without him. And she would not even have the option of following him to the afterlife. She carried their daughter and she must bring her into the world safely. She would have to seek shelter and protection from the Prince of their people. "Gabriel." She whispered his name in sudden terror. He could not leave her alone like that, not after he had dragged her back into a world she had given up.

"He would not have allowed the others to destroy me." Gabriel sounded as calm as ever, his voice soft and comforting. *"It is a game to him. No other can play it. Only I have the potential to defeat him. He would have liked me to attack him. He is probably disappointed that I did not."*

The pure, beautiful voice filled their heads. *"You have grown soft, Gabriel. I was prepared for such an action, yet you passed up the perfect opportunity."*

"You looked tired, Lucian. I did not want an unfair advantage." Gabriel's reply was gentle. *"You need a rest, you seek ever to find a resting place, a way to leave this world behind. Tell me where you are that I may come to you and aid you in your long-awaited journey."*

Francesca's heart jumped at the idea, fear racing through her bloodstream so that she actually felt physically ill. She waited for the answer, terrified that Lucian would call Gabriel to his side. They would fight to the death. She knew it as surely as she knew her own name. Gabriel would never go unscathed by so powerful a being.

The laughter that followed Gabriel's words should have been ugly and horrible to hear, yet Lucian's voice was a beautiful instrument filling them with a soothing, tranquil feeling. Their tranquility was quickly dispersed when he spoke. *"You seek to entrap me with your voice, brother. I do not think entrapment is possible between us."*

"I did once."

"Locking me to you beneath the earth was an interesting move and one I did not expect." There was a certain note of admiration in the beautiful voice.

"You were weak from loss of blood."

"Now you seek to anger me, hoping I will continue our conversation so you may follow my trail. I am incapable of emotion, brother, not even anger. The precious gift was not bestowed on me as one of the legions of undead. But I am glad to tell you where I am at this moment. I am bending over the child you claim as yours. She is unusual, a rarity in a world filled with carbon copies." There was a subtle threat, a subtle challenge.

Francesca cried out and without thinking dropped Brice's wrist. She had all but forgotten him. Now she could think only of Skyler lying helpless in bed with the vampire bending ever closer to her neck. She pushed Brice into a sitting position, issuing a command to awaken from his dream even as she dissolved into a million droplets of water and streamed back toward the hospital.

"I forbid this, Francesca." Gabriel's voice was quiet, authoritative. *"It is a trap."*

"I will not give her to him." There was a sob in her voice, in her mind. She knew Gabriel was already winging his way toward their shared destination.

"I am sorry, my love. I cannot allow such a threat to you." Gabriel's voice whispered against the walls of her mind like butterfly wings.

Without warning Francesca abruptly changed direction. Alarmed, she cried out to Gabriel. She was no longer in control of her motion, someone else was controlling her flight. Instinctively she attempted to fall to the ground, to shape-shift, but it was impossible. *"Gabriel!"*

"Do not fear so, Francesca, I am merely doing my duty. You will wait for me in the protection of our home."

The soft, taunting laughter came again, moving through their minds and bodies like a warm, molten spread of sunshine. The power of Lucian's voice was incredible. *"What safeguards do you think to use to keep me at bay? Have you learned much that you have not shared with your own twin?"*

"Do not think yourself invincible, Lucian. I have bested you once, I may do so again," Gabriel replied calmly.

His very calmness strengthened her, allowed Francesca to push aside her horror. She was shocked at Gabriel's strength, that he could command an ancient such as herself in flight, hold her course steady, safeguard her, yet continue his journey toward the hospital even as he conversed so calmly with his mortal enemy. His calm was not a facade. He was completely confident, an ancient warrior who had battled continually, fought his way through the long centuries. The forthcoming battle would be the culmination of those centuries of experience. At once she stopped fighting him, not wanting to make his tasks more difficult.

Francesca had to force herself not to plead with the vampire to spare Skyler further pain. Vampires thrived on the pain of others. It was one of the dark gifts of the undead. Through their victims, they could feel momentarily, a fleeting glimpse of what they had lost. Each emotion was dark and ugly, but it was emotion all the same.

She quieted her thoughts, centered herself. *"Skyler? Can you hear me?"* The teenager was asleep. *"Do not open your eyes. You are in danger."*

There was a slight stirring and the young girl was aware. Francesca was so familiar with her mind, she could actually feel the child scanning her surroundings much as the Carpathian people did. Her pulse rate stayed the same; her heart didn't jump in the least. *"I cannot be. He is here with me and I am perfectly safe."*

"Has he taken your blood?"

There was a long silence while Skyler puzzled over the question. *"He isn't a lab tech. I know he isn't. Why would you be afraid he would want my blood?"*

Francesca thought for a moment. Skyler had obeyed her: she remained still, breathing easily, feigning sleep. Yet for some reason she felt safe despite the threat of terrible evil. Skyler was gifted with a sense of danger. Lucian must not mean her any real harm. That was the only answer. He was baiting a trap to draw Gabriel to him.

She knew Gabriel could read her thoughts, was sharing her mind. She should have realized Lucian was sharing Gabriel's mind as well. His laughter came again, that soft musical symphony of beauty. *"Now you see the futility of struggling against one such as I. This human child, though she is rare in this world, cannot fool one such as I by pretending to sleep. You cannot protect her from me, not with your safeguards, and not by trying to hide her from me. What Gabriel knows, then so do I. When I wish to make her my slave, I will do so. Right now it is tedious to think of such a burden."*

"Lucian." Gabriel said the name softly, gently. *"You grow tired of your existence. There is nothing to hold you to this world. You chose to lose your soul and follow the path of darkness, yet you gained no emotions, no power you had not already wielded. Allow me to aid you in leaving this madness behind. You want me to aid you. You have always wished such a thing."*

"That was your vow to me, brother, and you can do no other than honor it. Yet I find this world different, much changed since last I arose. It is true it is tedious to continue when I have no one to match wits with, yet you remain. Do you then also seek the dawn?" He laughed softly, as if to himself. *"I think we should continue our game for a time in this strange world."* He was fading; Francesca felt it through her link with Gabriel. He had lured Gabriel to the hospital with the intention of battle, yet he seemed to have lost interest quickly, fading from Skyler's room, from the very air itself, leaving no trace of power behind.

Gabriel sighed with frustration. Lucian knew about both women. How could he not? The power, unmistakably female, was there for any to read. Already the undead were being drawn to the city, looking for the one thing that might save them. Lucian could not have failed to read the signs, would know that Skyler as well as Francesca existed. And he would know Gabriel had claimed Francesca, that she was an ancient Carpathian. He probably knew she was with child. What Gabriel knew, so did Lucian. Skyler was no longer safe in the hospital, away from his protection.

Gabriel shape-shifted as he landed, already striding across the hospital parking lot to the entrance. He blurred his image, not wanting to deal with humans while he checked to see for himself that Lucian had not touched Skyler. They had to move her as soon as possible. Lucian could use human minions to harm her during the day when Gabriel was unable to protect her. Skyler needed to be in their home where he could use safeguards. Where he could supply human bodyguards that could be trusted to watch over her when he was deep within the ground. In all the centuries they had battled, Gabriel had never known Lucian to use a servant in an attempt to destroy him during the day, but with Skyler to protect, he could take no chances. And there were others in the city, vampires of lesser power, but still evil and vicious. Any might attempt to acquire Skyler. He could not allow such a thing. Her mind could not take one more battering.

Skyler was lying quietly, staring up at the ceiling, when he entered her room. His shadow reached her first. Someone with fewer powers of observation would never have noticed the tiny shiver that ran through her small body. "Do you fear me?" Gabriel asked softly, giving her the courtesy of staying out of her mind. He knew he would have to "read" her to be sure Lucian had not taken her blood, but he was determined to respect her privacy whenever possible.

Skyler's fingers curled nervously in the sheet. "Not really." Beneath the thin covering, the outline of the stuffed wolf was visible close to her side.

There was honesty in her voice but her tone was a mere thread of sound. "Do you know why I am here?"

She looked at him then, her large gray eyes soft and wide, long lashes throwing thick crescent shadows across her cheek. She looked beautiful to him. Skyler swallowed hard and brought up her hand to cover the scar running along the curve of her face. Very gently Gabriel caught her wrist, preventing her from covering the thin, jagged white line. Tenderly he turned her hand over, ran his thumb over the myriad of scars crisscrossing her forearm, wrist, and hand. "We are family, child, *real* family. There is no place for embarrassment. I am proud of you, proud of the way you defended yourself and kept yourself true to your own soul. Do not hide your badges of courage, Skyler, not from me and not from Francesca."

Her large eyes moved over his face a little moodily. "I have always been alone, as far back as I can remember. Ever since my mother died, I have been alone. I'm not certain I know how to be with others."

Gabriel had a breathtaking smile and he used it shamelessly. "Welcome to the family then, Skyler. I have been alone far too long and so has Francesca. We will learn together." He stroked back her hair with gentle fingers. "We may be amateurs at it, but in the end we will be successful."

The smallest ghost of a smile flickered across her face. "You think so?"

"I know it absolutely. I do not fail in my tasks, not even those abhorrent to me. This is the first time I am undertaking something for myself. Believe me, child, I will not fail."

She studied him, more adult than child. "What tasks are abhorrent to you?"

His white teeth flashed at her, a small tribute to her insight, to her special gifts. "There are times I have no choice but to order the women in my family to do as I bid them," he answered mischievously.

Her soft gray eyes lit up briefly, a small victory for him. "And that is abhorrent to you? I doubt it, Gabriel." She felt very brave teasing him back.

He sat down so he wouldn't tower over her. It was important to him that he didn't intimidate her. Francesca's influence had helped Skyler to accept him, to see him as someone good, not an enemy, but his position with her was tenuous. He made certain his movements were flowing and graceful so he would not startle her.

"If I take your hand as Francesca does, I can read your thoughts," he explained softly, "much in the way you receive information about those around you. I do not want to frighten you with my touch, but it is necessary that I 'read' your memories of the other one who visits you so often."

Her long lashes fluttered, veiled her large eyes. "Will I be able to read yours?" There was a hesitation in her voice, as if she feared angering him.

"Would you like to?"

"I usually can." When he continued to look at her, Skyler twisted the sheet between her fingers. "I've always been able to read people if I touch them." She glanced at him, a quick surreptitious look. "I don't think it's the same way you and Francesca read minds though. I just seem to know things. I can hear and feel her talking to me. I know she's there with me." Her fingers continued to pluck nervously at the sheet. "Just like the other one is there when I'm afraid."

"Skyler," Gabriel said very gently, "if you do not wish to read my emotions or my thoughts, then you will be shielded from them. If it would reassure you to do so, then, by all means, let us begin."

Her large dove-gray eyes were very expressive as they moved over his face. He waited quietly, allowing her to make up her own mind. Eventually she nodded. Gabriel took her hand with extraordinary gentleness, leaned close so that his black eyes could trap Skyler's gaze in the dark depths of his. She didn't even blink. When the young woman made up her mind to do something, she threw her heart and soul into it and did it 100 percent. He would have to keep that in mind when he was trying out his nonexistent parenting skills.

She startled him with her laughter, not aloud, but in her mind. *"I'm reading your mind, too,"* she reminded him.

"Great, you are going to be a pain in the neck, just like Francesca," he groused, teasing her gently while flooding his mind with the extent of his love for Francesca, with his warmth and feelings of protectiveness toward Skyler. She felt his presence in her mind occasionally, but she didn't realize he had already shared her memories of her childhood. That would have humiliated her. He knew it instinctively and had no intention of allowing her to be embarrassed. She read what he wanted her to read. His desire to welcome Skyler into his family, his hope he would be a good parent, someone who would protect her and guide her and always make her feel safe. He shared his feelings of inadequacy as a husband, his fears he would somehow let Francesca down. He loved Francesca more than life itself and he allowed Skyler to know he would grow to love her the same way.

All the time, he was delving deeper into her mind in an attempt to find a trace of power, a hint that his twin intended to use her to strike against Francesca. He saw Francesca's work and it was flawless. He saw their combined safeguards, the strong protection they had wrought together, yet he could find no trace of Lucian, no hint of tainted power, no dark hidden agenda. Gabriel was careful, searching everywhere for the slightest anomaly, finding many, examining them all meticulously. She seemed to be free of all outside forces.

He sighed softly, releasing her before his sudden, unexpected surge of anger transmitted itself to Skyler. She had been hideously abused and the raw wounds in her mind would forever leave scars. She was an extraordinary young woman with rare insight and gifts beyond measure. But the man who should have loved and protected her had been the very one to initiate and perpetuate the abuse.

Gabriel was careful to breathe deeply, wanting to appear completely calm and in control. He knew that Skyler would be terrified by any masculine displays of temper. Lucian had already destroyed Skyler's abusers one by one. He had taken the girl's enemies as part of his little chess game with Gabriel, to show he knew what Gabriel knew.

"Did you see anything in there that changes your mind about wanting to take me home with you and Francesca?" There was a challenge in Skyler's soft voice but her gaze had slid away from his the instant he released her.

Gabriel caught her chin in two fingers and tipped it up so she had to look at him. "You have an astonishing mind. I stand in awe of you and the things you have accomplished and the things you are capable of doing. I am honored you would want me to serve as your guardian along with Francesca. Did you not see yourself through my eyes?" He asked it very gently.

A faint flush of color crept up her face. "I'm not like that. Not like you think of me—courageous and brave and beautiful. No one else thinks that." When he continued to look at her the color deepened. "Well, only Francesca, but she doesn't have a mean bone in her body. She would find something nice to say about a monster."

A small smile tugged at Gabriel's mouth. "You are very

likely correct, Skyler, in your assessment of Francesca. She would think the best of a monster, but she also is very astute. In you she sees what I see. You need to begin to see yourself as we do. We are your guardians, and you must learn to trust and rely on us. If ever you wish, you may examine my mind and I will share my thoughts with you openly."

"I wish to get out of this horrible place and go home with you and Francesca."

"She was securing the doctor's permission when we were interrupted."

Skyler bit her lip, started to speak, and then dragged the stuffed animal to her face.

"Tell me, little one," he encouraged softly. "In our home I will expect truth and respect to be given on both sides. If you wish to say something, I will listen and value what you have to say."

"You won't believe me, but I know I'm right." She dug her fingers into the plush wolf in her nervousness.

Gabriel gently placed his hand over hers and sent her a small wave of warmth and reassurance. "If you know you are right, Skyler, I will believe you."

She loved the sound of his voice, the accent she couldn't place, the funny way he twisted his words. Mostly she loved the conviction in him, the way he made her believe him. "I don't think the doctor is really good. Something's wrong with him."

Gabriel nodded. "He was very much in love with Francesca and he was not happy when I returned. You see, Francesca thought I was dead. I think the doctor is having difficulty overcoming his jealousy."

Skyler stared at him a long while, then shook her head. "It is more than that. I feel it when he touches me."

For a moment, the red flame of the monster danced in Gabriel's eyes and inside him, claws unsheathed. He took a moment to breathe before he responded. "What do you mean, little one?" His voice was quieter and more beautiful than ever.

Skyler felt the air in the room grow still, as if the earth itself were waiting for her answer. Her long lashes swept down, concealing her expressive eyes. "When he comes in to examine me, he tries to hide it, but I know something's wrong with him. He's twisted. It's more than jealousy, Gabriel."

"I am going to secure your release for tomorrow evening. Francesca and I will need to set things up at home so we can give you adequate care while you recover. In the meantime, Francesca has hired a bodyguard for you. He is *your* guard, not a hospital employee, and he will ensure you are safe in our absence. If you feel threatened, you tell him to get you out of this place and take you to our home." He pulled the key to the front door of Francesca's house from his pocket. Taking a thin chain of gold from around his neck, he secured it. "This is the house key, little one." He placed the chain around her neck. "If you need to come home, you have the key."

He felt her relief. She was lifting the key, turning it over, and holding it to her as if he had given her something precious. Gabriel stood up, towering over her. "Your room is ready and Francesca has outdone herself." He wrote the address on a slip of paper and tucked that into her hand also.

A small smile shaped Skyler's soft mouth. "I knew she would go crazy." The smile faded from her face, leaving her wan and pale. "Do you believe me about the doctor?"

There was an anxious note in her voice she couldn't conceal.

Gabriel regarded her gravely, his black eyes serious. "I believe you, Skyler. I have felt the same uneasiness around him. Do not fear for Francesca. I will do all within my very considerable power to keep her safe."

Skyler searched his face for a long while before her lashes drifted down and she subsided quietly in her bed, obviously satisfied with his reassurance.

Gabriel automatically scanned during his waking hours, and now he felt Brice entering the hospital. He glided away from the bed toward the door. A small gasp of alarm spun him around. "What is it?" he asked softly.

Skyler was staring at him as if he were a ghost. Self-consciously she forced a laugh. "Just now you reminded me of . . ." She trailed off.

He deliberately grinned, a boyish, mischievous grin. "A rock star?" he asked hopefully. Skyler's astuteness was far more than he had given her credit for.

She managed a nervous laugh. "Not hardly, Gabriel. A wolf. A big bad wolf." She held up the stuffed animal. "Just like him."

He laughed with her but took great care to appear more human as he left the room with a reassuring wave.

Chapter Fourteen

"The couple will arrive today, Gabriel," Francesca said. She was sitting at her desk, rather absently weaving together abstract designs. They looked a jumble of materials to Gabriel, but he could see how her fingers traced each swatch lovingly, even though her mind didn't seem to be on what she was doing.

Gabriel crossed the room to stand behind her, wanting the closeness of her slender body. "I am well aware of their arrival, Francesca. What is it you are trying not to say to me?" There was a hint of laughter in the richness of his voice. He was her lifemate, he had only to share her mind to uncover her worry.

Francesca took a deep breath. Her fingers sought a piece of cloth and unconsciously began to rub her thumb over it. "Aidan has requested we do not take their blood."

There was a small telling silence. The air was heavy with

the weight of his disapproval. Francesca understood completely. There were only a handful of humans who knew of the existence of the Carpathian people. Gabriel was an ancient, a hunter unsurpassed by any, other than his twin. He had remained alive by concealing his sleeping chambers, by blending in among the human race. Carpathians could easily control the behavior of humans they took blood from, yet Aidan had asked that they not do such a thing. If the human had knowledge of their race and lived in their home, he held power in his hands. To Gabriel it was putting the lives of his family at risk, trusting two people he did not know.

"What do you say to this strange request?"

Francesca felt her heart leap. "Gabriel." She breathed his name silently, held it to her. She had been her own person for so long, making her own decisions just as Gabriel had, yet he remembered it was important to consider her opinion as if she was his partner.

Gabriel found a smile curving his mouth. Francesca was his partner, his other half. Her opinion counted where no other ever could. He was extraordinarily proud of her achievements. She didn't seem to realize just how much she meant to him. That astonished him. She needed to see herself through his eyes. In his opinion she was without equal in the world. "Of course I value your opinion. You may not have mixed with our people all these centuries, but you have kept up with the news. You managed to hide your identity from those in power and from the evil ones continuously searching for females of our race. I believe you are better equipped to judge this strange request than I, who have been buried in the earth for nearly two centuries."

"I have heard it said that Aidan does not control this

family, has never used them to feed, that he respects them greatly. They have helped out other members of our race in times of need. Not all of them are privy to our secrets, but those who know have never betrayed us. If Aidan has recommended two of his human family to aid us, then I believe he must trust them implicitly. He has said this is the son of his housekeeper. This man has known of our people for some time. I believe his wife was told only recently, but she has proved to be loyal. Her husband has assured Aidan that she is trustworthy."

"I do not like the idea of the wife not being under our control," Gabriel admitted. "Obviously the husband has known for many years and has proved his loyalty, but this woman is a huge danger when we are under siege. She could turn into a liability."

Francesca nodded. "What you say is very true, especially now, when Lucian is here and hunting us, but I think we can monitor her thoughts well enough to control the situation. If we believe there is danger, we will have time to contact Aidan."

Gabriel's eyebrow shot up and Francesca turned away from him to hide her sudden amusement. Gabriel did not like her idea of consulting Aidan Savage over any matter, let alone one within his own household. It was all she could do to keep her face straight.

Gabriel reached out lazily and held her shoulder. "Are you laughing at me?" he inquired very softly. His voice purred with menace.

"Would I do that?" Her eyes were so dark they were black, and they glinted with laughter.

He wrapped his arm around her waist and pulled her right into the shelter of his body. "Yes, you would do that," he whispered, bending his dark head to the invitation of her neck. His mouth skimmed over her satin-soft skin. "Are you so busy with these people, you have no time at all to discuss my ailments? I need healing."

She reached up behind herself and circled his neck with her arm, leaning into him so that his every muscle was imprinted on her slender body. She found his mouth with hers. The earth seemed to stand still beneath her feet. For one heart-stopping moment breath ceased to be important. Their hearts had a single beat, their minds were fully merged, their souls one. Francesca melted into him, her body soft and pliant. He could do that with his kiss. Send molten lava coursing through her blood and raise her temperature several degrees in seconds.

"We have a child," she murmured softly against his throat. "She's moving toward us right at this moment."

Gabriel groaned softly. He had heard the soft pad of Skyler's small feet as she explored their home. At the first rising, Gabriel had hunted prey, feeding well for himself and for Francesca. They had much to do, seeing that Skyler was settled in her new home. Gabriel approved of the bodyguard Francesca had summoned. Jarrod Silva was a man of almost thirty who looked very capable. He wasn't the least bit intrusive and Gabriel easily read his desire to do a good job. Gabriel reinforced Jarrod's determination with a subtle compulsion and was satisfied the man would protect Skyler should the need arise.

Francesca turned all the way around in his arms, to press her slender body along the length of his. He laughed softly, holding her close. "I look at you, Francesca," he whispered softly as he framed her face with his hands, "and I cannot believe my good fortune. You are my life, my very breath. I hope that you always know that and carry the knowledge in your heart. You make the torment I endured all those centuries worthwhile."

Francesca felt tears gathering behind her eyes. She sensed his utter sincerity, the intensity of his emotion. Certainly he wanted her body, she could feel the heat and need in him rising like the inevitable tide, but even stronger and more intense was the love he felt for her. She told herself to breathe, just to take a breath and inhale his scent.

A soft sound had both of them turning their heads. "I love that about the two of you," Skyler announced. She was moving slowly, carefully, her small body still battered physically. "The way you look at each other. I've never seen anyone else do that. You look at each other with such love. It shines between you."

Francesca immediately held out her hand to the girl. "And you wonder if there's any room for you."

Skyler looked very fragile. Her skin was pale, almost translucent, her eyes enormous in her delicate face. She looked far younger than her fourteen years until one looked at her too-old eyes.

Skyler ducked her head, her long lashes veiling the expression in her eyes, but she moved forward and took the outstretched hand. Francesca drew her gently to them. Gabriel covered their hands with his. "We have enough love to go around, Skyler," he replied gently. "More than enough. We are family, the three of us, and we always will be, no matter what the future brings. It starts here, with us. Francesca has lived her life alone, as I have. You also. We do this together, helping one another." His voice was beautiful and compelling. He could command the heavens and make the very earth rise up beneath their feet. He made Skyler a believer without any hidden compulsion.

Francesca smoothed back the ragged ends of Skyler's hair. "Our housekeepers arrive today. They will be living with us on a permanent basis, we hope. Gabriel and I have many duties to perform and for a brief time during the daylight hours we will not be home and it will be difficult to reach us. I want someone I trust with you at all times so you feel safe. But you remember this is *your* home. If something is done or said that you do not like, I expect you to convey it to me so we can deal with it together. If you have fears or wish to change something in the household, please say so. Your happiness and comfort matter to us. It is no bother. We want to do things for you."

"My room is beautiful, Francesca," Skyler said, her voice still so soft and thin it made Francesca want to gather the girl into her arms. "Thank you for going to so much trouble for me."

"It was fun. Shopping together will be fun." Francesca laughed softly. "You turned pale at the thought of shopping. Most girls would be thrilled. I finally get my daughter, or younger sister, whichever label you prefer, and you do not want to shop for clothes."

Skyler brought a trembling hand to the thin scar on her face and rubbed it self-consciously. "I haven't been out in public in a long time," she confessed.

Gabriel took her hand gently and brought the worst scar to his cheek. "When you decide you are up to it, we will all go and look at the strange people out there together. It will be much more fun that way."

Skyler stared up at him for a long time, her eyes moving over his harsh, sensual features, studying every inch of his face. Her smile was very slow in coming, but when it did, it lit up her eyes. "I think you are almost as afraid of all those people as I am, just not in the same way."

Francesca laughed at Gabriel's wry expression, the joyful sound filling their home with love. She could do that, Gabriel thought. Francesca could fill up every inch of that huge house with love. Each moment spent in her company only deepened his feelings for her. There was so much light spilling out of her it fascinated him. Gabriel had lived in a world of darkness, of violence, for so long, he could only stare in awe at Francesca. His black eyes met Skyler's dove-gray gaze and they shared a small smile of mutual understanding. She felt the same way. Both of them wanted to bask in Francesca's healing light for all eternity.

Francesca slipped her arm around Skyler's waist, a gesture so natural to her, Skyler didn't think to pull away. "We won't have to worry about going out in public until you're ready, honey. I just want you to feel comfortable and safe here at home. I think you'll like our new housekeepers."

Skyler made a face and exchanged another quick look with Gabriel. He was making the same face. Francesca laughed at them. "I can see how it's going to be. You two are a couple of hermits. There will be no ganging up against Francesca, you two. Skyler, you like your bodyguard, don't you?"

Skyler shrugged. "I try never to look at him."

"Well, you should. He's quite nice-looking," Francesca replied.

"That will be enough of that," Gabriel interrupted. "You do not need to find any man good-looking other than me."

Francesca smiled very sweetly. "But then, I don't remember ever saying you were good-looking."

Skyler found herself laughing. For one moment in time, she forgot. She forgot the scars on her body. She forgot the scars on her mind and soul. She was a young girl enjoying a moment of happiness with two people she was growing fond of. It was nearly impossible to believe she could trust them so quickly, but she did. "Are you going to let her get away with that?" she asked Gabriel, her eyes sparkling. "You are good-looking and she's noticed. I know she has."

He shackled Francesca's wrist when she would have run, and dragged her close. "I am going to hypnotize her and plant all kinds of suggestions. You can help me, Skyler. I think she should revere me."

"While you're making suggestions, you can tell her no one else needs to take care of me, I only want her," Skyler said softly, more than half serious.

"No one else has authority over you, Skyler. These people are coming to *help* you during the hours I'm away," Francesca replied gently. "They are doing us a tremendous favor so that you will not be alone." Her voice was musical and seeped into Skyler's mind with a healing compulsion.

Gabriel made a rude noise, drawing Skyler's attention to him. "I noticed she used the words 'no one else.' Did you catch that, Skyler? Is she excluding me? I think I'm the authority in this house."

"You're not even good-looking," Skyler pointed out, laughing despite the seriousness of the situation.

"Oh, so now you need to be hypnotized, too," he threatened. "I should have known you women would stick together. Just remember this when you find yourself barking like a dog in your room and wondering how you got there."

"I'd be wondering why I was barking," Francesca contradicted. "The barking would be a bit much."

"I don't know," Skyler mused. "If the housekeeper came

in and found us all barking like dogs, she'd hightail it out of here and I'd be very happy."

"You will give them a chance, won't you, Skyler?" Francesca asked gently.

Skyler sighed softly. "I guess I don't have much choice. But I know I could stay by myself. I'm not a baby and I've spent most of my life alone."

"You have a point," Gabriel acknowledged. "Please do not misunderstand, Skyler. Francesca and I want you to have a housekeeper because we want to ensure your comfort and safety, not because we don't trust you. We are wealthy, little one, and you may become a target because of that. Francesca would spend an inordinate amount of time worrying if we did not adequately protect you."

Skyler's eyes were fixed on his face while she determined whether he was telling her the truth. Eventually she nodded. "I didn't think of that. I wouldn't want either of you to worry about me."

Francesca's touch was soothing, as always. "Try it for a while, honey. If they don't work out, we'll find someone you like."

Skyler made an attempt to ease the concern on Francesca's expressive face. "Aren't you worried about spoiling me just a little?"

At once Francesca smiled, her dark eyes brilliant with laughter. "I hope that we do. It will be such fun."

"You don't know the first thing about parenting, do you?" Skyler chastised. "I'm going to have to be the one to run things around here."

The doorbell cut off any further byplay between them, wiping the smile from Skyler's face. Francesca immediately circled the young woman's too-thin shoulders with a comforting arm. "They're here, aren't they?" Skyler whispered it, as if she were afraid to speak any louder. Francesca could feel her small body trembling.

She glanced at Gabriel, clearly worried. *"Perhaps we are pushing her too hard, expecting her to accept too many people in her life too fast."*

"She must be protected, my love. Our only other choice is to command her acceptance and we both agreed we would not do so unless necessary." Gabriel reached over to take Skyler's hand. "I do not like strangers in my home either, little one. Perhaps you will be my strength while Francesca performs her magic. If neither of us feels anything wrong with these people, we will attempt to integrate them into our home. Is that a deal?"

"What if I don't like the man?" Skyler asked, voicing her worst fear.

"Understand this, Skyler," he said softly. "If you ever have misgivings about any man, myself included, whether you have concrete reason or not, go directly to Francesca. Do not think about it, or worry about it, or hesitate in any way. Tell her immediately. Promise me you will do that." His voice was magical, so gentle and perfect it was impossible to resist.

Skyler stood still for a moment before she nodded solemnly. She found herself gripping Gabriel's and Francesca's hands as they moved through the house to the front door. Somehow, physical contact with them made her calmer. There was something extremely soothing about the couple. When she was between them, their peace seemed to fill her up and keep her fears at bay. She couldn't remember a time in her life when she wasn't afraid. Not until Francesca had found her huddled inside her own mind and had swamped her with waves of warmth and reassurance. Even the fact that Gabriel was a very overwhelming male didn't bother her. She knew he was powerful, she could feel it when she was close to him, yet Skyler found Gabriel's power comforting. He had given her his word and she believed him. She believed in both of them. They were determined to make her whole again, make her understand love and kindness and what true safety was.

Above Skyler's bent head, Francesca's black gaze met Gabriel's dark one in mute understanding. Both of them easily read the teenager's thoughts. Gabriel smiled his reassurance, wishing he could take Francesca into his arms and hold her close within the shelter of his heart and his mind, in the shelter of his body. She always thought of others, always wanted to help those in need, and her compassion was slowly rubbing off on him.

"I love you very much, Francesca." The emotion was so intense, the words spilled over from his mind, into hers.

Francesca felt the color rising in her cheeks. Gabriel could make her feel like a teenager, her heart fluttering at the brush of his hand. Sometimes he allowed himself to be so vulnerable. It was a very unusual trait in a Carpathian male.

His soft laughter echoed in her mind as she opened the front door. *"You do not know the first thing about the Carpathian male."*

Francesca gave him her haughtiest look when what she really wanted was to fling herself into his arms. Instead she smiled a welcome at the couple standing on her porch. "Please come in. Aidan sent word to expect you. It's very kind of you to help us out when we are in such great need."

The man stepped forward with an easy smile and held out his hand deliberately to Gabriel. "I'm Santino and this is my wife, Drusilla." He was clearly at ease despite the fact that he suspected what they were. He was completely unafraid to have Gabriel "read" him, and Gabriel liked him for that.

Santino was a good man with a sense of duty and a determination to do whatever it took to protect his family. He had been through sieges with vampires and their minions and knew the danger and what it took for the hunters to protect humans and Carpathians. He had willingly joined the ranks of the fighters by accepting the responsibility that came with knowing that vampires really existed. He had a quiet confidence about him, an air of capability that Gabriel liked immediately.

Gabriel could almost see Francesca's inward sigh of relief. Skyler was very quiet during the introductions, her face very pale, but both Santino and his wife were extraordinarily gentle with her. Drusilla was a small woman, with much the same build as Skyler, only rounder and soft-looking. She was more nervous than her husband, but neither Carpathian could detect anything other than sincere compassion for Skyler and determination to be of assistance to a child in distress. Francesca liked her immediately for that. Skyler obviously read only good in the couple because she began to slowly relax, loosening her death grip on their hands and even managing a faint smile once or twice in the course of the conversation.

Francesca showed the couple around the house, purposely excluding Skyler's bedroom. It was important the young woman felt she had her own privacy, a sanctuary no one would intrude on without permission or invitation. Drusilla was particularly happy with the kitchen and garden area. Santino was unhappy with the easy access from the street. To him protecting the household was a logistical nightmare. Both spoke French fluently with a distinctly American accent.

It was impossible not to feel at home and at peace in Francesca's home. There was something soothing and tranquil about the house. Drusilla smiled at her husband, suddenly happy with the decision they had made. It had not been an easy one. Their two children were in college and they were ready for a change, but coming to France had not been in their plans at all.

It had been the thought of the little girl so terribly abused and in need of someone to love and care for her that had tipped their decision in favor of the move. Still, it had been particular frightening for Drusilla. She loved Aidan and his wife Alexandria, but she had known them a long time. The things her husband had told her were so far-fetched, she was uncertain whether she believed them or not. It was true she had never seen either Aidan or his wife during the day, although her memories seemed to be vague. Before Santino had told her the truth about Aidan and Alexandria, she would have sworn she often had been with them during all hours of the day. Now she knew she hadn't.

She looked at Francesca closely, sneaking quick looks in an attempt to judge her personality. Would she be easy to work for? Drusilla wanted to make this house feel like her own home. She wanted to love poor little Skyler like a daughter. And she wanted to love Francesca and Gabriel as she did Aidan and Alexandria. Santino's parents had worked for Aidan all of their married lives. Santino had grown up in Aidan's home and loved him very much. She knew her husband's loyalty ran deep, a bond almost as strong as her marriage. Maybe stronger. She sighed and looked at her husband. Santino. She loved him so much. And she was very proud of him.

Drusilla caught Francesca smiling at her and hastily gave her a tentative smile in return. "I really love the house," she said, hoping to break the ice.

Francesca's smile reached her magnificent eyes. "Thank you, I've lived here a long time and it feels like home to me. I'm hoping it will feel the same to you. If the rooms aren't to your liking upstairs, or you need anything for the kitchen, please say so. It is, after all, entirely your domain."

"I can cook," Skyler said suddenly, surprising everyone. She had been very quiet, simply watching the others as they moved through the house. She stayed very close to Francesca and sometimes reached out and touched her arm as if to assure herself she wasn't alone.

"That's wonderful," Drusilla said immediately. "You'll have to show me all your favorite recipes. I know what Santino likes. Just about anything edible."

A ghost of a smile appeared on Skyler's face, but it didn't quite reach her eyes. This time she curled her fingers in Francesca's. Even as she did so, a strange look crossed her face. She leaned toward Francesca. "You asked me to tell you when the other was here. I can feel him right now."

Francesca went very still, her fingers forming a loose chain around Skyler's tiny wrist. "Do not look at anyone in the house, honey, just concentrate on something else to keep your mind occupied." *"Gabriel, he is with Skyler now. I am afraid he will use her to harm someone. Skyler couldn't bear that."*

"Do not enter her mind while he dwells there. I will do so and see what it is Lucian is seeking. More than likely

it is information and mischief. He does like his games." Gabriel smiled his reassurance at Skyler even while he sent a silent signal to Francesca to keep the conversation going with Santino and Drusilla.

"Be careful, Gabriel," Francesca said worriedly. She was very afraid of Lucian. She knew his power; knew he was a force unlike any other. *"You believe he will use Skyler against me, but I fear he will use her against you."*

Gabriel's only answer was a flood of warmth in her mind. "Come with me, sweetheart," he instructed very gently and took Skyler's hand in his, walking her to the den. As he passed the bookshelf, he handed her a book he had taken at random. "I am certain you will enjoy this very much."

Skyler took the book without question and opened it. She read in earnest, but even as she did so, a small smile was tugging at the corners of her soft mouth. "All this cloak-and-dagger stuff is interesting, isn't it, Gabe?"

Gabriel's black eyebrows shot up nearly to the ceiling. In all the long centuries of his existence, no one had ever thought to call him Gabe. "More respect, young lady, and less of this Gabe stuff." He merged his mind with hers quickly, not giving her time to think about it or tip off Lucian that he was joining them. Immediately he could feel the surge of power that signaled his twin's presence in the girl's young mind.

Lucian felt him at once. *"A little crowded for the two of us."*

"When were you reduced to using children to get your way? I thought perhaps you were strong enough to meet me face-to-face, but I see that your power has been slowly dwindling away." Gabriel spoke in a soft, pure voice, his tone hypnotic.

"You persist in taunting me. It has never worked, Gabriel. I doubt if I will be driven to accept your challenge. While you grow soft in that house surrounded by women, I am building a kingdom to rule."

Gabriel sighed softly. *"You sound like a child, Lucian. You would be bored ruling a kingdom. Find a monastery and read some books."*

"I have already done just that." Before Gabriel had a chance to "see" through Lucian's eyes and give him an idea where his twin might be, he felt the withdrawal. Lucian was gone from Skyler's mind that fast.

Skyler looked up at him. "He knew you gave me the book. He quoted from it and told me to look on page eighty-two. I looked up the quote and he'd repeated it word for word." She sounded awed by the feat.

"Lucian is a genius, Skyler, and he has a photographic memory."

She turned her wide eyes on him, old eyes. "You have one, too, don't you?"

Gabriel nodded. "Yes, I do, honey. Lucian is my brother, my twin. He likes to play games, not always nice ones. I do not want you to be afraid, but he has power and sometimes misuses it."

Skyler shook her head and handed Gabriel the book. "I'm not afraid of him, not at all. Why did Francesca tell me not to look at anybody?" She asked the question to see if Gabriel would tell her the truth.

His white teeth flashed and for the first time Skyler felt a small shiver run down her spine. She could see the predator in him clearly for a moment. "Lucian can do more than talk to you mind to mind. He is telepathic, but he also has other powers. He can use you if he is merged with you."

She hadn't expected this answer. Skyler stopped walking and stared up at him. "You really will answer my questions, won't you? No matter how bad it is, you will tell me the truth."

"What were you expecting, Skyler?"

She shrugged. "Most people lie to kids if the truth is difficult." Skyler ducked her head so that her hair spilled around her face. "I shouldn't have tested you like that. I suspected it was something like that."

"Is it too far-fetched for you to believe?" Gabriel asked curiously.

"Isn't it far-fetched that you and Francesca can talk to me in my mind? Isn't it far-fetched that I can talk to animals?"

He raised one eyebrow. "Can you?"

She nodded without looking at him, half afraid he might not believe her.

"I knew you had a built in barometer for trouble, but I did not realize how gifted you really are. We will have to work on that particular talent. Do you like animals?"

"Better than people," she admitted with a little grin. "Much better than people. I relate to animals. They have a code they live by. An honorable code."

"Some people have codes, sweetheart. Some people actually have honor and integrity. You should know that; you are one of them."

"Can you really help me speak to animals better?"

"I can help you develop what talent you have," he answered. "And it is very possible Francesca and I might be able to teach you to shield yourself from unwanted emotions when you are with other people."

"I'd like that." Her small teeth tugged at her lower lip.

"You have a different accent. It's nice. I like the way you twist your words."

"How did you learn to speak both English and French?"

Skyler shrugged again. "Languages are easy for me to pick up. I don't really know why, but I think my mother was the same way."

"She must have been a remarkable woman. I wish that I had known her, Skyler."

"Thank you," Skyler murmured. Her voice was soft and sweet, reminiscent of Francesca's. She did a peculiar little skip toward the stairs.

Gabriel moved through the house, silently listening to the sounds of the humans. It wasn't nearly as uncomfortable as he'd thought it would be sharing the same dwelling. He had touched Santino's mind and found him to be a loyal, courageous man. He had never spent much time among humans, could call none his friend. But Santino was solid and had a good heart. There was no hidden agenda in the man. And his wife was sweet and good-natured. She was uncertain whether or not she believed the things Santino had told her about Aidan and his lifemate, but she was willing to live with Santino anywhere he chose and she was determined to make his home a happy one.

Gabriel found himself smiling as he moved through the large house. The noises were becoming familiar, almost comforting. The different scents that filled the air made the house all the more homey.

"You like them." Francesca made it a statement as she slipped up behind Gabriel to circle his narrow waist with her arms. She rested her head against his broad back.

"Yes, I like them," he conceded. "I do not know whether

the woman will run screaming from the house if a vampire should actually attack us here."

"I don't know if I'd run screaming from the house," Francesca laughed. "Skyler has gone to bed. She's very tired. I sat with her for a few moments to be sure she was healing. But you know, my love, I'm incredibly hungry." There was a soft suggestion in her voice.

He placed his larger hand over hers. "Again? Just how often am I going to have to feed you?"

Her hands moved over his body, shaping his muscles, exploring the most intriguing places. "It isn't just for me," she reminded him. "In any case, you know perfectly well that isn't the hunger I'm talking about."

He turned around to pull her into his arms, cradling her as if her weight was no more than a child's. His black eyes burned over her face with such hunger and intensity it took her breath away. "And what kind of hunger would that be, Francesca? I love when you ask me for what you want."

"Gabriel." She breathed his name with a kind of wonder, drew a caressing hand along his stubborn jaw. Her Gabriel. Her legend. So incredibly sexy. "I am not asking, lifemate, I am demanding. My body hungers for yours. I'm burning inside and only you know how to satisfy me."

They were moving quickly through the corridor to their bedchamber. "I can do no other than please you."

"Hmmm, I think I wish to please *you*. I want you in my mouth, I want to see your face as you make love to me, I want to feel you hard and hot and so much a part of me I will never, never be able to get you out."

His mouth found hers, rocking her world while clothes littered the corridor. Already his fingers were deep inside her wet, welcoming core, pushing deep, stroking the heat, while he kissed her until she didn't know where he started and she left off. In the chamber she pushed at the wall of his chest, insisting on her own right to taste him, to tease him, her mind merged with his to share the experience, to allow him the heady satisfaction of knowing she wanted to drive him over the edge of control. Gabriel, who was always so controlled, was thrusting helplessly, a harsh cry torn from his throat as she tasted his essence. He pulled her into his arms and settled her onto his lap, filling her completely, his hands guiding her hips while he watched her slow, lazy ride, her hair covering her body so that her breasts could peek provocatively at him.

"You are the most beautiful, sexy woman on earth," he whispered softly. He had absolutely no intention of sleeping or allowing Francesca to go to sleep for a long, long while.

Chapter Fifteen

The doorbell let out a soft, melodious peal, announcing a visitor. Santino glanced at his wife and wished he didn't feel so apprehensive. Everything in Francesca and Gabriel's house was harmonious, even the doorbell, yet he had an ominous premonition of disaster. Skyler paled visibly and shrank into a little ball in the armchair. Her eyes seemed enormous in her small face as she hugged her stuffed animal to her. Santino wanted to put his arms around her and hold her, but she was careful to avoid any physical contact with him.

Drusilla glanced at him, then moved over to stand beside Skyler's chair, partially blocking the visitor's view of the teenager. They had both noticed that Skyler seemed to know when trouble was coming, and right now she seemed very apprehensive.

Brice stabbed at the doorbell again with his finger, determined to see Francesca. He had developed an obsession. He couldn't sleep at night anymore, certain she was in danger. He thought of her every waking moment, planning and scheming ways to get her out from under Gabriel's black spell. Now he knew just the right thing to say to make her listen, but it was a total stranger who answered the door. Brice heard a buzzing in his head. It was happening more and more frequently, a prelude to the terrible merciless headaches.

"Who the devil are you?" he demanded rudely. How many men did Francesca have in her life anyway? Was he going to have to resort to violence? Gabriel probably had a gang of some kind; maybe he really did belong to organized crime.

Santino raised his eyebrow. "I beg your pardon," he answered softly, his face an expressionless mask.

Brice clenched his teeth, his fingers actually curling into fists. "This house belongs to Francesca Del Ponce, a very close friend of mine. Where is she?"

"She is out at the moment. May I tell her who inquired after her?" Santino asked politely. He watched the other man closely, wondering about him. No one had warned him to expect trouble dressed in an expensive suit.

Brice swallowed his anger and pressed his fingertips to his throbbing temple. "I'm Skyler's doctor. I'm here to check on her."

Drusilla felt the young woman instantly grow still and she looked down at her. Skyler was so white she looked like a ghost. The child had buried her face against the wolf; only her eyes peered out in alarm. Drusilla reached down and put her hand very lightly on Skyler's shoulder. The girl's slight body was trembling.

"I wasn't aware Skyler had a doctor's appointment.

Francesca is usually very good about informing me of the day's schedule," Santino improvised smoothly.

"Francesca promised me she would bring Skyler to the hospital for a checkup."

Skyler made a small sound of distress, so low only Drusilla heard her. Santino glanced back at them, and his wife shook her head quickly. "I'm sorry, Doctor, but until Francesca returns, I'm afraid there's little I can do. I'll tell her you called," he said softly, easily.

"I'll take Skyler to the hospital myself," Brice volunteered immediately.

Skyler pressed back among the pillows, determined not to move one inch. She stared up at Santino helplessly.

Santino smiled his reassurance at the teenager. "I'm very sorry, sir, but as I haven't received any orders from Francesca, I cannot allow Skyler to leave the premises. I'm certain Francesca will make arrangements as soon as possible to bring Skyler in." He stood solidly in the doorway so that Brice had no chance to push his way in.

Color swept instantly up Brice's neck into his face, giving his cheeks a ruddy glow. His temples were throbbing so hard he dug his thumb into the pulse point to try to ease the pain. "She is my patient whether Gabriel likes it or not. I won't allow that man to dictate to me whether or not I examine my patients."

Santino continued to smile pleasantly. "I'm very sorry, sir. My French must not be very easily understood. Gabriel did not give me any orders concerning you at all. I was speaking of Francesca. She is the one who insisted Skyler remain indoors and without the stress of company. I'm certain she did not mean you, sir, as you are Skyler's doctor, but I cannot go against her direct orders. I'm sure she'll clear up this misunderstanding as soon as she returns."

Brice swore angrily, glaring daggers at Santino. "I don't even know you. Why would Francesca leave you in charge of my patient? I insist on coming in and speaking with Skyler. I want to make certain she is all right."

Santino continued to smile, but his eyes were flat and cold. "Are you suggesting I might be holding the young lady in captivity in her own house?"

"I don't know what you're doing. Francesca is a *close* friend of mine." Brice's tone implied all sorts of things. "She would have told me if she'd made arrangements for Skyler's care."

"Perhaps you are not quite as good a friend as you thought you were, sir," Santino replied very softly.

Brice stepped forward to crowd the man, fury ripping through him, nearly overwhelming his good sense. "How dare you?"

Santino didn't budge. He didn't flinch. He simply stood in the doorway, a solid, muscular frame impossible to move. Behind Brice a man moved out of the shadows. Skyler's bodyguard stood at the bottom of the stairs with his arms folded. Brice swallowed his rage and stepped away from Santino. "Skyler, get out here. You're coming with me. I mean it. If you don't come now, I'm going straight to the judge and insist you be placed in my custody immediately."

Skyler buried her face in her hands with a small moan of fear.

Beneath the earth in the secret chamber lay two bodies, as still as death. A single heart began to beat where before there had been only silence. Gabriel felt the strength of the girl's fear and it had awakened him. Instantly he felt his twin's presence. At that moment they were one being with one thought. Someone had threatened a child under their protection, and this wasn't to be tolerated.

Gabriel could not explain such a phenomenon to Francesca. This was what made Lucian unique. It was what made it so difficult to condemn and hunt him. Lucian merged with him and at once they were bonded, strong and lethal, of one mind on the hunt. Whatever his motive, Lucian was as determined as Gabriel that Skyler not be further intimidated. Gabriel could no more close himself off to his brother than give up protecting the women. At that moment, they were truly one being.

Gabriel disconnected with his body, his spirit rising above his body and moving swiftly through the earth upward toward the main house. It was a peculiar wrenching feeling to be out of one's body, disorienting and yet strangely exhilarating. Gabriel was at his lowest point of power in the afternoon, but he could travel without his body and he did so now, moving swiftly through the house until he was in the room where the disturbance was occurring.

Light was streaming into the room despite Santino's large frame blocking the door way. Gabriel flinched from the sunlight although he was without his body and the light could not blind him. He went to Skyler's trembling figure huddled so small on the couch, forlorn and lost without Francesca and Gabriel to protect her from the world. He flooded her with warmth and a feeling of safety, while Lucian lent his own strength and power so that she was instantly soothed.

Skyler lifted her head and looked around her, puzzled that she should sense Gabriel's presence even though he wasn't in the room with her. She glanced at Drusilla to see whether she felt anything. She wasn't going to go with Brice no matter what any of them said.

"Of course you won't, honey." It was a distinctly masculine voice, soothing, comforting, filling her with confidence. *"Neither Santino nor I will allow anyone to take you against your will from this house. Brice is ill."*

Skyler felt the presence of Gabriel, strong and powerful, in her mind. She recognized the touch of the other one, the one they all seemed to worry about, just as strong and powerful as Gabriel, his strength pouring into her along with Gabriel's. Skyler knew she would be protected. She had never felt part of a family before. It was a strange and even unnatural feeling to her, yet she wanted it desperately. She wanted to believe that Santino, Drusilla, and the bodyguard, Jarrod Silva, would protect her and be loyal to her in the same way she knew Gabriel and Francesca would. She had reservations about the other, only because she knew Gabriel and Francesca both were wary of him. She couldn't fathom why, although she had given it much thought and had even tried to "read" the couple when they touched her.

Skyler attempted to reach out to Gabriel, felt frustrated for a moment, then laughed softly at herself. All she had to do was think a reply in her head. *"I told Francesca something was wrong with the doctor. He doesn't feel the same as he used to feel. I am more afraid for Francesca than for myself. I think Dr. Brice is nuts."*

"You must have faith in me. I would not allow Brice to harm Francesca." Gabriel knew what her fear was, knew Skyler was afraid that Brice would hurt Francesca, would somehow separate them. *"It will not happen, no one will take you from us."* His voice was reassuring, so perfectly tranquil and soothing that Skyler regained her confidence

immediately and was able to peer around Drusilla to smile a little impertinently at the doctor.

"I think you are frightening Skyler, sir," Santino said more softly than ever. There was the merest hint of a threat in his voice this time.

Beside him, Gabriel stirred, a cold breeze washing over Brice, swamping him with fear such as he had never known before. He was choking on it, his skin crawling with the feel of tiny insects, thousands of them attacking his body so that he began raking at his own flesh in an attempt to rid himself of the things.

Santino exchanged a worried glance with Jarrod over the doctor's head. The man was acting as if he had the DTs. More than ever they were determined to protect Skyler from the doctor. The man needed a padded cell in a psych ward. Maybe a good detox center. Without warning, the doctor slammed his body into Santino's in an effort to get to Skyler.

Afterward, Brice could never remember why he'd done such a rash thing. His head was pounding abominably and his skin was crawling; he thought; he would go mad. His only coherent thought was Francesca. She echoed in his mind with each throb of his pulse. He literally bounced off Santino's chest and landed on his backside.

At once Jarrod was looming over him, his face an expressionless mask. "I think it best you leave, sir," he said firmly. "I do not want to embarrass you by calling the authorities to escort you off the property. I know you are a good friend of Francesca's and she would be appalled at this display. If you don't mind my saying so, sir, I believe you need to check yourself into a clinic." He bent down and with ease lifted Brice to his feet.

Brice was a wreck, physically and mentally. He could

hardly think with the terrible buzzing in his head. His body was jerking and twitching almost as if he were suffering seizures. Pills, he needed more pills, then his body and mind would calm down. He tried to be reasonable. Some shred of dignity and pride prompted him to walk away, yet he couldn't force his trembling body to do it. The bodyguard had to drag him off the property.

Skyler held her hands over her eyes, shutting out the sight of her doctor, almost foaming at the mouth. She had seen drool and spittle spraying as he talked. "What's wrong with him?" she whispered aloud, whispered it to Gabriel. Beneath Drusilla's palm, the teen was trembling, retreating. At once Francesca and Gabriel moved quickly to surround her, their warmth and love sending her waves of reassurance. She felt the other one, too, his presence strong and powerful.

Santino closed the door firmly on the distasteful scene. "I'm sorry, Skyler. I'm afraid that poor doctor has been sampling his own medicine. He's way gone on drugs."

"Why was he trying to get to me?" Skyler asked in a low voice. She was beginning to believe she might actually be safe here in this house.

Gabriel decided the truth would be best. *"I believe he thought to use you in some way to get to Francesca."*

"I don't know," Santino answered gently. "Perhaps he thinks in his twisted mind that you are in some kind of danger and he is rescuing you. He doesn't know me, I'm a stranger in this land. Whatever his reason, he can't take you from this house. You are perfectly safe here, Skyler. I gave my word to Francesca and I did not give it lightly."

Skyler was very confused. Why were all these people suddenly protecting her? They were all virtual strangers, yet they were willing to risk violence to protect her. Why?

She clutched tightly at her stuffed animal, the first gift she'd ever received.

"You are now a part of our family." It was said quietly and with great authority. There was no way to dispute Gabriel's beautiful voice. He spoke with such purity, Skyler could only believe him. At once she relaxed, allowing herself to breathe normally.

Gabriel's heart twisted at the sight of her. She looked very small, far younger than her age. Except for her eyes. There was something about her large gray eyes that held far too much knowledge, none of it good. Gabriel wished he could stamp out that look for all time, but it was impossible.

"You have grown so soft, Gabriel. This child you profess to feel such affection for should have been avenged."

Francesca, listening through Gabriel, went very still, touching Skyler's mind to learn whether Lucian was broadcasting to the teen as well. She could hear the vampire through his connection to her lifemate. But Skyler was unaware of the conversation, paying attention instead to Santino.

"I grow weary of your constant taunts, Lucian. Perhaps it is the only way you have left to torment me, but it is growing tedious and no longer bothers me. Revenge has never been our way. We do what we must to maintain the secrets of our race. We destroy the undead, but it is out of duty, not out of revenge. In any case, the man claiming to be her father had to be removed from this earth and you destroyed the others that were in her memories, saving me the trouble. You have forgotten the difference between justice and revenge. Meet with me, Lucian, that we may come to terms."

"I know what is in your mind, brother. You seek to hunt

me. You believe still that you can destroy me. If I wish it, I can kill the girl, your silly woman, and those humans you have installed in her house. You cannot prevent it with your safeguards. I taught you those safeguards."

Gabriel gave the mental equivalent of a shrug. He was floating back toward the chamber, away from the light of day into the earth that held his body for him. He saw Francesca lying there, although he knew her essence was not asleep. At once a sense of peace and warmth seeped into his soul. Without thought he projected it to his twin, a sharing of intense love. Even before he could register that he had done such a thing, before he could judge Lucian's reaction, his brother was gone.

Gabriel's cry of anguish at his brother's rejection echoed to Francesca. Gabriel settled into his own body beside Francesca, wide-awake but unable to move. His heart was pounding loudly in the underground chamber and his chest was tight and burning with pain for his lost brother.

Beside him Francesca's heart began to beat a slow, strong rhythm. She turned her head slowly and looked up at him. The movement must have taken tremendous effort, yet her expression was one of such love it robbed him of breath. She moved her hand, a slow process of pushing her fingers toward his so that they finally met.

"You are never alone, my love." Her words were clear and strong. *"It does not matter that he cannot feel what you share. He is undead, no longer your beloved twin brother. Mourn the one long gone from this earth. His empty shell remains behind, but the one you love so much, the one you honor is beyond pain and heartache now. I am here with you, our child grows in me, and our house is filled with warmth and promise."*

"Why would he merge with me and give me added

power to help Santino and Jarrod keep Skyler safe? What plan could he have but to use that child as a weapon?"

"His plans do not matter, Gabriel. Together we are strong enough to face him. We are a mirror he cannot look in." Her voice filled him with love and warmth. He felt so peaceful Gabriel wanted to stay there for eternity.

"I want you to see him as I once, did." Gabriel wanted her to understand his great sorrow in the face of their love. He wanted her to know he valued her all the more because of Lucian, never less. He opened his mind fully to her, sharing his past, the terrible battles, the endless loneliness that only his link to his twin had made bearable. He showed Lucian's endless strength and power, his great genius, his search for knowledge to understand the mysteries of their race. Time and again Lucian had risked his body and soul for Gabriel's safety, for the safety of their people and that of the human race.

Francesca watched the scenes playing out from Gabriel's memories. She could see Lucian as he had once been. Without the taint of a vampire. Intelligent. Always placing himself in danger to shield his twin, always taking the lead in every dangerous situation. Countless times he gave his blood when he was mortally wounded himself, countless times he dragged himself to his twin and healed him when he was close to death. Gabriel saw his twin as the most selfless Carpathian ever born and he shared that memory with Francesca. She understood and her heart ached all the more for her lifemate.

He had exchanged vows with Lucian, promising to destroy him should he lose his soul and become the very thing they hunted. Gabriel knew Lucian would never have rested until he had completed the task, and he could do no less. Francesca understood the enormity of that vow, knew it was a part of Gabriel as much as the lungs he used to breathe. She loved him all the more for his devotion, was determined to find a way to aid him.

Lucian was alive to her now. She had shared their lives and those centuries of loneliness they both had endured. Gabriel now had her, but Lucian was lost to them, lost to their people along with his great genius and his iron will and tremendous power. His loss was a senseless, terrible tragedy.

With effort, Francesca inched her body closer to Gabriel's so that their skin touched. Their limbs felt like lead, lethargic and heavy. Normally they shut down their hearts and lungs during daylight hours, sparing themselves the terrible knowledge of their helplessness and vulnerability to enemies. Francesca lay close to Gabriel for a long time before she spoke. *"When you felt the disturbance, Gabriel, and Skyler's fear, did you reach for Lucian?"*

Gabriel thought it over. *"I cannot honestly say. I felt him with me as I always do in moments when I need strength and power. It is an ingrained habit neither of us seems to be able to break."* He was silent a moment. *"If you think to find a way to exploit this strange phenomenon between us to defeat him, I have already tried. It is as natural as breathing. I do not know when I do it and neither does he."*

"Yes, but he is a vampire. An undead creature. He should not be able to travel while the sun is at its highest peak. You are the most powerful of our males and it was a great effort for you to release your spirit from your body. How could he do such a thing, being a vampire?"

Gabriel gave the mental equivalent of a shrug. *"His mind shared mine and he threw his power behind me. He could have just as easily attempted to stop me or kept me from reentering my body. It is just as well that whatever game he thinks to play requires our Skyler. His power is great, Francesca. I would have been happy throwing up a wall in front of the doctor, but Lucian was not. He twisted my power so that Brice felt thousands of insects crawling on his skin."*

"Don't remind me." Francesca was not happy with that at all. She felt guilty about Brice. Something was happening that she didn't understand. *"I tried to tone down his memories of me so that he would think of me only as a friend, but it didn't work. I've never had that happen before."*

Gabriel's fingers tightened around hers. He knew the reason she could not control the doctor's mind and Francesca must know it also. She simply wasn't ready to face the truth. Gabriel wanted to hold her close in his arms to protect her. In his mind he surrounded her with love and support. *"A vampire has somehow managed to ensnare him. There is no other explanation."*

Francesca wanted to shake her head in denial. *"There are other explanations. I saw him popping pills."*

"And why did he lead you to the cemetery where the vampires were waiting for you? He is in league with them and does not know it. They are using him to get you. That is why you cannot control him. He is controlled by the undead. When you attempt to reach his mind, there is nothing there but the orders they have given him."

"Is it Lucian? Has Lucian done this to punish me for my feelings for Brice?"

"You cannot imagine what it is like to be unable to feel emotion. Lucian has no need to punish. He feels nothing at all. He uses others as puppets in the hope of feeling amusement, but he cannot. I did not detect the taint of

his power, yet I cannot say for certain. Lucian prefers to work alone at all times. To my knowledge he has never brought another into what he refers to as 'the game.' "

"Can you undo what they did to Brice? Is there a way to make him whole again? This is my fault, Gabriel, entirely my fault because I became friends with a human. Now they think to use him against us. He is totally helpless."

Gabriel could not bear her unhappiness. He would do anything to take the sorrow from her mind. He tightened his fingers around hers even as he flooded her mind with love and warmth and comfort. *"You are so right, my love. We are not alone in our struggles and our tasks. We have each other to draw strength from. As long as we believe in each other, it will all come right. I will do what I can for Brice. If you wish me to try to save him, you know I will have to take his blood. Without a blood bond, I doubt if I can break what others have wrought."*

Francesca turned that idea over in her mind. The blood bond was a powerful weapon. Would it somehow put Gabriel in danger? Would the vampire, perhaps Lucian, expect such a move and somehow be able to use Brice as a weapon against Gabriel?

Gabriel, locked as he was to her mind, was enormously pleased that her first thought would be for him, for his safety. She loved him in the way of a true lifemate. For who he was and what he was. Unconditionally. She saw good in him where he was never certain it really existed, but he lived up to her expectations all the same.

"Do it then, Gabriel. Take his blood and I will see to his healing with you. I owe him that much. He is a great doctor and the world would lose much if his healing abil-

ities were destroyed." She smiled up at him even as her lashes drifted down.

Gabriel felt her smile in his heart. It was like that with her. She turned him inside out with one look. Just by closing her eyes. He lay for a long while beneath the earth, feeling its vibrations, allowing it to murmur to him, soothe and comfort him, rejuvenate his body with its nourishment. He left the chamber at the first setting of the sun and fed well before returning to awaken his lifemate. He lifted her body in his arms, floated to the bedchamber hidden in the rocks of the earth yet fitted with human comforts—the four-poster bed, the long, heavy drapes, and hundreds of candles.

The candles sprang to life with a simple wave of his hand, immediately enveloping the chamber in a soft, fresh scent. He inhaled sharply, then took in the sight of her body. She was so beautiful, so feminine. Gabriel bent over her and whispered softly, "Wake, my love, I want you so badly I do not think I can wait until you are breathing properly." His mouth moved over her neck, her small shell-like ear. He found her pulse and lingered as it began, as her body heated beneath his hands. His teeth scraped her exquisite skin. So soft, so perfect.

Gabriel liked the way the dancing flames played over her body. Her high, firm breasts were full and inviting, her rib cage narrow, her waist small. He bent his head to follow the clean line of her form, followed the dancing shadows with his mouth even while he created his own flames licking along her skin. His lips explored the small mound of her belly, the intriguing ridges of her hipbones.

Francesca smiled, her eyes still closed while her heart raced and her blood heated and her world contracted to include only sensuous, erotic feeling. His thick hair brushed over her body while his teeth nipped and his tongue stroked and her blood heated to molten lava in her veins. She felt him worship her with the gentle touch of his exploring hands, which lingered in every sensitive spot on her body. She lay quiet, simply enjoying the sensations he was creating with each stroke of his tongue, each time his silky hair moved over her bare skin.

How had she ever faced a rising without him? How had she ever wanted to open her eyes without the promise of seeing his beloved face? She knew every line, the strength in his jaw, the arch of his brow, the perfect shape of his mouth. She sighed softly in contentment and moved to give him better access to her breast. Her slender arms curved around his head, cradling him to her while he leisurely enjoyed her.

His scent enveloped her and her temperature soared. With it rose her hunger. She stirred beneath his strong hands, her body alive with needs, with a thousand secrets. She was a temptation, an invitation, an enticement. She buried her face in his neck, felt his body burn hotter against hers. Francesca's smile was frankly sexy with a woman's knowledge of her own power. Her teeth scraped his neck, her tongue swirling around in a small, lapping caress. She opened her mind more fully to him so that he could see her desire, share her feelings, the pleasure he was bringing to her body.

At once he responded to the erotic images in her head, his hand moving lower to find her hot pulsating entrance. She was creamy with need and excitement, wanting to share her body and heart with him. Gabriel couldn't help the shudder of pleasure moving through him when her hands shaped his body, her fingers tightening like a sheath, her mouth on his neck. She whispered something softly in his mind, a plea, a need, a hunger she couldn't ignore.

Gabriel caught her small hips in his hands to slide her beneath him more fully, to lift her body to his. His breath caught in his throat as he held her still for one heartbeat, one moment while he looked into her beautiful eyes. He saw her stark hunger, so sexual, so erotic, all for him. He wanted to capture the moment, keep it, prolong it, but then she slowly lowered her head to his chest and deliberately caressed his pulse with her tongue. It was slow and sexy and beyond anything his imagination could have conjured up.

He saw the beauty of her mouth as it slid over his chest, felt the heat of her call, wild and untamed, and then white-hot lightning sizzled and danced through his body, through his mind and heart, and he surged forward with one deep hard stroke, taking possession of her body while her teeth sank deeply into his skin. He heard his own husky cry, drawn from somewhere deep within his soul, and he felt tears burning in his throat and behind his eyes at the sheer beauty of it all.

She was fire and velvet, lightning and thunder, molten lava taking him to a place he hadn't known existed. His fingers dug into her hips, clamping her to him while he performed the most erotic tango of his life. She knew every way to move to please him, her body adjusting to his rhythm almost before he knew. Her mind was filled only with thoughts of him, of his body, of giving him pleasure, of the pure enjoyment he gave her. She lapped at the tiny pinpricks on his chest when she was finished feeding.

Francesca caught his thick hair in her hand and brought his head down to hers, finding his mouth and kissing him, sharing his exotic taste while she moved her hips ever faster, rising to meet each thrust with one of her own. Her muscles clenched tightly around him, a fiery friction, holding him, milking and teasing and luring him on so that he was as wild as she was.

He stretched her arms over her head while he took her again and again, while the earth shook and her body and mind went up in flames. Still he gave her no rest, lapping at the small beads of sweat, tasting their pleasure from the pores of her skin, wanting all of her in case this memory would have to carry over into the next world. This union with her, this was true mating. He wanted to give her as much pleasure as a man could possibly give the one woman he loves. He wanted the memory of himself in her skin, in her body, in her deepest soul.

When she was tired and lay passive in his arms he found her breasts, so full and seductive, filling his mouth with creamy softness until her nipples were hard and begging for more. He cupped her bottom, pressing her close to him, his hands everywhere, arousing, memorizing, simply worshiping. He would never get enough of her, no matter how long he lived, and if he had only a short while, he wanted to bring her every pleasure he could, give her every good thing she deserved.

Francesca lay quietly, knowing what he was doing, knowing he needed to be with her this rising before he went off to face the worst of his enemies. She wanted him to make love to her, to never stop. She wanted her body to hold him to her. She wanted him safe in their chamber, in their own world of pleasure and beauty and love, not out there in the night where something malevolent crouched and waited.

Once she found herself laughing on the floor, and neither of them had any idea how they'd got there. But as she went to climb into the bed, he trapped her against the mattress, leaning over her, his body possessive, his hands strong as he took her again, riding her until they both went up in flames. It was paradise, yet at the same time it was a kind of hell. Between them always lay the fact that he was going out; he must hunt the undead. Long after the candles burned low and the lights were barely tiny flickers on the walls, they curled up in each other's arms, holding each other close.

Francesca wanted them to be wearing the same skin, she wanted to be that close. She wished somehow she could prevent the future from happening. She wouldn't ask him not to go, he had to go. She knew it in heart and mind and soul. It was who Gabriel was. For the first time she truly understood why he had chosen to fight, to hunt. Gabriel was the only one capable of defeating Lucian. The entire world, human and Carpathian alike, depended upon him.

His hands were tangled in her thick hair, his mouth against her breast. "Listen to me, my love. Hear me. If I do not succeed this night, it will be all right. You will take Skyler and our child and go home to the Carpathian Mountains. Mikhail will guard you for me. *You* and only you will raise our child. I want our child to know you and to know me through your eyes. I know it will be difficult for you, but you are strong and I will dwell in your heart. Wherever I am, I will wait patiently for you, knowing you are carrying out the task that is so important to me. To both of us."

Francesca closed her eyes against the hot tears threatening to fall. She felt his breath so warm against her skin, his arms tight around her, locking her body to his. Their legs were tangled together and yet it wasn't enough. It would never be enough. She couldn't go with him, and if he was defeated, she couldn't follow him until their child no longer needed her.

Gabriel raised himself above her, looking down onto her beautiful face. "Francesca, you can do this thing for both of us. Give me your word."

"Do you have any idea what you are asking of me?" The words were a strangled whisper and with the stirring of her breath the last of the flames spluttered and went out. The chamber was once more inky black.

Gabriel could easily see her beloved face, the shimmering tears she was so valiantly trying not to shed. He bent his head to taste a teardrop. "You have given me more happiness than I could ever have dared to hope for. I want our daughter to know you, Francesca, your courage, your compassion, the essence of you. You are the best part of me. I love you more than life on this earth, more than my own life or that of my brother. I thank God every day for you." His mouth drifted lazily over her face, her long, wet spiky lashes, along her high cheekbones, the corners of her mouth, and down to her throat. "Please do not feel sorrow. What I have done, I have done to the best of my ability. I cannot regret my choices, nor would I change anything but the briefness of the time I have had with you. Eternity looks good when I know I'll eventually share it with you, honey."

Francesca clasped her arms around him, holding him tightly to her. Love was an overwhelming, all-encompassing emotion. *He* was her life; he had somehow become her life. "Come home to me, Gabriel. Do not make me face a life of emptiness without you again. I was strong the first time because somehow I convinced myself that we were working together, you hunting and me healing. We were apart, but for many centuries, you were still with me."

His tongue swirled over the creamy swell of her breast, then traced a line along her rib. "And I will still be with you. No matter where my body may be, I will be in your heart, in your soul." His mouth moved over her heart, a warm dance of flames.

"You have to believe you can defeat him, Gabriel. You have to know you can. I am willing to aid you. We can work together. I can at least share my strength and power with you."

Gabriel smiled against her satin skin, nuzzled her breast again, unable to ignore such an erotic temptation. "You will not aid me in any way. You cannot connect with my mind while I am hunting. It is dangerous, my love. Lucian will know the moment you are with me and he will use me to harm you in some way. That would be much more likely than your giving me strength. You have to trust me to know what to do."

Her body was a miracle to him. Everywhere he touched her, each time he touched her, it was an incredible experience. He shifted his body to blanket her once more, his thigh edging hers so that he could lie over her, his body easily, naturally pinning hers.

Francesca could feel him, thick and heavy, so hot with need there was an answering fire immediately in her body. She smiled up at him, raising her hips as he surged into her, leaving her breathless and beautiful and hungry for him all over again. "Just come back to me, Gabriel," she whispered softly against his throat. "I love you so much and I am no longer so very strong without you beside me."

He was tender and gentle, his body moving in hers with long, sure strokes to heighten her pleasure. "I will always be with you, Francesca. In this life or the next, there is only you. That is a promise I know I can keep."

Chapter Sixteen

It was well past midnight and the lights of the city were soft and muted by the layers of fog hanging in the night sky. Gabriel stood on the balcony looking not at the city but at the young girl asleep inside the adjoining room. She looked far too small for her large bed, a slight figure clutching a stuffed animal beneath the intricate quilt Francesca had made. His heart went out to the teenager. She looked so vulnerable and childlike in her sleep. She still was not completely safe. She was a rare gift to his people and she would be much sought after. It was a precious treasure he was guarding and the weight of the responsibility was tremendous. In her slender body and gifted mind, she might carry the life or death of one of their Carpathian males.

With a wave of his hand he closed the door firmly and the locks slid into place. His hands moved gracefully, weaving intricate safeguards at every entrance to the room. Skyler would be safe from all but Lucian. Gabriel did not fool himself into thinking his twin would be unable to get past what he had wrought. Lesser vampires would be hurt, trapped, and probably held until the dawn could bring them justice, but not Lucian. In two thousand years no trap had ever successfully held him and there was no safeguard that he could not unravel.

Gabriel rested his palms on the wrought-iron railing and stared down at the greenery below him. The garden was beautiful, colors exploding even in the night air. He found himself smiling. Francesca. She had a way of making everything she touched alive with beauty. Of course she would choose flowers that could bloom at night. She would want things pleasing and soothing in her house and in her garden, no matter what the time of day or night. It mattered to her that others were comfortable, were surrounded by beauty.

He filled his mind with thoughts of her, and of course she filled his heart instantly. She always put others before herself, before her own needs. She had tried to be so tough with him, but from the moment Francesca had entered his life, she had been the one continuously giving. She soothed those around her with her spirit alone. She didn't have to do anything other than simply be who she was, yet she did so much more. Even now, she was allowing him to go, knowing he might not return to her, selflessly giving him to the world when she wanted him so desperately beside her. She was with child. His child. If he were to die this night, she had promised to continue without him even though the separation would be agony for her.

His body ached for her even though he had just spent hours with her, precious, wonderful hours that had given him so much more than he had ever thought possible. His heart and soul ached for her. This house was his home. These people were his family. But out in the night, creatures were stalking the innocent and he had no choice but to stop them.

Gabriel watched the heavy fog moving through the city. It was not a natural fog, but one created to allow the undead to move unseen by their prey. He lifted his face to the shadow of the moon and drank in the beauty of it. He was a hunter of the night. A natural predator. He leaped easily onto the railing and spread his arms wide, embracing the air as he stepped into space.

At once his body shimmered, becoming transparent so that the heavy fog could be seen right through him. He seemed to dissolve into millions of droplets; which streamed through the sky, weaving in and out of the dark clouds and the heavy fog. He flew out over the city, scanning as he went, looking for "dead" spaces that might indicate where the enemy was hiding. The small group of vampires that had banded together in the city were hunting for victims, for live prey to be used and discarded.

Gabriel was determined to rid the city of the undead this night, and he wanted to find Brice. He knew Brice's fate weighed heavily on Francesca's conscience and he was determined that he would put things right. He freely admitted he had little use for the man, but Francesca felt affection for the doctor and the things he had done lately had been committed under the influence of a vampire. Perhaps even Lucian, although Gabriel doubted it. He would never have sent Brice to the house to take Skyler from them and then aid Gabriel in sending him away. There was no point in such a move.

A few nightspots were teaming with life, the perfect

hunting grounds for the vampires. They would find prey to their liking, young men and women they could manipulate into all kinds of deviant behavior just for the perverse pleasure of making them squirm before giving them death.

He moved through the city in silence, scanning for the undead even as he searched for a hint of Brice. Twice he moved over the hospital, knowing Brice often spent long hours there, but, instead, he found him in the cemetery, drawn, no doubt, by his connection to the unclean *nosferatu*. Gabriel stayed high in the fog, carefully examining the area for one of the undead. Brice was shuffling over the uneven ground, stumbling like a drunken man, muttering to himself, and constantly batting at his body as if he still felt the crawling of bugs over his skin.

Gabriel had withdrawn that illusion as soon as Brice was off the property, but one of the vampires controlling the doctor must have picked the memory out of his head and used it to punish his failure to obtain Skyler. Gabriel felt the malevolent presence of one of the vampires. Not an ancient, more likely one recently turned, running with a pack to learn as much as he could as fast as he could. They thought they were banding together for protection against the hunters, but more often than not, the ancient vampires used the lesser ones as pawns, to be sacrificed.

Had Lucian joined this group? The question nagged at Gabriel. He shook the thought away. It was much more likely that Lucian would control those around him from a distance so that they would never know what was happening to them. Gabriel had seen him do it often enough. His voice alone was one of the most powerful weapons Gabriel had ever encountered. Lucian had never allowed anyone else to intrude on their battles, he had disposed of other vampires in the areas where Gabriel had chased him. He never left evidence any other hunter would recognize. Lucian was not messy about his kills.

Gabriel streamed to earth, the tiny droplets coming together just out of sight of Brice. For a moment the large frame shimmered and sparkled like crystal before it solidified. Then Gabriel was striding through the cemetery to cut Brice off before he could make his way to the caverns where the vampire waited.

Gabriel could feel the compulsion the undead was using to call his victim to him. Brice was muttering to himself, his clothes disheveled and dirty. There were long scratches on his skin where he had attempted to dislodge the illusory bugs crawling on him. Gabriel tried to feel sorry for the doctor because he knew Francesca would be so horrified. But Brice had opened himself up to the vampire's compulsion through his own jealousy, and Gabriel could not forgive him for aiding the undead in his attempt to ensnare Francesca and Skyler.

Brice kept his head down as he hobbled determinedly forward. He didn't seem to notice Gabriel standing solidly in his way. Gabriel waved his hand to put up a block, one invisible to the eye, but strong enough to interrupt the compulsion in the air. Brice's blood had obviously been tainted by the vampire, so he continued to shuffle his feet although he was unable to move beyond the boundary Gabriel set for him.

The doctor's eyes were dilated, fixed, and staring. He was far gone under the spell. Gabriel entered his mind to counteract the compulsion and give the human some relief. Brice's face went slack and his muscles relaxed so that he stopped attempting to move toward his destination.

Gabriel very gently eased him into a sitting position and Brice complied like a lost child.

From somewhere close, Gabriel heard a shriek of rage. Vampires didn't like interference with their chosen victims. The puppet master was not going to let Brice go so easily. Gabriel smiled and turned his face up to the sky. The clouds were darkening to an angry black above his head, and small veins of lightning leaped from cloud to cloud. He shook his head slightly, and as the electrical charge began to build where he stood, he raised his hand and swept it in a small semicircle.

Anyone watching would hardly have noticed the gesture, but the lightning in the clouds reacted immediately, slamming to earth just beyond the gently rolling hill, out of sight. The clap of thunder was deafening, as was the bang as the bolts scorched earth and shattered gravestones. A scream of hate and vengeance rose with the whirling wind. The trees began to shake under the onslaught, first twigs and then branches shaking loose to hurtle through the sky toward Gabriel.

He blew softly into his palms and stood tall and straight, unconcerned as debris rained down around him. Brice sat at his knees, unknowing, uncaring of the danger. There was no warning as the wind suddenly reversed itself. The sky rained leaves and dirt and branches over the small hill. Gabriel leaped into the air with the largest branch, camouflaged by its bulk.

He was on the vampire before it had time to realize it was in deadly peril. Gabriel blasted out of the sky like a missile straight at the gaunt figure standing on the charred grass. Around him were broken headstones, shattered by the lightning bolts and the branches and wicked wind. The vampire stood frozen, trying to decide his next move even as he attempted to protect himself from the flying objects coming at his body.

Gabriel came in behind the branch, hitting the vampire so hard, the blow drove the creature backward with Gabriel's fist embedded deep in his chest cavity. He gripped the blackened, pulsing heart and extracted the thing, separating the organ from the body. Even as he did so, he leaped away to minimize his contact with the tainted blood.

The vampire's shriek of despair echoed through the cemetery so that the the bats rose up into the air in great clouds. The undead simply folded in half and sank in a heap to the bloodstained ground, flopping, dragging its body toward Gabriel, toward the dark, ugly thing he tossed upon a rock just out of the vampire's reaching claw. Almost without conscious thought, Gabriel built the charge of electricity and directed it at the horrible organ straining to return to its body. The thin white-hot lash incinerated the heart and leaped to the body of the undead, reducing it to ashes. At once Gabriel bathed his hands in the heat, removing every trace of tainted blood before checking that the ground was clean of all infection.

The vampire couldn't have turned very many years earlier; he'd been unskilled and slow. He couldn't have been the one to put Brice under such a well-hidden compulsion. The darkness in the doctor ran deep, it tainted his blood and was eating up his will and rotting him from the inside out. He wasn't a ghoul, feasting on the flesh of human dead and living for the vampire's blood, but the one controlling him was a powerful being.

Gabriel couldn't see Lucian's hand in Brice's corruption. Lucian would consider it beneath him to do such a thing. He might harm Brice, or kill him outright, but he wouldn't use the man to entrap Skyler and ultimately Francesca. He would not need to stoop to such a thing. Lucian was a true genius. He possessed a powerful brain that constantly thirsted for knowledge. Lucian needed difficulties for his mind to work on. Intellectual challenge was what kept him from going completely mad.

Gabriel shook his head, exasperated with himself. Lucian *had* gone mad; he had chosen to lose his soul many centuries ago. If Gabriel was going to protect his family, he could no longer think of Lucian as being part of him.

Francesca was his heart and soul now. He couldn't take the chance of Lucian harming her. Gabriel made his way back to Brice. He needed to take the man back to the house and put him under a strong safeguard to prevent the vampire from harming him further. Brice was so far gone, Gabriel wasn't certain the doctor could be helped. Obviously the vampire had been working on Brice subtly for a long while.

The doctor was huddled in a ball on the ground, oblivious to his surroundings, deep within Gabriel's spell. Gabriel knew no one but Lucian could break through the safeguard keeping Brice's mind intact. It was a gamble bringing Brice into Francesca's home. They would have to take him to the underground chamber so Skyler would not be frightened by the sight of the doctor. And if he couldn't be healed, it would be up to Gabriel to show him mercy; it was not something he thought Francesca would thank him for.

Gabriel lifted the man as if he were no more than a child. Under the strong hypnotic trance Gabriel had put him in, Brice was completely trusting. He lay passive as Gabriel took to the air with him. The cloud cover was heavy enough to prevent prying eyes from seeing more than a blur moving fast through the night sky.

Francesca was waiting on the balcony for him, an anxious look on her usually serene face. Gabriel hadn't attempted to keep the extent of the damage from her and she knew if she were to save Brice's sanity, they would have to work fast. "Thank you for trying, Gabriel," she whispered softly, her voice a velvet caress. Her eyes moved over him carefully, searching for any injury he might have sustained.

At once he felt that curious melting sensation he was becoming familiar with. She was worried about him, checking to be sure he was fine even when he was bringing her a human friend whose mind had been damaged by the undead. Francesca thought of him first, and her concern meant everything to him. "I have directed Santino and Drusilla away from the kitchen so that we can take him safely down to the chamber. Skyler is asleep in her room. See to it that she stays there." His voice was a little bit gruff, made husky by emotion he couldn't control. She was so beautiful standing there in the night, tall and slender with her long hair in a thick braid and love shining in her eyes.

Gabriel reached out to run his fingertip tenderly down her face. "I think there is a chance that he can be healed, Francesca, but it will be difficult. The poison is already well advanced in his system."

"Can the vampire reach him in our home?" She was worried about young Skyler. The girl had suffered enough at the hands of a human monster; she didn't need to witness what the undead was capable of doing.

"Unless the one using him is Lucian, there is no way he can penetrate the safeguards I have wrought. I do not believe this is Lucian's work. But it must be an ancient to have deceived both of us as he did. He must have taken Brice's blood some time ago. Brice is using drugs to counteract the pain in his head, but he does not understand what is happening to him. He thinks only what the vampire wishes him to think. He is a puppet now with none of his own thoughts. I warn you, Francesca, the damage is substantial. He may never be the same again."

"I will try," Francesca vowed as she followed him down the stairs through the kitchen and below the earth where the first chamber lay.

Gabriel placed Brice on the bed and turned to help his lifemate fill the room with the pungent odor of healing herbs. At once a frown replaced the slack expression on the doctor's face and he moved restlessly. Gabriel took Francesca's hand in his, brought her knuckles to the warmth of his mouth. "You know I must go back out and find this evil one. Without his death, Brice is lost no matter what we do. The vampire knows we have Brice and he is angrier than ever. We cannot keep the man a prisoner down here forever."

Francesca turned her face away from Gabriel in an attempt to hide her expression from him. He was going back out to hunt. They both knew he had to do it, but she didn't have to like the idea. Gabriel's arm encircled her slender shoulders and pulled her into the shelter of his body. "I am not going to allow any vampire to defeat me, my love, when I have so much at stake. I will remove the threat to Brice's sanity. Then we will see what can be done to heal him."

Reluctantly he released her, his hands lingering for a moment in the wealth of her hair, crushing the thick braid in his fist. He knew she was afraid for him, but he was pleased that she refused to voice her fears, rather gave him a tentative smile to send him off.

"Do not attempt to heal this one until I return. His blood is tainted with the vampire's blood. You cannot walk in his mind alone and unaided. Should I not return, you must get another healer to aid you before you make your attempt. Promise me, Francesca. It would be far too dangerous for you to go in without additional strength. Remember always, you carry our life within your body."

She gave him a quick look of reprimand from under the long sweep of her lashes. "It is not necessary to remind me of either fact. I do not care to dwell on the possibility that you might not return. And I have never, for one moment, forgotten I carry our child. She is a miracle to me. I would never risk the baby, not even for Brice. You *will* return to me this night. I will expect you very soon without a mark on your body. Now go and do what you were born for." She leaned into him, resting her body all too briefly against his, savoring the feel of him. Strong. Masculine. Powerful.

She had never expected to love him so much. And she had never expected to feel so loved. Gabriel wasn't shy about showing her his emotions. He hungered for her with an intensity she had never dreamed of. Not simply her body, but her company, her heart and soul. He liked to be in her mind, sharing her laughter, the way she looked at life. The way she lived. He had such pride in her, such a deep belief in her.

"Gabriel." She breathed his name, her body soft and pliant, molding itself to his. "Hurry back to me." She had no thought of seduction—the last thing on her mind was making love—yet she felt a terrible need for him.

Gabriel filled her mind with love and warmth as he held

her to him; then he was striding away, back through the tunnel to the upper stories. By the time he had reached the kitchen, he was invisible, moving fast, a cold blast of air.

This time Gabriel streamed under the door out into the garden, taking to the sky immediately. He had destroyed a minion of the vampire, had taken one of his puppets from him. The vampire would be in a rage and easy to locate. Already Gabriel could feel the disturbing vibrations in the air. They flowed through the sky, leading him like an arrow toward the vampire.

"You go to this one's lair like an amateur. He has set a trap for you, hunter."

Gabriel continued moving. Lucian sounded far too close for comfort. If he took a hand in the battle, there was no way to know which side he would come down on. *"Do you suggest another approach?"* Gabriel replied.

"Back off. You know better than to go into battle when the enemy is waiting for you." The voice was as soft and gentle as always, with no hint of a reprimand. Gabriel found himself smiling. Lucian's presence was so familiar to him, so much a part of him.

"I thank you for your advice, ancient one." The old taunt was a reminder that Lucian was older by a few minutes. Gabriel was unswerving on his path, but more alert now. He had no fear of the upcoming battle with the vampire, but his twin was a different matter.

"You are not heeding my advice."

"This one is not as powerful as those we have faced in the past."

"This one is an ancient."

Gabriel withdrew from the merge, his mind turning over the possibilities. What was Lucian up to? He shifted his course, turning in a circle to approach from a different direction, scanning below him as he went. He was over a river, where a vast bridge covered the water. Two tubes ran along the embankment, emptying their contents into the river. The tubes were quite large and surrounded by masses of reeds. He could feel the presence of the vampire. There was a dark, malevolent feeling in the air, heavy and oppressive.

Gabriel was very familiar with the foul stench of the undead. It clogged the air as nothing else could. They were masters of illusion, presenting themselves to their human prey as handsome or beautiful, but in reality they were gaunt and gray, with receding gums and sharp, stained teeth. Gabriel felt their presence like a blow deep in his gut; he abhorred the subversion of superior gifts and talents meant to be used for good.

Below him the region looked stable, but the wind told him different. The vampire was waiting, lurking in the shadows, unseen, bloated with his own power, enraged. The scent of blood reached Gabriel just before the soft choked cry that signaled a kill. The wind carried the tale, the fear and adrenaline in the blood of the victim that would give the vampire a rush, make him even more powerful.

The vampire had known he was coming, had baited the trap and waited like a spider in the midst of his web. He had human prey, kept alive and terrorized, so that adrenaline would flood the bloodstream. The rush was addicting to the undead. They believed it made them stronger and much more difficult to kill. Gabriel couldn't spot the exact location of the vampire; there was more than one suspicious "dead" spot in the air.

He took a pass over the area before settling to earth. At

once the ground shifted slightly and his feet sank into a black mire. It sucked at his shoes, the grip astonishingly strong as if the bog actually wanted to drag him under. Something moved toward him beneath the surface, fast, serpentine, large, raising the reed-choked mud. Gabriel dissolved quickly into droplets of mist, merging with the heavy fog. At once a ferocious wind began to blow, striking at the molecules hidden in the fog in an attempt to scatter them and stop Gabriel from bringing his body together. A foul dark shape hurtled through the fog bank directly at the droplets.

The shape hit a barrier before it could reach Gabriel's bodyless form. It fell from the sky into the bog even as Gabriel rose sharply to avoid the dark mass. The monster hidden in the mud attacked at once, dragging at the struggling form while Gabriel shape-shifted above the scene. He hadn't thought it necessary to throw up a barrier, so he supposed his twin had once again joined the battle, inserting his body between Gabriel and the vampire. Yet Gabriel could not detect his presence. That was Lucian's skill. He could go undetected while others could not. The wind would not whisper of his presence or give him away to any seeking him.

The vampire howled in anger and pain, hurling from him the wormlike creature he'd created. He extricated himself from the mud, whirling this way and that in an attempt to locate Gabriel. Gabriel dropped from the sky, one razor-sharp talon ripping across the vampire's throat. The creature screamed in rage and at once lightning arced in the clouds and the air boiled with dark malevolence.

They struck from all sides, dark-winged gargoyles ripping at Gabriel, clawing and biting at him, landing on his head and shoulders, weighing him down in an attempt to drive him to earth and the black mire. Calmly Gabriel dissolved beneath them, streaming into the rank air toward the vampire. He shifted into his form just as he made a thrust at the vampire's chest, his feet inches above the ground.

His fist penetrated the chest wall, but the vampire was already moving away from him, his voice a jarring cacophony of sound so hideous and discordant, it hurt Gabriel's ears. To protect himself, Gabriel immediately muted the sound and turned it back on the vampire. His hand was burning with the poisonous blood coating it. He had to keep moving to avoid the gargoyles. There was no standing in one place with the creatures constantly circling and darting at him. They raked at his skin and eyes, clawing and biting to aid their master.

Gabriel was patient. The vampire had two major wounds, draining him of his strength. In the muck and mire, with blood seeping below the ground, the worm creature was becoming difficult for the vampire to control. It was in a frenzy, snapping and biting at its creator, looking for flesh and blood. Gabriel had closed himself off to pain and fatigue. His entire being was focused on the battle.

As he prepared to launch another attack on the vampire, lightning erupted unexpectedly from the sky above. Gabriel hadn't felt the surge of power, so he was as surprised as the vampire when the lash of white-hot energy whipped across the sky, a jagged streak that cleared the air instantly of the malevolent gargoyles. They fell to the muck, scorched and seared, incinerated by the blast of energy. At once the worm creature rose up to consume them. Another bolt came out of the clouds, missed the vampire by scant inches, and reduced the worm to ashes.

The stench was incredible. Gabriel struck while the vampire was reeling from the shock of the lash of lightning. He blurred his image and moved with preternatural speed, slamming into the vampire, driving hard with his fist into the same wound, this time reaching the blackened, withered organ he was seeking.

As he began to extract the heart, he felt the warning in his mind, and shifted his body weight. Something hit him hard in his side, penetrating his rib cage, breaking bones as it went. The pain was excruciating; it drove the breath from his body. At once the entire sky lit up, as if the world were going up in flames. In the air was a feeling of dark foreboding. Gabriel had never felt anything like it. The dark sky went red and orange with flames storming across the black clouds. A network of white-blue veins sizzled and danced in the roiling clouds. All around, the ground seemed to explode as bolt after bolt of lightning hit the earth.

Gabriel calmly extracted the heart and tossed it into the fiery conflagration, turning as he did so to meet the threat behind him. The ancient undead had revealed himself, believing Gabriel to be occupied with his partner. The vampire was thin and gray, his skin shrunken over his bones. His hair was white and gray, a long tangle of frost. His eyes glowed red hot, a feral cunning in them. He backed away from Gabriel, his gaze darting from side to side, looking for a way out. He didn't understand the intensity of the storm raging around them. He didn't recognize the hunter confronting him. He had lived by knowing how to avoid confrontation with the hunters, by studying his enemies and picking his moments to fight.

There was a voice whispering in his head. At first he couldn't hear the words over the explosions slamming all around him. He watched the hunter back slowly away from him. The voice was pure and beautiful, moving through his mind almost gently. It was painful to hear that voice, to listen to the tone. It had been long since the vampire had listened to such purity, and his body cringed away from the sound.

The voice was the brush of black velvet, a soft whisper of death. The vampire didn't take his eyes from the hunter now, believing he would attempt to deliver the killing blow momentarily. He was ready for it. He had tricks, illusions, so much power. He was fresh, without real injury, while the hunter had been weakened battling his lesser servants. The undead knew he had scored a terrible blow to the hunter and the creatures had drained precious blood from him, yet the hunter stood tall and straight with the black eyes of death.

Was that his voice whispering in his head? Where was it coming from? No Carpathian male had ever exchanged blood with him. He had no connection with anyone, yet he could hear that soft whisper calling him to his death. The words were clearer now. They spoke so gently of death. Of hopelessness. There was no hope. This hunter would take his life. He would die this night after surviving where others could not. "Who are you?" The vampire shrieked.

"Death," the beautiful voice whispered.

"I am Gabriel," Gabriel replied. He was leery of the firestorm raging in the skies, his every sense flaring out to locate the one initiating the blasts. Their creator was definitely one of much skill and power. *Lucian*. There was no spillage, nothing to tell where the power came from, it simply surrounded Gabriel and the vampire, a force of great destruction.

The vampire snarled, his sharp teeth stained from years of tainted blood. "You think to defeat me with clever tricks. No hunter has defeated me in centuries, but you, an unknown, presume to challenge me."

All at once Gabriel was weary. He had played out this same scene on so many battlefields, in so many countries, in so many centuries. It was always the same. The vampire was attempting to use his voice to weaken Gabriel's confidence.

Gabriel's head went up, his dark features hardening into an expressionless mask. "You know of me, ancient one. You do not want to know me, as I have been named legend by our people. You cannot defeat me. The battle is already won and justice has finally come to you."

There was a curious whisper brushing Gabriel's mind. A soft note of censure almost, yet not quite. Gabriel was not using his own voice to defeat the ancient killer as he should have been. He was tired from blood loss; the stench of death filled his mind and heart. He was tired of destroying his own people time and time again. He would do what was necessary, but he did not have to enjoy it.

The vampire suddenly covered his ears and began to wail in a high-pitched tone, attempting to drown out the insidious whispering of that velvet voice. There was a quality to that voice that insisted on being heard. It was sapping his strength, taking his power, removing his abilities. Shrieking his hatred and fear, the vampire played his last card, jerking his arms wide and calling his minions to the kill.

At once the mire erupted with hundreds of huge leeches, boiling out of the mud to swarm at Gabriel. Even as they did so, the air groaned with a sudden infestation of owls, a black cloud of bodies that dove, talons extended, straight for the hunter. The vampire turned to make his escape and ran straight into the Carpathian. The hunter seemed to shimmer out of the air itself, his face a mask of granite.

The vampire looked down and saw his chest, wide open, his withered heart pulsing in the fist of the hunter. The man never changed expression, yet he seemed to be fading in and out, almost an illusion. Only his fist was all too real. The vampire screamed his hatred and defiance, lunging forward in an attempt to recover his stolen heart. He fell facedown in the muck of his own making, the leeches finding him immediately. They covered his body, filling the empty hole in his chest.

Gabriel had been forced to dissolve when the vampire sent his servants to attack. He had risen high above the ground, into the clouds themselves. Now he directed the electrically charged air in a thin whip along the ground to sear the leeches and fry the raptors right out of the sky. They rained on the earth, their blackened bodies plopping into the bog. He could see the vampire lying in the muck along with his minions and wondered for a moment what trick the undead thought to play. What good would it do to pretend death?

With his superior eyesight, Gabriel could see the vampire's heart several feet from his body, lying atop a rock. *Lucian*. He had definitely joined the hunt, removing all other players from their battleground. Gabriel could see that the vampire was dragging himself forward, inching his way ever closer to the withered heart. At once Gabriel directed the whip of lightning, reducing the heart to a pile of ashes, ensuring the undead could never rise again. The vampire let out a hideous hiss, a last protest just as the lightning bolt took him, incinerating his body, removing all evidence of his existence. There was nothing left to do but clean up. Gabriel took care to eliminate all evidence of the vampire and his work from the area. The bog would be a trap for animals and humans alike, and Gabriel used precious energy to eradicate it. It took a long time to extract every evil thing from that place, replacing it with good.

Whatever game Lucian was playing, it would have to wait. Gabriel's wounds were throbbing. He kept the pain at bay, but his energy was gone. He would not attempt to pursue Lucian this night. He could only find it in himself to be grateful his twin had come down on his side in the battle.

When Gabriel turned toward his home, weariness immediately set in. He was tired and his wounds could no longer be ignored. He needed blood and Francesca's healing presence. He was eternally grateful he had a home and a lifemate to go back to.

Chapter Seventeen

The moment he entered the house, Gabriel knew something was wrong. There was an oppressive feeling of danger. Some menace disturbed the usual tranquility. Automatically he touched Francesca and found her filled with fear. But the fear was for Gabriel and their unborn child, not for herself. Gabriel glided through the upper story, his feet barely touching the floor. There was blood oozing from the deep scratches on his arm, and the puncture wound in his side was throbbing with each movement. The pain in his ribs took his breath away. He was tired, his great strength drained.

Naturally Lucian would choose this time for their battle. He knew Lucian was in the house; there was no other explanation. Only Lucian was powerful enough to conceal his presence from the air itself. As Gabriel continued through the house, he shut off his emotions, his fear for

Francesca and Skyler, his doubt in his ability to defeat his brother, the pain of his wounds, and his fatigue. He became the emotionless robot he would have to be to defeat the greatest, the most powerful vampire ever in existence.

The large living room was empty, but he caught a glimpse of Santino and Drusilla lying together on the floor of their bedroom. He didn't bother to check if they were alive or dead; it wouldn't make a difference at this point. He accepted that he could do nothing for them until he had taken care of his greatest task. Lucian must be defeated. Gabriel scanned the house for Skyler's presence, and found her in her room seemingly fast asleep. He could sense Francesca's hand in that; there was a very feminine feel to the power that clung to Skyler's room. It was like Francesca to think of the girl even in her own moment of stark terror. If she could help Skyler sleep through this nightmare, then she would do so.

Gabriel scanned farther, checking the underground chamber where Brice slept fitfully. The vampire's tainted blood was still in his system, poisoning him, making him restless despite the healing herbs and the deep sleep he had been placed in, but he was not in danger from Lucian. Those safeguards were intact.

Gabriel continued moving through the house, making no attempt to hide his presence. Lucian was expecting him. He moved slowly into the drawing room. Francesca was seated in a high-backed armchair facing his twin. Lucian was in the shadows, his face hidden from Gabriel, but he stood tall, shoulders wide, his clothes, as always, immaculate.

"We have a visitor, Gabriel," Francesca announced, her voice matter-of-fact. "Skyler thought he was you when he came to the door."

Gabriel nodded. He merged with Francesca to "see" her memories, not wanting to ask questions in front of Lucian. Skyler didn't know she had allowed their enemy entrance into their home. Lucian, a powerful ancient, had easily changed his thought patterns and aura to those of his twin. He hadn't revealed his true identity to Skyler and neither had Francesca. Francesca had put her under compulsion to sleep in an attempt to save her from what was to come.

"Did he touch you, harm you in any way?"

"He asked me questions." There was a note in Francesca's voice that Gabriel couldn't define. *"Personal questions about myself. He did not come near me, but stayed in the shadows where I could not see him or touch him. He did not attempt to take my blood or the blood of any residing in this house."*

"I trust your greetings are satisfactory and are over now," Lucian said in his beautiful voice. It seemed to send out a wave of purity and goodness.

"You are welcome in our home, brother," Francesca said suddenly, softly. "Please come in and sit with us for a visit. It has been long since you and your brother have had an occasion to visit in a tranquil setting." She gestured toward a chair, her movements graceful.

Francesca had a way about her—her voice, the way her body moved, her very presence—that soothed and made those near by feel at peace. She was wielding her magic now, her greatest gift, in an attempt to reach Lucian. She knew it was hopeless. Once a Carpathian male had chosen to give up his soul, he was lost for all time. There was no going back. Even Francesca, with her great healing powers, could not do the impossible. Gabriel ached to gather her in his arms and hold her to him, both as comfort for himself and for her.

"You wish us to be civil before our battle." Lucian looked around the room. "This does seem a place of peace rather than war." He lowered his voice so that it became a compulsion. "Come here to me then, sister, and share your strength with me."

Gabriel inserted his body between his twin and his lifemate immediately. He crouched low, his stance that of a fighter. Behind him, Francesca watched with sorrow-filled eyes as the tall, elegant man approached them. He came out of the shadows, looking what he was, a dark, dangerous predator. His black eyes glittered dangerously. They were graveyard eyes, eyes empty of all emotion. Eyes of death. He moved with an animal grace, a ripple of power.

"Stay back, Lucian," Gabriel warned softly. "You will not endanger my lifemate."

"It was you who brought her to danger, Gabriel," the voice said softly. "You should have done what you vowed so many centuries ago. Now you have brought more pawns into our game. I did not have anything to do with that." The voice was sweetly reasonable. "I see you are injured. I trust that will not prevent you from doing your duty and destroying me."

"You were the one who destroyed the ancient undead."

"What do you mean? Lucian killed the vampire?" Francesca's voice was in his head, her voice thoughtful.

Instead of answering her mind-to-mind, Gabriel chose to throw Lucian off guard with his answer. "Lucian prevented the vampire from injuring me further and he used his voice to weaken him. I could not hear the murmuring, but I know he was there. He created a massive storm and eventually it was Lucian who destroyed the undead while I took to the air above the battle scene."

Lucian shrugged his broad shoulders and turned his empty black eyes on his twin. "You made me a promise, Gabriel, and you will now carry it out." The voice was a whisper of velvet, a soft command.

Gabriel recognized the hidden compulsion even as he leaped forward to strike, closing the distance to Lucian so fast even Francesca could not see him moving. An eternity too late, with his lifemate's cry of denial loud in his mind, he whipped his razor-sharp clawed hand at his twin brother's throat, even as it registered that Lucian had opened his arms wide in acceptance of the kill. *Lucian had given him a direct shot at his chest and jugular.* No vampire would ever do such a thing. The undead fought with their dying breath to kill everyone and everything around them. *To sacrifice one's life was not the act of a vampire!*

The knowledge came too late. Crimson droplets sprayed the room, arced over the heavy curtains. Blood poured in a steady stream from the gaping wound. Gabriel tried to go back, to reach his brother, but Lucian's power was far too great. Gabriel was unable to move, stopped in his tracks by Lucian's will alone. His eyes widened in surprise. Lucian had so much power. Gabriel was an ancient, more powerful than most on earth. Until that moment he had thought himself Lucian's equal.

Gabriel looked helplessly at Francesca. Her eyes were drowning in tears. *"Help him. Save him for me. He will not allow me to aid him."*

"He wants to end his life. I feel his resolve." Francesca moved, a slow subtle glide of grace and tranquillity. "You must allow us to aid you," she said softly. Her voice was crystal clear, soothing. She had a tremendous gift for healing; if anyone could prevent Lucian's death, she could. "I

know what you have done. You think to end your life now."

Lucian's white teeth gleamed. "Gabriel has you to keep him safe. That has been my duty and privilege for many centuries, but it is ended. I go now to rest."

Blood was soaking his clothes, running down his arm. He made no attempt to stop it. He simply stood there, tall and straight. There was no hint of accusation in his eyes or voice or in his expression.

Gabriel stood very still, his eyes alive with pain and sorrow for his twin. "You did this for me. For four hundred years you have deceived me. You prevented me from making the kills, gave me no chance to turn. Why? Why would you risk your soul this way?"

Small white lines of strain were beginning to appear around Lucian's mouth. "I knew you had a lifemate. Someone who would know told me many years ago. I asked him and knew he would not tell an untruth. You did not lose your feelings and emotions early, as I did. It took centuries. I was a mere fledging when I ceased to feel. But you merged your mind with mine and I was able to share your joy in life and see through your eyes. You made me remember what I could never have for myself." Lucian suddenly staggered, his great power draining away with his life.

Gabriel had been waiting for the moment when Lucian would weaken and the hold on him would loosen. He took advantage, powering through the barrier, leaping to his brother's side, sweeping his tongue across the gaping wound to close it. Francesca was at Lucian's other side, her small hand on his arm, gentle and soothing. She slipped her hand into Lucian's to connect them. "You think there is no more purpose to your existence."

Lucian closed his eyes tiredly. "I have hunted and killed for two thousand years, sister. My soul has so many pieces missing, it is like a sieve. If I do not go now, I may not go later and my beloved brother would be forced to hunt and destroy a true vampire. It would be no easy task. He must remain safe. Already I could not walk quietly into the dawn. I relied on his aid. I have done my duty on this earth. Allow me to rest."

"There is another," Francesca whispered softly. "She is not like us. She is mortal. At this moment she is very young and in terrible pain. I can only say to you, if you do not stay she will live a life of such agony and despair as we cannot imagine. You must live for her. You must endure for her."

"You are telling me I have a lifemate."

"And that her need of you is great."

"Skyler is not my lifemate. I merged with her repeatedly to spare her suffering when she was alone and the terrible nightmares invaded. But she is not my lifemate." Even as he made the denial, Lucian was not resisting as Gabriel's lifemate began to work on the savage wound.

"Nevertheless, I am not telling an untruth to hold you to this earth. I cannot tell you where she is or how I know, but she exists in this time period. I feel her sometimes and I know, now, she belongs with you. Allow me to heal you, my brother," she insisted softly, "if not for your sake or ours, for your lifemate, who has great need of you."

Gabriel filled the room with healing herbs and began the ancient healing chant. He cut his wrist and pressed the wound to his twin's mouth. "I offer my life freely for yours. Take what you need to heal. We will put you deep within the soil and guard you until you are at full strength."

Lucian was reluctant to take Gabriel's blood when his twin was already so depleted from his wounds. Gabriel pressed his wrist tight to his brother's mouth, ensuring that he fed. He was determined to save Lucian's life. He could not believe what his twin had suffered for him. He should have known, should have realized everything Lucian had done was for his protection. Lucian had always taken on the most ancient and skilled of their enemies, always inserted his body between Gabriel's and death.

"Do not feel such guilt." Francesca's voice was gentle in his mind. *"It was always his choice. He made each choice with full knowledge of the consequences. You would never have agreed. Do not lessen his sacrifice to ease your guilt."*

Francesca smiled up at Lucian as she applied precious soil from her homeland that she kept for dire emergencies. She had it stored with the numerous herbs she grew for just such an event. "You aided Skyler on more than one occasion. I thank you for that. And you brought to justice the men involved in harming her so that Gabriel would not have to do so. I could not understand, at first, why my lifemate had such trouble with the idea of destroying a creature he believed to be a vampire, but I understand now. A part of him knew you had not turned. Not his conscious mind, but his soul."

Gabriel helped to lower Lucian to the safety of the couch. Even as he aided his twin, he could feel his own great strength draining. They were in desperate need of blood. He glanced at the serenity of Francesca's face and at once felt better. She always knew what was needed and he could trust her completely with his life and with that of his brother.

"I need to heal your wound, Lucian," she informed Gabriel's twin gently.

Lucian closed the laceration in his brother's wrist and looked into Francesca's eyes. "I am no gentle man. I have killed so long, I know of no other existence. Tying any woman to me, Carpathian or mortal, is sentencing her to live with a monster."

"Perhaps a monster such as yourself is needed to protect her from the monsters who would destroy one such as she. Your first duty is to your lifemate, Lucian. You can do no other than find her and remove her from danger."

"The darkness is already in me; the shadows are permanent now."

"Have faith in your lifemate," Gabriel counseled, "as I have in mine. You were strong enough to sacrifice your life for mine. You are strong enough to live while you hunt for this woman of yours."

Francesca signaled to Gabriel and closed her eyes, shutting herself off from their conversation and all that was around them. She separated herself from her body and went seeking outside of herself into the body so mortally injured. She made the repairs with all the skill of a superior surgeon. All the while Gabriel chanted the healing words and the scent of the herbs filled the air.

Francesca removed herself from Lucian's body and immediately entered Gabriel's. She was not about to allow her lifemate to suffer needlessly. She meticulously attended every wound, every laceration, pushing out the poisonous cells the vampire had injected through his minions and repairing all damage from the inside out. It took time to repair his ribs, his lungs, the battle scars so deeply entrenched in his body. She was swaying with weariness when she emerged.

At once Gabriel put his arm around her. "Rest, honey, I will go out to hunt this night to replace the blood we need."

Francesca gave him one swift look of censure with her enormous black eyes. "I do not think so, Gabriel. You will stay right in this room. *I* am the healer and you will follow my instructions in this matter. You and Lucian will stay here where you both are perfectly safe in your weakened condition and I will return soon with the blood you need so desperately."

She rose with a little swish of her hips, a very feminine gesture of impatience with the male of the specres. She looked quite haughty. Gabriel didn't dare look at Lucian to see his expression. He watched her leave, his features carefully expressionless. It was only when he was certain she had left the house that he turned his head to meet his twin's black gaze.

"Do not say it," Gabriel said with quiet menace.

"I said nothing," Lucian pointed out.

"You raised your eyebrow in that obnoxious way you have," Gabriel replied. "You are already in enough trouble with me without adding a sneer to your sins."

"She is not like the women I seem to remember from our youth."

"You did not know any women in our youth," Gabriel told him. "Francesca is a law unto herself. She had hidden from the Prince of our people for as these long centuries."

"She hid from me," Lucian admitted. He slid farther down into the cushions of the couch, his large frame drained of its life-giving fluid. "I sensed her close on more than one occasion and often led you here in the hopes of discovering her, but she was always out of reach."

Gabriel was inordinately proud of Francesca for that.

When Lucian hunted the undead, none was successful in hiding from him, yet Francesca had done just that over several centuries. Lucian shook his head tiredly. "If she had not been so successful, we would have found her long ago and you would have been safe."

"And then you would have chosen to end your life and your lifemate would be without the one she needs so desperately," Gabriel pointed out rather smugly.

Lucian's empty black eyes gleamed for a moment, moving over his twin in a kind of warning. Gabriel grinned at him like a little boy. "You hate it when I am right."

"She is with child," Lucian said suddenly, his eyes closing. His long lashes softened the lines of strain in his face. "She cannot enter the doctor's body without endangering both of them, even with your aid. You know it is so."

"Yes, I know," Gabriel admitted. "There was no reason to tell her when I did not know if I would return to her. She gave me her word she would call Gregori in to aid her if I had failed to come back to her. Gregori would never have allowed Francesca to place herself or the child in jeopardy."

There was a small silence. Lucian had slowed his heart and lungs because his body was crying out for blood. Gabriel sighed. "You should not have done it, Lucian. You are correct, I was close to turning. I believe I felt Francesca's decision to withdraw from this world. She was able to find a way to live partially as a human. Her intention was to grow old and die in this time period. She had been experimenting, seeking ways to become more human for several centuries."

"She is an extraordinary woman. I was astonished by her strength and ingenuity." Lucian's voice was very low, a mere thread of sound. "You are the only reason I continued my existence, Gabriel. If not for you, I would have chosen to end my time in this world and go on to the next a long time ago. I did not believe there was ever hope for me. I lost my ability to see in color, to feel emotion almost immediately. I did not last the two hundred years our males usually have as fledglings. For years I used your emotions, but then you, too, lost them, and there was only one way for both of us to survive. I had to convince you I was a danger to the world or we both were lost. If you did not believe I was too dangerous to allow others to hunt me, you might have turned. And if that had happened, I knew I would not be able to destroy you."

Gabriel smiled. "You could have destroyed me. You are far more powerful than even I imagined."

"I *would* not have destroyed you, Gabriel. You are the one who sought to keep our vow. I would never have allowed anyone to kill you."

"You would have, Lucian," Gabriel said softly, knowing it was true in his heart. "You never have stepped aside from our chosen path and you never have gone back on your word of honor. You would have kept our vow."

"Your belief in me is greater than my own." Lucian lifted his head tiredly. "She returns to you, brother. She will attempt to replenish me as she believes I am in the most need. Take the blood and then give it to me. I have discovered you have a few flaws, and jealousy is one of your worst."

Francesca found the brothers stretched out on the couches in her drawing room, a small smile on Gabriel's mouth, Lucian devoid of all expression. She started toward Lucian, but her lifemate stopped her. *"Come to me, my love. I will feed and then care for my brother. We will have to utilize the soil beneath the chamber where the doctor rests."*

If Francesca wanted to argue with him, Gabriel couldn't find it in her mind. She went to his side instantly, leaning her body into his, her hands moving over him as if to assure herself he was in one piece. She was careful to stay clear of his wounds, although she passed her palm over the multitude of deep scratches and bite marks, leaving behind a soothing balm. Whether it was in his mind or real, Gabriel didn't know and didn't care. She made him feel alive and whole. She made his world right again.

He gathered her close, inhaled her fragrance. He could hear the blood flowing in her veins, beckoning to him. Her scent mixed with the heady temptation, and the untamed beast in him rose quickly, his need and that of his brother great. Gabriel bent his dark head to her slender neck, tasted her satin skin, the warmth of her pulse. His mouth drifted down the warm column to the hollow of her shoulder, his teeth grazing her skin gently.

Francesca felt the shiver run along her spine. Gabriel had a way of doing that to her no matter what the circumstances. His arms tightened around her as he fitted her body more closely into his. Despite the measure of his need, he knew they weren't alone in the darkened room and he wouldn't take sustenance from his lifemate in front of his brother. It was far too intimate a ritual for that. He moved her backward into the privacy of the heavy draperies. His mouth wandered lower, traveling over her shoulder toward the creamy swell of her breast, pushing the thin material of her shirt out of the way as he did so.

Instantly Francesca felt alive again. She had been holding her breath the entire time he was gone, her heart pounding with fear, but now it was pounding with excitement. There had been something wrong all along with the picture of Lucian as a vampire. He had intervened too often to protect Gabriel and those Gabriel loved. He had come to Skyler to soothe her, rather than harass and frighten her. She was ashamed of herself for not putting the pieces of the puzzle together much quicker.

Her head went back, her slender arms cradling Gabriel's head to her as the white-hot whip of lightning danced through her bloodstream. His teeth had pierced deep and he was feeding. A kind of drowsy contentment took the place of her leaping pulse. It was edged with sexual excitement; she couldn't have Gabriel touch her like this and not want him, *need* him, even crave his body in hers.

Gabriel dragged her closer, his hands moving over her, pushing her shirt farther from her shoulders to feel the heat of her skin. She was soft and warm, a haven in his world of dark, dangerous battles. He closed the tiny pinpricks with a sweep of his tongue and allowed his mouth the pleasure of tasting her skin for just one moment. He found the slope of her breast, the deep valley, drifted upward along her collarbone to her soft, vulnerable throat.

Beneath his palm her heart was beating with the same rhythm as his heart. Her mind was filled with desire for him, her body with liquid heat. "I am home." He whispered the words against the corner of her mouth. "Really home."

Francesca smiled as he kissed her face, her small dimple, her chin. "Of course you are, my love. Now kiss me and give your brother what he needs so that later you can give me the things I need."

Her voice was no more than a warm breath in his ear, but Gabriel's entire body tightened at her words. His mouth settled over hers, rocking the earth beneath their feet, whirling them together into another world, a time and place where they were alone with the heat of their bodies and pleasure uppermost in their minds.

Lucian coughed discreetly. *"I am trying not to share your mind, Gabriel, but you are close and your combined emotions fill this small room. I have been long without feelings and the temptation is strong."*

Gabriel pulled away from Francesca instantly, his black eyes glittering, but she was laughing, her face washed with color like a teenager. *"We were being thoughtless."* She pointed it out gently even as she adjusted her clothing and moved around him.

Gabriel loved the *way* she moved. Silent, very feminine, a symphony of motions that could rob him of breath. In his mind he heard a soft sigh, his twin's reminder to get on with the job. Francesca was bending over Lucian, touching the wound on his throat and neck, her fingertips gentle, her manner tranquil. Gabriel knew she was providing another healing session. She could not touch someone who was hurt or in need and not provide solace of some kind.

Lucian attempted a wan smile, although he did not open his eyes. "You are the miracle my brother has named you in his thoughts."

"Has he named me a miracle?" Even her voice was soothing and tranquil to Gabriel's ears. He wanted to touch her, bask forever in her beauty, in her serenity. After the chaos of a bleak, gray world filled with violence, she was a miracle.

"Yes, and for once, he was right." There was an edge of weariness to the beautiful pitch of Lucian's voice and it alarmed Gabriel. He had never heard his invincible twin sound so utterly drained of strength.

"I am right at all times," Gabriel corrected, moving at once to his brother's side. "It is a peculiar phenomenon Lucian finds difficult to live with, but all the same . . ."

Lucian opened his eyes to regard his brother with an icy stare clearly meant to intimidate. "Francesca, my dear sister, you have tied yourself to one who has a much inflated opinion of himself. I do not remember a time when he was right about anything."

Gabriel moved to the couch, seating himself beside his brother. "Do not listen to him, my love, he practices his intimidating stare in the mirror on a daily basis. He thinks to silence me with his glare." Very carefully he slit a long, deep gash in his wrist and pressed the life-giving fluid to his twin's mouth. "Drink, brother, that you may live. I offer to you freely for you and your future lifemate wherever she might be." Deliberately Gabriel reminded his brother of the woman waiting for him somewhere in the vast world.

He could feel Lucian's weariness beating at him. He was tired of the empty bleak existence he had lived for over two thousand years. His body cried out for blood; his eyes saw only the shadows, gray and dark; there were no emotions other than the few he borrowed when he merged his mind with Gabriel's. He had lived without hope, had sacrificed repeatedly that Gabriel would not have to kill, giving him respite from the endless battles.

Lucian took the ancient blood reluctantly, sparingly. He had spent his entire existence looking out for his brother and he wanted him strong and healed. Lucian felt his shriveled cells welcoming the fluids, building and growing in strength and power.

Once more he closed his eyes, not wanting the renewal of life. For so long he had been set on his future, but now it was necessary to make a switch. What if Francesca was wrong? How could she possibly know such a thing? She had no blood tie to this mythical woman. Was she simply saying whatever it took to keep him on earth?

"She could not," Gabriel assured him, weariness creeping into his voice. "Francesca could not possibly tell an untruth. If she says there is a lifemate in need, then it is so."

"And how do you know this?" Lucian asked Francesca.

A small smile curved her soft mouth. "I wish I could tell you, but in fact I cannot. For some time I have felt a connection to another being. She is very young, perhaps a few years older than Skyler, and she is experiencing great trauma, but her spirit is strong. She is far away, perhaps in another land, but as I touched you to heal you, she appeared in my mind. She is a part of you, Lucian. That is all I can tell you. I wish it was more."

Lucian closed the wound on his brother's wrist, careful of his twin's health. "Do not feel you have failed me, sister."

Francesca looked startled, her eyes flying to Gabriel. Her lifemate laughed softly. "He would have you believe he is so powerful he can read the thoughts of all Carpathians, but in truth, he is reading my thoughts and I am merged with you. He can feel your emotions through me."

Lucian raised his eyebrow. "Do not be so certain, brother. You do not know if I can read minds or not."

Francesca began laughing. "I can see the two of you are going to be obnoxious. Gabriel is right, Lucian, I would not lie to you about something so important as a lifemate. I am certain I am not wrong. This child cries out in the night. I feel her pain and sorrow even stronger than I felt Skyler's. She is connected to us as no other has been. We must put you deep within the soil to heal. You must be strong before you begin your journey of discovery."

"First I will take care of your doctor friend. You cannot do so." Lucian made it a decree. His black eyes glittered for a moment, sheer ice and menace.

Francesca glared at him, her black eyes sparkling. "I will do what is necessary. *You* have no say in it."

Lucian's empty eyes turned on his brother, one eyebrow arched. *"You will allow this lunacy?"*

"These things are difficult." Gabriel shrugged his broad shoulders as if to say Lucian didn't know anything about women.

Francesca tossed her thick braid over her left shoulder. "I realize you were born many centuries ago, Lucian. I should have not shown such impatience. Women no longer do whatever a man decrees." Her voice held a faintly haughty tone.

"Francesca!" The look in Gabriel's black eyes was something between laughter and censure. He could not remember anyone ever speaking to Lucian in such a way.

She turned away from her lifemate, trying desperately not to laugh. The two men were very old-fashioned in their manners. Courtly. Elegant. *Sexy.* That thought crept in unbidden and was hastily censored. She shared Gabriel's thoughts, knew it was in his mind to prevent her healing Brice until he had removed all traces of the tainted blood himself. Right now, Gabriel needed the healing earth, as did Lucian. Both ancients were wounded and weak.

"I have noticed for some centuries now, it is the women who take care of all the little details. I will ensure that Brice sleeps this day until the new rising. It is necessary to prepare the earth for your brother. He is in great need, despite his belief in his own omnipotence. Do not worry, I do have brains and have managed quite well without guidance of any kind for centuries. I will be able to handle all the details by my little lonesome while you poor boys rest."

"But you will not go near Brice," Gabriel said, trying to make it more of a statement than a command.

Francesca swept past her lifemate and glided down the hall toward the kitchen and the underground chambers. Of course she wouldn't risk her unborn child trying to heal Brice without aid. Did they think she was a dolt? The two of them could sleep in the underground chamber together!

"I will not be sleeping with my brother, woman, believe me. I will be sleeping right alongside you where I belong." This time there was distinct laughter, a drawling male amusement in the deep timbre of Gabriel's voice. His voice always held that lazy, sexy note she couldn't ignore.

"Do not count on your charm to get you out of this one." Francesca opened the earth, a section of deep rich soil large enough to accommodate Lucian's powerful frame.

"I am much gratified to know you find me charming."

"Was I thinking that? I do not think so. I believe what I was thinking was how irritating the males of our race are and I am certain I had good cause to hide my existence from them all these centuries." Deliberately Francesca kept her voice as haughty as ever. Teasing him. Loving him. Wanting to be alone with him. Gabriel.

"You were thinking about making love to me, not sentencing me to a lonely bed."

"You think much of yourself, sir."

"Only by reading your thoughts. I find I like the way you view me far better than the view I have of myself."

Francesca scattered healing herbs across the dirt floor and added precious soil from her homeland from the small treasure box she had guarded over the centuries. The soil was what Lucian needed more than anything else. *"It is ready."*

Gabriel reached for his twin, helping him to his feet. It felt right to be with Lucian again. They moved the same way; their expressions were totally alike. It suddenly occurred to Gabriel that perhaps Francesca couldn't tell them apart.

"Do not be so silly. You are part of me, the other half of my heart. You think the silliest things, Gabriel." The whisper of her voice was an invitation. It heated his blood as nothing else ever could.

Gabriel guided Lucian past the chamber containing Brice. The twins touched the mind of the sleeping human at the exact same time, sharing the knowledge without thinking about it, a well-rehearsed action.

Francesca stepped to one side to allow Lucian into the narrow opening leading to his sleeping area. "Sleep well, brother."

Lucian looked down at her with his empty black eyes. "I thank you for your kindness to me, sister, but most of all for the way you care for my brother." He said it sincerely.

There was pure magic in his voice. Francesca found herself smiling up at her lifemate's twin. She believed him far too powerful for his own good, but she knew he loved his brother, and that reassured her as nothing else could have.

Gabriel locked his arm around her waist the moment Lucian had floated to earth and the soil had closed over his head. "Alone at last. I did not think it would ever happen."

She gave him her snootiest look. "You seem to forget poor Drusilla and Santino. They deserve an explanation of tonight's events. I protected them as best I could and I suspect Lucian probably did also, but Santino is not one we control. We gave our word to Aidan. Besides, you went out and got yourself hurt. That was uncalled for."

He leaned down to nuzzle her neck, inhale her fragrance. "I love the way you smell. The moment I entered our house, it was filled with your presence and I knew I was home."

Francesca's hand crept up to his face. "I love you very much, Gabriel. I do not appreciate gray hair at this stage in my life when I am about to become a mother."

"You would look very sexy with gray hair," Gabriel replied, holding her hand to him so that he could turn his face and press a kiss into the center of her palm. "And I would like to go upstairs and see young Skyler before the night is gone. You can see Santino without me."

She bit his palm, a little nip of reprimand. "You will not go without me, and you will not leave all the tiny details of our life to me."

He managed to look innocent. "Was I doing that?"

Francesca laughed, her heart light and happy now that he was beside her and they were safe within the walls of their home.

Chapter Eighteen

Francesca woke in Gabriel's arms. Gabriel had remained below the earth for two days, but now his wounds were completely healed and Francesca felt safe calling him to her. She felt she had been patient long enough when everything in her cried out for him. Above them the night was stirring to life and the comforting sounds of her household were settling into the rhythm of the night.

Skyler was laughing in the kitchen with Drusilla. Francesca lay for a moment savoring the wonder of that. Skyler didn't laugh often, and when she did it was brief, but the sound was incredibly beautiful. Francesca was already becoming fond of Drusilla. She was a motherly woman who ran the house very efficiently. She had an open, loving personality. There was ample room in her heart for young Skyler.

Santino was a miracle. He had immediately set to work

with the bodyguard to ensure the house was protected inside and out. It would be necessary to change Francesca's manner of living to accommodate a high fence around the grounds now that there were humans to protect also. Santino was quick to find a design that fit the old-fashioned architecture. He had incorporated the safeguards Francesca had chosen to build into the fence itself.

It was already well under construction; Santino didn't believe in procrastinating. Francesca was certain Gabriel and Santino would become good friends in time.

"You are certainly accurate in your thinking," Gabriel murmured, his heart already finding the perfect rhythm of hers. She was his world and he loved waking up with the knowledge that she was there, waiting for him, so cool and serene and beautiful.

Francesca smiled as she turned in his arms, her body molding itself to his, already soft and pliant, her skin warming as his blood thickened and heated. She reveled in the feel of his body; how different he was from her, his muscles so defined and hard. With her hands she sought his hips, the columns of his thighs, smoothed over his chest, lingered over the area where he had been wounded. "You hunger." She made it a statement. She had known he would awaken ravenous, and she was more than willing to provide for her lifemate. She could feel the hunger in him, a growing, living thing.

Gabriel buried his face in the hollow of her shoulders, his mouth moving over her scented skin. His hands shaped her slender body, tracing her perfect form, her lush breasts and rounded hips, her small tucked-in waist. Their child lay beneath his palm and it excited him to think of it growing there, another binding tie between them. A rush of heat hit him with the speed of a fireball, exploding in his lower belly as her fingers danced over him.

"Francesca." He breathed her name against the creamy mound of her breast, his warm breath teasing her nipple into an answering erotic peak. His lips kissed the vulnerable line of her throat, found her mouth, fastened there, his mouth dominating and very male. She was everything to him. "Everything." He whispered it into her mouth, sliding his tongue along hers in a fiery tango.

He closed his eyes to feel her with his body, his hands exploring while his mouth moved along her neck back to the deep valley between her breasts. His body was growing hard and uncomfortable with wanting her, his hunger rising sharply. She murmured something softly against his skin, a little endearment, an enticement even, while her hands moved over his hips and settled with teasing, dancing fingers along the hard evidence of his growing need. His breath seemed to explode out of his body as she moved over him, her breast an invitation beneath his seeking mouth.

Fangs lengthened, grew as his teeth teased and scraped her skin over her pounding, beckoning pulse. Her fingers were inflaming him, teasing and shaping, even as she arched her body closer to his. Fiery heat streaked through her, through him as his teeth sank deep. Whips of lightning danced over their skin as he fed voraciously, her blood, hot and sweet, flowing into the starved cells of his body.

His body. Wracked with fires. Flames that could never be put out. He was so hot he burned with need. Even as he fed, he caught her slender hips and pinned her beneath him so he could surge forward, a powerful thrust, burying himself deep in her tight sheath. She was hot and slick with need, with hunger. Colors whirled and danced and the fire raged out of control. Gabriel just let it happen, let it consume him. Her body was all that mattered in that moment. He would plumb every secret place, delve deeper and deeper until he found complete sanctuary from the host of demons forever haunting him.

He moved harder and faster, long sure strokes designed to inflame her, to bring her to the same burning fever he felt. He whispered her name as he stroked his tongue across the tiny pinpricks, closing the wound in her breast. He gathered her to him, reveling in the mysteries of her wondrous body. He was lost for all time; she was his world and everything good in it.

Francesca looked up at his face above her, etched in sensual beauty, his black eyes glittering with the intensity of his wild lovemaking, swimming in unexpected tears. She gasped, touched a teardrop on his impossibly long eyelashes. His perfect mouth softened, curved in response. "You are just so beautiful, Francesca. I still cannot believe I am here with you, sharing your life, sharing your body. You have no idea what you mean to me."

She leaned up to capture his mouth with hers, merging her mind more fully, offering total acceptance of his wild nature, matching his fiery demands with her own. Long afterward they lay together, listening to their combined heartbeat, savoring the luxury of simply lying in each other's arms, in the differences of their bodies and their ability to be so entwined.

"I love you, Francesca," Gabriel told her solemnly. "I cannot express in words what you are to me."

She smiled up at him. "You do a fairly good job expressing yourself."

His eyebrow shot up. "Fairly good?"

"I think your ego is already far too large. I am not about to call you the greatest lover in the world."

His hand cupped her soft breast, his thumb stroking small caresses over her taut nipple. "But you would if it were not for fear of my ego?"

Each stroke of his thumb produced an answering rush of liquid heat and Francesca shifted, rising above him, flinging her abundance of hair over her shoulder as she slowly straddled him, lowering her body over his. He gasped aloud, his eyes closing for a moment in ecstasy, then opening to watch her body as she began to slowly move.

"I booked Brice in at a medical clinic in Milan. I have friends there who will back up my story. I told them he was recovering from an addiction and we were helping him here. They owe me a favor or two," Francesca added when Gabriel frowned. He wasn't used to relying on humans for aid but Francesca slipped easily between the two worlds. She knew the value of money and social position. She knew medical clinics relied heavily on wealthy benefactors. She was very generous in that regard and rarely asked anything in return. If she wanted one of her friends, particularly a great physician, to be booked in as recovering from a violent flu, the clinic was more than happy to help. "And yes, I know you and Lucian will aid in destroying the vampire's hold on him. I read your mind easily, my love; nothing will harm our daughter. Either of our daughters. I will wait until Brice is free of all shadowing before I aid in his healing."

"Yes, you will," he said softly, his hands going to her waist.

She moved her body a little faster to accommodate the sudden erotic picture in his mind. Francesca smiled, a slow seductive smile as she sensed the fire building in his body.

"You believe it is wise to involve another clinic?" Gabriel had to work at keeping his voice natural when she was tying him up in knots again. Her waist was so narrow and her breasts jutted so temptingly over him. "Surely he cannot simply pick up and leave his job when the whim comes upon him."

"Of course not, but it wasn't too difficult to put in a phone call from the clinic inviting Brice to speak at a fictitious seminar. Brice often does such things. I had his secretary arrange for other doctors to take over his patients and then simply followed up with another phone call saying he had become ill but the clinic was taking good care of him. When we heal him, he will still be in good standing in the medical community." She was trying not to smile at his reaction to her body teasing his, at the way his eyes had gone smoky and glazed as he watched her so intently. He was striving desperately to follow the conversation, to maintain interest in it when his body was in ecstasy.

"Do you fix everything for everyone so easily?" Gabriel asked her, bending his head forward to the temptation of her inviting nipple. He couldn't help himself. He had to touch her, to taste her. Her skin reminded him of warm honey. His hands caught her around the waist as she undulated her body, so beautiful she robbed him of the ability to think. He loved her face, her eyes, her lush mouth.

Francesca tossed her head back as she began to move faster, her body hot and demanding, her breasts bare to his sight, while her hair spilled around them in dark silken clouds. She watched his breath shorten and she smiled, moving a little harder, her body tightening around his in response to his evident pleasure. "Actually, yes, I do," she answered slowly. "Particularly you. For instance, I know you like certain things."

He could barely breathe, watching her ride him with that sexy little smile on her face. "What things?" he dared to ask.

She leaned back, moving deeper, teasing him, enticing, watching him watch her. It was wildly exciting the way Gabriel gave her so much power over him. She loved being his partner. His other half. She loved to be in his mind while they were making love, loved the way he thought about her, the way her body pleased him.

"You please me," he contradicted, suddenly moving his own hips into a hard, rhythmic surging. He watched her ride him, the sight adding to his intense pleasure until he could only thrust at her almost helplessly, reaching higher and higher, building, forever building. Her hair brushed his sensitive skin, scorching him, burning him. Nothing mattered except her body over his, sliding wildly, rocking and teasing until he was crying out her name to the very heavens and she was clinging to him somewhere between laughter and tears.

Neither could breathe normally for the longest time. They simply held each other tightly, savoring these moments alone together. Overhead the sounds of the household were comforting to Gabriel. Brice would be seen to as soon as they were able. Skyler was forming bonds. Lucian, his beloved twin brother, slept safely beneath the soil, healing, gathering strength, his iron will renewed. Francesca was in his arms, his body and soul wrapped deeply in hers, and all was right with Gabriel's world.

Chapter One

To Sarah Ashton, Lady Clevancy, chaos seemed to swirl in the damp night like leaves in the wind. The last place she wanted to be this evening was locked in a carriage with George and his mother. Huddling into the musty squabs of red velvet as the Beldons' lumbering barouche inched through the crush of carriages converging on Carlton House, she shivered. It might have been because of the chill in the spitting October air. Her life was unraveling.

"I don't care what you say, Sarah," Lady Beldon remonstrated for the hundredth time, pulling her lap rug more securely over her knees. "These dreadful murders strike fear into one's heart." The many ostrich feathers on her massive aubergine turban shivered in dread.

Sarah didn't care about the murders. She had come to London to see Mr. Lestrom, her solicitor. She would have seen him today, but the coach had lost a wheel on their way into London from Bath. The letter from Lestrom's son, its crumpled pages now carefully refolded inside her reticule, *must* be a mistake. How could there be a challenge to her ownership of Clershing? She had just paid off the debt her father left when he died, finally almost escaped her genteel penury. If she lost Clershing, what would she do? The house in Laura Place would go as well with nothing to support it. Cousin Amelia, her servants Addie and Jasco, they depended on her. What would become of them? And of Sarah, herself? Would she become a governess, a housekeeper? She could never take orders from some haughty, thoughtless creature; she'd be sacked within a week.

"George, how can you take your own mother into a metropolis where I am like to be killed at any moment?" Lady Beldon poked her second son's knee with one plump finger.

George Upcott did not even turn from looking out the window. How could he be calm, Sarah wondered, when she thought she might scream at any moment? "If you like," he said, "I shall order John Coachman to turn around."

"But I cannot miss the Prince's ball," the dowager almost wailed. "He's opening Carlton House for the first time since the Nash renovations. People are begging for cards. If one were not to go . . . well, I hardly think one would be considered fashionable at all."

George shrugged. "As you choose." He was a well-made man of medium height, his hair a sandy blond, his eyes translucent gray-blue. He was a handsome specimen; everyone told Sarah so. His lips were thin and straight like his nose, his complexion rather wan since he spent most of his waking hours in a laboratory. He was serious and single-minded, a promising man of medicine. All Bath had expected him and Sarah to make a match these three years and more. It should be natural to confide her dilemma to him. It wasn't. He had never approved of her managing her affairs herself, with only the aid of dear Mr. Lestrom. If she lost Clershing, George would claim it was her own fault. And if her penury was not even genteel? What would George say then?

"I wouldn't miss being in London now for the world," he remarked, unmindful of his mother's nerves. "I can't for the life of me see how the blood is entirely drained from the victims' bodies. Once the heart stops beating, the blood ceases to flow."

"How can such crimes be committed in the most civilized city in the world eighteen years into the nineteenth century?" Lady Beldon complained.

The coach lurched to a stop. Horses snorted and stamped around them. Coachmen shouted. A young woman shrieked with laughter. Sarah heard the noise only dimly.

What kind of challenge to her ownership was there? Her solicitor's letter gave few details. She had never heard of this dreadful Julien Davinoff who laid claim to her land. Her thoughts stole to her grandfather's disastrous propensity for gambling. Had he lost Clershing gaming? Surely a note of hand so old could not be brought to a court of law. Well, she would never relinquish Clershing without a fight.

Sarah had no desire to go to the Prince's ball. She had tried to stay home tonight, pleading that her head ached, but Lady Beldon had insisted. Since Sarah needed Lady Beldon's chaperonage to stay in London while she conducted her business, and Lady Beldon required an entourage at every social occasion, Sarah was going to Carlton House, whether she would or no.

She didn't even have the satisfaction of knowing she looked well. She wore the only dress she owned fit for a ball. The tiny puff sleeves and high waists that were the height of fashion were not always kind to women with voluptuous figures. The dress was rich looking, to be sure, but the cream-colored lace would have been better stark white for Sarah's dark hair, green eyes and pale, almost translucent skin. The cream color pulled the freshness from the lavender satin and muddied it somehow. George had helped her choose it, had insisted on the fabric. The lace tucked modestly into the neck and cascading over the hem was his suggestion, too. The deep rose silk he had so disparaged rose to mind, with a daring Austrian neckline and a black beaded fringe. He was probably right. It would have seemed fast.

"We'll never get there at this rate." Lady Beldon complained.

George finally looked exasperated. He leaned out the window and called for the driver to take an alternate route. The carriage swung into a side street and the going got better. But shortly before Hyde Park Corner the barouche pulled up again amidst the noise of a crowd.

George thrust his head out the window again. "Why are we stopping, John?"

"The way is blocked by a mob, sir," came the answering call.

"Well, push through," George ordered and sank back inside. "What could induce a crowd to gather? Everyone is either locked indoors in terror or on their way to the ball."

"I don't know and I don't care," Lady Beldon declared. "Tell him to hurry, George."

There was nothing to be done, however. The carriage crept into the gathering. Those in the crowd craned their necks to look ahead. The streets were wet and black. Bare branches clicked in the wind. What could all these people be looking at?

As they came to the center of the throng, Sarah began to dread what she might see. Two very official-looking men stood in a pool of light cast by one of the new gas lamps. One held a notebook in which he was writing. The other questioned a beautiful girl, wrapped only in a shawl of Norwich silk over a diaphanous gown, in spite of the chill night. She was red-haired, with wide lips and blue eyes. Sarah was struck by a sly quality in her expression. One would never forget that face. A few feet away a woman lay supine on the cobblestones.

Was this a murder? The woman on the cobblestones was very still. Instinctively Sarah put her hand to her mouth. "George," she whispered. He must have come to the same conclusion, for he leapt out of the carriage without a word to his companions and elbowed his way through the crowd, shouting, "I am a doctor, let me through."

"George, don't leave us," Lady Beldon cried. When she saw that she was having no effect on him, she rapped her cane on the inside of the roof and ordered the driver to pull ahead.

Sarah leaned out the window as the barouche pulled up to the barricade. All thoughts of her own predicament seemed instantly insignificant. She didn't want to know what had happened here, yet she could not turn away. Lady Beldon sank back into the cushions with a low moan.

George pushed his way through the barricades into the circle of light.

One of the constables, the younger and stockier of the two, blocked George's path to the corpse with a broad shoulder. "This 'ere investigation is official." Sarah strained to hear.

George pulled at his cravat. "Of course. But you must require a physician's opinion."

"We know what we got 'ere. Same as the other twelve." George was being dismissed. Sarah realized with a shock that this was one of the murders they called the "Vampire killings."

"Are you a fool, man?" George protested. "I'm a specialist in blood transfusion."

"What's that you say?" the stocky one asked, suspicious.

George mastered his impatience enough to snap his reply without actually shouting. "Draining blood out of healthy people into sick ones."

"Then," the thinner constable interrupted in more cultured tones, "we could use your perspective, doctor." He held up a hand against his cohort's protests. "My name is Chaldon, sir, and this is Barnett." He gestured an invitation toward the body. "What do you make of it?"

George pushed past and knelt over the body. Sarah could see a dark stain on the walk. The too-pale countenance had already begun to sink in upon itself without the support of filled capillaries, so the body had a shrunken look. Even Sarah knew that its blood had been drained. Her mouth went dry. She couldn't look away from the dead girl's staring eyes. George didn't seem perturbed at all. He turned the woman's chin. She wasn't stiff.

"Well, what do you think?" the constable named Chaldon asked. His voice almost trembled.

"I see no possibility that these two small puncture wounds could account for this woman's death," George pronounced, wiping his hands as he rose to his feet. "So much blood could not be drained, even using my new invention. I call it a syringe," he added.

The two policemen exchanged disappointed glances.

"Is this how the other bodies were found?" George asked.

"Aye," Barnett answered. " 'Cept one where the throat was just ripped open, like by an animal, maybe. He bled to death more natural-like." Sarah was shocked; this fellow thought bleeding to death was natural.

"Can you think of no way someone could drain the blood?" Chaldon pressed.

"Well"—George rubbed his chin—"perhaps if there were some sort of pump connected to the syringe to create a greater suction . . ."

"You sound as if you have the beginnings of a theory, doctor," Chaldon encouraged. "May we prevail upon you to come down to the magistrate's office in Bow Street tomorrow? We are quite anxious to learn how these murders were accomplished." He paused and looked down at the corpse. "If we know how it was done, we are one step closer to catching this madman."

George gave a gratified smile. "I shall place myself at the Magistrate's disposal."

"May I go?" The red-haired woman the constables had been questioning broke in upon their contemplation of the body. Sarah had almost forgotten her. Now all eyes turned her way. Her ruby lips were fascinating. Her flaming hair gleamed.

"Well, miss, since you have seen his face and can identify our murderer, it might be best for your own safety if you came with us." To Sarah's surprise, the girl chuckled.

"I am enough safe. There are never two deaths in one night, yes?" She had an accent. Continental. Germanic?

"Never been a witness before," Barnett rejoined.

"You saw the murder?" George asked. His gaze was rapt upon her. "How was it done?"

"I cannot say," the woman replied as the fingers of the chill evening breeze caressed her hair. "I saw the man's face. I heard the girl scream. But while the deed was done his back was turned. His cape covered all. Me, I hid myself in the shadows. But I have told all this."

This woman should be frightened, Sarah thought. Death had barely passed her by tonight. And you should want to take her hand and soothe her, Sarah told herself, reassure her. Instead Sarah shuddered when those cold blue eyes scanned the crowd.

"Even drew us a pi'ture." Barnett waved a page of his notebook. The drawing was a few lines merely, but evocative. "Tall, well-made, dark, 'air, dark eyes, 'igh cheekbones, dressed in an evening cape," Barnett recited.

"With your kind description, we will set the Runners out to comb the city and beyond. He cannot escape." Chaldon apparently felt he needed to reassure the cold-eyed woman with lies. She hardly seemed to need it. And they *were* lies. Hundreds fit the description she'd given.

Barnett looked up from his notebook. "You sure that's all, are you?"

"Really, gentlemen, no more. I will go home now."

And they let her, in spite of the danger, in spite of their questions. Sarah couldn't believe it. They all looked into her eyes as though they had been turned to stone and watched the only witness in a string of grisly murders walk off alone.

Sarah put her hand to her forehead. The whole scene was like a play revealed by the garish glow of the street-lamps, the emotions stirred yet drifting in the wet air. George, the officers and the beautiful woman were actors on a stage at the denouement. The climax done, they played out their parts by rote, flattened by the light. The people who pushed and shoved for a better view of the tragedy were a dim chorus, a surge of humanity in the darkness between the lamps.

George came to himself. "I say, I hope you know where to find her."

" 'Course we do." Barnett shook his head. "Bristol Court, off Dean Street." He flipped through his notebook to read the address.

Chaldon snatched the notebook from him. "Did you say Bristol Court?" The two constables looked at each other for a long moment, surprise and then dismay crossing their faces in turn.

"What is it?" George asked.

Chaldon snapped the notebook shut and tossed it to Barnett in disgust. "There is no such address off Dean Street."

George returned to the carriage. Looking smug, he swung into the seat next to his mother and patted her hand. As the coach inched away Sarah sat forward and craned to see the constables still standing over the body. She couldn't relinquish her awful fascination.

A countenance in the gloom at the edge of the crowd jerked Sarah back. The man was tall, well-made, with dark eyes, arched brows, and high cheekbones, with sensuous, curving lips and wild, black hair against pale skin. A cape swirled about him. The evocative lines of the red-haired drawing flashed into Sarah's brain. Could this be the man who had murdered here tonight? His eyes burned as he surveyed the scene. They were hard, unforgiving. He had seen everything, forgotten nothing, and he was obviously angry. The crowd shrank back from him. He seemed to float in his own space. Sarah strained to see, leaning over to press her breasts against the door of the coach. He was beautiful, she thought, but like the forces of disorder, he lurked at the edge of the tenuous circles of light. This man could kill; she was sure of it. She shuddered. *Be sensible. Your mood is coloring your thoughts.* But she could not look away from that face. Was it fear that wound its way into her heart, or fascination? Before she could decide, his cape swirled and the man disappeared into the darkness.

Sarah stared after him, wondering if he had ever been there at all. *Foolish girl.* There was nothing to connect this strange man to the victim lying in the circle of light. The drawing could have been anyone. Behind her George apologized for having left them. His mother revived and began to scold. It didn't matter. What mattered was one face in the dark, barely discerned. The face of anarchy, perhaps the face of evil, infinitely repellent, infinitely attractive.

Sacrament
SUSAN
SQUIRES

Strange, twisted carvings adorn the *palazzo* of the great Scarletti family. But a still more fearful secret lurks within its storm-tossed turrets. For every bride who enters its forbidding walls is doomed to leave in a casket. Mystical and unfettered, Nicoletta has no terror of ancient curses and no fear of marriage . . . until she looks into the dark, mesmerizing eyes of *Don* Scarletti. She has sworn no man will command her, thinks her gift of healing sets her apart, but his is the right to choose among his people. And he has chosen her. Compelled by duty, drawn by desire, she gives her body into his keeping, and prays the powerful, tormented *don* will be her heart's destiny, and not her soul's demise.

___52421-X $5.99 US/$6.99 CAN

Dorchester Publishing Co., Inc.
P.O. Box 6640
Wayne, PA 19087-8640

Please add $2.50 for shipping and handling for the first book and $.75 for each book thereafter. NY, NYC, and PA residents, please add appropriate sales tax. No cash, stamps, or C.O.D.s. All orders shipped within 6 weeks via postal service book rate.
Canadian orders require $2.50 extra postage and must be paid in U.S. dollars through a U.S. banking facility.

Name____________________
Address____________________
City____________________State________Zip__________
I have enclosed $__________ in payment for the checked book(s).
Payment must accompany all orders. ❑ Please send a free catalog.
CHECK OUT OUR WEBSITE! www.dorchesterpub.com